A Step So Grave

CATRIONA McPHERSON

A Step So Grave

HODDER &
STOUGHTON

First published in Great Britain in 2018 by Hodder & Stoughton
An Hachette UK company

1

A CIP catalogue record for this title is
available from the British Library

Hardback ISBN 9781473682351
eBook ISBN 9781473682375

Typeset in Plantin Light by Palimpsest Book Production Ltd,
Falkirk, Stirlingshire

Printed and bound in Great Britain by Clays Ltd, Elcograf S.p.A.

Hodder & Stoughton policy is to use papers that are natural, renewable
and recyclable products and made from wood grown in sustainable forests.
The logging and manufacturing processes are expected to conform to
the environmental regulations of the country of origin.

Hodder & Stoughton Ltd
Carmelite House
50 Victoria Embankment
London EC4Y 0DZ

www.hodder.co.uk

This is for Lori Rader-Day,
with love and thanks

List of Characters

In Perthshire

Dandy Gilver, detective
Hugh Gilver, Dandy's husband
Donald Gilver, elder son
Teddy Gilver, younger son
Bunty, Dandy's Dalmatian

Miss Cordelia Grant, Dandy's maid
Mr Pallister, the Gilverton butler
Mrs Tilling, the Gilverton cook
Becky, head housemaid

Alec Osborne, Dandy's Watson
Barrow, Alec's valet cum butler

Inspector Hutcheson, of the Perthshire Constabulary
Rev. and Mrs Arnethy, of Dunkeld

At Applecross

Lachlan Dunnoch, Viscount Ross
Lavinia, Lady Dunnoch, Viscountess Ross, née Mallory.
The Hon. Miss Mallory Dunnoch, elder daughter
Mrs Cherry Tibball, younger daughter
Martin Tibball, her husband

Biddy Tibball, Martin's mother, secretary to Lavinia
Dickie Tibball, Martin's father, nurse to Lord Ross
Captain David Spencer, a guest in the house

Samuel McReadie, gardener
Mrs McReadie, his wife, the cook
Roddy McReadie, son

Lairdie, footman
Mackie, footman

Ursus, Lord Ross's cat

Gaelic Glossary

A'Chomraich: old name for Applecross. Lit. 'sanctuary'

Aporcrosan: Gaelic origin for 'Applecross'. Lit. 'the meeting of two rivers'

bealach na bà: pass of the cattle, the new road from Lochcarron to Applecross

bean-nighe: washerwoman – a harbinger of doom

bodach: old man

cailleach: old woman

ciste-ulaidh: Lit. 'treasure chest', the sea.

cù sith: black dog – a harbinger of doom

eolas: knowledge of charms

feannag an dubh: black crow – a harbinger of doom

mo ghoal: darling. Lit: 'my girl'

sithichean: fairies

'Marriage is a step so grave and decisive that it attracts light-headed, variable men by its very awfulness.'
Robert Louis Stevenson, *Virginibus Puerisque*

'See how love and murder will out.'
William Congreve, *The Double Dealer*

Prologue

Snow lay, faint as feathers, each flake alighting by one tip upon the flakes below, making lace. Under the lace, the earlier snow nestled like a quilt, blue in its shadows. Under the quilt, the first fall grew heavy and wet in the dark.

Hard against the cold ground, the corpse lay hidden. Blood fanned out across unyielding earth, seeping upwards and blooming. Rose-red turned rose-pink as gently as a petal fades. Rose-pink became the faintest blush of apple blossom as softly as a season slips away.

And all around, above the stain, the snow lay in its perfection, lace over quilt over carapace. Undisturbed, untouched, unstepped-upon, it hugged its secret close until the first drips melting from the branches of the trees began to tell.

PART I

Winter

I

13 February 1935

Lavinia, Lady Dunnoch, Viscountess Ross, née Mallory, was loved by everyone. Those who knew her well, those who encountered her now and again, those who merely caught a glimpse of her angelic face and beatific smile in passing: all were in thrall. All but me.

My hatred was quite unfounded – which dented it not one whit – for no one chooses when to be born. I daresay that even Lady Love herself would have preferred a birthday in the gentler months, when she might have celebrated with picnics and garden parties. Be that as it may, Lavinia Mallory had been born upon St Valentine's Day and so it was in February that I journeyed, along with Hugh, my husband of over twenty years, and Donald and Teddy, our two grown-up sons, to Wester Ross, first by terrible road in the midst of hammering rain and now by rickety boat in the teeth of a howling gale, to mark her fiftieth birthday.

'Lady Love indeed!' I said, through clenched jaws, both my hands clamped on the lip of the bench and both my feet braced hard against the gapped floorboards that made up the deck, as the little vessel creaked and yawed and splats of rain came straight at me from her portside. If I had seen rain like this on a picture show I should have laughed. I should have scoffed at the notion that stagehands heaving buckets of water across in front of a camera would fool anyone. As another couple of gallons were heaved with gusto towards the side of my head, I only wished I *were* at the pictures. I could have got up and left.

'Ah, but wait till you meet her, Dandy,' said Hugh. The boys were standing at the prow, sodden and frozen and loving every minute. Hugh cast the odd wistful look in their direction, but stuck by my side from some mixture of duty and contrition. He had told me that we were to embark at Plockton on the banks of a sea loch and traverse something he called 'the inner sound' to land in Applecross Bay and so I had been expecting a boating pond. In truth, the sea loch was choppy, the height of the waves in the 'inner sound' made me quake to think of the 'outer sound', and if the skipper managed to find the mouth of a bay and insert his craft into it, I would doff my drenched hat to him. I shot him a quick glance, there in the wheelhouse. He was standing with his feet so far spread that, when one added the tall hat and sturdy coat, one was somewhat reminded of Toulouse-Lautrec; hardly the last word in reliability. On the other hand, I could still see steady puffs of smoke rising from him and surely an imminent shipwreck would cause the captain to knock out his pipe.

The other passengers did not look concerned. Three of them were sheep, to be fair, and sheep are famously stoical, but there were four women as well – all dressed in black from boot-soles to headsquares – wedged in a row onto the opposite bench, holding parcels and packages on their laps and conversing in low voices. Such low voices, indeed, I wondered they could hear one another at all. I should almost have said they were muttering prayers to themselves if their eyes had been closed and if any Scot would have given way to such excess as public prayer outside a church or, in a pinch, a graveyard. Besides, every so often one of them would hiss with suppressed laughter at something another had said. They did not actually look at Hugh and me as they delivered their bon mots, but I had my suspicions.

4

'Do tell,' I said to Hugh. 'Regale me with the source of Lady Love's belovedness. Take my mind off my innards.'

'Well, you know,' said Hugh uselessly. I moaned low in my throat, by way of encouragement. 'She was just a very jolly, pretty, friendly sort of girl.'

I snorted and immediately regretted it, for my face was wet with rain and salt spray and introducing a snortful of it to my nasal passages did not add to my comfort. But really! We were *all* jolly, pretty, friendly girls. We had had the jollity and friendliness ground into our fibres by battalions of nannies, governesses and tutors until any of us being trampled by a runaway horse would shrug off all enquiries and leap up to check that the poor dear thing had not loosened a shoe. As for the prettiness: we were eighteen and had maids. We were at our prettiest whether we knew it or not. We should have listened to those who tried to tell us so.

I sighed and closed my eyes. Perhaps Hugh was right that there was something special about Miss Mallory as was; she had been snapped up quick enough, at any rate. Therefore, while she was the same age as Hugh, married at eighteen and long gone before I came out, she now had a child of thirty.

Well, I knew she had a child of thirty, for that was the reason I was in this soap dish being buffeted and lashed and half-wishing we would capsize and sink to the peace of the bottom of the sea. The Hon. Miss Mallory Dunnoch, if you please, thirty or not, had captured the unguarded heart of my dear daffy Donald. The purpose of this visit was to see what could be done about it.

That is to say: the Dunnochs' purpose in inviting us all was to take stock of Donald and the rest of the Gilvers before the engagement was announced. Hugh's purpose was to talk settlements with Lord Ross. My purpose was to find out Miss Dunnoch's darkest secrets and put him off her, or even to share a few of Donald's less edifying exploits and see if *her* ardour could be cooled.

The trouble was, Donald had so few unedifying exploits from which to choose. (If it had been Teddy now . . .) He was not the sharpest pin in the cushion; even as his own mother I could not deny that much. But if Mallory Dunnoch and he had spent half an hour tête-à-tête she must know it already. He was very young at twenty-three to be marrying at all, even absent the age difference, which was a gaping chasm. But I could hardly argue that he was too inexperienced, for his romantic life had begun when he was a tiny little boy in his sailor suit. He had marched up to an equally tiny little girl after church one spring morning, handed her a fresh-picked daffodil and planted a kiss on her mouth before she could stop him. After that, he lurched from one passion to the next, eternally lovesick for some village girl, chum's sister or film star. He had been lucky so far – which is to say we had never had an awkward audience with a burgeoning girl and her furious parents – and it occurred to me that perhaps I should fold my hand while I had some chips left. If I detached Donald from the elderly Miss Dunnoch and the next passion he lurched to was even older – or a barmaid or something – I would look back on this day and kick myself for ever.

I sighed and opened my eyes again. Something had changed while my mind was wandering. The roar of wind, wave and boat engine had lost a note from its chord. As I looked around myself, the skipper turned from the wheelhouse and grappled with an anchor, heaving it up and over the side. It sent up a great spout of water that missed me by an inch as it fell back down onto the deck. My shoes caught a little of the resulting flood washing by on its journey to the stern and a little more on its return journey to the prow again. I noticed that the four women opposite had snatched their feet up out of harm's way and

6

were tittering again. The skipper pulled on his foghorn, three long blasts, and then came towards us.

'Here we are!' he said, a toothy grin showing amid his beard and around his pipe. He pegged about in front of me like a drunkard as the boat pitched and rolled. The anchor, in my view, was doing precisely nothing.

'Where?' I said, turning into the wind and searching in vain for a harbour mouth or jetty anywhere in the endless grey.

'Applecross!' said the skipper. Then he added an utterance that sounded like a sneeze. It was, I would shortly learn, Applecross's Gaelic name, spelled *A'Chomraich*, and it was pronounced exactly like a sneeze; there really is no more helpful way to describe it.

I peered around again, bewildered. The four women were on their feet and Donald and Teddy were racketing along the side of the wheelhouse, with great shouts of hilarity about the way the deck twitched and bucked under their feet and the likelihood that one or both of them might be pitched over the side at any moment.

'We've arrived?' I said. I tried standing, as though a bay and a village might be hidden from view by the side of the boat somehow.

'Aye,' said the skipper. 'Here comes the wee boaty to fetch you in.'

I twisted round, squinted into the murk and could just glimpse a couple of darkish blobs I might have taken to be shadows on the undersides of the highest waves, except that there was not enough sunlight penetrating the storm clouds to throw shadows on this wretched morning. As I watched I saw one of the blobs grow a crest or plume of some strange kind, and with one blink I finally understood I was looking at a man waving his arm at us from a dinghy that was just about to draw up alongside the soap dish and into which Hugh, Donald, Teddy, the four women in black, the three sheep and I were expected to descend.

I turned to Hugh in disbelief. 'Did you know about this?' I said. 'Did you know, from your maps, that Applecross has no harbour?'

'One of Lady Love's current good works is a pier for the village, you know,' said Hugh. 'They hope to dedicate it before the year is out. Of course, the building work can't start until spring. One couldn't bring the necessary iron and stone by sea in the winter—' He bit off his words.

'God forbid,' I said. 'Heaven forfend! I'd hate to think of great lumps of stone or loads of iron girders being risked. Wives, though? Wives are a different matter.'

'Dandy,' said Hugh, 'children take this boat to school every week. Those crofters's wives have taken it to market and back their whole lives. And look at the boys!'

That was my undoing. I could have stuck like a barnacle to my suddenly precious bench on this suddenly acceptable boat until the skipper delivered me back to Plockton, were it not for the sight of my firstborn son straddling a rail on its starboard side, then disappearing. Teddy was after him like a ferret, of course, and then there was nothing for it. A sharp maternal tug somewhere in my middle, that portion of myself already thoroughly discomfited by the journey, drew me to the rail, the ladder, the dinghy and quite the most wretched ten minutes of my entire life. Teddy and Donald, in contrast to me, were even more exhilarated by the rearing and slapping of this even more minuscule vessel. They shouted with joy all the way to shore. The sheep took it quietly. The four black-clad women carried on their murmured gossiping. I kept my eyes and mouth closed and sent up silent pleas. Hugh, I am delighted to recount, was sick.

2

The means of disembarkation from 'the wee boaty' was yet another surprise. I had expected us to pull up to a jetty of some kind – perhaps an inadequate jetty, given the current plans for a new one, but a jetty nonetheless – and was prepared to scramble up some slippery stone steps, skidding on seaweed and ruining my gloves by clutching the rusty bar that served as a banister. I have clambered out of vessels by means of many sets of slimy green steps in my years of Scottish life. What I had never done, before that grim morning at Applecross, was wait in a dinghy that had been grounded on a beach and then been lifted over the side into the arms of a burly stranger, to be carried ashore like a damsel in distress, or rather – I suspect – like a week's washing.

'How d'you do?' I said from under my hat to under his. We both had our heads bowed, he to watch his step in the shallows and I to avoid giving him a crack in the bridge of the nose; my hat brim was stiff and had a peak at just the wrong point on its circumference.

'Ach bash mash buch,' said the burly stranger.

'Indeed,' I said, to the luxurious red sideburn half-obscuring his right ear. 'Well, thank you awfully much. Gosh, how strong you are. Thank you.' That got us to dry land, or at least far enough up the beach that the water was all rain puddles and no waves. He set me down, touched a gloved hand to his hat brim and waded back in to fetch the next one. I trudged up the beach and across a muddy track to take shelter under the eaves of a stone shed. From the acrid smell and the blackened earth criss-crossed with footsteps that led to its locked door, I guessed it was a coal store and I spent the minutes it took Hugh, the boys and our luggage to be brought ashore daydreaming of the fires fed by all that coal, fires that would warm my bathwater, my bedroom and my winter nightclothes just as soon as we could get to Applecross House and put this dreadful day behind us. I had quite forgotten it was not yet luncheon time.

'Now, the village itself – they call it "the street" – is down there,' said Donald, pointing into the curtain of rain in one direction, 'but Mallory's house is that way, round towards the clachan.' He gestured again. 'And someone will be on his way to fetch us. That's the system, Mother. The skipper blasts his horn and that tells everyone the boat's here.'

'What's a clachan?' I said, feeling a pang to hear him speak of 'Mallory's house' and its habits in that familiar way. I could not help but notice that a cart had come for the four women and that a young lad dressed in oilskins had driven the three sheep away up the hill and yet we Gilvers were still waiting, foghorn blast or no.

'Good grief, Dandy,' said Hugh. 'Have you learned nothing after all these years? Please try not to be such an out-and-out Sassenach around the Rosses, won't you?'

I sighed as loudly as I could manage, although I expected the rain drumming on the tin roof of the coal store drowned it out. I have never understood the one-upmanship of Scots regarding longitude. Why should the most northerly-dwelling Scotsman in any gathering be the top dog? London, Paris and Monte Carlo are all to the south, as is Edinburgh if we are scraping barrels, and the farther one goes from them the worse life gets. I hoped these Rosses would not be the type of Highlanders who would look down on Hugh and Perthshire and thereby nudge him into endless accounts of his grandmother's childhood on Skye to even the score. For northerliness is only one of the winning cards in the game:

an island carries a hefty bonus. Of course, Skye is quite a southerly island and the ferry journey to it is a brief one. If a Ross grandmother had come down from some speck in the Shetland Isles, Hugh would be trounced completely.

At last I thought I could hear a motorcar engine and the raindrops off to our right began to sparkle as a pair of headlamps shone through them.

'I wonder who it is,' said Donald, peering at the blurred shape of the approaching motor. 'I hope it's Lady Love. She's a terrific driver, Mother. She's driven through a mountain pass in the Alps, you know.'

'We know,' said Teddy. 'You told us.' He had taken it very badly to have a brother so besotted he overflowed about his sweetheart's mother's driving prowess.

'But it might be Biddy, or Dickie, or Mitten, or Cherry or—'

'Uncle Tom Cobley,' said Teddy.

'Who's all that?' I said. 'Who are all they, I mean. It sounds like a litter of puppies.'

'They're Tibballs,' said Donald, hardly helpfully, as the motorcar emerged out of the rain. It was a Daimler and quite a new one. The driver's door flew open and a figure in tweeds and sou'wester leapt down.

'Gilvers?' the man shouted, with grin that showed very white teeth in a very brown face. 'David Spencer, at your service. Bundle in out of this filthy weather. Never mind the bags, I'll get them. Go on, in you all get. There's a flask on the back seat and a few hot water bottles and what have you. What a day!'

'And who's *that*?' I asked Donald once we were squashed into the back seat, hugging the bottles and starting to steam.

'No idea,' Donald said, sounding a little crestfallen to be caught out.

'Competition?' said Teddy. 'He's a fine-looking chap and looks about Mallory's vintage.' This was unfair as well as unkind. The man was much older than thirty. On the other hand, he was the right sort of age for a thirty-year-old bride, unlike poor Donald.

'Shut up,' Donald said. He had flushed brick red and I did not think it was just the warmth of the bottle or the nip of whisky from the flask lid that had done it.

'Please don't use that ungentlemanly expression, Donald,' said Hugh, twisting round from the front seat, where he had taken up position. 'And Teddy? Please don't be uncivil to your brother.'

I boggled at the back of his head as he turned to face the front again. Donald and Teddy had been telling one another to shut up, get lost and much worse since they were lisping it all through their baby teeth. Hugh always left it to Nanny to scold them. If he had suddenly taken it upon himself to hand out etiquette lessons he must be very keen on this alliance indeed.

Before I could apply myself properly to the puzzle of it, Mr Spencer flung himself back into the driver's seat, slammed the door closed and we were off.

'It's only a minute or two round the bay,' he said over his shoulder. 'You'll be warm and dry in no time. What a pity though. Lady Love and Lach are so proud of the place and you're not seeing its best side today. I'm tempted to ask you to shut your eyes and wait till the sun's out to take your first look around. They said on the BBC it's to clear up later and be fine tomorrow.'

I was looking around with great interest already. We had rolled through a gate and were now crunching up a drive of red gravel chips towards a pretty, white house, freckled all over with little windows, topped off with crow-stepped gables and flanked by cottage-like side-wings. A liveried footman with two umbrellas came out as we approached and when the motorcar stopped I could see, through the open door and the lower windows, warmth and light, paintings and flowers, crackling fires and glittering chandeliers. My spirits lifted.

Inside, the house smelled of daphne blossom, from a great wide bowl of it on the table in the hall. I drank it in as I went over to the fireplace to warm my hands. It was an applewood fire, I thought, from the fragrance, and quite deliciously hot. I turned my back and unashamedly toasted my rear. Nanny Palmer would have fainted and Hugh gave a quick frown, but I looked around at the paintings and ignored him.

'Don? Is that you, darling?' A silvery voice sang out and a slim figure came skipping down the stairs, landing with a light thump at the turn and skipping down the next half-flight to the ground floor. 'How did I miss the boat horn? Did Sandy give three blasts? Do forgive me. And welcome, welcome, welcome home!'

I bristled like a hedgehog, unable to help it, unable to say what was most annoying. 'Home' was an outrage, of course. But 'Don' was not much better. No one had ever called Donald anything but Donald in all his life. And she did not sound the least bit genuinely sorry that she had escaped having to go out into the rain on such a day.

'My eye,' I muttered to myself, and scowled at her back as she kissed Donald on both cheeks and then held his two hands in hers and stood back to inspect him. I had never seen such a bumptious young woman in all my days, I decided. Greeting him first and ignoring his parents was atrociously ill-mannered. My heart sank to see how Donald looked at her, with his brows drawn up and his eyes wide, his mouth open and his throat going up and down as he gulped.

Then she turned round and beamed at me. My first thought was that she had spent too much time out in the sun without a shady hat on. Her face was as dark as a gypsy's and her hands were the colour of walnut shells. She looked every day of her thirty years and more. Much more, I realised as she came forward. She had wrinkles round her eyes and lines down either side of her mouth. This was not Mallory.

'Lavinia Ross, Mrs Gilver,' she said, confirming it as she grasped my hand. Her palm was calloused and her fingers were rough with scratches. 'Excuse my paw,' she went on, 'I've been pruning.'

'Dandy, please,' I said. 'And you remember Hugh?' I nodded to where Hugh stood, his face a grim mask. He had seen what I had seen, then.

We do not often commune, my husband and I, but as Lady Love went scampering over to grab his hands and effuse at him, he caught my eye and a question, an answer and an agreement passed between us. If there was any doubt, the arrival of Mallory herself removed it. She came downstairs, skipping just like her mother, although the effect was somewhat more definite since she was twice as heavy and a head taller. They were definitely cut from the same cloth, nevertheless. Mallory's dark head glinted with the coppery threads that, by the addition of much sunshine, had turned her mother's as bright as a polished kettle.

'Hello, Donald,' she said, offering a cheek to be kissed.

'Hello, old thing,' Donald replied, obliging with a peck. His eyes did not widen, nor did he gulp. 'Here are my olds to meet you. Mother, Father, Ted: my intended.'

'Aren't they awful?' said Lady Love, back at my side and squeezing my arm. 'Olds! Intended! I thought we were slangy in our day, Dandy, but we're the *Shorter Oxford* compared with this lot. Let me show you to your room. The bags should be up by now. Would you like help to unpack? I'll send someone. Are you too travel-worn to notice our Fragonard? Just at the bend in the stairs here. Terribly sentimental, of course, but I've always rather loved it and it's wonderful for masked balls.'

I murmured about the Fragonard, although I have never cared for those eighteenth-century paintings that look like boxes of sugared almonds. At least, though, it served as acclimatisation for the first floor, where the walls were pink with white swags picked out and the carpet runner had rosebuds on it. Rosebuds. My room was worse: pink striped wallpaper to the chair rail and Chinese silk above depicting a bower of fantastical botanical splendour and lots of little pigtailed gardeners rushing around with wooden rakes and flat barrows. Despite the busyness of this, all the upholstery and hangings were deep pink with enormous white cabbage roses and there were bowls of forced bulbs in moss-pots on the dressing table, bedside table and chest of drawers. Lady Love took a huge breath in as we entered.

'Don't you just adore hyacinths?' she said. 'It smells like heaven in here.'

'Mm,' I said. I had always thought one bowl of hyacinths near an open door was plenty. 'What a delightful room. Thank you.'

'I shall send up some coffee,' she said. 'Come and find me when you're ready, won't you? I'll be in the garden room until lunch at one.' Now it was my turn to be beamed at. 'I'm absolutely delighted about our youngsters,' she said. 'Isn't it marvellous?' She squeezed my hands and left me.

As soon as she was gone, Hugh rapped on the connecting door and marched in. 'What's that smell?' he said.

'Hyacinths,' I said. 'They smell like heaven. Fragonard is wonderful and the engagement is marvellous. There doesn't seem to be room for discussion on any of it.'

'Fragon . . . What?' said Hugh, distracted. 'Dandy, my dressing room is like Madame de Pompadour's boudoir. Perfectly nice Highland manor house and they've got it dolled up to the nines till you can't see the bones at all. Poor old Ross, living in this. I wonder why he doesn't put his foot down.'

I shushed him as a movement at the door told me someone else was approaching. I did not want the Applecross servants to hear us traducing their beloved mistress's taste as early as this. It was Teddy, however, who came into view after a quick knock. His face was solemn and his eyes looked troubled.

'Ma,' he said, 'I don't quite know how to broach this and I don't want you to tell me I'm imagining it, but I think there's a bit of a problem here. With Donald and Mallory, I mean.' He cleared his throat. 'And Mallory's mother.'

Good Lord, I thought to myself. If the frisson between Donald and Old Mother Dunnoch had penetrated even Teddy's skull, there was nothing for it.

'Don't call me "Ma",' I said.

'We came up Plockton Sound on the coal boat, Teddy,' said Hugh. 'Not up the Thames on a cracker. Leave it to your mother and me. We shall take care of everything. And do not say a word to Donald or I shall revisit some of our happiest memories of your childhood. Just you, me and a slipper. Understood?'

It was a rare moment for the Gilver family: three of us in accord and Hugh taking charge. I rather liked it, even as the cause of it made me feel even sicker than the wee boaty and chilled me even more than the freezing rain.

3

Luncheon made a great many things a little clearer, and a few things much clearer than I would want them. We gathered in the dining room just as the clouds lifted and parted. In fact, a rainbow was laid on for us, stretching right across the bay from the quaint row of village houses beyond the coal store to the quaint little church inside its graveyard wall on the other side. In between, frilled ripples played along the edge of the tide and left the pebbles glittering. It was hard to believe that merry spangled water, so harmless now, was the same expanse that had frightened me and sickened Hugh not two hours ago.

Lord Ross was rolled into the dining room in a wheeled chair, a shawl on his shoulders and a cat in his lap. He was a handsome man, with a long humorous face and a shock of silver hair, but his eyes had the strained look that comes with pain long borne, and even the blanket over his knees did not disguise the withered thinness of the legs underneath it.

'Hugh, my boy,' he said, lifting a hand gnarled with scars from its resting place on the cat's luxurious fur. 'How long has it been? Whose pheasants have you been shooting all these years when you might have been shooting mine? Oh yes, I still keep a shoot going,' he added, at Hugh's look. 'And I can still pot a few, even from this contraption and even with these trotters where me hands should be. Dickie here – this is my nurse, Dickie Tibball' – he waved one of his shiny fists at the man holding onto the chair's handles

– 'wheels me up a paved path to the grouse moor and we all have great fun.'

'Oh, tremendous fun,' said Dickie Tibball. 'And I've got muscles like Tarzan of the Jungle from the shoving.'

He sounded like one of us, rather than a medical nurse of any sort, and he was dressed in the kind of ancient country tweeds that only a friend would dare be seen in. An employee of the usual sort would be sacked for them. My hunch was confirmed when Lady Love appeared with another woman, in equally ancient tweeds and with her hair frizzing out around myriad hairgrips, whom Lady Love introduced as, 'Biddy Tibball, Dandy. My secretary and right hand. And you've met Dickie and Lachlan already, I see.'

'So, a paved path to the moor, eh?' said Hugh, who can always be relied upon to bend towards estate management.

'Unusual, I know,' said Lord Ross, 'but needs must. I can cope with sleeping on the ground floor of me own house but if I couldn't get up to me moor, life would barely be worth living.'

Ah, I thought. The poor man was banished from the bedrooms and Lady Love had gone berserk with rosebuds in his absence. And as for Biddy and Dickie Tibball? Lachlan's nurse and Lavinia's 'right hand' were, as I had guessed, a couple of old pals down on their luck who'd been taken in as paid companions, for all they might be called 'secretary' and 'nurse' to soothe their pride.

The mysterious David Spencer arrived a moment later and was absorbed into the general sitting down, flapping of napkins and passing of bread – for aside from the footmen carrying in salmon and potatoes, the household shifted for itself. I glanced around, wondering if there was a pained butler in the background somewhere, his fingers twitching at an invisible pair of serving spoons. Our own Pallister would go into a sharp decline if *we* were ever to begin treating every meal like a picnic this way. I took a sauceboat that Mr

Spencer handed to me, slopped some of it over the piece of fish on my plate and handed it on up the table to Lord Ross on my other side. Hugh, opposite me between Lady Love and Biddy Tibball, looked black enough to start the rain again. I noticed that the cat had a seat of its own, a tall stool at Lord Ross's side. It stretched and stepped off his lap, settling down on the stool and watching the fish plate's progress with interest. I could not look at Hugh for fear of what I might see on his face now; he who scoffs at me for my dog sitting quietly over my feet, hidden from view by the tablecloth.

'Are you on a visit, Mr Spencer?' I asked. 'Or do you live here?'

'Just a flying visit, I'm afraid,' he said, with another flash of those white teeth. 'A birthday visit for LL. I'm an old chum of both and I do like to pop up and see them every so often.' He sent a speculative glance up and down the table as he spoke and I wondered if he had a specific worry.

'Pop up from where?' I asked, merely to keep him talking. 'Are you a neighbour?'

'Ha, hardly,' said Spencer. 'I pop up on the sleeper from King's Cross.'

'Gosh,' I said. 'You *are* a good friend. That sleeper blighted years of my life. It's the one drawback of marrying a Scot.' A quick frown tugged at his dark brows as I mentioned marriage and it occurred to me that the specific worry I had imagined might concern Lavinia's future son-in-law.

At this moment, however, Donald was talking quietly with Mallory and I had to admit they made a handsome pair, her glinting dark head close to his fair one and their faces solemn as they murmured softly to one another. Perhaps I was fretting over nothing. I could just catch the odd word if I tried hard.

'. . . wool prices, you see,' Donald was saying. 'These New Zealand sheep farms have the kind of acreage that . . .'

19

My heart sank. Even Hugh had not started talking to me about the market price of sheep wool and foreign competition during our engagement. I leaned forward to catch Mallory's reply.

'. . . very modest mixed farming, rather than just sheep, and although they sell the surplus . . .'

I sat back, not sure whether I was comforted, alarmed or simply astonished. Before I had recovered and could cast around for another source of chat with Mr Spencer or manage to attach myself to one of the general conversations going on around the table, a tremendous clattering and thumping began somewhere in the hall. Pelting footsteps and ragged breaths reached our ears and then the dining-room door banged back on its hinges. Two people tumbled in and caught each other in an embrace just before they sprawled headlong onto the carpet.

'Oh! Oh!' said the female part of the tangle of arms and legs. 'Daddy! Mummy! Dickie! Biddy! Mallory! Donald! Oh! Oh!'

'Thank the Lord!' said the male part, detaching himself. He turned to the girl and hissed, 'Don't say any more.'

'We were up on the moor! We saw—'

'Don't tell them!' This hiss was so loud I wondered if the boy had had theatrical training.

'Oh dear,' said Lady Love. 'Dandy, I'm afraid these two reprobates are my younger daughter and her husband. Cherry and Mitten. Mr and Mrs Martin Tibball.'

'Tibball?' I said.

'Yes!' Biddy Tibball exclaimed. 'Can you imagine the joy of two old chums like Lady Love and me when our children tied the knot?'

I could imagine the relief of two impoverished parents like Biddy and Dickie when their son landed a Dunnoch, certainly.

'Cherry?' Lady Love was saying as I dragged my mind out of the gutter, or at any rate out of the accounts book. 'Mitten? These are our dear Don's parents come to stay. Come to see what sort of family their son is marrying into. Thank you for all your help, darlings.'

They did not look old enough to be married. I would have put the girl Cherry at seventeen or eighteen, although the hair ribbon that was sliding down a lock of her chestnut curls was more suited to a nine-year-old. She was dressed in a tea-gown and a mackintosh and the tops of a pair of lumpy knitted socks showed above her gumboots. Her husband, if it was really true that this pair of puppies were married to each other, wore a cricket jersey of equal vintage to his parents' tweeds and under it a set of brown overalls, like a labourer; the collar showed above the V-neck and the legs were tucked into a pair of gumboots even muddier than his wife's.

'How d'you do,' said Cherry. 'Welcome to Applecross. Failure dawn *Chomraich*.'

'Please don't speak Gaelic in the dining room, darling,' said Lord Ross. 'Or if you must, please try a little harder to pronounce it properly.' Then he made a noise as though he had swallowed a fly. 'Your fricatives are too breathy, Cherry. You sound like a fairy.'

Now the girl started making the rumbling noise too, and Lady Love joined in along with one or two others until it sounded as though a light aircraft were just about to take off from under the table. Biddy Tibball broke first, collapsing into giggles. Then the footman, disappearing out of the room with the empty fish plate, said, 'Fuchsia cabin marmoset coal-cake', which finished off the rest of them. It ended with Lord Ross wiping his eyes with his napkin.

'Dandy, you must forgive our servants,' said Lady Love when the tittering had died down. 'I've told them until

21

I'm blue in the face not to lapse into Gaelic in front of southern guests but we were all brought up together and went to Miss Alva's school until we were ten so they take no notice of me. All he said was that we sounded like cockneys.'

Hugh – included among the 'southern guests' – wore a frozen mask of offence, but all I could think was how surprised I was to learn there was a Gaelic word for 'cockney'. Besides, there was a much more interesting conversation to be had. The elder Mrs Tibball had begun it.

'What did you see up on the moor, Cherry darling?' she was asking her daughter-in-law. 'Don't leave us on tenterhooks.'

'I was mistaken,' Cherry said.

'What did you think you saw, Cherry?' said Lord Ross.

'Don't tell them,' said Mitten. 'As your husband, whom you promised to obey – in front of most of this lot, not even a year ago, I might add – I forbid it.'

'You *are* funny,' said Cherry. 'Well, Daddy, since you ask—'

'Cherry!' That was Mitten again.

'I thought I saw,' she went on, 'to my horror, up on the moor—'

'I'm not joking, Cherry,' her husband said. 'It's not safe. A shock like this could—'

'—with my own two blue eyes . . . a *ghost*.'

Mitten breathed out, as though in relief. I said nothing, minding my manners, but I waited with a small smile on my lips for the chorus of snorts to begin. Not even a solo snort was forthcoming.

'A morning-time ghost?' said Lady Love. 'So not the grey lady then?'

'Not the grey lady, nor the lost child, nor the riderless horse, no,' said Cherry. 'It was . . . someone we know. Most alarming.'

'Was it perhaps a marsh-gas mirage?' said Donald. I was proud of him.

22

'Yes,' said Mallory. 'If someone was cutting peats and broke into a particularly oily patch.' I was proud of both of them.

'This was no cloud of gas,' said Cherry firmly. 'It looked exactly like a person we know, clear as day, striding out across the moor, fit as a fiddle and large as life.'

'A person we know who is *dead*?' said Biddy Tibball. 'Who?'

'No,' Cherry began, then she clapped her hands to her mouth and moaned.

'Now do you see?' Mitten asked her.

'Oh no!' said Cherry.

'Please don't say any more,' Mitten said. 'The shock of it could cause all sorts of collapse. Think for a minute. Do you want to be responsible for a heart attack?'

'A harbinger,' said Lady Love. 'Which one, though? The coup she?'

'No, Mother,' said Cherry.

'The what?' I asked.

'The coal yak?' said Lady Love.

'A yak?' I said.

'No indeed,' said Cherry. She turned to me with the perfect social smile of a nicely brought-up girl chit-chatting to a stranger. '*They* are bringers of death,' she said, spoiling the effect rather. Then her face clouded. 'We merely saw – or thought we saw – someone we know, someone we love – looking rather different and so we thought it was a spirit. We rushed back here to check and we were immensely relieved to see everyone alive and well. I'm so stupid! It didn't occur to me that what I saw was so much worse than a ghost.'

'What are you saying, Cherry?' said her father. He leaned forward in his wheeled chair, making the basketwork sides creak. 'Do you mean it was one of *us*? You saw someone at this table? His voice was stern enough to make the large cat pause in its demolition of its piece of salmon and turn yellow eyes on its master.

23

Cherry Tibball lowered her eyes and spoke in a small voice. 'Don't ask me, Daddy. It was a mistake, wasn't it? Everyone is fine. And here comes Lairdie with the lamb.'

'Lairdie with the lamb' sounded like another harbinger, along with the coal yak, but the dining-room door opened just then and the Gaelic-spouting footman backed in, turning to reveal an enormous platter, upon which about half a yearling sheep was shining and steaming.

He cocked a look at the silent party around the table and let off another stream of gulps and rasps in his native tongue.

'Miss Cherry has seen a vision up on the moor, Lairdie,' said Lady Love. 'A death is foretold. Let the servants know.'

She made it sound as if she was issuing a bad-weather warning to a chauffeur to make sure he fastened the window flaps on a motorcar. Hugh was shaking his head in rueful wonder.

'Neigh neat furt,' said Lairdie, widening his eyes and glaring at the cat crouched on the high stool at Lord Ross's side. I took it to be more Gaelic at first until Lady Love piped up.

'What on earth do you mean "no need for it"?' she said. 'No need for a *harbinger*?'

'Reckless,' Lairdie said. He slid the lamb onto the table and passed Lord Ross the carving knife, then left the room.

'And what does he mean by "reckless"?' said Lady Love.

'Oh dear,' said Biddy Tibball after he was gone. 'Look, LL. Look around.'

Lady Love let her gaze pass around the table, nodding at each place. She was counting. I counted along with her. Donald, Teddy, Hugh and I were four. Lord and Lady Ross were five and six. The three Tibballs brought the figure to nine, David Spencer made a round ten and the two Dunnoch daughters took us to a dozen. Eventually, Lady Love's eyes settled on the cat.

'Not Ursus!' said Lord Ross, putting out one of his scarred

fists and stroking the creature's back. 'Cats don't count, do they?'

'He's in his own seat and he's eating the same food,' said Lady Love. 'I think Lairdie is right. There are thirteen of us. Cherry, darling, this is too grave to be trifled with. What – *Whom* – did you see, walking on the moor?'

'I can't tell you,' said Cherry. 'I can't say who it was. My heart will break from the grief of it!'

She put her hands against the table and shoved her chair back, but her mother and her husband each shot out a hand and clamped her by both arms.

'Don't,' said Biddy. 'Just in case, Cherry. Just in case the cat counts. Don't do it, darling, please.'

'Don't worry, Biddy,' said Cherry. 'It wasn't *me*!'

I was now staring at Hugh in a paroxysm of embarrassment and irritation. I had expected Highlanders perhaps to be a little more romantic than I had been used to in my Northamptonshire childhood, but I had never seen anything like this in all my days. Not even a few years ago on a case in Fife, when I had met some women who felt themselves to be true witches, had I ever witnessed such a carry-on.

'Is that us at a stalemate, then?' said Mallory. I noticed Hugh give a nod of approval. She did not believe in ghosts and she played chess. Despite her peculiar family, those were two marks in her favour. 'Do we just sit here until one of us dies of old age?' Hugh stopped nodding. He does not care for impertinence in the young. I, on the other hand, liked the girl more and more. I glanced at Donald, hoping to see a look of devotion, or even appreciation, upon his face, but Donald was gazing at Lady Love again, God rot him.

'We could count to three and all stand up together,' said Teddy. 'After pudding, I mean. Would that work?'

'You are all very kind,' said Lord Ross. He lifted the cat into his lap, earning a low growl for separating the creature

25

from the last shreds of salmon. 'But a harbinger cannot be outwitted. Besides, I've rather lost my appetite, truth be told, even if this is to be my last meal.'

A small sorrowful noise escaped Cherry's lips.

Lord Ross put his hands down to the wheels on his chair and propelled himself back from the table. 'You are a sweet child, Cherry my darling, but we all know there's only one of us you'd be surprised to see striding out across the moors, fit as a fiddle.'

'Oh Daddy,' his daughter said, with another small sob, as he wheeled himself slowly away.

I shared a look with Hugh, unable to say which idea was most troubling: that the Rosses believed in the old superstition of thirteen at table; that the Rosses believed in visions and harbingers; or that mysterious strangers were wont to stride about the moors rattling everyone.

4

The rest of luncheon passed more sedately than one would imagine possible after such torrid exchanges. David Spencer discovered army connections in common with Hugh, Lady Love and Mallory began a long discussion on the subject of wedding flowers and Donald and Teddy ate steadily, looking neither to right nor left, leaving the Tibballs to me. I discovered that the youngsters, Cherry and Mitten, had a flat in one wing of the house and the elders, Dickie and Biddy, lived in a cottage on the estate.

'Oh, I adore our little hovel!' said Biddy with excruciating good humour. 'It's so easy to run! I flit round with a feather duster in one hand and a cup of coffee in the other and I can be over here with LL's correspondence before the sun is up.'

'It sounds idyllic,' I offered.

'A walk across the heather with my beloved at dawn and at dusk?' said Biddy. 'Even as a girl I never dreamed of anything so delightful.'

'And how long have you been here?' I said.

'I, all my life,' said Biddy. 'My father's estate – Rue No Fern – was just round the headland to the next promontory. LL and I shared a piano master and had our coming-out dresses run up by the same little woman in Plockton. Do you remember— Oh, she's not listening. Dickie was a slave to his father's bank in London, pinstripe trousers and a rolled umbrella: can you imagine? Until a few years ago when we escaped.'

'How lovely,' I murmured.

I decoded it before passing it all along to Hugh afterwards. We were taking a turn on the west terrace, making the most of the hour and a half of watery sunshine before the afternoon gave up completely. This far north the February days were still depressingly short. 'The wife's family lost its estates and the husband's family lost its bank. They lodge in a cottage and live off scraps. Poor things.'

'I wonder how they're set for the future,' said Hugh. 'Donald doesn't have the faintest idea whether this place is entailed on a male heir somewhere. If not, and if Mallory comes down to us with a good wedge—'

'Hugh, really! A "wedge"?'

'. . . leaving this place free and clear to Martin and Cherry, then his parents have nothing to trouble them, even once old Ross drops off his perch and doesn't need a nurse any more.'

'Assuming Lady Love shifts into a dower house,' I said. 'And she might not. If there's no entail.'

'Oh, I think she'll be long gone before that,' said Hugh.

'How can you possibly know such a thing?' I said. 'We've only been here five minutes.'

Hugh took me by the elbow and hurried me round the side of the house to where the broad sweep of the bay was laid out before us. I shivered as he pointed to the north, where great grey lumps of hills rose up above the shore.

'Behold, the clachan,' he said.

'Don't be so tiresome,' I retorted. 'What on earth *is* a clachan? What am I supposed to be looking at?'

'"Clachan" is the old Gaelic word for a village,' said Hugh, 'as I have told you many times, but you never listened. That church over there is the Clachan church and the house I'm pointing out to you is the Clachan manse, although no doubt they'll have the minister in some cottage somewhere. Like Mr Arnethy at Dunkeld.'

28

'Oh Lord, Hugh, not Mr Arnethy at Dunkeld. Please!'

Hugh and Mr Arnethy had plotted and grumbled away for many an evening, but the Presbytery ignored them roundly and the manse was sold to a businessman from Perth whose daughters' ponies had broken out of their field and eaten all the leaves off a new ash planting in our lower copse.

'*Mrs* Arnethy,' I added, 'is probably delighted to have a neat little villa to run instead of that sprawling beast of a house, with ice on the inside of the windows and all the servants three flights away from the drawing room. She's probably jumping for joy to be done with the place.'

'There's not even a spare room for guests,' said Hugh.

'I daresay Mrs Arnethy is jumping even higher for more joy that she no longer has a houseful of African missionaries on rotation. What on earth would one feed them?'

'Cassava,' said Hugh, who had never in his life heard a rhetorical question he did not answer. 'Returning to the point: look at the front door, Dandy. There's a ramp.'

I squinted at the distant frontage of the Clachan manse. It was a pretty white-painted house, almost a miniature version of Applecross House in a way, except that humble sheds to its either side took the place of the sweeping wings here. There was indeed a new-looking wooden ramp beside the steps.

'I see it,' I said. 'Now, since it's freezing cold and about to rain again any minute, might we go in?'

'Snow,' said a voice from behind us. It was Biddy Tibball. I cast my mind back over the last few minutes' conversation and decided that, while she might think us feeble-minded to be arguing about African food and the Abernethys, she probably had not heard a word on the Dunnochs. 'I wouldn't venture up onto the hills, but if it's a turn round the bay you're after, you'll be fine. The road is paved for Lach's chair to run on, you see.'

'Yes, I do see,' said Hugh. And indeed the road that followed the shoreline around from the little stretch of cottages that made the modern village to this ancient 'clachan' at the other end of the bay was a smooth metalled surface, very different from the ragged stretches of rocks and potholes we had seen while journeying to Plockton yesterday. 'As I see the provision made for him to enter the house over there.'

'The old manse,' said Biddy, causing Hugh a small triumph.

'Are Lord and Lady Ross planning to move?' I asked.

'When Mallory is married and no longer needs a home here, Lach and LL are going to retire from their duties as laird and lady.'

'It's onerous enough running an estate when one is in rude health,' said Hugh. I was not sure I agreed with this well-worn sentiment, for although his factor and steward put in long hours, Hugh spends a great deal of time standing in the river communing with his salmon, striding about nodding at the gamekeeper's handiwork and sitting in his library with a heap of dogs. I said nothing.

'Oh, don't we know it!' said Biddy. I noticed that we seemed to have begun walking the shore road without anyone making the decision. 'Cherry and Mitten wouldn't know where to begin! Lucky they have his father and me to help. And lucky we'll be free to offer it. LL won't need a secretary once she gives up the estate and of course Lach won't be needing a nurse any—' She bit off her words and bent her head.

We walked a few yards in silence, before she piped up again. 'Because of all the wonderful work LL has done on the house, you know. That ramp is only the beginning. Rails and rings abound. He'll be quite independent. And there's a lift!'

Ah, I thought. Not because a harbinger of doom had foretold his imminent death, then?

Hugh might ordinarily have been enthused by the thought of a lift, for he loves any kind of engineering feat, from canal locks to cattle crushes, but he was sunk in contemplation of what it might mean for Mallory's portion that her sister was to be given all the estate as a playground. It was up to me to keep the conversation going.

'I assume you've known Mallory all her life,' I said. 'I'm very much looking forward to getting acquainted with her. Donald's estate abuts ours.'

'I remember when she was a tiny little thing. She had the dimpliest knees of any child I've ever known. We used to count them. She had five dimples on one and six on the other. It was quite remarkable.'

It may have been, but I could not dredge up a single remark on the strength of it. Thankfully, we had drawn abreast of a field gate by which a bent-backed man of great age was employed in some mysterious task at an upturned boat, balanced on a crooked stick to hold it off the ground at one side.

'Good afternoon, Michael!' Biddy exclaimed.

Michael straightened as far as he could, to a stoop instead of a hairpin, and said something that sounded like 'whisker', touching his cap with a blackened finger.

'It's not much of a day for boat-mending,' said Hugh.

'English, is it!' said the old man. 'Aye well, 'tis nut a boaty till spring. 'Tis a hutty a while.' He kicked at the stick and the little dinghy fell to earth again, as Michael bent and swiped up two orbs, one in each of his hands.

'They all use their boats as sheds in winter,' said Biddy. 'Very practical. Michael has his turnip crop earthed up under there. But it's a surprise to see you fetching neeps, Michael. I do hope Nellie isn't abed. We never heard that she was ailing.'

'Naw,' said the old man. 'She's up the top field clearing stones.' He waved one of the turnips at the ridge behind us, and right enough we could see the figure of a woman with a creel on her back, making her slow way along, bending and straightening, flinging her arm up and tossing objects backwards over her head. 'And so I've stirred myself from my chair to help her. She'll have the tea ready fair time with me laying it all on like this.'

'That's quite a job for her on her own,' I could not help saying.

'Aye, 'tis not like the old days when the children could help,' said Michael, nodding nostalgically. 'They're all away at the school living the high life now. And poor Nellie has another acre to go before the snow comes.' He tutted and shook his head.

'Yes, perhaps we should turn back too,' said Biddy. 'Lots to do for Lady Love's birthday, Michael.'

'Tell her I was asking for her,' the old man said as he tucked a turnip under each arm and prepared to mount the hill towards his cottage. 'We've all got a lot to be thankful for. You mind and tell her I said so.'

Biddy nodded uncertainly. There was something above the commonplace about the way the old man spoke.

'Can I ask you something?' I said to him. He turned round and skewered me with a sharp gaze that belied his creased face and bent back. Hugh made a little movement with the hand nearest to me. Perhaps he thought I was about to berate the chap for the division of labour in his household. Hugh believes that my detecting career has turned me into some kind of Bolshevik. 'Why is your turnip clamp so far from your house?'

For I made it about five hundred yards from this field gate to the cottage nestled in the hill with its chimney comfortably smoking. It would be a bind, even on a day one were not clearing stones from a ploughed field.

'I dinnat grudge the shaken a bite, but I'm glad they're afar,' he told me and with that he was off.

'Sometimes,' I said, 'I can't tell if they're speaking English or if I'm hearing things. Did he say he doesn't grudge the *shaken*?'

'She-heech-un,' said Biddy. 'S-I-T-H-I-C-H-E-A-N. It's a . . . fairy, more or less.' I could not help my eyes widening. 'They know the fairies will take the odd turnip and they don't mind, but they don't want them near the house, you know.'

'I see,' I lied. 'Have you heard of such a thing before, Hugh?'

'It's similar to the way the churches are kept apart from the villages,' said Hugh. 'Look how far the clachan is from the village proper, after all, "The Street" as they say. In case of unrest in the graveyard. Dandy is English,' he added and Biddy Tibball grinned at me.

'And I'm afraid I didn't follow what he said about thanking Lady Ross either,' I went on, as we made our way back towards the gates to Applecross House. 'Has she done something in particular?'

'She has done a great many things in particular,' Biddy said. 'And she is going to do even more.' Her voice was surprisingly grim, given the words she was speaking. Then suddenly she seemed to recollect herself. 'Or perhaps it was just a birthday wish. The crofters are all very fond of her. She's been good to them, with the shop and the school here for the little ones. And now the pier. That will make a tremendous difference in the long winters.' There was still a rasping quality to her voice and I was not sure I believed her.

'What surprises me,' said Hugh, before I could think of a way to quiz Biddy any further, 'is that there are crofters here at all to be spoiled with schools and shops and a pier. That there's a crofter's cottage right there by the big house, cheek by jowl. Was this land never cleared?'

'Ah,' said Biddy. 'Now, you're getting to the heart of it all. Our little corner of Wester Ross *wasn't* cleared. Lady Love's family have been good stewards and good landlords for many hundreds of years.'

'Lady Love's family?' I said. 'Not Lachlan's?'

'He brought the title here but it's her family's estate and has been since the days of Maelrubha himself.'

'Who?' I said, predictably ignorant.

'That's the seventh century!' said Hugh, just as predictably well-informed. 'Irish monk, Dandy. Killed by Vikings and got a sainthood for his troubles.'

I was impressed. Vikings belonged to very ancient history and, while the Lestons of Northamptonshire have a long pedigree, it was nothing in comparison.

'Scotland wasn't even a kingdom then, was it?' I said, trying to raise my stock with a pinch of knowledge.

'And yet that's when the Mallorys first built a house and settled here,' said Biddy.

Hugh gave her a sceptical look. 'Mallory is a French name,' he said. 'There were no French around until much later. But it's a quaint story. Like the *sithichean*.'

'It's a corruption,' said Biddy.

'Of Maelrubha!' I said. 'Golly! Imagine being descended from a saint. How thrilling. Weren't monks celibate in those distant days?'

'Lady Love never speaks of that side of things,' said Biddy. 'Understandably. But she's very, very passionate about the place, as you can imagine. Now, if you'll excuse me . . .' and she ran off up the front steps, leaving us on the drive.

'She's rattled about something,' I said.

Hugh was not listening. 'And so she named her firstborn child,' he said. 'Mallory was no doubt meant to inherit the place where her forebears have been living for twelve hundred years.'

'Nonsense,' I said. 'They can't have known then there would be no son.'

'Twelve hundred years, Dandy,' Hugh insisted. 'How on earth can a "Mitten Tibball" take over? A child whose father . . .? Dickie Tibball isn't even Scottish!'

'What's it to us?' I said, although I had a horrible feeling I knew.

34

'Donald needs to be encouraged to—'

'Oh no,' I said. 'No, no, no. Donald lives half an hour from my sitting room and that suits me very nicely. I do not want to have to get on that dreadful boat every time I want to see my son, Hugh.'

'But a thriving croft system,' Hugh said. 'An estate that missed the clearances completely. The soil must be a wonder to behold!'

'Quite apart from the fact that we decided immediately and in complete agreement that Donald should be detached and removed.'

'Twelve hundred years of continuous cultivation. I wish I'd had a closer look under Michael's turnip clamp. And we agreed no such thing. My aim was and is merely to put the kibosh on any unsuitable fancies Donald might be harbouring about Lady Love.'

We turned a corner of the house and all but fell over Lady Love herself, apparently coming to look for us. Hugh harrumphed into his collar, as if any amount of throat-clearing would undo the horror if she had overheard.

'There you are!' she exclaimed, 'and just where I wanted you too. Look at that sky.' She pointed up beyond the roof of the house at our backs. I could see nothing more remarkable than the usual heaping bolls of grey that made up the winter sky in Perthshire, but Hugh drew his breath in over his bottom teeth and tutted.

'Snow coming and no mistake,' he said. 'Will it lie, this close to the sea?'

'Heaven knows,' said Lady Love, 'but just in case it does, I thought I'd grab you. This might be your only chance to see the gardens!'

I suppressed a sigh. I am very fond of my dog, proud of my detecting, and was quite beguiled by my sons when they were tiny, with heads full of curls and little piping voices. Still, I have never dragged a guest in my house to coo over

35

a puppy or a baby, or made him listen to me recounting my triumphs, without a single word to indicate interest. Keen gardeners, though, need no encouragement. I could not count the number of rockeries, shrubberies, bluebell woods and grassy paths between mixed borders I have been driven through like a sheep for dipping, Latin names pouring into my ear and insects feasting upon me. I had, though, expected to be safe from any such fate in February.

'Splendid, splendid,' said Hugh. 'I can tell from guide it's a triumph.'

Lady Love beamed at him and took his arm to guide him down a set of stone steps leading from the terrace to her playground and domain.

It was, to be fair, quite something. The grass was free of moss even on this soggy coast and at this soggy time of year and we only had to traverse a few yards of it before we found ourselves with gravel underfoot. Overhead was the real marvel, though. The garden was a perfect warren of arbours and pergolas, loops and knots arching over the pathways making a kind of covered labyrinth. The plants trained up it were bare at this time of year and so I did not know what had arrested Hugh when he stopped dead and peered at a nearby upright from inches away.

'Good Lord!' he said. He spun and looked back along the way we had come, then spun again and looked ahead. 'Good Lord above!'

Lady Love clapped her hands and gave a little chirrup of delight. I smiled blankly.

'How long have you been working on this?' Hugh said, in awed tones.

'*I've* been working on it for forty-six years, since my grandmother taught me to brush the blossoms with a paintbrush to help the pollination,' said Lady Love. 'But the family has been breeding apples since Georgian times. Since this house with its high garden wall was built.'

'All *Malus*?' said Hugh. I knew it would come to Latin sooner or later.

'Nothing so restrained, I'm afraid,' said Lady Love. 'Nothing so austere. You should hear my gardener on the topic.' She turned away from us and shouted. 'Sam? Are you in here?'

A loud grunt came from somewhere deep in the labyrinth.

I took the chance while she was distracted to ask Hugh in a whisper, 'What is it? What's so special about—'

Hugh turned a look of familiar incredulity upon me and answered me out loud in his lecturing voice, the one he uses when instructing tenant farmers in wonderful new agricultural discoveries and when scolding the boys about clashing gears in his motorcar. 'This is not a work of construction, Dandy,' he said. 'Look closely. This pergola is a living thing. These are rooted trees! There must be . . .'

'Oh, thousands of feet of it all told,' said Lady Love.

'But it's latticework,' I said, leaning close and inspecting the nearest section of what I had taken to be a trellis. It did look rather lumpy at close inspection.

'Exactly!' said Lady Love. 'They are apple trees. Grafted into—'

'Crosses!' I said. 'Oh golly, now that *is* clever!'

'But as I was saying,' Lady Love went on, ushering us round a corner and into another stretch of the – now quite mesmerising – bower. 'It's not all apple. Some of it is sour cherry, hence the name of my younger daughter – and how she used to complain until I pointed out that she could have been named "Apple". Some, I'm afraid, is *Rosa rugosa*. We have bred some beautiful roses, my gardener and I, over the years, and I can't resist poking some in here and there.' She pointed at where a thorny cane had been woven up through the applewood and out into a fan shape round a corner. 'Sam!' she shouted again. 'Are you at the cross?'

37

A second grunt came back in reply, from rather closer this time.

'McReadie and I have our worst quarrels about the cross,' she said. 'Hugh, if you're a gardener, perhaps you'd give me your opinion.' She had got my number, clearly; she did not even pretend to want my opinion on anything.

'But what variety are they, this far north?' said Hugh. His tone of wonder had not let up any. 'I struggle down in Perthshire unless I have them trained on a south wall and even at that they're better cooking than eating.'

I nodded knowledgably, for many's the time I have heard Mrs Tilling, our cook, on the matter of what to do with another enormous basket of sour apples when her store cupboard is already full of apple jelly and dried apple rings and the sight of another baked apple stuffed with raisins would make everyone scream.

'They're our own, of course,' said Lady Love. 'They're the Applecross apple cross! My great-grandfather was a terrific breeder.' She gave a tinkling laugh and Hugh joined her. 'He started with crab-apples and the very hardiest dessert variety and spent a lifetime winnowing and discarding until he struck gold. And it's carried on down to McReadie and me. We've grafted some of these eleven times.' She bent down and pointed to some very gnarled lumps at the base of the nearest trunk.

'Well, I take my hat off to you,' said Hugh. 'I thought I'd seen everything. Do you tape the grafts? Some of these new chaps use a kind of gum to guard against canker.'

'My lips are sealed,' said Lady Love. She dropped her voice and leaned very close to Hugh before whispering, 'In case McReadie hears me. I'll tell all after dinner.' Then she drew back and spoke at a normal volume again. 'And here we are!'

We had walked out from under the pergola and found ourselves in a small knot garden. At its centre, of course, was an apple tree; this pruned into the shape of a goblet. An intricate little dovecote was cupped in its branches, octagonal in shape and topped with a weathervane. The frames of the knot-garden beds were made of more apple branches, instead of the usual box hedges or willow hurdles. These had been forced to grow along the ground in a series of swirls, making one think of that poor Mr Van Gogh. Hugh gave a low whistle of appreciation, but I felt rather sorry for them.

The rest of it was bare earth but for the first pinkish tips of something pushing through, and in one of the sections a gardener was kneeling on the wet ground. He was dressed in a mackintosh coat, against the filthy weather, and had gaiters of sackcloth tied over his trouser-legs, as well as an apron of the same covering his front. For all that, he looked frozen; the tips of his ears were blue under his cap and his fingers red under a coating of mud, as he unrolled what looked like a bolt of mattress stuffing over the soil.

'Oh Sam!' said Lady Love. 'What have you done now?'

'It's for Miss Mallory's widding. Nut fur you.'

Lady Love cuffed the back of his head, dislodging his cap until it covered one of his eyes and gave him a rakish air quite at odds with the surly expression he wore. 'McReadie thinks I interfere far too much *in my own garden*,' she said, laughing. 'What have you planted now that will die before it blooms, Sam?'

'Peonies, isn't it?' said Hugh, scrutinising the pink tips just as the mattress stuffing fell on them. 'Or hellebore?'

McReadie gave a snort and shuffled along to the next bare strip.

'Nothing so pretty and reliable!' said Lady Love. 'It might be hibiscus or bougainvillea or even lotus blossom. Sam brooks no nonsense from our climate. If I had any say at all these beds would have snowdrops, daffs, summer bedding, asters, pansies and snowdrops again.'

'Not even a lily?' McReadie said.

'I'll give you the lilies,' Lady Love replied. 'They're no fuss and bother and we wouldn't need to have them muffled in blankets from October until May.'

McReadie sat back on his heels and looked up at her. Now, with his head raised, I could see that he was no ancient worthy but a chap probably the same age as Lady Love herself. His face was lined and brown, but his eyes were clear. They were Highland eyes and no mistake, as blue as the sea on a cloudless day when he smiled and as dark as the sea on a stormy night when he frowned. They crinkled with long-held affection as he regarded his mistress. No doubt they had gone to dame school together. Certainly as he unleashed a torrent of 'fuchsia' and 'marmoset' on her he did not sound like a servant, even to my ears; I who am far from being mistress of my own staff at home.

'And if Mallory chooses to have a tiara in her hair and to pose for photographs on the front steps I shall be laughing at *you*!' Lady Love retorted and stuck out her tongue.

McReadie looked past her and up at the sky instead of answering and a shadow passed over his face. I followed his gaze and saw a bird, huge and black, come flapping down over the roofs of the house to land on the weathervane. It was only a crow but I had never seen such a large one so close up and never seen such a glossy and vital-looking one at all. I am more used to the poor ragged creatures game-keepers leave in the traps on the high moor. This one, free and proud, excited alarm instead of pity. Its legs were posi-tively muscular, clenching as they took a tighter hold of the swinging arm of the vane.

'The Fiona hag,' whispered McReadie, as the bird rattled and rustled its wing feathers and turned its bright black eye upon us all. It opened and shut its beak as though tasting the air, then it hopped down onto the ledge at the dovecote door and popped inside with a single darting lunge.

'A second warning!' said Lady Love. She gasped as a scuffle and squawk rose from inside and a pair of doves came bundling out at the opening on the far corner. Shedding breast feathers as they went, they flapped off towards a distant stand of fir trees. The little tufts of down they had left behind came whirling to earth and just then there was a gust of wind that brought the first snow flurries too, just as light and soft, whirling down after them. From inside the dovecote, the crow gave one single raucous caw.

5

It was falling heavily, straight down in intricate flakes the size of saucers, before we were back through the labyrinth, across the terrace and in at a side door.

Lady Love shook herself like a dog, laughing. 'It's going to lie, I think,' she said. Mr Spencer was crossing the hall towards us and she called to him: 'Have you looked out the front windows, David darling? They do say if it lies on the beach an hour it'll lie on the land a week. I don't give much for my party now.' She gave a mischievous look. 'Or is it supposed to be a surprise? Well, too bad. I'm going to go and tell Biddy to telephone around and dissuade everyone from making the attempt.' She said something else, about a bee of yellow that ended in a cough. Gaelic again, I assumed.

'Fat chance,' said David Spencer when she had skipped up the stairs and away along a corridor. 'The neighbours will come, by land or sea. She inspires devotion and the most wondrous thing about it is that she doesn't even know.'

'That is indeed a rare trait in a— person,' said Hugh. I was sure he had been about to say 'woman' until he caught my eye. 'We have just seen evidence of devotion out in the garden. What a marvel. What a display it must be in blossom and in fruit.'

'Oh, so you've met Samuel McReadie, have you?' said Mr Spencer. We had drifted into a library, where a fire was burning. A large hound of indeterminate breed was slumbering before it. I went over to make its acquaintance. 'He has good reason to be devoted to Lady Love. To be grateful. Care for anything, old man?'

Hugh took out his watch and looked at it, then stared out of the window at the incessant snowflakes dashing past and seemed to decide that three o'clock on such a filthy day was late enough. He nodded at the tantalus of whisky.

'Why should Samuel McReadie be especially grateful?' I said, when they had settled into two armchairs with their drams. I had a cigarette and this darling of a dog to warm my feet and was quite happy. 'For steady employment, do you mean? Or is it more? Carte blanche with the bulb catalogue?'

'He's not just a gardener,' Spencer said. 'He's a renowned plant-hunter.'

'He's *that* Sam McReadie?' said Hugh.

'Indeed,' said Spencer. 'He has travelled all over Europe and Africa at LL's bidding and brought back some decent stuff. She went too once or twice, before Lachlan needed her here. But the famous lily was all his own.'

'He mentioned a lily,' I said. 'Played it like a trump card.'

'Good grief!' said Hugh. '*Agapanthus Mallorium*!'

'He'll be delighted that you've heard of it,' Spencer said. 'It's rather obscure, having no particular beauty to add to its rarity, and he has his heart set on bigger fish now.'

'Oh?' said Hugh.

'A black one,' Spencer said. 'A true black lily.'

'The holy grail,' Hugh said, without any irony. 'And you think this gardener . . .?'

'He's a fine plantsman. It's the Highland tradition: a lowly birth doesn't get in the way of learning. In the sciences as in the arts.'

'Ah yes,' said Hugh. 'The Ettrick Shepherd, the excise man . . .'

'But James Hogg and Robert Burns were lowlanders,' Spencer put in. 'Allan Ramsay too. Although Lord Byron was brought up in Aberdeenshire.'

'Gosh,' I said. 'I wonder what they made of him.' Hugh shook his head at me and I affected not to notice. 'But why,' I went on, 'would being sent to darkest Africa to dig up bulbs make one grateful?'

David Spencer gave me a grave look. 'Lachlan saved their son's life in the war,' he said. I was chastened, of course, but felt a little sulky with it. How was I supposed to know that?

'*Their* son?' said Hugh.

'Mrs McReadie is the cook. Daughter of the last cook. She's lived at Applecross all her days, like Sam too. They have just one son, Roddy, and he was a corporal in the Fusiliers. It was the Somme he got caught in. Lachlan shouldn't have been anywhere near the front, of course. He was almost forty for one thing and he was a major. But he happened to be on a visit to the trench, boosting morale or something, so the story goes, and there was a push no one had been expecting.'

Hugh nodded sagely. All I could think was that I was glad Alec Osborne was not here to sit through this boorish rehashing of battle stories. My fellow detective, the other half of Gilver and Osborne, is a good-natured soul but his hard war is still with him. To be fair, Spencer must have discovered Hugh's own, rather milder, war record over luncheon and so knew there were no dark chasms to avoid. Had Alec been here, no doubt – one soldier to another – Spencer would not have been so plain.

'The way it's told, a couple of men came back from no-man's-land, bleeding and broken, one carrying the other, and shrieking that McReadie was lying there awake and unable to move.'

'Shrieking,' I repeated softly. It seemed a slur on the poor men – or boys, quite possibly – ambushed and terrified.

'My apologies,' said Spencer. 'We are supposed to pretend otherwise for our womenfolk, aren't we? Dandy, I sobbed like a child throughout Arras and I was not the only one.' I concentrated hard on the dog. Its fur was black and sleek, like velvet loosely dropped over its warm muscles.

'So McReadie's lying on the field,' said Hugh. 'What then?' I could not have looked at him if God had commanded me. For of course he *did* pretend that all soldiers were heroes. This was the first of shrieking and sobbing I had ever heard.

'The lad still on his feet made to go back out and fetch McReadie once he dropped off the other one,' said Spencer. 'But he was bleeding heavily from one shoulder and an eye and his mates managed to overcome him and keep him in the trench. No one noticed that Lachlan had slipped away. No one knew a thing until he came back. There was an almighty bang closer than ever and a hideous bellow, and young Roddy McReadie came rolling over the sandbags like a dead weight to be followed a minute later by Lachlan, hauling himself by his hands and somersaulting into the trench. He had carried the boy almost all the way before a shell caught his legs. Then he rolled him the last few yards and tipped him in. Bravest thing anyone had ever seen, so the story goes.'

'And for a gardener's boy,' I said.

'Indeed,' said David Spencer.

'Despite the fact that he had a wife and two daughters at home,' I added.

Hugh glared at me. 'A wife and girls safe at home and a boy you've known all his life lying out in the shelling? There's not a soldier born who'd do it differently.'

'And what happened to his hands?' I said, ignoring Hugh. I am used to being scolded. It runs off me like water by now. 'Lord Ross's burnt hands.'

'Young McReadie had been trapped under a plank that had caught alight, perhaps, or a puddle of oil set off by a shell, I'm not sure,' said Spencer. 'But Lachlan beat out the flames with his bare hands before he lifted the boy. The lad's

45

legs are scarred, I believe, but they work. It's Lach who's paid the price.'

We were all silent a moment then. The beautiful dog turned onto its other side to warm a new patch of skin.

'What's its name?' I asked, stroking its flank.

'No idea,' said Spencer. 'I haven't met this beast before now.'

'And is young McReadie here at Applecross with his parents?' said Hugh. He disapproves of my silliness about dogs.

Spencer gave a bark that might have been laughter. 'No indeed. Roddy McReadie, if you please, is at Oxford. Balliol. Courtesy of Lady Love.'

'Gosh,' I said. 'Although I suppose if one saves a life it makes sense to ensure it's a life well lived. What's he reading?'

'I have no idea,' said Spencer again. He spoke rather grimly. 'But I think his Applecross days are over, no matter how much his parents might miss him.'

I nodded uncertainly. As a mother myself, I think I would be happy to know my son was safe. If he was leading a soaring kind of life to my modest one, I do not imagine it would trouble me, as long as he wrote regular letters anyway.

'No doubt he'll be back for the wedding,' I said.

David Spencer looked as though he was going to say something more than a conventional remark and I sat forward. But all he did was set his glass down on the table and get to his feet, with a rather ostentatious glance at the clock upon the mantel.

'I hope you'll excuse me,' he said. 'I want to beard Lach while LL is busy. I've come all this way to talk to him and I can't ever catch him without either his wife or that nurse of his.'

'Of course,' said Hugh. 'We're quite content to sit on. Send Donald in, would you though, if you see him on your travels.'

46

'No need,' said Spencer, as he left. 'Here he is.'

Donald was wandering past the library door with that very specific look upon his face and with that very specific aimless gait. To be a houseguest, especially a male houseguest, in a country house in bad weather when the womenfolk are planning a party is to be more bored than humans were ever meant to be.

'Mother,' he said. 'Father. Any idea where Ted's got to? I'm dying for a game of billiards and he's vanished.'

'Sit down, Donald,' said Hugh. 'We want to talk to you.'

'Sounds ominous,' Donald said. 'Have you found something to disapprove of, Father? Might I point out that you're drinking whisky in the afternoon and Mother is lolling on the floor hugging a dog. If that's not feeling at home I don't know what is.'

'I've found nothing whatsoever to disapprove of,' said Hugh.

'I have,' I said, but Hugh drowned me out.

'I thoroughly approve. But I'm rather in the dark. Of course, I'll talk man to man with Ross, but I want to talk to you first. You know you'll inherit Gilverton when I'm gone.'

Donald had flung himself into an armchair in his usual fashion, but now he straightened up. 'Hello!' he said. 'It's that time, is it?'

'Not necessarily,' I said. 'Nothing is announced.'

Hugh glared at me and I withdrew my gaze and concentrated on the dog instead, who appreciated me. Its ears were the most wondrously silky things I had ever encountered and it groaned with pleasure and thumped its whip of a tail as I rolled them up on top of its head and then let them unfurl again.

'But Gilverton is one thing and this place is something else again. Do you happen to know why it's earmarked for young Cherry? She doesn't seem the type to take land stewardship seriously.'

'You divined that from one luncheon she arrived at late, did you?' I said. Dog's ears or no, I could not let that pass.

'Whereas your Mallory is clearly a sensible girl.'

'Very sensible,' Donald said. It was a deathly compliment for a young man to give his betrothed and I wondered for the first time how Donald had come to the current pass. Heretofore, he had been swayed by glamour and giggles.

'Is it your upcoming marriage that's leaving the way clear for the younger girl?' Hugh said.

'I don't know, Father. It never occurred to me to wonder. I've got an estate now and another, some distant day in the future, and Applecross is stuffed to the gunnels with Dunnochs and Tibballs. Why would Mallory and I think of squashing in here?'

'Exactly,' I said. 'There's such a thing as being too close to one's family.'

'That's what I think,' Donald said. 'I shall be very happy just to visit a few times a year and perhaps have Lady Love down at Benachally sometimes. Lord Ross doesn't travel but there's no reason *she* couldn't.' His face had lit up as he spoke of it.

'Well,' said Hugh, 'when Lady Love and Ross move out to the Clachan manse, there will be no need for two of the Tibballs. And as for the other two . . .'

'They love Applecross,' said Donald. 'They adore it. They've got their own sheep.'

'I don't know what weight that's supposed to bear,' Hugh said. '*You* have sheep, Donald. *I* have sheep.'

'No, I don't mean they've got five hundred ewes and followers and a shepherd with a cottage. I mean they've got their own little flock of hefted blackface sheep that they shear and dip and drench with their own four hands. Cherry's in the rota for turning all the sheep back up the hill for the local crofters if they wander.'

'Like Madame de Pompadour and the Sun King,' I said. 'How do the crofters take it?'

'Tremendously well,' said Donald. 'Mitten tried drying his hay on the fences last year, as they do in Norway, and it was a revelation. Even the oldest and stodgiest crofter had to admit it was efficient.'

Hugh was nodding. 'It makes a lot of sense,' he said. 'Get the wind through it without it blowing away.'

'Hugh!' I said. 'We are not here to talk about drying hay. We are here to decide on the wisdom of an alliance between the Gilvers and the Rosses.'

Hugh's mouth dropped open and Donald, after an initial start, burst out laughing. 'You sound like something from Shakespeare, Mother,' he said. 'What on earth do you mean?'

'Do you love her?' I said.

Hugh shot to his feet and banged down his whisky glass. 'I just remembered a letter I need to get in the late post,' he said, hurrying out.

'There's only one post,' Donald called after him. 'And you've missed it.' But Hugh had made his escape and did not return.

'Well?' I said, when I was certain we were alone. 'Do you love Mallory Dunnoch?'

Donald shrugged. 'Of course,' he said. 'Why wouldn't I? She's a good sport and very chummy. Not always sulking and simpering like some girls.'

'She's quite a bit older than you, darling,' I said and, to my horror, Donald grew red in the face and stammered as he answered.

'What difference does age make? Who's to say that the chap must be older than the lady? What would it matter if she were even older? What would it matter if she were forty instead of thirty? What if she were fifty?'

The dog by my side was looking up at him from under troubled brows, worried by the raised voice.

'Oh Donald,' I said. 'Oh darling. She *is* fifty, isn't she? But you can't marry her daughter, just to be near her. It isn't fair on anyone.'

Donald stared at me, absolutely aghast. It took two swallows before he was able to speak. 'Are you talking about Lady Love, Mother? Where did you get such an extraordinary notion?' He went over to the drinks table and poured himself a goodly measure of whisky. I heard the tantalus neck knock against the rim of the glass. 'I wish you'd told Father your mad imaginings before you told me,' he said. 'Or told Teddy, even. They'd have laughed you out of it and we wouldn't be having this embarrassing—'

'They think it too,' I said. 'Teddy asked your father and me to do something.'

Donald swung back round to gape at me, as shocked as I had ever seen him. 'Ted did?' was all he said, but his face showed that this was the ultimate betrayal, by his lifelong co-conspirator and chum.

'Look,' I said hurriedly, for I was sure I could hear footsteps approaching. 'It's Lady Love's birthday tomorrow. Don't say anything to spoil her party. Then we can all go home and your father will write to Lord Ross and you can write to Mallory and the whole episode will be behind us by spring.'

'I can't do that to Mallory!'

'Better that than what you were planning to do,' I said. 'Let the poor girl meet someone who adores her.'

'She's thirty,' Donald said. 'No one has shown up so far.'

'That's terribly unkind, darling,' I said. 'I'm shocked at you for that, I have to say.'

'And *I* have to say I'm shocked at *you*, Mother,' Donald said. 'You of all people. Lecturing me because I've decided airy-fairy love and marriage don't need to go hand-in-hand.' The dog by my side was shaking now. It stood up and shivered, its flank bumping against my shoulder.

'How dare you!' I said, scrambling to my feet. 'How dare you speak to me that way.'

Donald's eyes had a glint of triumph in them. 'I notice you don't ask what I mean,' he said quietly.

'I—' I put a hand up to my throat and straightened the neck of my shirt, which had got disarranged from my sprawling. 'I don't care what you think you mean. I have not brought you up to be impertinent and unfeeling.'

'No,' said Donald. 'You've brought me up to be sensible about my domestic arrangements and discreet in affairs of the heart. And now you scold me for learning my lessons well.'

I tried hard to speak, but my mouth opened and shut like that of a goldfish and no sounds emerged. The dog was growling.

'All I can say is if I get the chance I shall try not to disappoint you any more,' Donald said.

'What?' I managed to croak.

'If the vision Cherry and Mitten saw on the moor turns out truly to be a harbinger of death,' he said. 'If she should suddenly be widowed, perhaps I shall follow my heart. As you suggest.' I blinked in astonishment. Donald laughed. 'I don't mean it,' he said. 'I don't believe in any of that nonsense.'

'Nor do I,' I said, trying very hard not to think about the black crow ousting the doves from their cote. 'I don't believe that you meant a single word you just said and I am willing to disregard it. Let's just be good guests until Friday morning and we shall discuss this when we get home.'

Before he had a chance to answer me, whether in agreement or in more of this most uncharacteristic belligerence, a gasp from the open doorway hooked my attention away.

It was Cherry, standing there framed in the light from the hall, staring – or so I thought – right at me. She had the cat Ursus in her arms.

'Did you bring that with you?' she said. 'Is it yours?'

Donald and I frowned at one another.

'Did we bring . . .?' said Donald.

'The dog!' she cried. 'The black dog. Is it yours?'

'Isn't it yours?' I said.

51

The dog had put its head down and its tail was curled right under its body. A low growl rumbled through its ribcage and made the floor under my feet start to thrum. Ursus, with one single unearthly yowl, scrambled out of Cherry's grasp, clawed his way up and over her shoulder, then ran down her back and shot across the hall and up the stairs.

'It's the coup she!' Cherry cried. 'Right in the house. The coup she!'

At her words, the dog stopped growling and, instead, put its head back and gave a long hollow howl that set every hair on my head standing on end. Then it turned and loped across the library floor towards the windows.

'What's it do—' Donald had time to say before the creature took a leap at one of the lower panes and broke through with an almighty crack. It landed out on the terrace in a shower of glass and a whirl of snowflakes and then took off into the gloom, leaving behind only its paw-prints – three damp and one bloody – as the snowstorm swallowed it up.

'What *was* that?' I said, as we stood boggling at the hole in the window and the swirl of snow coming in and melting on the polished floorboards.

'The coup she,' said Cherry. 'The coup do. It's a harbinger of death. And it's the second one today.'

I did not tell her it was the third. I did not believe in such things. I was holding on very hard to my certain knowledge that no such thing could possibly be true.

6

A hastily summoned estate carpenter boarded up the window and a muscular housekeeper swept and swept the terrace until every splinter of glass was gone. Meanwhile, Donald, Teddy, Hugh and David Spencer made off across the garden in pursuit of the *cù sith*, (as I shortly found out was the creature's true name) Lachlan took to the brandy bottle and soda siphon in his business room with Dickie Tibball in close attendance, and the Dunnoch and Tibball women took to the fireside in the hall to twitter.

'Poor thing,' I said. 'It must have been in a terrific fright to plunge through a closed window that way.'

The Highlanders simply shook their heads and muttered inaudibly.

'The *coup she* is an even clearer sign than the Fiona hag, Dandy,' said Lady Love. Cherry gave a little cry. 'Yes, mow howl,' said her mother, 'I'm afraid we saw the Fiona hag Anna doo in the garden just a while ago. And you saw . . . it *was* Daddy, wasn't it? Up on the high moor. Not the coal yak?'

'Please, *please*, speak English,' I said. 'I'm getting dizzy.'

'I said the black dog – the *cù sith* – is a stronger sign than the black crow – the *feannag an dubh*,' Lady Love said obligingly, 'and I want Cherry to admit she didn't see the *cailleach* – the old woman – earlier. *Mo ghoal* means darling.'

'It was Daddy,' said Cherry, when the lesson was complete. 'And yet it wasn't.'

The housekeeper, who had now finished with her broom and shovel outside on the terrace, brought in a tray groaning with tea things. Perhaps she was also the cook. A plate piled high with some food I did not recognise dripped butter onto the tray cloth.

'I've made a batch of my bannocks for you,' the woman said, muscles rippling on her forearms as she bent to place the tray on the tea-table. She was truly Amazonian and between her *ligne* and her air of command I would have pegged her as a games mistress or, if a servant at all, then a governess. 'And there's the end of last year's gooseberry jam I've been saving,' she went on. 'But you've all had a shock and you need a wee treat.'

'Thank you,' said Mallory. 'Dandy, do take one, but do take a napkin too. That's a lovely dress and Mrs McReadie believes in butter.'

Ah, I thought. This then was the distaff half of the plant-hunting gardener and barely a servant at all, bound instead by long years and close connections to the family.

'And please stay, Mrs McReadie,' said Lady Love, confirming my view. 'Sam will have told you about what Cherry saw earlier.'

'Daddy but not Daddy,' Cherry said again. She did not take a bannock but she spooned three spoons of sugar into quite a small teacup and drank thirstily. 'He was walking, for one thing.'

Mrs McReadie turned her head to one side and, with her black hair pulled so tightly back from her brow and her bright black eyes sparkling, looked rather horribly like the crow as she waited for Cherry to say more.

'He was striding out like a man in his prime. Poor Daddy, but you know what I mean. It was definitely him, though, in the way that it wasn't anybody else and it wasn't a stranger. Do you see?'

Lady Love nodded calmly. She looked up at her cook and gave a smile. 'What do you say to that, Mrs McReadie?'

''Tis the way,' Mrs McReadie said. ''Tis good news usually. When we pass over we are whole again. No longer halt and lame.'

'I always wonder about that,' said Cherry. 'If I were to die—'

'Hush, hush,' said her mother.

'No, but if I were to die in childbirth or something,' Cherry went on. 'At thirty, say. And say Mitten lived until he was an old man of eighty. When we met again in heaven, wouldn't it be odd? Would I age? Or would he be thirty again too?'

'And what about the baby?' said Mallory. 'Would it grow up in heaven, or would you be looking after a tiny baby for all eternity. With no nanny.'

'Oh I think all nannies go to heaven, don't you?' I said. Mallory grinned at me and, not for the first time since we had arrived, I felt a little pang that this girl – if I could help it – was not to be my daughter-in-law. I liked her.

'So what shall we do?' said Lady Love.

'I'll get busy,' said Mrs McReadie. 'You should all get yourselves along to the church and I'll have them ready before you're back. Will you speak to his lordship or will I, my lady? He won't like it.'

'He'll take it better from you.' Lady Love turned to me to explain. 'You wouldn't mind wearing a little bit of wool twisted round your neck until the sun comes up, Dandy, would you?'

'What?' I said.

'Just a little braid of coloured wool my good Mrs McReadie's going to plait. One for each of us. One of our old customs here.'

'It can't hurt, I suppose,' I said.

'Exactly,' said Lady Love. 'Make one for Ursus too, won't you?'

Mrs McReadie frowned at that. 'Lairdie was saying you counted the cat at the lunch table,' she said. 'I wouldn't count the cat. It was only twelve. Unless . . .' She turned to Cherry and fixed her with another bird-like look. 'Why are you thinking about childbirth, Miss Cherry?'

Cherry was in mid-sip of her sweet tea and she spluttered a bit. 'Mrs McReadie, really!'

'Oh Cherry,' said her mother. '*Are* you, *mo ghoal*?'

Mallory leapt up and went over to squeeze her sister hard. 'Am I to be an aunt?' she said. 'Remember my plan for what a marvellous maiden aunt I'd be? With a walking stick and an ear trumpet and changing my will a lot to keep all your children on their toes!'

'I was waiting until after your birthday, Mummy,' Cherry said. 'I didn't want to steal your thunder.'

'But I can't think of a nicer birthday present,' said Lady Love. 'I am going to be a grandmother at fifty. Wait until I tell—' Her face fell as she remembered. 'Yes, we will all wear the wool, Mrs McReadie. Cherry can wear two. Ursus will be livid – he's never had a collar on – but he will have to lump it. And we'll all go to church and pray hard. I refuse to be widowed on the eve of my birthday. I simply refuse.'

At that, Mrs McReadie took herself off to go about her mysterious business and before the ladies were done billing and cooing about babies, the men were back, bursting in at the front door with snowcaps on their heads and wet feet, full of news.

'Dratted thing scaled the wall by the peach houses,' Donald said.

'Surely not,' I said, for it sounded fantastical.

'Thirty-foot wall,' Hugh said. He was limping.

'It didn't bite you, did it?' I asked him.

'If I'd got close enough to be bitten, we might have caught it,' Hugh said. 'No, I tripped over a roller in the dark.'

56

'It's a raker, not a roller,' said Lady Love. 'I've told Sam not to leave it lying out.'

'I wish he had listened,' said David Spencer. 'The beast probably climbed it to get a head start on the wall. It left a smear of blood round about there.'

'It's really gone, though?' said Cherry.

'I never even saw it,' said Teddy disconsolately. 'The Hound of the Baskervilles and I missed it completely.'

'It was a perfectly nice dog,' I said. 'I fondled its ears and it wagged its tail.'

'Although, Dandy,' said Hugh, 'you never think a dog is anything but an angel. Nice dogs don't leap through glass for no reason.'

'It got upset at raised voices and the cat was the last straw,' I said. 'But Baskervilles didn't come into it, Teddy, I assure you.'

'Raised voices?' said Lady Love mildly and I felt myself flushing. Donald concentrated hard on untying his soaked boots. He took a folded newspaper from a small table and, after checking the date on its front page, began screwing up its pages and stuffing them into the toes. Mallory watched him for a while and then turned and gave me a questioning glance.

Oh Lord, I thought. She's good-natured *and* she's clever. If only things were more straightforward I would be cock-a-hoop.

We all dispersed to our rooms to rest, with Lady Love telling us that the gong would summon us to the hall again when the car was ready to take us to the church. I looked uncertainly out of my bedroom window and wondered if the motorcar tyres would be equal to the snow that was piling up in treacherous mounds as the onshore breeze swept it against the wall at the side of the lane.

'That's where a metalled road is a problem,' said Hugh, standing at my side. 'A good ash track gives a bit of purchase.'

57

I said nothing. Hugh would love to metal the roads at Gilverton but the lowest road-maker's estimate had made him open his eyes so wide his spectacles fell off into his porridge as he read his letters one morning. He was waiting for the Corporation to pave the road that passes us by, hoping to catch the men and offer them a little something to take a detour through Gilverton on their way.

'I had the most startling conversation with the ladies while you were scampering round the garden,' I said, subsiding onto my dressing stool. 'The cook is busy making some kind of charm out of wool for us all to wear. So Lord Ross won't die. Can you believe it, in this day and age?'

'A knotted wool necklet,' said Hugh. 'Yes. I've seen them on farm animals when there's foot-and-mouth. I've seen one on a horse for the staggers.'

'Well, you're going to see one on a cat tonight,' I said. 'Shall you wear yours?'

'It would be rather churlish to refuse, don't you think?' said Hugh. 'No worse than touching wood or throwing salt, after all.'

We both turned as a knock sounded at the door. I called out to whoever it was to enter and Mallory came in.

'Ah well,' said Hugh, patting me on the shoulder in an affectionate way. 'I shall see you later, Dandy. Bang on the door if you don't hear me moving.' And he took himself off to his dressing room, leaving the girl to me.

'Sorry to beard you,' she said, coming in and sitting on the end of the chaise by the fireplace. 'But I did just want to catch you alone. I can't even imagine what you must think of us all.'

'Not you, dear,' I said. It would have been more diplomatic to pretend that I did not understand her.

'You are kind,' she said. 'Donald told me you were kind. And he told me too about your . . . would you say it's a job? Gilver and Osborne? I hadn't heard of it, I'm ashamed to

58

say. We're so cut off up here. We were worse before the bee yellow oak banana, of course.'

I held up a hand to stop her. I was learning that whenever someone appeared to lapse into utter gibberish, it was probably Gaelic. 'Bee yellow oak banana?' I asked.

Mallory blinked and then threw back her head and went into paroxysms of laughter. When she had wiped her eyes and cleared her throat she explained, speaking the words much more slowly. 'The *bealach na bà* is the new road up from Lochcarron. It's not passable in winter but it's made a big difference overall. Still, we don't bother with newspapers much, because they're so out of date by the time they come off the coal boat. Especially now with the BBC signal so much better . . .'

'We haven't been mentioned on the news bulletins!' I said, horrified by the very idea.

'But,' Mallory said, 'you are detectives? You and Mr Osborne. I was hoping he'd be here, actually. Might he come up for the engagement party in spring? And the wedding? I'll invite him and you twist his arm. But meantime, is it *infra dig* to talk to you without him?'

'Mallory, my dear,' I said, uncrossing my legs and sitting up as straight as Nanny always told me to, 'do you have a matter you need to put before Gilver and Osborne?'

'I hope not,' she said. 'I fear so. I was hoping you'd listen on spec, as it were, and then we'll see.'

'Tell all,' I said. 'I'm very happy to help.' Quietly to myself, though, I was wondering if I had got to the bottom of the engagement, such a bloodless kind of engagement from what I had seen. Had this young woman accepted Donald just to get a free crack at his detective mother?

'It's about Applecross,' she said. 'The estate, I mean. Or rather, it's about my mother. And my father. It's not really about Cherry and Mitten. It's more about Biddy and Dickie. It's about that ghost, you see. And the *feannag* and the *cù*

59

sith. Oh, I wish everyone would just talk to one another! Have you ever read *Cyrano de Bergerac*, Dandy?'

I had been trying to follow each little dart of speech as she pecked and ducked back again and the last change of subject unseated me. I thought it was yet more Gaelic until my brain caught up with my ears. 'No,' I told her.

'Or *The Mill on The Floss*,' she added. 'Or just about any Hardy. All those sad tales that would have come out quite differently if people would only just talk to one another instead of sitting with their lips buttoned and their hearts breaking.'

'I quite agree,' I said. 'I'm glad to hear you being so sensible. There's something I want to broach with you, along the same lines. But let's discuss your business first, shall we?'

She looked intrigued, as how could she not, but she shook her head and pressed on. 'No one has to die,' she said. 'Everything could be all right. We could all just be very sensible and level-headed about it, instead of this . . . this . . . nonsense!'

She appeared to think she had said enough to put me in the picture. She was certainly waiting for me to weigh in, an expectant look upon her pretty face. There was only one subject I could think of that would fit the bill.

'Are you talking about dissolving something?' I said, carefully. 'About scandalising society a little instead of a lot? Toughing it out? Facing them down?'

'Yes!' she said, sitting back with a great rush of relief. 'Exactly. Oh, I am glad you understand.'

'I shall be your ally,' I said. 'Unlikely as that might seem. A divorce is much worse than a broken engagement.'

'But far preferable to a murder,' she said, nodding. I felt my face, which had relaxed into a smile, freeze again. 'Cherry is so suggestible, you see. Heaven knows what she really saw out on the moor. But *someone* sent that terrible crow into the garden. And someone definitely brought that dog into the library.'

60

'Mallory,' I said. My voice had dried to a croak worthy of the *feannag* itself. 'Are you telling me you think someone is planning a murder?'

'What did you think I was telling you?'

I was so shocked that I blurted it out. 'I thought you wanted to break your engagement.'

'What?' she cried. 'Why?' Her eyes had filled with instant tears. 'What has he said to you?'

'Nothing! Nothing at all,' I assured her, kicking myself. I took a deep breath. 'But his father and I both have serious reservations.' I heard a floorboard creak just on the other side of Hugh's dressing-room door. He had been listening to this conversation he did not have the stomach to join and he had just run away at hearing himself mentioned.

'About me?' Mallory said. One of the tears trembled on her lower lashes and splashed down onto her cheek. 'Is it my age? Or, what has Daddy said about a settlement? Is it my dowry?'

'It's the fact,' I said, hardening my heart and reminding myself that she did not care for romantic novels, that she preferred cold reality laid out at everyone's feet while they squirmed, 'that we think he is unhealthily infatuated with your mother.'

She had taken a breath to say more but it stilled in her breast and she sat with her mouth open. Then, to my astonishment, she laughed. 'Oh that!' she said. 'Well, yes of course. Everyone is in love with my mother. Daddy, still.' Her face clouded briefly, but she went on. 'Dickie and Mitten, to be sure. And then there's David Spencer. He has been in love with my mother for decades. Sam McReadie adores her. And every crofter on the estate would walk over coals for her. I'd be worried about Donald if he hadn't lost his heart. I'd think him a cold fish indeed if he wasn't mesmerised by Lady Love.'

'I see, I see,' I said. 'And so, setting that aside and returning to what you were saying. You think someone who loves your mother is planning to kill your father . . . to clear the way?'

Mallory stared at me for a long while before she answered. 'Not necessarily that,' she said. 'And my mother has plans of her own besides. But something. Still, we don't have to sit in silence waiting, do we? It can't be true that Cherry and Mitten saw my father's ghost. And so I want you to interview them – interrogate them if it comes to that – and find out what they really did see. I don't like the idea that someone is acting like a kind of horrid puppet-master, setting those harbingers to pop up. And even if *that* person doesn't follow through on the threats, I don't like the way everyone is now expecting Daddy to die. It feels dangerous. It feels like the kind of thing that might plant an idea in the wrong mind and then it will come true. Please Dandy, can you stop it coming true?'

I had never missed Alec Osborne more; him and his interminable pipe, his drawling dismissal of all my most fanciful imaginings. I needed his sharp brain hacking through the clouds in mine. I needed someone who was not hog-tied by motherhood and crippled by being a houseguest. For although we had often worked rather closer to home than Hugh was happy about, this was something else again and I needed Alec to keep an eye on the jagged rocks below the surface and pilot me. I needed him so much that when my bedroom door handle started to turn I was convinced that he had somehow magically arrived.

Of course, he had not. In the doorway stood Mrs McReadie, staring stolidly at Mallory. I wondered how much she had heard and whether she would go straight to Lady Love to report it. I had seen enough earlier to know they were extraordinarily close for mistress and maid.

'I've your wools for you,' she said, holding up a fistful of coloured strands wound into loops. 'I wondered where you'd got yourself to, Miss Mallory. I've got yours too,' she added, glancing at me.

'Thank you, Mrs McReadie,' Mallory said, leaping up and

holding out her hand. The older woman sorted through the handful, peering closely at one or two necklets before selecting one.

'And then you, Mrs Gilver,' she said. 'I know which one is yours. I was most particular about winding yours.' She held out a loop of hairy-looking heather-hued wool on one of her fingers. I took it and gave it an uncertain look before putting it round my neck.

'I have the jealous,' said Mrs McReadie. At my look, she explained. '*Eolas*. A strong ken of charms. It came down my mother's side. You've no need to fear my wools round your neck. You or those boys of yours.' She could not have dreamed up anything less comforting to say if she had tried. 'If his lordship had worn the wools I had given him when he went away to the war he'd not have been sitting in that chair since he got back,' she went on. 'Fine and sure my Roddy was wearing his and came through, didn't he?'

I was speechless. To credit a twist of wool instead of the courage and sacrifice of the man to whom she owed her son's life, and to do so out loud in front of the man's daughter, marked her out as a heedless fool. And her wool was scratchier than horsehair. I put a finger underneath it to pull it up over my collar.

'Next the skin's best,' she told me. 'For his lordship's sake. I'll see you at the kirk, Miss Mallory,' she added, making her way back to the door. 'I've a drop of broth to hand in at the shop. Mr Spencer was along the street buying baccy and said the Logans are all bad with the whooping cough, and wee Mrs Logan is still in her childbed yet a few days.'

When the woman was gone Mallory laughed and shook her head. 'She's not as bad as she seems,' she told me. 'That broth of hers could raise the dead, for one thing.'

I fervently hoped that it would not need to.

7

I was never sure afterwards who cancelled the plans to go to the church. The gong did not sound and, after a while, the thought of that broth began to shove its way to the front of my mind, although I did not know whether I would rather fortify myself with it and then venture out or brave the elements with broth and a toddy to come home to.

When Hugh rapped on the door and came in, I was looking out of the window again at the snow dashing down into the black salt water of the bay and at the way the walls and gateposts were softening as I watched, their edges disappearing under the constant dredging. The lane was invisible, with just a few scribbles of bracken strands and brambles showing its borders.

'Unless they've got a sleigh I don't fancy our chances of getting to the clachan and back tonight,' Hugh said.

'They might be adamant enough to make us tramp along there in snowshoes,' I said.

'Did I ever tell you of the Boxing Day I came down the hill with tennis racquets on my feet and a newborn foal over my shoulders?' said Hugh.

Of course he had. When one has been married as long as I have been married to Hugh, one has been told everything, at least once.

'I had forgotten!' I said with a smile, terribly wifely tonight for some reason. 'For goodness' sake don't mention tennis racquets to the Dunnochs. I wouldn't put it past them.'

But when we ventured downstairs, it was to find the family

gathered at the hall fire once more and we could see lit candles and a white cloth through the dining-room doorway.

'Well, now, here we all are,' said Dickie Tibball. 'Aren't we just! All present and correct.'

I managed to stop my lip from curling, but could not help a glance at Lord Ross. It would be annoying enough to be stuck in a wheelchair, but to be nursed all day every day by a man who came out with twaddle like that would be excruciating. And he could not sack his daughter's father-in-law, presumably.

'Except Mummy,' said Cherry. 'We can't go in without Mummy.' She had shed her wellingtons and retied her ribbon, making it even more bedraggled for the extra manhandling. In her tea-gown and a cardigan she now looked simply dowdy rather than eccentric. Her husband had put on a tie and a pair of brogues. Donald, Teddy and Hugh had divined that we were not changing – men always seem to find out somehow – and were in their tweeds. Mallory and I alone looked as though we were about to eat dinner, in velvet and satin with a few jewels here and there. I had brought a shawl against the draughts I expected and I swathed myself in it now to damp down my splendour.

'Didn't you say she was having a tray, Mallory?' said Biddy Tibball.

'When we have guests?' said Lord Ross.

'Headache, Daddy,' Mallory said. 'And you know LL's headaches. She needs to get in front of it tonight so it doesn't spoil her birthday.'

'Poor Mummy,' said Cherry.

'I shall take her an oat pillow later,' Mallory said. 'Lairdie?' The footman had come to the dining-room door. 'Can you ask Mrs McReadie to put an oat pillow on the back of the range, for my mother, for after dinner? Thank you.'

'Let's go in then,' said Lord Ross. 'Would you mind pushing, Dickie? I'm finding myself tired tonight.' Cherry

65

and Mallory both turned troubled eyes upon him and he hastened to dispel their fears. 'It's just fatigue, my dears. It's nothing more than the upset of the day. I'll be fine after a good night's sleep. Dandy?' he said.

I fell into step beside him to be taken in first as guest of honour, although his low seat in the wheeled chair meant that he could not take my arm. I glanced behind and saw Hugh take Mallory's arm. Donald took Cherry, and Teddy and Mitten made an elaborate show of not fighting over the last remaining lady, who was Biddy. She looked coldly furious about it too. Perhaps she had thought that with Lady Love hors de combat she would rise up the ranks.

Dinner was uneasy and, while not silent, was marked by conversation desultory enough to be more tiring than a whirl of chatter. The food was good, although the fabled broth made no appearance. We dined off sea trout, pigeon and something with pineapple and a great deal of sweet syrup; a hefty enough meal to make me long for coffee and bed. Perhaps Mallory was exhausted too, despite her youth. Certainly when Lairdie, bringing in the wine for the pigeon, told her that her mother was not to be disturbed she hardly argued.

'Has she got an oat pillow already?' was all she said.

'Dinnat ken. Jist that she's tucked up and doesn't want anyone knocking.'

'That's my Lady Love,' said Lord Ross. 'She's always been the same the night before her birthday, even when she's not laid low with a bad head. Christmas Eve too. Alone in her room, communing with the spirits of Applecross. All those ancestors.'

I nodded with as little encouragement as was polite. I had had enough of the spirits of Applecross, be they black dogs, crows or turnip-eating fairies.

My sons were nicely brought up though. Donald murmured with feigned interest and Teddy found a conversational ball to bat back. 'It seems odd that Applecross has an English name,' he said, 'when everything else is so very Scottish.'

'It's a bastar—' Lord Ross began, then cleared his throat and flushed a little. 'Excuse me, ladies. It's a corruption of *Aporcrosan*. Similar to all our "Aber"s around the land. It means the confluence of two rivers. Nothing to do with apples actually.'

'The things we can say when Mummy's not here!' said Cherry and there was a ripple of laughter.

'My wife prefers the older name,' said Lord Ross. '*A' Chomraich* – "sanctuary".'

'But any place where rivers meet *is* a lucky spot,' said Hugh. He had told me that many times early in our marriage, standing on the hill top behind Gilverton, showing me where the Tummel and the Dun met at Lochaber.

'But the rivers no longer run in their old beds,' said Lord Ross. 'We had to divert the River Applecross and the *Allt Mor* when we made the new roads, a culvert being so much more affordable than the bridges it would have taken to span and re-span them. These days the *Allt Mor* empties into the river upstream.' He waved a hand behind him. 'It was hard for my wife when the luck drained from the place she loves so much. I think that's when she started making her plans.'

'Her plans?' I asked.

'Such as looking at the Clachan manse with new eyes.'

'For sanctuary?' said Hugh. 'Does Lady Love think Applecross is unlucky then, without the rivers meeting?'

'She's as fey as a crofter sometimes,' said Lord Ross. 'She heard so many tales from the *cailleachs*, sitting in those black houses.'

'She sat in a what?' I said. 'And listened to . . . Do you mean the cries of ravens?' I was sure that the coal yak was what they had all called the crow in the dovecote. Their laughter told me I had got it wrong again.

'A *cailleach* is just an old woman, Dandy,' said Hugh.

'A crone,' said Dickie Tibball. 'Of which Applecross has many.'

'And my darling wife was in and out of their cottages for a bowl of crowdie and a bite of oatcake all her childhood through. Listening to them talk. Just like her mother before her and her daughters in their time.'

'They're called black houses because the fire's in the middle of the floor and the smoke goes up through a hole in the roof,' said Donald. He turned to Lord Ross. 'But they've all got chimneys now, sir, haven't they?'

'Indeed they have, thanks to Lady Love's efforts and pockets,' he said. 'And yet there are those on the estate who say they're plagued by coughs and colds now that they don't have the "good peat smoke" in their lungs any more. Ungrateful wretches.'

'But they still make crowdie and oatcakes and they still spin and they still have lots of stories,' said Cherry. 'It added to the atmosphere no end, hearing "Rapunzel" and "Sleeping Beauty" from an old lady in a lace cap, spinning yarn while spinning tales.' She grinned at me. To be fair, she had made it sound charming.

'Enough of the local crones,' came Dickie Tibball's voice, and I saw Cherry's smile fade. '*The cailleach* – definite article – is something else again, you know.' Cherry's smile was now completely gone. 'It's an avoidance of her real name, you see. The washerwoman. A Highland version of the grim reaper. Isn't that about right?'

'Not exactly,' said Mallory.

'Anyway, we didn't see her,' said Cherry. 'We told you at lunch. Now, let's talk of happier things. Has anyone started trying to prise a few blooms out of McReadie's grip for Mummy's party?'

'Flowers?' I said.

'Oh ho,' said Mallory. 'Haven't you seen McReadie's hothouses yet? They're at the far side of the apple crosses garden, against the west wall. And they're a sight to behold, aren't they Daddy?'

'Lady Love's birthday is just about the only time the old curmudgeon will put a hand to his secateurs,' Lord Ross said. 'He treats every bud as if it's his firstborn child.'

'That's gardeners for you,' said Dickie Tibball, with great good humour. Since he did not have a gardener now and, presumably, if he had ever had one the loss must be a painful memory, it seemed a strange choice of banality to deliver.

'Does he grow fruit?' said Hugh. Donald, Teddy and I all laughed.

'Oh, he patrols the *fruit* with a rifle cracked over his arm,' said Lord Ross.

'Because our old chap at home was a fiend,' said Teddy. 'He's retired now, but one year I had to steal a basket of grapes so we had dessert for a dinner party. Do you remember, Ma?'

'Very well,' I said. 'Poor man. He was looking forward to a rosette at the flower show and all he got was an assurance that you'd be punished.'

'It's McReadie's pineapples that consume him,' said Mallory. 'We're only getting one tonight because it was bashed.'

We all laughed and the conversation ran on along these harmless lines until the pineapple cake had been reduced to crumbs and the pot of coffee in the drawing room was wrung dry. Donald and Teddy went to play a quiet game of billiards, and Mallory and Cherry had some unspecified preparations to make for their mother's birthday morning, but the rest of us went gratefully to bed.

I looked out again just before retiring. The snow had stopped but lay thick on the ground. A crystalline drift of it was piled up on the windowsill and the transoms of the window itself were ruffled as though with lacy shelf-edgings, like a cottage dresser. Gratefully, I pulled the curtains closed and climbed in between my warm sheets.

★

I have always loved waking up on a snowy morning. The cold white light, the muffled softness of the usual daily sounds, the eerie transformation of one's humdrum surroundings into a stage set: all of these turn me back into a girl again. Add blue sky and sunshine and a snowy morning is a holiday indeed. I met Mallory coming back from the bathroom with her sponge bag as I sallied thence with mine and the beaming smile I gave her took no effort.

'Poor Mummy,' she said. 'Have you peeked yet? We were hoping against hope that the Marshalls and the Dents would be coming for her party, but it doesn't look very likely. It must be two foot thick out there. We'll still have the minister and his wife and the Miss McIntoshes from the street, of course. They always come hours early and stay till the bitter end. They have skis and it won't be the first time, but arriving on skis is their most entertaining moment, I'm afraid.'

'I shall do my valiant best,' I assured her. 'And I'm sure your mother will be happy with her family. Is she going down for breakfast or does she have it in her room?'

'In her room today, Mrs McReadie told me,' Mallory said. 'She went up with poached eggs and coffee just a minute ago.'

'Up?' I said.

'The tower room,' said Mallory. 'It was Mummy's nursery and she never gave it up. Cherry and I threw fits of envy when we were children – it's like something from a fairy tale and we coveted it like anything – but it's so very much Mummy's room it would seem odd now. I still can't believe she and Daddy are moving out, after—Well, after the summer.'

After the wedding, she meant. 'One party at a time,' I said.

'We shall all certainly do our best.' Then she sidled closer and spoke in a whisper. 'I want her to have a perfect birthday. One glowing day. And then we'll speak to her tomorrow, as you and I laid out.'

I would not have said that our peculiar discussion had laid anything out, exactly, but I could readily agree to the

70

plan to make Lady Love's fiftieth birthday a proper treat for her. I went into the bathroom wondering how I could add some celebratory touches to the rather dull cashmere scarf and suede gloves I had bought to serve as a birthday present from Hugh and me. Grant, my maid, had wrapped the box very nicely and tied it up in ribbon, but it was still a scarf and a pair of gloves.

Donald was waiting in the passageway when I came out. He had his towel round his neck as though he had just played a set of tennis.

'What on earth?' I said. 'Have you been lounging there waiting your turn? As if it were a bus stop?'

'Only five minutes,' he said. 'You were nice and quick.'

'What if it hadn't been me?' I said. 'Donald, really. You are not one of the family yet and I must insist on better manners than that. What would Nanny say?'

'I knew it was you,' said Donald. 'You were singing that song you and Alec always sing when you're puzzling something out.'

I knew Alec Osborne had an irritating habit of humming 'The Entry of The Gladiators' at moments of distraction but I had no idea I had caught it from him.

'*Are* you puzzling something out, Mother?' Donald said.

'Not really, 'I said. 'What did you get Lady Love for her birthday?'

'A wooden apple that comes undone like a puzzle, with a secret compartment,' said Donald.

'And Teddy?'

'A box of playing cards with botanical paintings of apples on the backs. Why?'

'Good boys. Never mind,' I said and went on my way.

Lord Ross was still in the breakfast room, with Dickie Tibball at his side, as ever. 'Good morrow, good morrow,' Tibball said. 'How do you like us in our winter cloak?' It was all I could do not to shudder. He was so horribly proprietorial about the place.

'You got here all right through the drifts then?' I said, and was rewarded by his grin lessening from maniacal to merely insufferable. 'It looks awfully deep.'

'Oh, we bunk here when it's as bad as this,' he said. 'We have a hammock in an attic, you know, and no pig or parrot at the cottage. The aspidistra will survive until it thaws and we can venture home again.'

'And a thaw never takes long, this close to the sea.' said Lord Ross.

'It's very pretty while it lasts,' I said. 'Even just glimpsed from a window.'

'You're not tempted to take part in the snowball fight?' said Tibball. 'The children are planning a battle royal, so Biddy tells me.'

'Where?' said Lord Ross. 'Not in the apple crosses, I hope.'

'Oh, Daddy,' said Cherry, who was just coming in at the door. 'It was once and it wasn't a snowball.' She gave a comically exasperated sigh and turned to me. 'Once upon a time, Dandy, back in the primeval mists, Mallory and I broke a graft on one of the apple crosses larking about in the snow and we've never been forgiven, even though the tree recovered and Mummy couldn't find the scar now if she had a week and a magnifying glass. I ask you!'

'Your mother likes to see the virgin snow in the knot,' said Lord Ross. 'You can scuffle around out the front, building snowmen and throwing missiles. But if you break a window it comes out of your dress allowance.'

'My dress allowance?' said Cherry, looking down at the pair of balding corduroy riding britches and Fair Isle jersey she was wearing. 'I think I'm in funds, Daddy. I could prob-ably spot *you* some in a pinch.' She had finished buttering a slice of toast. Now she wrapped it in a napkin and, dropping a kiss on her father's head, she made to leave the room again.

'But Cherry, now I think about it,' her father said, 'you shouldn't be in a snowball fight at all! Good gracious, no!'

'Oh Daddy, really!' Cherry said, wheeling back and giving him a look of wounded innocence. 'What have you heard? Who told you?'

'Mummy, of course. Who else?' said Lord Ross. 'And I'm going to insist. No snowball fighting for you.' The words 'in your condition' were unspoken but they hung in the air anyway. Dickie Tibball looked on with interest, but in ignorance. Clearly his wife had kept the news to herself.

'Very well then,' said Cherry. 'I shall sit on the sidelines and catch my death of cold instead.'

'Or there are the flowers,' said Dickie Tibball. 'For the party. They're all ready and waiting.'

I had no room to speak because my maid Grant is so far above herself I have despaired of ever getting her back in her place. Still, it seemed very odd to me that this man, whether one thought of him as Lord Ross's nurse or as Mitten Tibball's father, should be telling Cherry how to prepare for her mother's birthday.

'I shall do them once I've cheered the snowball fight,' she said. This time she really did leave the room.

'You should sit and eat a proper breakfast,' Lord Ross called after her.

She did not answer but Mallory appeared in her place and grinned. 'No time, Daddy,' she said. 'Are there boiled eggs? Oh good – very portable and very apposite for a snowball fight too. We've just got time for one almighty set-to and then we're going to start decorating. Mrs McReadie has promised to try to winkle some orchids out of the old grump. And I'm going to ski up to the blasted oak and cut some ivy with my little machete. We can twine it round the staircase and put some ribbon through it if McReadie won't give up any carnations. I know there are some in flower in those hothouses somewhere because the

73

smell just about knocked me over when I took Donald to show him the melons.'

Hugh had entered during her speech. 'Pinks?' he said. 'Sweet williams? Or true carnations? I'd love to see what he's got them growing in to have them in flower for St Valentine's Day.'

'Oh,' said Mallory, putting a hand against her chest in an astonishingly unconvincing gesture of surprise. 'Is it Valentine's Day? I had quite forgotten.' She gave a giggle and trotted out, juggling three boiled eggs expertly as she went.

'I don't blame Spencer for taking off out of it,' said Dickie Tibball.

'Has he left then?' I said. It struck me as odd that he would journey all this way and leave before the party.

'Not left,' Lord Ross said. 'Just off somewhere on the early market boat. Mysterious tasks related to Lady Love's birthday, no doubt.'

'He'll be back before the fun begins,' Dickie added. 'Wise man, skipping the preparatory nonsense.'

'Yes, all the womenfolk are going to be skittish today,' said Lord Ross. 'Do pardon them, Mrs Gilver.'

I smiled tightly, rather offended not to be included amongst the womenfolk. On the other hand, gushing and skittishness were not in my repertoire and I was glad to be excused joining in with it.

Biddy Tibball had the gushing well in hand anyway. I caught sight of her in the drawing room as I was leaving to return to my own room and write Lady Love's birthday card. Hugh had been instructed to join me and sign his name to the thing. He did not dare to argue in front of Ross and Tibball, although I knew he found such behaviour sentimental.

'I'm not dusting, Dandy!' Biddy sang out. She was standing by the piano with a duster in her hand and a

74

great sliding heap of silver-framed photographs piled up one on top of the other on the closed lid. 'Or rather, yes of course I *am* dusting, but only incidentally. I'm setting out fifty years of our darling Lady Love. These are usually kept in the top attic, except for this one day.' She caught her lip and seemed to consider saying more, but in the end she merely pointed to a few of the topmost photographs, which showed Lady Love and a spaniel on a gusty hilltop, Lady Love and McReadie standing in a village hall with a beribboned cup held between them and Lady Love and Lord Ross sitting in an open-topped motorcar of ancient pedigree, both of them with darker hair and smoother faces.

'Look at this one,' said Biddy, selecting a small frame with a tinted picture of an enormously fat baby in frills and flounces. 'Wasn't she a poppet? And then there's the first one of her and me together.' Lady Love was still as plump as a peach, sitting on a tired-looking pony with a slim and sleek Biddy on another pony at her side.

I tried to select a remark that touched on how much prettier Biddy had been than her chubby friend but everything seemed to carry with it an unspoken coda regarding how things had changed now that Lady Love was the centre of this adoring household and Biddy Tibball was no longer slim and sleek, but instead dishevelled and scrawny. I failed of course. There was no such remark – and besides, there were more important matters to be spoken of.

'Do you know Dickie's plans for the day?' I said. 'Is he to be swept up in the preparations for the party or will he be by Lord Ross's side?'

'I can fetch him for you now if you need him,' Biddy said. 'I think he's still at breakfast.'

'No, no, it's not that,' I assured her. 'It's just that I promised Mallory I would make certain her father was carefully watched. For a day or two. After yesterday.'

75

'Mallory?' Biddy said, in a voice so surprised the word came out like a squawk. 'Don't tell me she's starting up with all that too? I mean to say, we adore Cherry. Of course we do. She's a darling. But she's never heard a fairy tale in her life she didn't believe. Besides all this Garden-of-Eden frivolity.'

I frowned. I had never thought of the story of the Garden of Eden as being one of rampant frivolity. A certain mis-guidedness, perhaps; a lack of forethought . . .

'I see you've escaped hearing about it,' Biddy said. 'Enjoy it while it lasts. You'll be lucky to get through another day without a lecture from one of them.'

'One of them,' I repeated. 'Cherry or . . .?'

'Mitten,' she said and sighed. 'Oh, that boy!'

'But not to harp on it or anything,' I went on. 'If you would just drop a word in your husband's ear about sticking close to Lord Ross for a bit, until the memories fade. It would soothe Mallory's troubled breast, which would soothe Donald's, which would in turn soothe mine. And his father's.' I gave a smile into which I tried to inject as much soupy maternal devotion as I could muster.

'It *was* odd. That dog. Wasn't it?' Biddy said.

'Poor thing,' I said stoutly.

'And the crow,' she added. 'Arriving like that. Has anyone checked to see if it's still there, I wonder. It's when it flies off that it takes souls with it, in the old legends.'

I said nothing and kept my face as blank as a skating pond. But perhaps my thoughts showed there anyway, for she gave me a sheepish look.

'Highlanders we are for good or ill,' she said. 'In fact, there should be a picture of Lady Love and Lachlan's wedding day here somewhere.' She clacked through a few silver frames and then drew one out with little cry of triumph. 'Here we are! Now look at that and tell me what you see.'

I saw a young-looking Lavinia in a frock with a bustle and a silly little hat practically falling over one eye, and Lord

76

Ross tall and handsome in full regalia. A youthful Biddy, with hair just as frizzed and a smile just as wide, stood at Lady Love's side as she did today. There was only one remarkable figure in the group.

'Is that a washerwoman?' I said, peering at the plump figure in a shawl, with a linen bundle under one arm.

'Yes, that's the *cailleach*,' said Biddy. 'The bent knee.' She took pity and said it very slowly. '*Bean-nighe*. For luck.'

'I thought the . . . I thought she was a bringer of death,' I said.

'Yes,' said Biddy. 'But better to invite her and keep her happy, than scorn her and risk her wrath, you see?'

'I think so,' I said. 'One's friends close but one's enemies closer?'

I wondered if I imagined the little twitch of a frown that plucked at Biddy's brows for a second before she smiled again.

'Are you all right?' said Hugh, arriving in my bedroom minutes later. 'You look a bit fed up.'

'Just reflecting on life and its disappointments,' I said, not the most diplomatic thing to say to one's husband, I admit. Thankfully, Hugh – as ever – was not really listening.

'Yes,' he said. 'Can you believe Ross wants me to go outside the wall and struggle round through the snowdrifts to get to the hothouses instead of walking on the paths. The garden, if you please, is not to be sullied by my footprints.'

'Not *your* footprints,' I said. 'Not specifically yours, and I think I might agree, actually. Let's go for a look from the landing window. I bet it's lovely.'

We went together up the next bend in the stairs and stood at a tall window that looked down over what the Dunnochs appeared to call the apple crosses garden. It was exquisite. The snow had landed on every filigree of twig and turned the criss-cross of the pergolas into something magical. The paths underneath were as perfectly blanketed with snow as the knot garden itself had been blanketed with ticking by McReadie the day before. The dovecote had a cap of snow on its roof and the arms of the weathervane were dusted with a few flakes too, like sugar on a little cake.

'Oh,' I said. 'It's beautiful. You see, Hugh? She's right, isn't she?'

Hugh hates to be corrected. He grunted into his collar and then brightened when he saw something he could point out to me that I had missed. 'McReadie's going to be in trouble!' he said. 'Look at that. The man's left his spade sticking out of the ground right in the middle of the garden. Ha! If no one's allowed to walk on the precious snow, we're going to be looking at that shovel handle until it melts, aren't we?'

'It's not exactly an eyesore,' I said. 'I wouldn't have noticed it if you hadn't drawn my attention to it. And I think it's a broom. It doesn't have the handle of a shovel.'

Hugh, corrected again, harrumphed even harder and I was glad to hear someone approaching who would break up our tête-à-tête.

Mrs McReadie was coming downstairs with a laden breakfast tray in her hands.

'Hasn't eaten a bite nor drunk a sip!' she said. '"Breakfast in bed, please, my good Mrs McReadie." *My good Mrs McReadie*! As if her and me weren't bairns together. Then she eats not a bite of it. As if I haven't got better things to do than tramping up and down all these stairs on a day like today!'

'It's very kind of you,' I said. 'Couldn't a maid do it?'

'No maids at Applecross,' said Mrs McReadie. 'Just the footmen.'

'Ah,' I said, as if I understood. In truth, it struck me as beyond odd to hang on to footmen and let the maids go. 'Do you have daily girls?'

'Women,' said Mrs McReadie. 'No maids in this house, like I just told you.' Then she stumped off down the next

78

half-flight, still tutting over the wasted effort of the breakfast tray.

I turned my gaze back out of the window towards the restful scene laid out below us, but there was movement there now, catching my eye. One of the pop-holes in the little dovecote had darkened as the crow, startlingly black this morning, hopped out. It took two more hops to the edge of the platform, looked down, looked up and then spread its wings – they looked five feet wide from up here although they could not be, really – and flapped away, setting the weathervane gently spinning and sending a flurry of snow-flakes down to settle on the mounds and drifts of the knot garden.

I shivered, standing so close to such a large window on such a cold day.

8

I need not have spoken to Biddy Tibball of my fictitious concerns after all, as matters transpired, for Hugh elected to spend the day with Lord Ross. He had legitimate business with the man, of course: thrashing out a settlement for Mallory. He also had a deep desire to keep out of the way of the party preparations.

The girls and boys came in flushed and boisterous about eleven o'clock. Teddy was crowing about a decisive victory over the others, since he had been unencumbered by a maiden to protect and defend. Cherry had, it seemed, ignored her father's admonitions and all thought of delicacy and had plunged into the fray with the rest of them.

'We've made a snowman too,' she said. 'I tried to make it look like Mummy, with one of her old hats and a trug, but it looks more like Mrs Tiggy-Winkle, if I'm honest. Have a peep at it out of the window, Dandy, and tell me honestly if you think I should knock it down before the Miss McIntoshes and the Rev. all get here.'

I wandered through to the dining room, which had the best view, and looked out at the snowman squatting in the middle of the lawn.

'It doesn't *scream* Lady Love,' I said. It was completely round with a completely round head, as is the way of snowmen, and since the snow was falling again, the hat and trug were beginning to blur. What it looked like, more than anything, was another version of that washerwoman from the wedding picture, the trug full of snow in place of the linen bundle and the snow on the hat rendering it indistinguishable from a white cotton cap. 'Why not ask your mother?' I said. 'But don't knock it down if she disapproves. Just put a bowler on top and pipe in front and turn it back into an archetype.'

'Oh, I don't want to bother Mummy,' said Cherry. 'She always keeps strictly to herself whenever we're planning a treat for her. She's such a rewarding person to lay things on for. Now, if McReadie really has agreed to furnish us with some of our own flowers, as Daddy said, I shall begin on the dining table. Are you a flower arranger par excellence, by any chance, Dandy?'

'I can just about put daisies in a milk bottle the right way up.'

'Splendid. Mallory and Donald are too busy nuzzling and whispering sweet nothings to be any use, but you and I shall manage.' She put an arm through mine. 'If we spin it out a bit we might miss the first couple of hours of the Miss McIntoshes. They always come miles early for anything. They see it as a wasted journey unless they get two meals out of us on any visit. But then they taught Mummy piano and they're not to be snubbed.'

'I'm happy to help,' I assured her.

But when we went along a side passage and arrived in a little stone-floored flower room with a sink and a shelf of vases, I quailed at the task ahead of me. Here, plunged into deep buckets, lying in towering heaps with wet paper over their stem ends, and filling two wheelbarrows besides, was a profusion of hothouse flowers the like of which I had never seen. Their perfume was enough to render one dizzy and the colour was an assault on the eye.

'I'm thunderstruck,' said Cherry. 'McReadie never forks over this much loot. Not for Armistice Day, not for Daddy's first Christmas back at home. Hmph! Not for *my* wedding.'

'Everyone keeps saying how much he adores your mother,' I said. 'Here is the proof.'

Cherry was unbuttoning her cuffs and rolling up her sleeves. 'Righty-ho,' she said. 'We need something massive for the middle of the dinner table and we could have two fairly biggish lots on either end of the sideboard too. Then how about a garland for Mummy's chair in the drawing room, for when she's opening presents? We've got these very natty little vials around here somewhere. They're for fancy buttonholes really. You put the stem in a sort of test-tube . . .' She had gone over to the dresser and was rootling around the shelves, '. . . then fill it with water, and a thingumajig like a hairgrip keeps it in place. There should be a box of them.'

But all I could see on the shelves were a great many bound volumes, each stamped with a date in gold upon its spine. These, I assumed, were Lady Love's garden journals. 'Perhaps in here,' Cherry said, wrenching on a drawer handle. 'Now then, let's see.' The drawer had sprung open at last, despite how the damp of this room had warped and swollen its wood over the years. She stood staring down into it.

'Is something the matter?'

Cherry turned to me and swallowed. 'No,' she said. Her hands were behind her as if she was steadying herself on the lip of the open drawer. 'At least, I think it might be the smell of all these flowers. I feel a bit sick all of a sudden.'

'It's to be expected,' I said gently. 'A cup of tea usually helps.'

'Rotten luck for it to start today of all days,' she said. 'I've been fine up till now.' She wiped her forehead and smiled. 'I think I'll take your advice and ask Mrs McReadie for a "nice cuppa".' She sidled past me and swept out.

It was subtle but not quite subtle enough. Cherry Tibball had just seen something unexpected in that drawer. She had palmed it quite adroitly. But she had not been able to hide the fact that it had shocked her.

I went over and looked down into the jumble of string ends, seed packets, blunt penknives and the papery detritus of many flower bulbs. There was, naturally, nothing left to be seen. I could follow her and ask her what she had found. On the other hand, I had no standing here to be quite as inquisitive as all that. I decided to stay put and try, valiantly and alone, to turn this monstrous harvest into a selection of floral arrangements that could be plonked in vases and dispersed around the house. Wreaths and garlands were not necessary for a woman of fifty in my view. I attacked the drawer on the other side of the dresser, still hoping for the test-tubes, and it sprang open. There was another identical tangle of plant labels, envelopes, bulb skins and a sprinkling of sunflower seeds that had escaped their packet.

There was also – or so I very firmly believed – another object to match that which had just been found in the first drawer. I considered it closely without touching. It lay on top of the disordered contents in a way that could not be chance. I put a hand to my neck and remembered the scratchy feeling of the wool necklet I had worn last night. What lay in the drawer of this dresser was something quite different, although it was made of the same stuff. *This* wool had been worked into a little figure like a corn dolly. Its face was blank, although my fancy supplied some shadowy features from among the heathery light and shade of the yarn itself. Its arms were thick plaited straps and its hands had been formed by knotting the plaits and burning them into charred lumps. Its body was a stiff barrel shape made by wrapping the wool round a bobbin. Its legs were two single strands wisping off to nothing at their raw ends. It was crude but its meaning was clear. This was Lachlan, with his scarred fists and his withered legs.

I reached out a hand to the nasty thing, then I remembered Biddy Tibball's words about the crow – 'It's when it flies off that it takes souls with it' – and my hand froze halfway to the drawer.

'Oh nonsense!' I said to myself. I snatched the figure up, closed the drawer and left the flower room.

But who to ask? I could hear the low murmur of Hugh's and Lachlan's voices through the library door and was loath to bother them. Lady Love was nowhere to be found and not to be disturbed if one did track her down. Donald and Teddy would never let me live it down if I spoke to them of such a ludicrous superstition. The Tibballs were strangers to me. Cherry was already too upset for a girl in her condition, Mallory had been rattled last night and did not need me rattling her further. David Spencer had gone out for the day. I was standing at the foot of the stairs, wondering where to turn, when my eye landed on the telephone.

Alec Osborne is as English as English can be, hailing from the Dorset coast, but he has taken to Perthshire life with gusto and can match Hugh, fact for fact, when it comes to the ancient traditions and surviving ways. If there was anyone I could ask about this without sinking myself in his estimation, it was Alec.

I sat down on the hard chair beside the telephone and rang the exchange. With a great many clicks and buzzes and three or four of those ghostly conversations one used to hear all the time before the Perth exchange was modernised, my call was put through.

'Dunelgar,' said Barrow, Alec's valet cum butler, in his usual way. That is to say as if one had just opened his tomb and shaken him.

'It's Mrs Gilver, Barrow,' I said. 'Good morning. Is Mr Osborne around?'

'Good after*noon*, Mrs Gilver,' said Barrow. It was, I saw with a glance at a nearby grandfather clock, just gone twelve. 'Mr Osborne is at Gilverton.'

'Really?' I said. 'Why?'

'Dealing with the correspondence,' Barrow said witheringly. Fussing over my dog, I interpreted. Molly, Alec's spaniel, had finally lain down in her basket one night just after Christmas and breathed her last and I had a Dalmatian pup of great beauty and intelligence, who adored Alec and who was offering so much succour to him through his mourning that at times I felt a bit green about it all. If only we had not procured her, Bunty the second, from the single-end of a Glasgow gangster, I would have been tempted to go back and see if there was perhaps another litter with another such angel in it.

The exchange was quietly disapproving of a second call so shortly after I'd abandoned the first one, but the girl relented after a bit of coaxing and soon the bell rang out. I saw in my mind's eye the set in my sitting room and the set in Hugh's business room and Pallister, our butler – who could teach even Barrow a thing a or two about sounding recently disinterred – padding calmly towards one of them.

But when the receiver was dislodged it was Grant's voice I heard, cheerful to the point of cockiness, coming down the line.

'Gilverton. Good morning!' she said.

'It's afternoon,' I told her. 'Why are you answering the telephone?'

'Hello, madam,' she said, unbowed. 'How's it all going? Mrs Tilling said she'd heard on the BBC that the weather's atrocious up there.'

'The weather is beautiful up here,' I said. 'Snow underfoot and blue sky above. Where's Pallister?'

'I am here, Mrs Gilver,' said Pallister's voice. 'But I shall "hang up" now if I am not needed and deal with the matter later.'

There was a short burst of knocks and rattles as he put down the other telephone.

'Well, Grant,' I said. 'You are what the boys would call "for it" and I can't say I'm surprised. What on earth's going on down there that you're answering telephones?'

'I'm in your sitting room,' she said. 'Mr Osborne asked me to take dictation.' I waited. 'Well, not true dictation, with a shorthand notebook or anything. But he said what he wanted me to write and I scribbled it down. There were ten letters between yesterday and today and he got overwhelmed. So I'm helping.'

'And is Mr Osborne there now, too overwhelmed to chip in?'

'He just stepped out with Bunty,' said Grant. 'Do you want me to call for him?'

'Do I want you to hang out of the French window in my sitting room and halloo for Mr Osborne that he's wanted on the telephone?' I said. 'No thank you. I do not have time to interview new butlers once Pallister drops dead.'

'Is it anything *I* can help with?'

I sighed quietly. We have all learned, since the advent of the telephone, the knack of sighing with little enough force to avoid making the line crackle. 'Probably,' I said. 'What would it mean for a little model of a person to be made and then stashed in a drawer?'

'With pins in it?'

'No.'

'A noose round the neck?'

'Grant,' I said, 'if either of those two features had been included, don't you think I might have mentioned them? No, just a model of a person, in a drawer.'

'Can you tell who it is?' she said.

'Oh yes. It's . . .' I looked around, peering up through the banisters and into the open doorways of the downstairs rooms. The Dunnochs were very insouciant about draughts. I turned away to the wall and put my hand round the mouthpiece. 'It's Lord Ross,' I said, looking down at the little object, which sat in my lap looking blankly up at me from its featureless face. 'He has withered legs and burnt hands from an act of heroism in the war, and this doll's legs are single strands of wool and its hands have been charred to lumps. It's him.'

'And you're sure about the act of heroism?' said Grant.

'What do you mean?'

'Well, how long ago was the doll made? What order did the single strands and the withered legs happen in?'

I shuddered. 'You are a ghoul,' I said. 'It was lying on top of a drawerful of bits and bobs in a flower room. It can't have been in existence long.'

'It can't have been in the *drawer* long,' Grant said, which was a fair point.

'Let's assume it's a recent creation, depicting Lord Ross after the fact. Without pins or a noose, what does it mean that it's in a drawer? Anything?'

Grant kept a thinking silence for a moment or two, then sniffed. 'There are some old superstitions about writing a person's *name* on a scrap of paper and putting it in a drawer,' she said. 'Death within the year, supposedly. But voodoo dolls – that's what it is, madam; whether you gasp or not – are harmless until the harm is evoked by a weapon.'

'*Weapon*?' I yelped.

'Symbolic,' said Grant. 'Such as pins.'

'And have you ever heard of two dolls being made, in case the first pins don't work? One up the sleeve, as it were?'

'No,' said Grant. 'Why?'

'Never mind,' I said. 'When Mr Osborne gets back with Bunty can you ask him if he's soaked up any Highland lore about all of this? The other signs have been northern in origin.'

'What other signs?' said Grant. Her attention had been wandering but now she was avid again.

'A vision of Lord Ross walking on the moor, a black dog in the house and a raven in the dovecote,' I said. 'They've all got unpronounceable Gaelic names and they've put the willies up the entire household. The cook has been making charms out of wool for us to wear round our necks.'

'She has the *eolas*?' said Grant. 'Nice to hear there's a force at work on the side of good. Oh!'

'What?' I said, boggling rather at the idea that forces were at work on any side.

'Did you say the dolly was made of wool? Its legs at least? And there's a woman tying knots of protection? Perhaps the doll is a charm to protect Lord Ross, madam. Where did you find it? A drawer in the flower room? Stone-floored, is it? Tile-walled? I'd put it back, madam, if I were you. It might be there to keep him safe.'

I rang off. I am not ashamed to admit it. While I was replacing the handset and standing up, though, I somehow managed to let the little doll fall out of my grasp. It hit the floor head first and as I stooped to pick it up again, I am afraid that I even got as far as kicking it with the pointed toe of my elegant shoe. It rolled over twice and ended up under the telephone stand.

'Oh God,' I muttered, hurrying back to the flower room with it cradled in my arms like a kitten, hoping to make things balance out again. As I passed the closed library door, I listened for the groans and sounds of astonishment that would accompany Lord Ross suddenly pitching out of his wheeled chair and rolling around on the floor as though some giant were kicking him.

The gold dates on the garden journals winked at me as I wrenched the dresser drawer open again. I stuffed the doll back in and scuttled off to my bedroom. I was sitting staring at myself in the mirror when Hugh strode in.

'Trouble, Dandy,' he said.

I knew my eyes went wide and my mouth dropped open. I did not believe in voodoo or any of its Highland cousins, but if Hugh was about to report Lord Ross's sudden collapse my lack of belief would take a deep dent.

Hugh was staring out of the window. 'And the worst of it is,' he said, 'that Mallory's portion wasn't too bad. A goodly heap of hard cash and a share of the rich soil to boot.'

'A share?' I said, aghast at him. 'A *share*, Hugh? I hope you demurred.' The only way for Mallory to be awarded 'a share' of the ground that Maelrubha himself staked out and that the Mallorys and their tenant crofters had been enriching for over a thousand years since was via the most egregious enormity known to any countryman: splitting the land. Splitting the land was something the French did – carving up nice estates amongst enormous families until gentlemen were peasants; it was something Americans did – those forty acres and their single mules; it was something the avoidance of which had kept the English in soldiers and vicars for hundreds of years, as the younger sons were mopped up and the land kept intact.

'She was to be given one of the crofts, Dandy,' said Hugh in icy tones. 'She was to be responsible for a croft.'

'Oh,' I said, suitably chastened. Then the odd phrase he had used struck me. '*Was* to be given?' I said. 'Is the wedding off?'

'I think it will have to be,' Hugh said. 'There is, I am sorry to say, going to be a divorce in the family.'

'Ah,' I said. 'Yes, I thought there might be. Well, there are worse things.'

'Not among distant cousins,' said Hugh. 'Among the very closest members of the family. The girl's parents. Lady Love is divorcing Ross.'

'Yes,' I said. 'Both he and Mallory hinted that she had plans afoot. Actually, Mallory *hoped* that she had. The poor child was worried that her father might be bumped off to get him out of the way. As I said – there are worse things.'

Hugh was blinking rapidly and standing as rigid as he must have in his parade-ground days. 'You knew?' he said. 'You didn't think of mentioning it to me? Have you no sense of propriety left at all, Dandy? Or did you imagine we would have her birthday party anyway, with neighbours in, and then just toast to absent friends when it came to the bit?'

I turned round then, in case looking at his reflection in my dressing mirror had somehow made me misunderstand him. 'What?' I said. 'Has she actually bolted already? Left her family on her birthday?'

'What do you think I'm trying to tell you?' said Hugh. 'She left a note and legged it.'

'Oh, poor Lachlan!' I said. 'Dear God, did a footman bring it to him on a salver?'

'She didn't leave it for Lachlan,' said Hugh. 'She left it upstairs in her bedroom. For her cook, if you please.'

'But does Lachlan know, at least?' I said.

'I was there when Dickie Tibball came to tell him,' Hugh said. 'He is dumbstruck. He's sitting in the dining room at the head of an unset table staring into space like a stone statue. Cherry and Mallory are wailing into Mitten and Donald's necks in the morning room. I think Teddy has locked himself in a lavatory out of sheer discomfiture. And, oh Lord!'

He had leaned in towards the window and I stood up to see what had happened. Down on the snowy drive a pair of ladies, well wrapped up in Alpine jackets and britches, knitted caps on their heads and knitted mittens on the hands clutching their poles, were pegging up the sweep on skis. The Miss McIntoshes arriving for Lady Love's birthday party.

As we stared, there was a knock at my door and Biddy Tibball came in, like a dog looking for forgiveness after a mess and a kick.

'Dandy?' she said. 'Have you heard? Yes, I can see it in your faces. I hardly know what to say. But Dickie suggested I come and tell you that there's a dinghy going out to meet the late boat in just under an hour. If you think you'd like to go home. And really, who could blame you?'

I thought about being hefted into the arms of a strange Highland man and carried over the shallows, about that dreadful boat, Toulouse-Lautrec at the wheel and sheep in the stern, about being pitched around and buffeted by the elements all the way to Plockton with nothing to look forward to but the long dreary motorcar journey home. Then I thought of facing Lachlan and making chit-chat with his friends and family.

'I'll pack,' I said. 'Hugh, gather the boys and let's go.'

9

Half of me thought Donald would refuse to leave and all of me was unsettled by how easy it proved to sway him. Applecross ought to have exerted its hold over him through Mallory. The presence or absence of Lady Love ought to be of no consequence. And yet, there he was in his hat and coat, his packed bags around his feet, waiting for Hugh and me in the hall.

'Are you sure you want to come back down with us?' I said. 'I would understand if Mallory wants you to stick around and . . .'

'I think they want to circle the wagons,' Donald said. 'Different if it had been announced and was official.'

'Indeed,' said Hugh. 'It has not been announced and is not official. You should think very carefully about your next steps, Donald my boy.'

Donald frowned at his father but before the message could be decoded, all of our attention was drawn away by Mallory arriving, deathly pale and solemn, with a handkerchief clutched in one hand.

'I'm glad I've caught you,' she said. 'I'll write very soon. Or I'll ring. Once things get a bit better sorted out.'

'Jolly good,' said Donald. 'I should be around to be rung except for the odd day's shooting.'

Teddy was skulking about in the shadow of the stairway overhang and he snorted at this exchange. Coming forward, he addressed Mallory in much warmer words. 'It'll all shake out, old thing,' he said giving her a squeeze. 'You'll see. You'll end up with a doting stepfather to spoil you and a wicked stepmother to keep you entertained. It'll all shake out in the end.'

Mallory gave him a watery smile and a peck on the cheek.

'Or,' said Donald, roused into something approaching adequacy, 'I can stay, if you like.'

'No, that's all right,' said Mallory. 'I'd run away *with* you, if I could. I certainly don't expect you to stay. It's bound to be excruciating. Oh, Mummy!'

And with that, she put her face into her handkerchief and gave way to a series of gulping sobs. Donald, Teddy and Hugh all turned beseeching eyes upon me.

'There, there,' I said, moving forward and patting her shoulder. 'There, there, my dear. Remember what we said. About how much worse it could be?'

'How could it be worse?' came a voice from upstairs. I craned my neck and saw the gaunt face of Lord Ross staring down through the banister rails.

'Daddy?' said Mallory. 'What are you doing? How did you get up there?'

'Dickie helped me,' said Lord Ross, wheeling himself forward. 'I had to see for myself. I couldn't believe it until I saw for myself. But it's not some kind of off-colour joke. She's really gone. Clothes gone, writing case gone. That silly little dressing trunk – all gone. She's even taken this year's diary, so you know she means it. She's truly left us.'

The front door opened then, and there was Dickie Tibball himself, clapping his hands together in a cheerful way and telling us that the dinghy was in the water, ordering the footmen around and organising the removal of our bags. In the bustle of leaving, Lord Ross withdrew from the edge of the landing. When I looked up again, he was gone.

We passed David Spencer on our way to the boat, his dinghy headed in as we headed out.

'Gilvers?' he called over, understandably perplexed.

'Oh dear,' I said, as my menfolk stared ahead of themselves with set jaws. I waved back at Applecross House, trying to signal that answers were there for the finding. Then I gave him an awkward smile as we were borne away from each other by our two lots of oarsmen.

I am drawing a veil over the rest of our journey. The still, blue day was already turning rugged when the little dinghy pulled alongside the boat and matters only worsened after that. By the time we were at Plockton, there was a lashing rain and a howling gale blowing it northward.

'At least the snow will melt,' said Donald, dolefully, when we were on our way to Inverness again, all steaming gently in the powerful blasts of heat thrown out by the radiator in Hugh's Rolls. 'And they'll be able to get out and about by road again.'

'That's a thought,' I said. 'How did she get away?'

'On the water,' said Hugh. 'Lady Love has been coming and going by boat her whole life.'

'Unseen?' I said. 'Out on a dinghy to a waiting boat with three pieces of luggage, unseen by everyone in that row of cottages, who have nothing else to look at all day?'

'Why "unseen"?' said Donald. 'The villagers and crofters might have thought it odd that she was leaving on her birthday, but none of them would have rushed out to stop her and none of them would have imagined the family didn't know and gone beetling along to tell tales. Even if they had smelled trouble, they adore her. Their loyalty would not have wavered.'

'Well, just her own household then,' I said. 'It was a very bold thing to do under so many noses.'

'Easy enough to buy silence when you hold the purse strings,' Hugh said. 'And the household's loyalties are to her too, not to Lachlan.'

'Poor old man,' I said. And we all lapsed into a bleak silence that lasted until Hugh turned in, after midnight, at the gates of Gilverton.

Of course, we had expected the house to be in darkness, save perhaps for one lamp in one window. Hugh had sent a telegram from Plockton warning Pallister of our arrival but assuring him we would shift for ourselves until morning. But, as we turned the last corner of the drive, it was to see lights on all over the ground floor, the door standing open and Alec's motorcar as well as a large ramshackle Renault I did not recognise sitting on the gravel. Pallister came out onto the step, still in his full livery, as we drew up.

'What's wrong?' I asked, stepping out and feeling the grip of dread clutch at me.

Alec appeared by Pallister's side, with Bunty at his heels. She gave a short yip and came down to greet me, weaving round my legs like a cat and whacking me with her tail. 'Bad news from Applecross,' Alec said. 'We've been waiting for you.'

'Is Mallory all right?' said Donald, much to my gratification.

'She . . . yes, in the way you mean,' Alec said. 'But . . .'

'Oh Lord,' I said. 'Did Lachlan harm himself?' I could not get rid of the image of him there behind the banisters of the high landing, pinched and white from the misery of his wife deserting him. Would he have enough strength in his arms to heave himself over the rail and plunge down to the stone floor of the hall?

'Do you want to tell them?' said Alec, looking over his shoulder. A figure came forward and, as he moved into the porchlight, I recognised Inspector Hutcheson from the Perthshire Constabulary.

'The snow melted in all that rain,' he said. 'And Lady Lavinia was discovered lying dead in her garden, a rose in her hand and a blade in her skull.' There was a short moment of utter silence. 'Aside from that, it's good to see you again, Mrs Gilver. How have you been keeping?'

★

95

'On her birthday!' Grant said. She was brushing my hair and pinning it into flat curls, with extra squirts of setting lotion to tame it after the adventure of the rain and salt spray and then the close fug of the motorcar. 'On the day of her fiftieth birthday! Every time I think I've heard the worst depravity in this world, I hear some more.'

'I don't think I'd find it less depraved that someone murdered her on any other day,' I said. 'And I'm far from sure it *was* her birthday, anyway. It might have been on the eve. Before midnight last night.'

'The eve of her fiftieth birthday!' said Grant, exactly as much appalled by this new idea. 'Such wickedness.'

'There I can agree with you,' I said. I had needed a stiff brandy and some strong sweet tea before I recovered from the shock of what Hutcheson had told me at the front door. And Donald had been beyond the reach of either. He had been taken away by Becky, the head housemaid, and put to bed with hot bottles. It had been left to Teddy to telephone to Applecross and try to convey a little of our dismay and our wholly inadequate good wishes.

Inspector Hutcheson had been waiting for us to arrive, hoping he could conduct interviews and wire the results through to Applecross in the morning, whence a party had been dispatched from the Inverness police station, by train, coal boat, dinghy, crofters's arms and dog cart to the scene of the crime. It had only taken him one look at us, demented from exhaustion, before he set out for home, promising to return bright and early.

'What a scunner that you left,' Grant said, fitting my sleeping cap over the pin curls.

Alec had touched on this point too. 'A murder, Dandy, and you right there in the house where it happened! And in such a remote spot that the police would probably be happy for your assistance, rather than coming over all snooty the way they sometimes do. And you just pack your traps and take yourself off! Are you kicking yourself? I'd be booting myself hard, if it were me. I could have been up there tomorrow to join you and help. Rotten luck.'

'As you say, Grant,' I replied. 'A pure scunner.'

Grant gave a soft laugh. It always amuses her to hear me talk Scots.

'And whose idea was it for you to leave?' she said. I caught her eye in the mirror and saw the gleam.

'Exactly,' I said. 'I don't think that occurred to Mr Osborne. He lamented it as though it was mere chance. He didn't wonder if it was something else.'

'He'll get there,' said Grant, with withering condescension.

'It was Biddy Tibball who suggested it to me,' I said.

'Who?' said Grant.

'Lady Love's childhood friend and companion,' I said. 'Her husband is Lord Ross's nurse and her son is married to the younger Dunnoch daughter, Cherry. Oh dear.' I had just remembered. 'Cherry is in the early days of her first pregnancy.'

'Or she was when you left at lunchtime,' said Grant, sepulchrally. 'Who knows by now. Biddy Tibball, then?'

'Mallory also suggested to Master Donald that we should leave,' I said. 'At least I think so. Of course, someone else might have fed the notion to Mallory and Biddy and encouraged them to pass it on.'

'Who else is there?'

'The devoted husband,' I said. 'Those three devoted Tibballs, or four if you count Cherry. Devoted servants, inside and out. Devoted crofters for miles around. Devoted neighbours. And Mallory.'

Grant put my hairbrush down and folded her hands in a tremendous display of meek virtue. 'What happened to *her* devotion?' she said. I had not been aware of failing to apportion her any, but I have had reason often enough to trust

97

my instincts. I tucked this little point away in a corner of my mind to examine later.

'Oh!' I said, remembering. 'And there was someone else. A David Spencer. Captain Spencer. Old friend of the family, they said, but absolutely as devoted to Lady Love as the rest put together. But he was out all day.' I put my head in my hands and groaned. 'I'm too tired to hold it all in my brain and I'm much too tired to turn it into notes,' I said. 'I shall just have to trust that Inspector Hutcheson has lost none of his bite and can winkle it all out of my memory in the morning.'

Inspector Hutcheson had not only retained his bite, but had honed his fangs and strengthened the powerful muscles of his jaw. After half an hour with him the next day, I felt like an elderly dishrag, well wrung out and good for nothing.

He started in on me gently enough, asking me for a general impression of Lavinia's state of mind and for my view of her household. We were in the inner sanctum of my own household; to wit, my sitting room, my erstwhile retreat from masculinity and now, with the advent of a telephone, a door to the garden and a desk for Alec, the base camp of Gilver and Osborne. It was just after breakfast and a bright fire burned in the grate. Bunty sprawled before it on the hearthrug, almost dozing but occasionally thumping her tail at the sound of my voice.

I thought carefully before answering but could not improve on what I had told Grant the night before.

'Beloved by all,' I said. 'A loyal wife to her crippled husband and just about to make even greater sacrifices in the name of his comfort. A loyal patron of old friends who're down on their luck. A benefactress of astounding generosity both to individuals and to the world at large. Everything from a scholarship at Oxford for the gardener's boy – whom a less saintly woman would have reason to resent rather than reward

98

– to roads and piers and rent rebates. She was her daughters' great chum too and quite elderly women came along from the village on skis to say happy birthday. Beloved by absolutely all.'

'Aye,' said Hutcheson. 'Mr Gilver didn't have a bad word to say about her either.'

'Well, they're old pals from the London season when she was presented,' I said. 'She was quite a hit, I believe.'

'Well now, I haven't got as far as your good man yet,' said Hutcheson. 'I'm doing it in order. It was Mr Donald Gilver I was meaning. He had nothing but bouquets for the lady.'

I inclined my head in acknowledgement of the point he had not quite made. It was useless to try to hide anything – no matter how private or embarrassing – from the inspector. 'Yes,' I said. 'Donald had a little crush on his future mother-in-law. A little pash. Mallory knew about it and found it charming. One gathers it wasn't the first time and it would have been thought odd if he'd been indifferent.'

Hutcheson nodded and made a few marks in his notebook. I wondered what he would think if I took out my notebook and did the same.

'Although,' I said, 'there *was* something. Her husband and her old friend both made veiled reference to a plan Lavinia was hatching. Not the pier, not Donald's wedding. Something else entirely.'

'That's the ticket,' Hutcheson said. 'Now I smell motive. But we must eat our greens before our pudding. Let's carry on: to the younger Mr Gilver. Or is he still Master Gilver?'

'He's in his twenties,' I said. 'He wouldn't thank you for it. I don't know that I actually saw Teddy with Lady Love at any point during our short visit. You'd have to ask him.' Then a thought struck me. 'What do you mean "in order," Inspector? How is Donald first and then me "in order"?'

'He knew them best,' Hutcheson said. 'And you're the one with the trained mind.' I sat back in some surprise. Hutcheson had had no high opinion of my mind when we crossed paths before. 'Ah but, you've had ten long years at the sharp end since then,' he added, reading my thoughts. 'I follow your career with interest, Mrs Gilver. And you've racked up a fair few wins.' I held my preening down to a tiny smirk and waited for more. 'So,' he went on, 'who did it?' His eyes were twinkling, but it was not entirely a joke. 'No such luck, eh? Well then, let's go round the long road.' He turned over a page in his notebook and licked his pencil. 'When did you see her last?'

'At teatime on Wednesday,' I said. 'We women were all gathered in the hall while the men, except for Lord Ross, were out in the garden hunting . . . Now, Inspector, this is going to sound quite mad when I tell you. But a stray dog had got into the house and—'

'Left by a closed window, yes,' he said. 'I heard.'

'The men gave chase and the women waited by the fireside. Then Lady Love went up to her room to rest before . . . Well, it was supposed to be before church, but we didn't go in the end. And I never saw her again. She ate her dinner in her bedroom, owing to a headache. Then she breakfasted in bed too, staying out of the way of party preparations so as not to spoil the surprise. But wait a minute. No she didn't.'

He raised his eyebrows, waiting as instructed. They had been impressive eyebrows ten years ago and a further decade's progress towards old age had rendered them magnificent.

'The people downstairs – Cherry and Mallory – thought she was breakfasting in bed, but Mrs McReadie, the cook, brought the tray away untouched. I think she was already dead.'

'"Brought" the tray away?' said Hutcheson.

'Mr Gilver and I were standing on the stairs looking out at the garden and the cook came down towards us, grumbling. Yes, she was definitely dead by then. We saw the virgin snow and the handle of the weapon.'

'What time was this?'

'Nine-ish,' I said. 'But it had cleared up late the night before. The moonlight was beautiful on the bay and the snowy land made it seem like a stage set. I stood at my window and drank it in. Yes, it had definitely stopped snowing the night before, so she must have been dead by then. So how did Mrs McReadie get the message to go up with a breakfast tray?'

'"Message" might be the word,' said the inspector. 'A note on the door maybe? Two notes even: one at night and one in the morning.'

'But she can't have been all alone from tea one day to luncheon the next,' I said. 'She would have been missed.'

'Keeping a low profile so as not to spoil her party, you said.'

'But not as low as all that! It beggars belief that no one spoke to her at all.' I was disturbing Bunty with the vehemence of my words and I could not help remembering another dog by another fire and the beastly end to what had been a peaceful scene.

'A hot oat pillow was in the offing for a while, then, in the end, cancelled,' I added, remembering. 'There must have been an exchange or two over that.'

'So there must.'

'But can't we narrow it down from looking at the body itself – I mean, of course, can't the Inverness police do so? I shouldn't get carried away. But when you ring up – from here if you like – ask them if she was wearing a piece of wool round her neck.'

'A scarf, you mean?' Hutcheson said.

'No, a strand of wool, with knots and twists. A kind of charm. Mrs McReadie was making them for everyone. She handed mine to me before we all came down for dinner and the church service that never was. If she gave one to Lady Love, it would be on the body.'

'The church service that never was,' said Hutcheson. 'Who cancelled it? Because I'm thinking, Mrs Gilver, that Lady Lavinia's absence from a church service would be harder to explain away.'

'I have no idea,' I said.

'And when you say a charm—' Hutcheson began, then bit off his words at my gasp.

'I know what was in the other drawer!' I said. 'It was her mother. When you ring up, ask Cherry Tibball if the dolly in the left-hand dresser drawer was her mother. I'll eat my blotting pad if it wasn't. Ring up from here, Inspector, and ask just that, of Cherry – what was in the drawer? Of Mrs McReadie – did she hand over the wool? Of Lairdie – who said Lady Love would eschew the oat pillow for the sake of peace? Of them all – why didn't we go to church as planned?'

Inspector Hutcheson rose and went to the telephone on my desk. He was waiting for the call to go through when a light tap came at the garden door and Alec Osborne let himself in.

'Who's on the other end?' he whispered with a nod at Hutcheson's back. 'Hello, sweet girl. Hello, darling. Hello, hello.' Bunty rolled on her back and wriggled, giving little whines of delight at his greeting.

'Quite the sulkiest exchange girl I've ever come across just at this moment,' I said. 'And that's a strong field, as we both know. But once he's charmed his way past her board, it'll be Applecross. We've thought up some very searching questions to put to them.' I filled him in in a whisper, while Hutcheon cajoled and entreated and eventually commanded the telephonist to put him through.

'Ah, Inspector Snell,' he said at long last. He was speaking very loudly, practically shouting, and I surmised that whatever the weather was doing across all the peaks and in all the glens between Perthshire and Wester Ross, the line was atrocious. 'I haven't finished the interviews down here but some early points have arisen. Some questions. I thought it best to have a chinwag with you at the earliest poss— What?'

Hutcheson jiggled the receiver up and down a few times and shook the earpiece before trying again. 'This line is playing tricks on me, Snell,' he said. 'For a minute there, I thought you said you'd— *What*?'

Alec and I were silent now. Quivering with interest, we trained our eyes on Hutcheson. He was standing up straighter. He was pacing. He could only take three steps in one direction before the phone cable was at its full stretch and then three more the other way before it jerked at his hand again. 'But that's . . .' he said. And: 'Look here!' And even: 'Is this your first murder, Snell?' Alec and I shared a look and a shrug, then turned back to Hutcheson, who was now saying, 'The Chief Constable of the County is going to hea— Oh, he is, is he? Oh he did? Well that's that then.' Without saying goodbye – without any leave-taking whatsoever – he crashed the earpiece into the cradle and glared at Alec and me.

'Have they solved it?' I said, even though I could not imagine why a speedy resolution would have upset him so.

'They have solved it to their satisfaction,' Hutcheson said. 'To the satisfaction of her immediate family, their connections, the village, the estate and that shower of boobies at Inverness that call themselves a police force.'

'Whodunit?' said Alec. His interest was academic, which excused the frivolous word and the jocular tone. My mind, in contrast, was ricocheting around them all trying to decide which name it would be most shocking to hear.

'*Whodunit*?' repeated Hutcheson grimly. 'Who journeyed to the wilds of Wester Ross, to a spot unreachable by road in the winter, needing two boats and a willing helper? Who navigated a landing without a harbour or pier, in full view of a row of cottages, in the middle of a snowstorm, and there killed a lady who was out in her garden in that same snowstorm sans hat, sans coat and in her slippers? And who then

103

departed the garden leaving no footprints, embarked once more in an invisible boat and sailed away? For no reason *whatsoever*?' His voice had risen until he was almost shouting.

'Who?' I said. I could not imagine what individual, except Mrs Hutcheson, could upset the inspector so.

'A passing tramp,' he said, his voice finally falling as he threw himself, exhausted by emotion, into a chair.

'Passing?' I said. 'Passing on the way to where? There's nowhere to pass to.'

'What's this about, Hutcheson?' said Alec. 'Did we hear you aright: that the CC of the county has put his stamp on it?'

'There are eyewitnesses,' said Hutcheson. 'They saw an odd-looking chap lurking about earlier in the day. They reckon he got into the house, or at least his dog did, and he lay in wait for Lady Lavinia, who went out to truss up an apple tree that was waving in the wind. I've never heard such nonsense in all my days.'

'Hm,' I said. 'Well, it's not completely at odds with the facts. Cherry and Mitten did report a stranger out on the moor, although they didn't mention a dog accompanying him. But there *was* a dog in the house that didn't belong there. And, strange as it sounds, if there was any woman in the land who would nip out into a snowstorm in her carpet slippers to tie up an apple tree, that woman is – was – Lavinia, Lady Ross.'

'You don't say!' said Hutcheson.

'No, of course I don't say,' I shot back. 'It's a pretty story woven from a few incidental facts lying close to hand. They've all put their heads together and agreed on a version that suits them. Once they got rid of the four of us, that is. What a cheek. What a blasted nerve! I wonder they managed to keep their faces straight until we were gone.'

'But why on earth are the Inverness police falling for it?' said Alec. 'And with such unseemly haste.'

'Ah,' said Hutcheson. 'The small matter of a public road laid using private funds. Mallory money put that pass through the hills. And another small matter of a public pier built by smashing another Mallory piggy bank. They know what side their oatcakes are buttered.'

'He . . . He said all that to you?' I was aghast.

'Not him!' said Hutcheson. 'I took the chance to find out about the family and their place in the county yesterday, while I was waiting for your return, Mrs Gilver. I half-wondered if there might not be a little convenient looking-away. But I couldn't have imagined the likes of this!'

'Well, that's decided it then,' I said. 'I already thought Donald was too young and Mallory was too old. I will not have my son connected to murderers. I shall go to tell his father this straight away and then we shall compose a very stiff letter.' I frowned. 'After the letter of condolence, I mean. And a decent interval.'

Hutcheson was looking at me with his eyebrows positively rippling. They looked like two lively caterpillars crossing a pathway.

'What?' I said.

'Condolences,' he said. 'And perhaps attendance at her funeral? Would you even go as far as to let the engagement survive long enough for another quiet house party?'

'Oh, Dan!' said Alec. 'I could come along too. And Hugh needn't kno— Well, I suppose it would be hard to hide it. But Hugh surely couldn't countenance this travesty of justice. He might be just as keen.'

'To throw my firstborn son into a den of villains so we can crack a case?' I said.

'He can't jilt the poor girl when her mother's body's not yet cold,' Alec said.

'You have children, Inspector, don't you?' I said. I do not often play the parental card to quash Alec, but these were desperate times.

105

'Two boys, like yourself, Mrs Gilver,' he said. 'Two fine boys who both did their duty to king and country and came home safe. They're in the force now, just like me. Fighting injustice wherever they find—'

'Oh, give it up!' I said. 'Very well, I'll go as far as this. We shall lay it before Hugh and before Donald and, in the event of unanimous agreement, back to Applecross we shall go.'

PART 2

Spring

IO

Hugh, cloaked in righteous indignation as well as a measure of true sorrow for Lady Love's demise and his usual desire to see fair play, was happy to go along with the plan. Donald – his breast heaving with a sorrow all the greater for its being new to him, young as he was was – stirred to a manly conviction that he must soothe Mallory's broken heart and dry her tears and that he could only do it by sweeping in like Robespierre and unmasking the serpent. Not that serpents wear masks. I was greatly relieved that his own heart was not broken and that Mallory was uppermost in his thoughts. Teddy was unmoved by the death of a woman older than his mother whom he had met only once, and he did not set such great store by fair play nor by manly sweeping, but he was loath to miss out on all the fun. Likewise Grant, who blithely inserted herself into the roster for attendance at the funeral and would not be denied.

The Dunnochs, however, outwitted us all. Less than a week after Valentine's Day, when we were still waiting for the black-edged card to arrive, Hugh had spluttered over his coffee at breakfast one morning and shaken his newspaper at me.

"'The funeral has taken place, privately at her home at Applecross, of Lavinia, Lady Ross, née Mallory, beloved wife of Lachlan Dunnoch, Lord Ross of Wester Ross, mother of the Hon. Miss Mallory Dunnoch and of Mrs Martin Tibball (Cherry). May she rest in peace.'"

'They've made a mistake, surely,' I said. 'They meant it to be a death notice and intimation of the funeral and the newspaper office has mixed it up somehow.'

'Dandy,' said Hugh. 'This is the *Scotsman*. Think what you are saying.'

I nodded. 'So. They've bundled her away,' I said. 'Could anything smell fishier?'

Hugh looked down at his plate of kedgeree and grimaced, pushing it from him. We were alone at the breakfast table, as we usually are these days. Donald was over at Benachally, eating his own breakfast, cooked by his own cook, and it was nowhere near time for Teddy to wake.

'Did Donald know?' Hugh demanded. 'About the private funeral?'

'I can't imagine so,' I said. 'He rushed straight off to his tailor for a new suit, didn't he? But, equally, he's been on the telephone to Mallory every day, so I don't quite see how she could have kept him in the dark.'

'Not accidentally anyway,' said Hugh grimly. 'I absolutely see how she could have lied through her teeth until the deed was done.'

'Oh, Hugh!' I said. 'You can't suspect Mallory. Surely.'

'I suspect everyone until they earn their way off my list,' said Hugh. 'And you'd do well to follow suit.'

It was the first indication of how deeply Hugh meant to dig into this case. He had tended theretofore to wait on the sidelines finding fault until Alec and I had teed up an easy shot, which he then took. By the time Easter came, in mid-April that year, he was champing so hard at the bit that both Alec and I began to wonder if we should abandon the whole enterprise. Hugh galumphing into the middle of things, alerting our suspects and destroying our chances, would be hard to stomach.

Thankfully, we made the trip to Applecross for the announcement of Donald and Mallory's engagement in two motorcars, so Alec and I had hours on our own to plot and plan.

Spring had changed the countryside entirely and some of the glens were almost pretty, with blossom on the bent hawthorns, ranks of daffodils nodding in the shelter of the field walls and everywhere a fresh carpet of new grass, upon which the great resurgence of life was played out in all its glory. Lambs were wherever one looked. The newborns, tiny knock-kneed creatures, stood wobbling and bleating while the ewes whickered their love and licked the babies clean; little balls of scrubby fluff scampered here and there, testing this new world in which they found themselves before taking fright and huddling into their mothers' flanks again. Best of all to watch were the sturdy little fellows, full of milk and already beginning to dot their heads down and take nibbles of grass, who were filled with an abundance of energy and such sheer joy at being alive in the sunshine that they rushed around the field as though it were a racetrack, infecting all the other lambs with their exuberance until there was a solid pack of them, stampeding at breakneck speed and bursting out into little explosions of jumping.

Alec leaned against the bonnet of his Daimler watching a lively gang of them while we enjoyed our last cigarette before the final leg of the journey, over the 'new road' from the banks of Lochcarron. Bunty was locked inside, for even an angel such as she could not be trusted with spring lambs gambolling. She whined a little and I am sure that had I turned I would have seen her beseech me with enormous eyes. I did not turn.

'Look at that dark one!' I said to Alec, pointing. 'He sprang three feet straight up into the air. Look! Look! There he goes again.'

111

'He's right at the far edge of being adorable,' said Alec. 'A few more days of such exercise and he'll begin to look delicious instead.'

'Are you practising to talk to the crofters?' I asked. 'Or have you been farming so long now that you can't see this as a landscape any more? You'll end up like Hugh.'

'With acres of land in good heart, healthy forest plantings, sound fences, happy tenants and a case full of silver cups from the local show?' said Alec. 'There are worse fates.'

I grunted. It often chastens me to be reminded what a good countryman Hugh is. When the reminder comes from Alec it is irritating too.

'Anyway,' he went on. 'I wouldn't be so crude as to talk of these sheep to the crofters.'

'What do you mean?' I dropped my cigarette end and ground it out with the toe of my boot. Then I lifted my face and turned out of the breeze to feel what I was sure was a trace of true warmth in the sunshine.

'This is cleared land,' said Alec. 'I think this might be part of His Majesty's estate, as a matter of fact. But, in any case, the crofters are long gone from this glen.'

'Cleared land,' I echoed. 'It sounds so innocent.'

'One of the more ticklish jobs ahead of us is to find out from the Dunnochs whether Lady Love's bounty to her crofters has survived her death. *Cuo bono?*'

I nodded. We had talked long into many nights about it. 'If Lachlan is now free to run the estate on more conventional lines and stop giving such heaps of cash . . .'

'But he couldn't have done the deed from his wheeled chair,' said Alec. 'Although Mitten, with an eye on his future prosperity, might have been willing to help.'

'Any of the Tibballs,' I agreed.

'All that said,' Alec went on, 'Spencer's the one I want to get my teeth into.'

'Why?' I said. 'You keep saying that but you've never offered a wisp of a motive.'

'Because there was no reason for him to be there. It was a party for neighbours and he came all the way up from London for it.'

'Meaning that we would have to go all the way *down* to London if we were ever to find out why,' I said. 'For the next few days, we need to put David Spencer out of our minds and concentrate on the family. If we can satisfy ourselves that they are innocent, then we'll get him in our sights.'

'Agreed,' Alec said. 'Very well then. Gawping at baa-lambs won't get us anywhere. Let's go. I'll open the door slowly and you grab her collar, Dandy.'

As dreadful as the coal boat had been, I almost missed it as we turned off the low road and began the climb up the *bealach na bà*. It rumbled along the lochside for a while, then switched sharply, rose, switched again, twined around the side of the hill for a while and finally reared up ahead like the neck of a bucking horse. Alec shifted down into a lower gear and set his teeth grimly. I hung on to the door handle and braced my feet against the floorboards. Bunty, wisely, got down off the back seat and curled herself into as small a ball as she could make behind me.

As we pulled and pulled up to the summit, the spring retreated. There were no blossoming hawthorns up here, nor any daffodils. The green blades thinned and disappeared until the grass at either side of the track was as grey as the rocks that stuck up from the thin soil. More and more of them stuck up, until it was all rock and only a very few tufts of straw-coloured stalks whipping in the wind. Up here, the sheep were still fat and waddling and I was glad to see it, shuddering to think of a lamb being born into such a comfortless world.

At long last, with Alec in second gear and the engine straining, the road levelled and we were teetering on the edge of a dizzying drop, looking out over the bare, brown slopes to blue water and distant islands.

Alec whistled and let go of the steering wheel to shake the cramp out of his hands after gripping so tightly. Then he took an even tighter hold, lifted his foot from the brake and began the descent.

When we arrived at the metalled road that ran along the side of the bay and turned in at the gates to Applecross House, we were astonished to see, helping to untie trunks and cases from the back of Hugh's motorcar, none other than David Spencer.

Hard on the heels of that surprise came another sight to drive it out of our minds: Lord Ross stood on the doorstep, leaning on a stick to be sure, but with his wheeled chair nowhere in sight.

He told us all about it over tea by the hall fire. Teddy had disappeared somewhere with Bunty but the rest of us were there, trying not to boggle too obviously.

'It was my birthday present to Lavinia,' Lord Ross said. 'It was to be a surprise for her. Me getting out of me chair and walking at her party. We had hoped I'd be able to dance, hadn't we Dickie, but I wasn't quite there. Not by Valentine's Day. I shall dance at your party tomorrow, Mallory. A slow foxtrot. And by the wedding I shall be doing reels again, just like the old days.'

I could not have summoned a polite response for a gold bar and a mink stole. Alec looked equally stunned by this bombshell, and Hugh shot me a quizzical glance. Thankfully, one can always rely on Donald to miss most of the import of what he hears and he answered Lord Ross with cheerful words and a ready grin.

'That's good news, sir,' he said. 'I came up ready to say I was willing to wait if you thought it was still too soon, but

I'm glad to hear you talk about the wedding. We both are, aren't we Molly?'

Lord Ross looked as surprised at 'Molly' as I had been at 'Don' but he nodded. 'It's been two months,' he said. 'And it's only a few friends and neighbours, not as if we're opening a London house and dyeing ponies pink. By midsummer we'll all be ready for a happy occasion, shan't we?'

'Are you the only friend who's made a long trip?' I said, turning to David Spencer.

He spoke lightly as he replied but there was a glint of steel in his eyes. 'I've settled here, Mrs Gilver. For a while anyway. So, you see, I'm one of the friends and neighbours.'

'And how are dear Cherry and Mitten?' I said. 'And are Biddy and Dickie coming for the party?'

'*Coming*?' said Lord Ross. 'They're here, Dandy. They'll be in for their tea in a minute. Nothing has changed except for the loss of our darling. Everyone else is still here. As before. Everything continues and we have all been of great comfort to one another, I'm glad to say. If my friends had started deserting me I don't know how I could have borne it. But with them I still have so very much to be happy for.'

That, in my estimation, was something of an understatement. And it skirted very close to the notion that Lady Love had had some scheme in hand that her death had scotched. Thankfully, before I had to drum up an answer, I recognised the smart clip-clop of Grant's feet on the stairs and then she swung into view with an enquiring look on her face.

'I've prepared—' she began, then stopped. 'Oh, you're having tea *first*?'

Mallory flushed and got to her feet. 'Forgive me,' she said. 'I should have thought. Of course, you want to wash and rest. I'm sorry. I still haven't—' She took a deep breath and started again. 'My mother was such an effortless hostess,' she said. 'And I'm such a boob in comparison.'

There was a flurry of denials from Lord Ross, Donald and Hugh and in the midst of it I escaped.

Grant and I said nothing until my bedroom door was shut behind me. Then we both exploded into chatter. Grant, having some theatrical training, exploded more effectively and held the floor.

'I can't believe it!' she said. 'Standing there bold as brass. Large as life! No wonder he took the vapours at luncheon on Valentine's Day, after Miss Cherry and Mr Mitten saw him out on the moor! What a nerve!'

Grant's outrage was close to irresistible, but I did my best. 'I don't think Lord Ross's halting steps could be described as "striding out" even now, Grant,' I said. 'But otherwise, I agree.'

'Do you think they told the police that he was only pretending to be crippled and really he was perfectly up to the job?' said Grant. 'Did they all know? Did every one of them cover it up?'

'Too bad if they did,' I said, nodding. These points were well made. 'It's uncovered now. I shall ring Inspector Hutcheson with the news as soon as I can be sure of a quiet moment at the telephone.'

'And why's that Captain Spencer still here? That's very suspicious if you ask me, madam. The whole thing is very suspicious. A *party*! When I was a girl they'd still be in black crêpe and not even thinking of a grey hat or a purple glove, never mind a party! Do you think they think two months is really plenty of time for mourning before they go throwing parties and dancing the night away? Or do you think they think we think there's something up?'

'I can't follow that,' I said. Then: 'Grant, were you listening?'

'Very handy, serving tea under the landing,' she said. 'The sound carried up the stairs quite nicely and I have sharp ears, madam, as you know. Someone's coming,' she added, as if to prove it to me.

116

There was just a suggestion of a knock at my door and Alec sidled in.

'Well,' he said. 'What do you make of that then?'

'How did you find me?' I said. 'Alec, for heaven's sake don't tell me you asked a servant which bedroom was mine!'

'I'm like a homing pigeon, Dan,' Alec said, throwing himself into a little sofa. 'I can always find you. But never mind that. How did you stop your jaw from hitting the floor?'

'When Lord Ross admitted that he was secretly able to walk the day his wife was killed by a non-existent passing stranger?'

'For starters. But also, what do you think of them throwing a party and setting the date for this summer? Is it just me being too sentimental or does it seem a bit callous?'

'It seems like the most heartless outrage I've ever heard of,' I said.

'Me too,' said Grant. 'Can I start unpacking, madam? Or would you rather I waited?' She waggled her eyebrows in Alec's direction.

'Avert your eyes from my undergarments, Alec dear,' I said. 'I don't know that the callousness is suspect, though. It's so blatant, I don't know if it doesn't perhaps scream innocence.'

'But whose?' said Alec. He was averting his eyes by way of filling and lighting his pipe. I thought of vetoing it in my bedroom, but it does help him think. 'If one innocent person says "Lady Love would want it" perhaps the guilty person or persons can't work out whether to agree or demur.'

He had just got to the end of this speech when my door opened again and Teddy appeared.

'Ma?' he said. 'Oh, a party. Listen, talking of parties . . . have you heard that the Dunnochs are pushing for a June wedding? That footman, Lairdie, just told me. Doesn't it seem a bit off to you?'

'It does,' I said. 'Don't call me "Ma".'

'It's a bit tight too,' he said, ignoring me. 'I mean, I'm assuming that you're not going to actually wheel Donald down the aisle before we've found out if one of this lot bumped off the old girl?'

'Teddy, your language!' I said. 'And no, of course not. We're going to be very sure to detach Donald from Mallory if we find out that one of the Dunnochs "bumped off the old girl". Rest assured.'

'Or Tibballs,' said Teddy. 'They're all as thick as thieves and it would make no odds. Maybe they're all in it together. Should we be locking our doors at night in case they're not finished?'

I opened my mouth to scold him, but before I could begin my door was opening again. Hugh's body appeared, leaving his head out in the corridor, then quick as a fish he pulled his head in and slammed the door shut. He turned the key.

'Dandy?' he said, turning. 'Oh!'

'We know,' I said.

'Do you think anyone told the police?' Hugh said. 'That the stranger striding about out on the moor, who looked a bit like Ross, was probably Ross himself practising for the big birthday surprise?'

Alec whistled. 'I never thought of that bit,' he said.

'Surely Cherry would recognise her own father?' I said.

'She *did* recognise him,' said Grant. 'You said as much to me, madam. She came pelting back because she thought she'd seen a vision of her father, foretelling his death.'

'Will this be enough to tip the police out of their "passing tramp" nonsense?' Alec said.

'There is much to be learned,' said Hugh, sounding like an ancient oracle. I saw Grant bite her cheeks.

'And let's make sure Donald doesn't hear any of what we're saying,' I said.

'Why not?' said Hugh. 'Surely the boy needs to be on his guard.'

'Because,' I said, 'he's not that good an actor.'

'He did a pretty splendid job acting the lovesick pup when we arrived,' Hugh insisted.

'As I said, I think, with Lady Love out of the picture, he has really and truly lost his heart to Mallory.'

'He can't marry her,' said Hugh. 'Not with all of this hanging over their heads.'

'Of course not,' I said. 'We shall solve the murder and then we shall see. But, while I've got you all here, I need to say this. Leave it to Alec and me. Do not meddle.'

'I wouldn't know where to start,' Teddy said.

'Hugh?' I said. 'Promise me you'll keep out of it. It's not that you aren't capable, but if we go asking the same questions you've asked already, the suspects will begin to smell a rat.'

'I shall keep my mouth shut, my ears pinned back and my eyes peeled,' Hugh said.

'And you, Grant,' I said.

'But I'm an assistant detective,' she said. 'I'm only undercover as a lady's maid these days.'

It was news to me. But I had had enough years with Grant to know her weaknesses. 'Very well,' I said. 'Only I was thinking, with your role as lady's maid to the fore, you might offer your services to Miss Dunnoch. Her with her wedding coming and no mother to help her.'

Grant's eyes gleamed. The thought of a wedding dress and honeymoon trousseau was irresistible.

'I shall report to you if I hear anything,' she said. 'From undercover, as I suggested.'

'And now we'd better get back out,' said Alec, 'before we're all missed.'

They left in reverse order: Hugh slipping away first, then Teddy, Alec next, followed by Grant and finally me. As I shut the door and walked towards the head of the stairs, though, I felt that prickling sensation I knew came from eyes

119

following me. I took my handkerchief from my pocket and dropped it, then tried surreptitiously to take a good look around as I bent to pick it up again.

An indistinct figure stood in the shadows at the turn of the passageway. It was female. I was sure of that much. But whether it was Biddy, Mallory or Cherry I had no idea. As to what whoever it was would make of the mass exodus from my bedroom, that was anyone's guess.

When I was halfway back to the ground floor, a shiver passed through me. It was undoubtedly caused by a draught from the tall and uncurtained landing window, but it might have been helped just a touch by a sudden notion that it was the ghost of Lady Love who had been standing in the shadows there.

I I

The next morning dawned bright and clear, as fine a Good Friday as I had ever seen in Scotland. When I looked out of my window, the bay was like a duck pond.

'I wondered if you'd care to take a turn around the policies with me, Hugh,' Lord Ross said at breakfast. 'I'd appreciate your advice about some of my newest saplings. My steward assured me there was no need to drain – we have natural drainage down a dry waterfall to a deep pool below it – but they're not looking very happy.'

'I can't think of anything I'd rather do,' said Hugh. I knew he meant it. To march about a forest telling its owner where he had gone wrong was pretty much a trip to Paris for the spring modes to my husband.

'I'll take my chair if you don't mind helping,' said Lord Ross. 'Dickie is needed elsewhere this morning.' He waved a hand as Dickie Tibball started to offer apologies. 'I'm all right on the way up, strangely, but coming down the steep bits sets me wobbling.'

'Glady, gladly,' Hugh said. 'How about you, Osborne?'

'Oh, I'm promised to Dandy,' Alec said, hastily. 'Isn't that right?'

I gave a stiff smile. The Dunnochs knew that Alec and I were detectives but I did not care to draw attention to our partnership too baldly. 'Yes, thank you Alec,' I said. 'I wanted to take a walk to the graveyard to pay my respects and I'd rather not go alone.'

Lord Ross nodded solemnly and Hugh gave me a look as though I were one of his dogs and I had just been caught napping in an armchair.

'She's in the family plot,' Ross said. 'Top of the hill behind the house, Dandy. And take some flowers, won't you? McReadie will tell you what's ready to cut.'

I was glad to have the excuse to go out into the garden and find Mr McReadie. For one thing, a devoted servant was at the top of the list of people I needed to speak to, and I also wanted to see what the turn of season had wrought in Lady Love's precious apple labyrinth.

Even expecting something wondrous as we were, it took my breath away when Alec, Bunty and I stepped out of the door onto the terrace and drank in the view before us. The winding arbours and pergolas that had been bare branches in the snow when I saw them last were now a riot of blossom, sweet-scented and alive with early bumblebees. A very light breeze sent just a few petals swirling down now and then and so, as I stepped onto the beginning of the labyrinth path, I felt like a bride walking below crossed swords and showered in confetti.

'It's heartbreaking that she's not here to see it,' I said.

'And smell it,' said Alec. 'I've never thought of apple blossom as particularly strong but I suppose when you get so much of it all together like this.' He breathed deeply. 'And the bluebells too.' Right enough, all along the feet of the apple trees, hiding those ugly knuckles where the grafts had been done, there were nodding bluebell heads.

'It's very early,' I said. 'I wonder if these are a special Applecross strain or if it's just a sheltered spot.'

'You sound like Hugh,' said Alec. 'Will this path take us right past where Lady Love died?'

'Unless we divert now and go round the edge,' I said. 'But I want to see what if any marker they might have put there.'

Another couple of turns brought us to the little knot garden at the centre of the orchard. I supposed it was an orchard in its way. I stopped walking and felt Alec stiffen beside me.

'Who's that?' he said softly.

McReadie, the gardener, was where I had seen him last, kneeling on the path, reaching over one of the little woven apple hurdles to work at something in one of the beds. He must have heard us approaching but he did not rise or even turn. His back was bent and his head bowed.

'Good morning,' I said and, as he sat back on his heels, I discovered why his head had been so low. The man had rivers of tears pouring down his weather-beaten cheeks.

'She loved this time of year more than any other,' he said.

'I'm terribly sorry,' I replied. 'Alec, this is Samuel McReadie. Lady Ross's gardener.'

'It must be awful,' Alec said. 'The first blossom season without her.'

'Aye, home's bad,' said McReadie. 'But journeying will be worse. I was to find the plant she had hoped for all her days and I cannut face it now. But then staying put would like to break my heart.' The old man rubbed the back of his hand across his face, removing the tears but introducing a smear of mud in their place. 'I cannut imagine what the harvest'll be like,' he said. 'We've got three good trees out in the testing ground we've been waiting to taste the fruits of. I could just take an axe to them some days.'

I felt my eyes open wide. After all, someone *had* taken an axe – or some sort of blade anyway – to Lavinia. McReadie sniffed and wiped his eyes again, spreading the mud. Bunty, the darling that she was, saw that here was a fellow creature in distress and tugged on her lead until I let go. She went over and leaned against the old man, rubbing the side of her head on his shoulder and making the snuffling noises that were her deepest expression of affection and sympathy.

'But Miss Cherry's coming round to it,' McReadie said, rallying a little. I thought he was responding to Bunty's succour without even knowing it. 'She'll never be half the gardener her mother was but she cares enough about the place to keep it going at least.'

'Doesn't everyone?' said Alec. 'Surely all at Applecross will work to keep Lady Love's legacy alive?'

McReadie opened his mouth to answer but then, just in time, seemed to realise that he was about to wash dirty linen. 'They've all been very good to Mrs and me,' he said. 'You'll have heard about our boy.'

'Indeed,' I said.

'And never a word about his lordship's ailments all these years since. Never a word about what it costs to keep the lad down there for his studies. Yes, they were very good to me and mine.'

He was holding a hand trowel and he stuck it into the earth with a savageness that did not match his words. Bunty wrinkled her brows and came back to stand beside me. I took the loop of her lead over my hand again. Of course, I knew little of gardens and perhaps he was chopping some creeping pest into two bits before it could feast on the lush shoots of new growth that were peeking out of the earth, but it looked rather more as though he was chopping at the lush shoots themselves. In fact, the basket at his side was full of roots and bulbs and tender little plants that he had dug up and discarded there.

'Are you having a change?' I said, nodding at it.

'I am,' he said. 'Lady Love had some fanciful notions about what would grow, and it never mattered how many times her latest effort got frosted off or washed out, she was just as bad the next year with those blessed catalogues. I got that sick of her mourning over some spindly wee thing I could have told her was too tender for up here.'

124

That did not accord at all with what Lady Love had said, but I was familiar with how two gardeners were wont to bicker over a shared patch. Broth cooks were nothing to them.

'What's that you're grubbing out?' I said.

'Ach, something with a tongue-twister of a name,' McReadie said. 'I'm planting some primrose for now and I'm bringing on some petunias for later. They'll do without a lot of fuss.'

'Jolly good,' I said. 'Speaking of bringing things on, McReadie, can you point Mr Osborne and me in the direction of something that might be ready for cutting, please? We were thinking of visiting Lavinia's grave.'

'What about some boughs of apple blossom?' Alec said. 'What could be better?'

McReadie rose up onto his knees and fired off a volley of Gaelic. Alec took a step back. McReadie cleared his throat and touched his cap. 'You'll forgive me,' he said. 'But these are pruned to a principle. There's no "boughs" can just be lopped off. Go in the far end of the hothouse and help yourself to lilies and glads.'

Alec and I beat a hasty retreat and before we were many yards away we heard the slice and scrape of McReadie's trowel digging into the earth once more.

'That is very strange, if you ask me,' Alec said. 'I wonder if the family know he's grubbing out Lady Love's last ever spring garden. Don't you think it odd, Dandy?'

'Grief is a strange thing,' I said. 'I would have expected him to nurture it, it's true. Perhaps even think kindly of her optimism and do his best to make it work this year. But what I think is interesting is the rage. If he really believed a passing tramp killed his mistress would he be as upset and confused as to hit out at her plants? Or is he . . . promise you won't laugh . . . is he laying waste to a bit of Applecross because he believes Applecross – someone *at* Applecross – is responsible?'

125

'He's a gardener,' said Alec. 'Not an Austrian psychologist.'

'He's a man who knew Lady Love from when they were children together,' I said. 'And it's not as though he could tell anyone, if he harbours suspicions. He and his wife, and his son most of all, are still dependent on the very people he must suspect.'

We had reached the hothouse door and Alec held it open for me to enter.

'Although he certainly is a gardener,' I said. Look at this!'

A true Victorian, I had seen some impressive hothouses in my life but this was a marvel. The staging along the walls was six shelves deep and every shelf was crammed with bright fleshy plants, and huge garish flowers, so that one's eyes were assaulted with colour. It heaved with life, the plants seeming to pulse, although that must have been just the heat and the humidity. I pulled my hat down over my ears to save my hair a bit.

Alec had taken a pair of shears from a hook by the door and was snipping them in the air.

'Which ones are lilies?' he said. 'And what are "glads"?'

I pointed out some thick stalks of striped Turk's caps and a few spears of gladioli that were just about to burst into full flower.

There was a back gate out of the garden, as Lord Ross had told me. It led to a path past a neat brick cottage I took to be the McReadies' and, after a short steep rise, out of the trees onto heathland. I looked up the hill with my hand across my eyes to shade them from the sun. It was going to be quite a climb to the family plot, even with Bunty dragging me. I took a deep breath and put my best foot forward.

'Where have you stashed our book of hours?' Alec said after a few minutes. He sounded out of breath. 'Under lock and key, I hope.'

I grunted. He knew I disliked the nickname he had given my notebook for this case. It was blasphemous to my ears. But when I tried to say as much, he teased me; saying my few days in a convent a year or two back had made me terribly pious all of a sudden. The book of hours – I could reluctantly agree that it was a good title for the document – had taken me a week of hard brain-racking and quite a few sessions of memory exercises that were almost hypnosis, but in the end I had filled in everything I knew about the day, night and morning around Lady Love's death. I had a fair idea of who was where when and I had left gaps to fill when we gleaned more. It would have been incendiary reading for any one of the Dunnochs, innocent or guilty, and so it was locked in my writing case, which was locked in my dressing case, which was locked in Hugh's gun bag in his dressing room.

'Have you added anything to it since we got here?' Alec said.

'Ssshh,' I said. 'I hear voices.'

Alec took a couple of big steps up the verge at the side of the track and held onto the capstones of the drystone dyke to see over to where the voices seemed to be drifting from.

'Crofters, Dan,' he said. 'Gaelic.'

'They *use* Gaelic,' I said, 'but they understand English even if we don't understand them when they speak it. Come down before you pull the dyke to bits; there's a gate just here we can see over much more easily.'

The gate was a worn wooden affair, smooth and shining on the top from years of elbows resting on it. We took the chance of a breather and a cigarette, and stood watching the crofters at work. There appeared to be a goodly number of them for the size of the field and from all that I could see they were replacing the stones they had toiled away removing in February. Seven men were stumping up the field, digging holes into the wet earth, and seven women were following them with creels on their backs. They were dropping stones in the holes, I was sure of it. After the women came packs of little children, some of them quite tiny, who scraped the earth back over the holes and stamped it down. It was utterly mystifying.

'Dandy!' came a voice and one of the women straightened and waved.

I squinted through the cigarette smoke, then almost dropped my gasper as my mouth fell open.

'Cherry?' I said. 'What are you doing?'

She threw another stone into a hole and then stepped aside. 'Tattie planting!' she said. 'It's Good Friday. We always put our tatties in today.'

It made more sense than stones but I was still flabbergasted. 'Is that basket on your back full?' I said. She laughed and said something in Gaelic to the women around her, who replied with soft whickering laughs of their own. 'Does Mitten know you're carrying half a hundredweight of potatoes?' I said. The man who was digging holes in Cherry's row took off his hat and waved it at me.

'Good morning, Dandy,' he said. 'Don't worry about the *cailleach*. She's fine.'

'*What* did he call you?' I said.

'It's affectionate,' said Cherry. 'It means old woman, but it's a term of endearment. And all the women call their husbands the *bodach* – "old man" – but it's said with love.'

'Does your father—' I began, but they were laughing again and I bit my words off. I was glad, nevertheless, to see Cherry swing the creel down to the ground and come over to the gate, wiping her forehead on a square of red flannel she pulled from a pocket. She was still very trim-looking, although she had lost her waist and turned lozenge-shaped under her brown overalls.

'Hoo, it's hot!' she said, sticking her hand out to Alec. 'You must be Mr Osborne. Mallory told me you were here. Sorry about missing you at dinner last night but we were driving the sheep down to the fank for drenching tomorrow

128

and then we were just so exhausted, we fell into bed after a crust of bread and a hunk of cheese.'

'But why are you driving sheep at all?' I said. 'Or planting potatoes?'

'Janet there is planting behind her man,' said Cherry, waving at another woman with a very full creel on her back, 'and she's as fat as a tick. Her baby is due any day now.'

'You astonish me,' I said. 'These women are used to it, Cherry. They were brought up to it. They are made for it.'

'I was brought up to it,' Cherry said. 'I got my first little calf and a plot to plant up when I was six. Mallory loves the sea and the mountains and she adores Applecross as a place, but all I've ever wanted is to be a crofter. I thought I'd have to be a spinster because I never believed Daddy would let me marry a local man and I didn't think any-one on his approved list would share my dream. I never dared to imagine that someone like Mitten would come along.'

I let Alec cast around for words of congratulation about her extraordinary good luck. They would have stuck in my throat. All I could think was that Mitten Tibball had 'come along' when Cherry's hobby was something to smile at while his parents-in-law aged and ownership of the estate came inexorably closer. I watched him awhile, sticking his spade into the earth and throwing off clods of soil. He looked happy enough. But if he had got away with murder, then he had good reason to be happy.

'Well, we'll let you back to it,' Alec was saying when I started paying attention again. 'We are taking these flowers up to your mother's grave.'

Cherry glanced at them. 'Her favourites,' she said. 'She loved lilies. They grew like weeds in the walled garden and she just kept lifting them and splitting them year after year until we were almost overrun with the things. Mummy was such a sentimental gardener. If a little bit of thrift managed to find a home in between two stones on a path she couldn't bear it to be pulled out. She'd water it in dry spells and put a flowerpot over it in the frost. I've seen her pick her way across a meadow without disturbing the dandelion heads. No plant was too lowly for her to love.'

It was a third view of Lady Love as a gardener, according neither with what McReadie had said about her ambitions for these northern climes nor her self-description as an avoider of fuss. But perhaps Lady Love had been a woman of caprice. Or perhaps she showed a different face to the various people in her life. I have often thought that someone who is universally adored must be duplicitous.

'Would it throw off the potato planting if you were to come with us?' I said. I needed to speak to everyone here and if Cherry could both be ticked off the list and be spared a morning's physical labour, it would all be to the good.

'Far from it,' she said. 'There are battalions of understudies.' With that she climbed the gate and, straddling the top spar, she put her hands to her mouth and yelled. 'Morag! Take my creel, *mo ghoal*. I'm going up the crow road, Mitten. I'll be back before elevenses.'

Then she swung her leg over to the lane side and jumped down. I winced. If Nanny Palmer had been alive to see such a thing, she would have dropped dead: a girl four months pregnant with her first child jumping off a five-bar gate? I felt her turn in her grave.

Four months pregnant or not, it was Cherry who set the pace on the way up the hill. First, she greeted Bunty with showers of kisses and baby talk, and then she strode off. Bunty, eager for more of both, pulled so hard I was obliged to catch up. Alec, unwilling to be a straggler, hopped and trotted and eventually fell in beside us.

'Why do you call this the crow road?' he said, puffing a little.

'It's the local expression for the path to a cemetery,' said Cherry. 'Sometimes people say it when they mean "dying", you know. Walking the crow road.'

'I am so very sorry about your poor mother,' I said, and I had to take a breath in the middle of it. 'That was a terrible thing.'

'Poor Mummy,' Cherry agreed. 'On her birthday. And when Daddy had such a lovely surprise for her.'

'Yes,' I said. Then I thought a while. There were so many things I did not understand about Lady Love's last days, I hardly knew where to start. 'One does wonder,' I plumped for eventually, 'about the ramp. At the Clachan manse. I mean, your father watching carpenters build a ramp to the front door and all the while knowing he wouldn't need it.'

Cherry laughed softly and shook her head. 'We used to tease Mummy mercilessly about her ramps,' she said. 'There's one into the library on the east side of the house. That was supposedly for Daddy too.'

'Supposedly?' said Alec.

'It took Mummy a week to start using it for her wheelbarrow,' Cherry said. 'It was springtime, and she brought in a load of bean seedlings to prick out and pot on. Out of the wind and listening to the gramophone. She put a ramp on the door to the flower room too.' She caught her breath a moment at that and I am sure she was thinking of the day she and I had been there together, when I had found that strange little doll.

'It didn't strike me as odd at the time,' I said, 'but now I think of it, wheelbarrows in the house are rather unusual.'

'So the manse ramp wouldn't have gone to waste,' Cherry said. 'Golly, walking is hotter work than planting.' She stopped and shrugged off her cardigan, tying it by the sleeves round her middle. 'We're halfway there,' she said. 'It's just hidden by that stand of gorse. Not far.'

'Speaking of the flower room,' I said, and I was sure that Cherry started walking even faster, as if, without being aware

131

of it, she was trying to get away from me. 'That day – your mother's birthday – when you and I were in there with the wheelbarrows of flowers, what did you see in the drawer?'

Cherry glanced at Alec and then turned a miserable face on me. 'Drawer?' she said. 'In the flower room?'

'Yes, you saw something in the drawer and went rushing out,' I said. 'You seemed upset.'

Cherry knitted her brows and twisted her mouth to one side, in a parody of concentration. 'I can't think what you mean, Dandy,' she said. 'I can't remember what you're referring to. Of course it was weeks ago – months really – and we've all been through such a time of it since.'

'I wondered if it was something connected to your mother's death,' I said.

Cherry's bewildered expression began to look rather fixed. 'What?' she said.

'Evidence of this "tramp" who was hanging round. With his dog.'

'Putting things in flower-room drawers?' said Cherry.

'Not necessarily,' I said. 'When I said you saw something, I didn't mean that you found something that didn't belong there. It could just as easily been that something that should have been there was missing. Stolen. By the tramp.'

'Yes!' said Cherry. 'Yes, that's it. I remember now. It was missing. Mummy's garden diary was missing. I went to find out what had become of it.'

'Missing from the drawer?' I said. 'Not the shelves above?'

'No,' said Cherry, shifting her feet a little. 'The complete volumes from all the earlier years are on the shelves. She keeps – that is to say, she kept – the current one in a drawer.'

'With old seed packets and seldom-used bud vials,' said Alec.

'Yes.' Cherry did not make the mistake of saying too much but she could not help colouring.

132

'Why didn't you check the other drawer?' I said.

Cherry swallowed. 'I should have,' she said. 'That would have made more sense than to go racing off like a startled rabbit.'

'Did your mother keep money in between the pages?' Alec said. 'Why would a tramp break in and steal a garden diary rather than silver or jewellery?'

'No, not money,' said Cherry. 'But it was irreplaceable. It had notes from years of her work. Hers and McReadie's.'

'And, of course, at that time,' I said, 'we knew nothing of this tramp, did we?' Cherry stared, aghast. 'So why were you so concerned that the journal was missing?' She looked close to tears now and Alec took pity.

'Did it turn up?' he said.

'Yes,' said Cherry. 'It was in the *other* drawer, as you said, Dandy. We found it . . . when we were doing the funeral flowers. A few days later.'

'It wasn't,' I said. 'I looked there.'

Cherry stared at me, frozen in the twists of her lies. If I had looked in the other drawer, as she well knew, then I would have seen the little woollen figure so cruelly suggesting her father.

'Tell me,' I said gently.

'The dolls,' she said. 'I take it you found Daddy on the other side after I found Mummy? They were benign. White magic at worst. They simply bound my parents to Applecross, to keep them safe.'

'Why then did you startle?' I said.

'It's hard to explain,' Cherry said, turning away. I thought she was hiding her face from me, until I saw the latch-gate set into the stone wall. We had arrived at the graveyard. I looked around. We were at the summit of the hill with a little lochan nestled into a dip ahead of us before the land rose again in a steep crag to the high tops. I could see sheep clinging to the sides of this crag like nesting seagulls.

'Beautiful,' I said.

'The Linn?' said Cherry. 'I suppose so, if you don't know what it once was. The waterfall dried up when the road builders diverted the burn.'

'Bad luck, they say,' Alec put in.

'Do you dispute it?' Cherry said, gesturing towards the graveyard gate and walking in. On the other side, the grass was long and grew in uneven tufts at the feet of many plain grey granite headstones.

'Mitten was supposed to open the gate and let the sheep in,' said Cherry. 'They do a better job than any scythe. But it's been left over-long. This is cow grass, this length.'

'Don't you have cows?' said Alec.

'Beautiful cows,' said Cherry. 'Highlands and Belties. Mitten and I have seven, all in calf. But we can't let cows in here. They lean against gravestones to scratch and they could topple them.'

You could pick them up again,' Alec said.

'Yes,' said Cherry. 'But they might trap their legs or flatten a calf, you see. We'll scythe it.'

She untied her cardigan from round her waist and put it on again, buttoning it to the neck. The wind was keen up here. I put my hands deep in my pockets and shrank my neck down inside my collar. Bunty snuffled around, no doubt enjoying the scent of many rabbits.

'Mummy is over here,' Cherry said, leading us to the far wall. 'Beside Granny and Grandfather. I don't remember Grandfather at all, but I remember standing here when Granny died. It was a perfect July day. Angus Lairdie – our Lairdie's father – played the bagpipes and all the sheep and cows came off the hill to listen. I remember being handed over the top of the wall to someone because the cows were gathered round the gate. I scraped my little patent leather shoe on the capstone. Just here.' She put her hand to the top of the wall and stroked it. Then she turned and faced me with a defiant look upon

134

her face. 'I know you don't believe in the tramp, Dandy. I know you're laughing at us over the death notice.'

'*Laughing* at you?' I said. 'I don't think there's anything to laugh at there.' I pointed rather brusquely to the gravestone as I spoke but then I caught myself and turned to pay my proper respects.

Lavinia Ernestina Pauletta Dunnoch, Lady Ross

said the bright letters newly etched into the stone.

The last of the Mallorys. Beloved wife, mother and friend. 14 February 1884–14 February 1934. In my father's house are many castles.

'Death came for my mother,' said Cherry. 'He sent his herald disguised as her own husband.'

'The vision you saw out on the moor?' I said. 'But don't you think, Cherry, that that *was* your father? Practising his walking for your mother's birthday surprise?'

'It wasn't my father!' said Cherry. 'I'd know my own father. But it was enough like him. I thought death was coming for *him*, it was so like. I know now I was wrong about that.'

'But Miss Dunnoch,' Alec said. 'When you say "Death came" . . . ?'

'Mrs Tibball,' she said. 'But call me Cherry. Of course Death came. He sent a warning vision of Daddy and then he came with a crow and a dog and he took her. We called it a tramp because we didn't want the world to know all our black business.'

Alec looked at me and I looked at Alec. Cherry looked at her mother's gravestone. She seemed quite sane and very calm.

'And what about your mother packing her bags and planning to leave?' I said gently at last.

135

'I believe she would have,' said Cherry. 'To protect us. To draw him away from the people she loved. She set everything in place. She had it all worked out. Daddy to live in sanctuary at the manse with Dickie to take care of him. A croft for Mitten and me. Mallory going down to Benachally with Donald where she would be safe and happy. She knew what she was doing.'

'You really and truly believe this?' I said. 'That Death came to take your mother?'

Cherry held her hand out towards the grave as if it were evidence.

'What black business?' Alec said. 'Why would your father have to go to the manse for sanctuary? Why would Mallory have to leave Applecross to be safe? Why would you be safe here if she wasn't?'

'I don't want to tell you if you're just going to laugh at me,' she said.

'As I said already,' I told her, 'nothing about this strikes me as a laughing matter.'

'The Clachan church is still used,' Cherry said. 'Even though the congregation has moved along to the street for every day. We have services there sometimes. Mummy's funeral was there. Mallory's wedding will be there. This little one will be christened there.' She rubbed the front of her overall and her face softened. 'There where Maelrubha himself preached. It's a very holy place.'

'A sanctuary,' I said.

'Yes,' said Cherry. '*A' Chomraich.* The whole of Applecross has a sanctuary.'

'Really?' I said.

'Well, there's a legend, anyway.'

It came as absolutely no surprise to me to hear it.

'When Maelrubha came here,' Cherry said. 'He was thrown ashore on rocks and his ship dashed to splinters.'

'Rotten luck,' I murmured.

'And so, to stop it ever happening again he prayed for a bay to be carved out of the rock. But God told him that his prayer would go unanswered and that he should set to work. "Whatever your hands find to do, do it with all thy might." Ecclesiastes, I think but don't ask me what verse. So, Maelrubha tried to mould the land into two arms to cradle the sea, but the rock was too stony and, tired out from trying, he fell asleep and while he slept a ship of many souls was wrecked. And so he buried the bodies on the top of the hill and wept. He wept so hard that he flooded the land from the hilltop to the open sea. And the flood of his tears wore away a narrow bay and so he called it a sanctuary and built his church there.'

'Well, that all sounds rather marvellous,' I said. 'My nanny would have hated it, of course: a story that hinges on lying down and crying until one gets one's own way. Still, it makes Applecross sound as safe as the Bank of England. And I must ask you again: why should Mallory leave?'

'We diverted the rivers,' Cherry said. She kept one hand on her overall front. 'Maelrubha's tears don't flow as they did. Look, I don't want to talk about it. Whenever I talk about it, this little one goes very still. I hate the feeling of it lying like lead instead of jabbing at me. Ask Daddy. If you really want to know.'

'Answer one more question,' I said. 'The warnings you say Death sent? The little figure in the drawer has another one, hasn't it?'

Cherry flushed and rubbed her nose. 'I've never been any good at lying,' she said.

'What did you do with it?' I asked.

'That's another question,' she said, but she was smiling. 'We buried it with her. To be on the safe side.' She turned and looked at Alec. 'Are you going to give her the flowers?' she said. 'She loved flowers. Well, you've seen the house. You should go into *my* old room. I think Teddy's got it this visit.

137

There's a painting of my wedding bouquet above the bed in there. Mummy made the bouquet, of course. And then she painted it before it wilted so I'd have the memory of it for ever. You should see it, Dandy, before you go.'

Alec had put the stems of lilies and gladioli into the stone pot that sat in front of Lady Love's gravestone and now he unscrewed the lid of the bottle he had brought and filled the pot with water.

'There you are, Mummy,' said Cherry. 'Beautiful lilies for Easter.' She turned her head to the side and spoke to Alec and me. 'No doubt you think it's silly sentiment for me to speak to her. Or blasphemous or something.'

'Not at all,' I said. 'You must miss her dreadfully.'

'Did you get the chance to say goodbye?' Alec asked. 'That last day?'

'Goodbye?' said Cherry. 'Whatever do you mean? Of course not. She didn't know she was going to be killed.'

Alec raised his eyebrows and nodded furiously at me, telling me to take over. 'But she was planning to leave,' I said. 'With bags packed and all the rest of it. Didn't she say goodbye to Mallory and you?'

Cherry shook her head. 'It wasn't until afterwards I found out her bags were packed,' she said. 'Of course, she must have *planned* to say goodbye. She wouldn't just take off. But in between deciding to leave and getting away, she was murdered.'

Alec started at the girl's bent head in disbelief and I cannot say that I blamed him.

'When *did* you last speak to her?' I said.

'I tried just then,' Cherry said. 'As soon as I found out she was leaving.'

'But how did you find out she was leaving?' Alec said.

Cherry boggled. 'The doll,' she said. 'You don't bind a person to a place unless they're trying to get away.'

138

'It doesn't sound quite so benign when you put it that way,' I said. 'This "white magic" of yours.'

'And what do you mean you "tried"?' Alec said.

Cherry said, 'She had locked her bedroom door and when I knocked she called out "Not now, my sweet" and I went away again. So I suppose you'd say it was teatime the evening before, when we all went up to rest and change before dinner, that I last actually saw her. After the *cù sìth* in the library. We went up arm in arm – Mallory, Mummy and me – talking about . . .'

'About what?'

'Ask Daddy,' she said, as she had before. 'If you must. My mother is dead and my father is all the more precious because of it. I don't want to lose him or make him . . . Or make anything worse. But yes, if you really must ask someone, ask Daddy. About everything.' She took a deep breath. 'And now I need to get back to the tattie planting. I've missed the hard work and I'm just in time for the scones. Perfect timing.' She patted the gravestone and turned away. 'You should join us,' she said. 'It's such a beautiful day and there's nothing like it, as long as you don't mind very strong tea.'

12

'No one older than five can be that innocent,' I said. 'Surely.'

'You say innocent. I say gormless,' said Alec. 'What did you make of the conversation through the door?'

'Impossible!' I cried. 'Lady Love was dead by then under a blanket of virgin snow in the middle of the knot garden. So either Cherry is lying about the whole thing, or she's embellishing what she took to be her mother ignoring her by adding a few kind words, or . . .'

'Someone else was in the room and shouted through the door. "Not now, my sweet" would do for just about anyone in the house except the servants, wouldn't it?'

'But,' I said, 'why doesn't Cherry know that her mother was dead by noon on Valentine's Day?'

Alec thought a while as we skirted the house towards the front door, then stopped, raised his hands and clapped them down at his sides again. 'Let's do what she kept suggesting,' he said. 'Let's ask "Daddy".'

'Do you think she said that because she knows, deep down, who's most likely to kill a woman before she can flee her marriage . . . perhaps "Ask Daddy" was Cherry sending as clear a message as she could bear to.'

'I think so,' Alec said. 'She almost said it straight out. Her mother is dead and nothing will bring her back, so why betray her one remaining parent?'

'Good grief,' I said. 'I didn't hear her words that way, but I see what you mean.'

'Because it seems to me that there's only one character

left to cast in this macabre Highland death scene. There are the harbingers. The dog and the crow. There's the victim herself. But if the vision out on the moor *was* Lord Ross, that makes him . . .'

'The murderer.'

'Something is certainly rotten here,' Alec said. He sniffed as he spoke, even though the air was sweet with apple blossom and fresh spring grass and piquant with the salt tang of the sea. 'They do say anything that rots rots from the head down, don't they?'

'How to manage it, though,' I said. 'A pair of houseguests buttonholing the host and pretty much asking him if he murdered his wife and got away with it? Bad form, wouldn't you say? I half-wish I hadn't forbidden Hugh meddling.'

'Perhaps he disobeyed you,' Alec said, pointing at where a paved path came twisting down the hill to meet the ash path we were on. Hugh was trundling Lord Ross's wheeled chair at a lively clip, his mouth set in a grim line. Ross himself was hanging on to the arms of the chair by hooked elbows, bouncing stiffly at every bump. His expression, too, was far from sunny.

'I think you're right,' I said. 'No discussion of bogged-down saplings can have put those looks on their faces. Hugh! Hu-ugh!' I waved and hallooed him. My husband of over twenty years looked back at me as though I were a card sharp. His disgust was palpable. Whatever had gone awry between Ross and him, it was clearly to be laid at my door. At a guess, I would have said Lord Ross had betrayed his guilt in the matter of his wife's death and Hugh blamed me for dragging him here to find out about it. I looked forward to scoffing at him for his fastidiousness later when we were alone. For the moment, I just set my jaw as firmly as his and ploughed on towards the junction of the paved planation path and the crow road a few yards further down.

'Why not drop me off here?' Ross said, through gritted

teeth, when we converged a moment later. 'I'm sure Osborne will oblige until we're down on the flat.'

Hugh let go of the chair handles, grabbed Bunty's lead and took off without another word. The three of us watched his departing back in silence until, realising that the chair was still moving – was, in fact, gathering pace – Alec lunged forward, grabbed it and brought it to a halt.

'I feel,' I said, tentatively, 'that is, I think . . . I mean, it looks as though perhaps we should talk.'

Lord Ross started trembling. His shoulders shook and his breath came in gasps. It was disconcerting, but it looked more like some kind of seizure than the onset of murderous rage and there were two of us, even if he *were* about to go on the rampage. I walked round to the front of the chair and looked down at him. He was laughing.

'I'm sorry!' he said, wiping his eyes. 'Oh, do forgive me for shocking you. I'm not laughing at Hugh or at my darling girl or my poor dead wife or any of the mess. I'm laughing at you, Dandy.'

'Oh,' I said. 'Oh well then.'

'Perhaps we should talk!' he said, whimpering as his breath gave out and then collapsing into another round of helpless giggles. Alec was smiling too now and a snort escaped him. At length, Lord Ross recovered himself. He took a handkerchief out of some remote pocket in his waistcoat or cardigan, and blew his nose with a final-sounding trumpet. 'I need a whisky,' he said. 'If you would wheel me through the apple crosses and in at the terrace door, young man. It's the quickest, but I don't trust meself on the gravel without me stick.'

We made a little desultory chat as we went; about the beauty of the blossom and the dedication of McReadie. I touched on the marvel of Cherry planting potatoes but, detecting a slight chill, I swerved away again and back to the early blooming of the bluebells and the glory of the

142

hothouses. That got us up the ramp onto the east terrace and in at the library door.

'I've had enough of flowers, if I'm honest,' said Lord Ross, as he lifted himself out of his contraption and, with a couple of tottering steps, let himself drop into his armchair. The cat, Ursus, rose from a window seat, stretched and padded over to take up his lap. 'The upstairs here looks like a Balinese brothel, for one thing. Just a splash of soda in it, Osborne, if you wouldn't mind obliging?'

Alec made an enormous whisky for the old man, took a tiny one for himself, poured a small sherry for me and then settled down as alert as a pointer at the first drive. I hoped I looked a little less eager for whatever juicy meat was coming, but inside I was aquiver.

'I have shocked Hugh with worse than laughter, I'm afraid,' Ross said. 'I have shocked him to the core. He very much wanted to break up Mallory and Donald, but he didn't want it to be mutual. I don't want the marriage to go ahead any more than he does. Than you do.'

I took a sip of my drink to cover my attempts at bringing my face back under conscious control. 'Why, might I ask?'

'It's not the boy,' Lord Ross said. 'Donald is a fine chap. But weddings, you see, attract attention. Press attention. And I don't want society, the world, the newspaper-reading public – call it what you will – to read that Mallory has married a chap so much her junior and scuttled off to Perthshire. They would take it as an admission of guilt. It would invite more shame and scandal. And we're drowning in that already.'

'You – you know that?' I said.

Lord Ross closed his eyes and shook his head, laughing softly. 'I'd have to be a cretin not to know it,' he said. 'No one believes in this "tramp". Good grief. Do you?'

'But do you mean you actually suspect Mallory?' I said. 'You suspect Mallory, specifically, of killing your wife? Her mother?'

143

'What else could make me give my dear wife that hasty, furtive funeral?' Ross said, speaking savagely. 'What else would make me go along with this travesty of justice but my child? And make no mistake; I'm outraged by it even as I court it. The stupid inspector and those craven pups on the county council. For the upkeep of a road? For a bally pier and a village hall? Even for the promise of a new school building so the little ones can live at home until they are twelve. That's all very touching, I'll grant you. But none of that – or even if we had promised to build a hospital and a library and a . . . and a . . . an opera house! Things like that shouldn't be enough to have them winking at murder and letting us off with it. Should they?'

Since he appeared really to be asking, I answered. 'No, of course not. And speaking of "your child", I think you should know that your other child believes you're saving your own neck. At least, we got that impression, didn't we Alec? Cherry thinks it was you, Lachlan. You should tell her it wasn't and set her mind at rest.'

To my surprise, he was shaking his head. 'No, thank you,' he said. 'I don't want to draw her suspicion towards her sister. If Cherry thinks I did it, we can leave that sleeping dog alone.'

Alec was watching the old man closely and steeling himself to speak. I sat back and let him. 'You're not forgetting,' Alec began, 'in all of this, what Dandy and I do for a living. Are you?'

'The detective agency?' Lord Ross said. 'Not at all. I couldn't think of anything that would make us look more innocent than inviting detectives back to the house.'

'What makes you think Mallory did it?' I said. 'I ask because the fact of having two detectives in your house is not *only* useful for thumbing your nose at the gossips. We could actually detect.' Lord Ross had been holding his whisky glass up to the light, admiring the glints of amber and gold through

144

the crystal, but now he put it down on one of his knees and cocked his head at me. 'We could find out if she did,' I went on. 'And if she didn't, then you wouldn't have to go along with this tale any more. You could . . . do whatever it is you want to do to avenge your wife's murder.'

'Cry havoc and let slip the dogs of war,' said Lord Ross. 'I want to breathe fire and brimstone and bring calumny down on the head of whoever took my Lady Love away from me. Unless it was Mallory.'

'Lay the evidence before us then,' I said.

'Motive,' said Lord Ross. 'Mallory has waited so many years for the right young man to come along. And then, when he did, Lady Love cast her spell and bewitched him.'

'If that's all it is,' I said, 'you can put it out of your mind completely. Mallory spoke to me about it on the evening before your wife's birthday. She was laughing about it. Well, smiling about it. She didn't mind. She hinted that she'd have been concerned about any red-blooded male who didn't fall a little in love with her mother.'

'She always was a sweet child,' said Lord Ross. 'But motive's not all. Not by a long chalk. You know the tale of apparent flight, don't you? That Lady Love was supposed to be leaving me?'

'Yes,' I said. 'Mallory told me. Oh! *Mallory* told me.'

'Quite,' said Lord Ross. 'And then the tale became that she *had* left me. Packed her bags and gone.'

'Yes,' I said again. 'That was why we left. Hugh came to my room and told me that she had gone and we had better make ourselves scarce to let you all lick your wounds in private. You yourself told me about her packed bags, if you remember. From up on the landing.'

Lord Ross nodded. 'The thing is, I think Mallory packed them.'

'She told you that?' said Alec. 'Or was she seen?'

'No, but you see the thing is, she knew what was in them.

145

Afterwards, days later – when we were talking about a funeral – the question came up of what LL was going to be dressed in, for her burial. And Cherry suggested this one frock that my wife was always very fond of. She looked like an angel in it. Mallory agreed and said it was such a shame and it would have been perfect but that her mother had packed it when she was preparing to leave.'

'I think I'm a bit less swayed by that single fact than you are, Lord Ross,' I said. 'I concede that it's odd but it's far from conclusive.'

'I'm working up to the truly damning stuff,' he said. He looked down at his glass.

'Another snifter, perhaps?' Alec said. 'To get you through it?'

Ross nodded. Once his glass was charged once more, and he had soothed himself with a stiff swig and a stroke of his cat, he went on. 'When we found her . . . When we found my wife's body, that dreadful, dreadful day. It was just after dark. Raining like the opening day of a second flood and black as pitch out there. I was in here with Dickie and Biddy. Cherry had cried herself to sleep. And all of a sudden there was a piercing scream. It was impossible to tell where it came from, except that it was outside somewhere. Have you ever witnessed a pig-killing? I suppose not. But that's the only sound I've ever heard that came close to this.

'Biddy and Dickie leapt to their feet, dashed out of the French window there and belted round into the garden to see what the trouble was. I was left behind. I was so exhausted by then I couldn't have hauled myself out of this thing if the house was on fire. I've never felt more useless. So I did the only thing I could. I opened the curtains and put the lights out. Then at least I could see what was going on.'

'You can't see the middle of the criss-crosses from here, can you?' Alec said. He got to his feet and went to check,

146

leaning in close to the glass and squinting out. 'I can't see a thing and it's broad daylight.'

'And what I saw,' Lord Ross went on, as if Alec had not spoken, 'was Mallory coming along the terrace from the front of the house, wheeling an empty barrow.'

He looked at me and then at Alec to see how that item of news had struck us and then he began talking again. 'She was taking it round to put her mother's body in it and dispose of it, you see. Having killed her.'

'And what was the noise?' I said. 'The piglike screaming?'

'At first, I thought it was the sound of my darling wife's death throes,' said Lord Ross. 'That's what I thought that night. One would. There was a scream and then a body. But the next day the police told me she had been dead for hours. Hours on end.'

'And why do you suppose Mallory – if she were guilty – would have left her mother's body there for those "hours on end" before she brought the barrow to move her?'

'As I said,' said Lord Ross. 'It had just got dark. She had to wait for cover of darkness. There are windows all over the back of the house and besides that, there's McReadie. No day is too foul for McReadie to suddenly decide he needs to do something out there. While the snow lay, all was well. No one would dare set foot upon it. But when it started to rain it was a race to see what happened first, the snow melting or the sun going down. In the end, she almost made it.'

'And might have, but for the scream,' said Alec, 'which alerted everyone. Who was it?'

'None of *us*,' said Lord Ross. 'Biddy, Dickie and I were in here. McReadie, Mrs McReadie, Lairdie and Mackie were in the kitchens together. Mallory was at the front of the house, as I said. Cherry was upstairs in her room. She came dashing down a moment later. David Spencer was along at the post, sending telegrams. He found out when he heard the police whistle and saw Constable Petrie pedalling along here like a bat out of hell. He ran all the way back.'

'So who was it?' I said.

Lord Ross heaved a sigh. 'It might have been a vixen,' he said. 'Except that the garden gates were closed and there are no holes burrowed under them. If you believe in unquiet souls and pilot ghosts—'

'Pilot ghosts?' said Alec. 'The ferryman and all that, you mean?'

'*If* you believe in them, you could say it was unearthly. It certainly sounded unearthly.'

'What did Mallory do when she heard it?' said Alec.

Lord Ross nodded in appreciation of the question. 'She stopped dead in her tracks,' he said. 'She let the barrow handles go and put her face in her hands. Of course, she didn't know I was watching. Then she turned and disappeared round the corner of the house the way she had come. She reappeared about five minutes later, soaking wet, saying she had rushed out when she heard the scream but she had thought it was coming from the shore side and she'd been searching and calling out round there. All lies. My poor girl.'

It was pretty damning. I am ashamed to admit that my first thought upon hearing it was that I would have my son to myself for a few years yet. He was not going to marry this murderess. My second thought was that it did not fit with the conversations I had had with Mallory in February, when she – apparently – opened her heart to me. She had been twisted up with worry that someone was going to kill her father. I remembered her pleading voice: *No one has to die. Everything could be all right.*

Then, with a shudder, I seemed to hear her words again, as if played in a different key. She wished everyone would be sensible. She wished everyone would talk plainly. Otherwise, to protect her father, someone – to her infinite regret – would have to die.

148

'Do we have your permission to speak to Mallory?' I said.

'No.'

'If I were to promise not to overrule your decision to protect her, would you give it?'

Lord Ross said nothing.

'If we were to promise we'd tell no one but you what she says. On that understanding, might we talk to her with your blessing?'

Alec was staring at me from saucer eyes: such an assurance as I was dangling before Lord Ross was directly at odds with everything Gilver and Osborne stood for. We were servants of truth. We did not take the law into our own hands. We never had. That is, we had from time to time decided not to join together two stray thoughts to make a third. And we had from time to time decided that justice had been served without the need for courts and juries. We had never, though, until that moment, assured anyone that their secrets, thus far unknown, would be safe with us. That is, I had; but not in front of Alec. And I assumed he had, but not in front of me.

Lord Ross nodded. Then he passed a weary hand over his eyes. 'Leave me awhile, would you please?' he said. 'I need to rest. And to sober up before luncheon too.'

Alec started in on me before the library door was closed at our heels.

'What on earth do you think—'

I held up a hand to silence him. 'Let me write it all down before I forget,' I said, walking away. 'You can ponder this in the meantime. What happened to the bags?'

'A good question,' said Alec. 'I *shall* ponder it. And then you answer mine, would you?'

13

I scribbled for a minute and then screwed the point of my propelling pencil safely back into its body and sat up. I was startled to see Alec sitting on the edge of my bed, but when I looked at the little sofa I saw Bunty stretched out there on her back with her head hanging down and her paws waving.

'Well?' said Alec. 'Since when exactly do we assure clients that we are their tame dogsbodies and they have nothing to worry about from us?'

'Ross isn't a client,' I said. 'We don't need his permission to talk to Mallory.'

'True,' said Alec. 'In that case why did you ask for it?'

'To make sure he didn't warn her off.'

'You are a very different woman from the one I first met.'

'Thank you,' I said, choosing to take it as a compliment. 'Shall we go and find her right now? In case her father lets something slip, after all. Or in case Cherry does. Or in case she kills someone else. Such as Donald.'

'You think she did it?' Alec said.

'You don't? After hearing that she was seen going to fetch the body with a wheelbarrow before anyone except the murderer knew it was there?'

'There's something in the book of hours that's bothering me,' he said by way of a reply. 'I wouldn't mind running through it one more time before we beard her.'

'There are a great many things in it that are bothering me,' I said. 'Where will I start?'

'Top of page one,' said Alec. 'Where else?'

*

I rapped at Hugh's dressing-room door and when only silence came in answer I went in. I opened the gun bag with my own little key, opened my writing case with another and withdrew back into my bedroom with the notebook I had selected for the purpose. I cracked its spine and bent the board back.

'Five o'clock, Wednesday, 13th February,' I read. 'Tea by the hall fire. All present. Dispersal of party at quarter past five. This is the last sighting of Lavinia by any of the Gilvers. Twenty past five, Mallory to Dandy's room to speak of worries that someone might die. Hugh in dressing room. Half past five, Mrs McReadie to Dandy's room, with woollen necklets. Question!'

'Was the corpse of Lady Love wearing one when she was found?' Alec said.

'Quarter to seven,' I resumed. 'Dandy and Hugh downstairs to gather for expedition to church. Question!'

'Who cancelled church?'

'Seven o'clock. Dinner. All present – except for Lady Love, who was dining off a tray.'

'Says who?'

'Mallory.'

'So she might already have been dead, if we only have her murderer's word that she wasn't.'

'But Mallory suggested an oat pillow and it was the footman who reported that Lady Love was not to be disturbed. You think . . .' I riffled forwards in the book, '. . . Lairdie's lying about the pillow and Mrs McReadie's lying about the breakfast in bed and Cherry's lying about hearing her mother's voice the next morning, all because they think Mallory is guilty and they want to protect her? A sister, I can just about see. But why would a cook and a footman?'

Alec screwed his face up tight and searched for an elusive thought. I waited. He made a creaking noise through his strained throat, as though he were literally physically stretching to try to reach something. Then, just as his brow smoothed and his face cleared, a shout came from through the connecting door.

'Who's done this?' Hugh sounded halfway between rage and panic. 'Who's done this?' He battered open the door to my room and stood framed in the doorway, his eyes wild. 'You're safe, Dandy! Where are the boys?'

'Why?' I said.

'Someone has broken into my gun bag and made off with – Well, let me check what's gone.'

'Oh dear,' I said, rising and hurrying after him. 'Nothing's gone. No one broke in, Hugh. It was me. I put something in there for safe keeping and I'm just having a look at it. I should have closed the bag again, though. I do apologise.'

'You put something in my gun bag?' said Hugh. 'What?'

'Just a notebook.'

'Why such precautions then?' said Hugh.

'Because it's full of incendiary libel about our hosts,' I replied.

'You should keep it about your own person in that case,' Hugh said huffily.

I turned to Alec. 'That reminds me . . . why take a garden journal from a place if you're leaving?'

'Or why, if someone was faking her departure, would that person bother to do the same?' said Alec.

'Were the bags properly packed?' Hugh said. 'Or were they just stuffed with the nearest things to hand to get the weight right?'

'That is an excellent question that no one has answered,' I said.

'Well, now I've helped you by stating it clearly,' said Hugh. 'Please don't leave my gun bag open, Dandy. In fact, I think I shall go and find Ross, get my guns put away properly downstairs. Keep things tidy.'

He did not so much leave as sweep out. I turned to Alec.

152

'What are the chances you still remember the elusive thought you just managed to pin down?'

Alec sighed in reply, which told me everything.

A little light sleuthing below stairs – to wit, putting my head round the kitchen door and asking Mrs McReadie – earned us the information that Mallory was on a mercy mission along at the grocer's shop cum post office and we would be doing the cook a kindness if we went along there and dragged her back in time for luncheon. Since Alec wanted some baccy – this case was already shaping up to be a drain on his pouch – thither we went.

It was a charming route for a walk on a fresh spring morning, especially when compared with hauling ourselves up a steep stony path with a graveyard at its end. The tide was coming in with rippling little rushes and, behind the row of cottages that made up the village, lines of washing were cracking like whips in the breeze.

'Isn't it odd that they've got clothes out to dry on Good Friday?' said Alec. 'And that they're working in the potato fields. I thought these Highlanders were holier than holy?'

'On Sundays,' I said. 'Marking Fridays – this of all Fridays – is rather popish for their tastes. Note that the grocer's shop is open, for instance, for whatever Mallory is doing there as well as for bags of sugar and packets of tea.'

The grocer's shop was easy to pick out of the row: it had a pair of battered advertising signs affixed to its front wall and a bench under one of its windows, where a trio of crofter men too ancient to be part of the potato planting were sitting in calm contemplation of our approach.

'Mad in varr,' one of them appeared to say to us as we drew near.

'Good morning,' I replied, taking a wild guess. Then I clutched Alec's arm as an unearthly howl arose from inside the dark interior. It sounded as though someone was being

153

murdered, and the recent tale of the scream from the garden on Valentine's Day was too fresh in my mind to allow for any sanguinity.

On the other hand, the three ancient men rocked with gentle laughter on hearing it, their mouths wide around a few yellow teeth.

'Let's go in,' I said. 'I'd rather know than wonder.'

'Be all nut leave,' said another of the old men to our backs. I was going to have to try to get to grips with a little Gaelic, if only to spare myself the bewilderment.

Inside, the shop was pungent with the smell of village grocers' shops throughout the land, perhaps even the world over: paraffin and tallow candles were the base notes, carbolic soap and lye gave a sharp top note, camphor lent some depth to it all and there was a light whiff of fresh newspaper ink, like a garnish. It was dark in here, but by squinting I could see a woman of solid construction, her hair scraped back as tightly as her shawl was tucked in, standing behind the counter, with both fists balled on its surface and her eyes squeezed shut.

'Are you all right?' I said. But as another long yodelling howl of agony broke out from somewhere unseen, I realised she was not its source.

'What can I do you for?' she said.

'We're here to see Miss Dunnoch,' I said. 'Is that her? Is *she* all right?'

'She's a saint,' said the woman. 'Away by if you can bear to.' She waved a hand and then put a knuckle to her mouth as a third wave of howling broke out, emanating, I now realised, from a back room beyond a curtained doorway. With a glance at Alec, I stepped behind the counter and drew the curtain aside.

I do not know what I had been expecting: perhaps a village girl in the throes of childbirth, although the old men's laughter suggested otherwise. Perhaps a feeble-minded individual

154

caged or chained and Mallory here to let his usual keeper go out for some fresh air. What I saw was neither so dramatic as the one not so heart-rending as the other. Lairdie, the footman from Applecross House, was sitting on a kitchen chair in the middle of a comfortable living room. Mallory Dunnoch stood behind it with Lairdie's head held in a firm grip, while a man in a white apron over his tweeds applied a pair of pliers to the deep recesses of Lairdie's wide-open mouth. There was a white-cloth-covered trestle table set up just to one side and on it was a row of gleaming instruments, including even bigger pliers as well as rolls of cotton wool and stoppered bottles of coloured liquid.

'Aaaaaa-AA-aaaoowwww,' Lairdie howled, his eyes rolling and his limbs thrashing.

'Nearly done,' said the dentist, with terrible bonhomie. He leaned into the job and the muscles of his forearms rippled.

'Be brave, Lairdie,' said Mallory. 'It'll all be over soon.'

Alec and I watched, wincing, as the dentist almost pulled himself off his feet with the effort he was applying. Then there was an almighty crack and the man stood back, his arm raised high in triumph and a grisly trophy held in his pliers.

Mallory let go of Lairdie's head and grabbed a swab from the instrument table, stuffing it into the wound before the bleeding could start. Lairdie's outpouring of agony was muffled by it but no less heartfelt.

'Will it need a stitch, Mr Craven?' Mallory said. 'It's bleeding like billy-o.'

'Och, just bite down, lad,' said the dentist. He was far more interested in the tooth than the patient. He turned it this way and that and admired it. 'I knew the root would be deep,' he said. 'I remember the last one. But this is a magnificent beast. I shall put this in a bottle of alcohol on a shelf in my surgery.'

It was just as well that Lairdie's mouth was full of cotton wool swabs because I did not want to understand the volley of one-syllable words he aimed at the dentist's back. Mallory understood them. She flushed and shot a glance at Alec and me even as she tried to suppress her giggles.

'And which one of you is next?' the dentist said, finally putting down his pliers and rubbing his hands with anticipation at what adventures Alec and I might offer up for him.

'Sorry to disappoint you,' Alec said. 'We're here to see Mallory.'

'And offer Lairdie an arm on his walk home,' I added. Lairdie scowled at me. He had recovered himself somewhat. He was a man again, not the boy who had howled and let Mallory cradle his head, and he set off ahead of us alone.

'Are there any more outside?' the dentist asked, craning for a look.

'There are three elderly men on the bench,' Alec said doubtfully. 'But . . .'

'Ocht, them!' the dentist said. 'They've not got a mouthful of teeth amongst them. They're just sitting, not queueing. Well, Miss Dunnoch, it looks like that's it for another visit.'

Lairdie had finally staunched the flow of blood from his gum. He sat forward and spat out a gob of bright, soaked cotton wool and looked at the dentist with disgust. 'It's well seeing you charge up front,' he said. 'For you'd have to set the dogs on me to get your money now.'

'You're welcome,' said the dentist. 'A wee rub of . . .' He looked at the curtain separating us from the shop '. . . of whisky on it now, a good swish out after eating and before you go to bed, and tomorrow will see you right as rain. Chew on the other side for a day or two though, mind.'

'Oh, I think I might just remember that!' Lairdie said.

'Don't worry,' said Mallory, 'there'll be plenty of suitable liquids for you to gargle with at the house this weekend.'

'I'm not listening,' came the shopkeeper's voice. 'I'm not hearing a word about strong drink flowing. And at Easter-time too.'

'I was hoping you'd stop in at the party, Mrs Marshall,' Mallory called back through. 'We're hoping everyone will come and have a wee dance and a bite. It would mean a lot to me after how dreadful things have been lately.' She walked through to the front shop as she spoke and I followed her. There was no mistaking the look of exasperated affection the little round woman bestowed upon the girl. This was a friendship of years. Mallory had no doubt been toddling along to this shop with a penny in her hand to buy a twist of barley sugar since before she could reach the counter. I wondered again about her willingness to leave this place to her sister and come down to dour, dull Perthshire where the shopkeepers sniffed their disdain for one and all, no matter how many years of daily meetings were racked up.

'Are you walking back along to the house?' I asked.

'I am,' Mallory said. 'I'm ravenous for my luncheon. A morning being screamed at by croft hands and bitten by frightened children has worked my appetite up beautifully.'

We stepped outside again and she put her hands up and ran them through her hair, drinking in the sparkling sunshine. One of the three old men rattled off a stream of Gaelic, making the other two laugh.

Mallory chortled too and rattled off a good string back at him. Then she grinned at me and set off along the road. She was evidently hatless and coatless on this outing.

Alec fell into step with us but was no help at all. He busied himself with his pipe in a way I have come to know and left it to me to start the interview.

'It's nice to see you in such good spirits,' I said.

'I've been nagged and cajoled into good spirits by Miss Grant,' said Mallory. 'She has swept in and taken over. She's a marvel, isn't she?'

'Grant?' I said. I had half-forgotten she was there, if the truth were known. I had not seen hide nor hair of her since before breakfast.

157

'She has taken charge of my party dress, my wedding dress, my bridesmaid's dresses and my trousseau,' she said. 'And one of the first things she scolded me about was frowning and turning my mouth down. It ages one, apparently. She told me she knows someone, not yet fifty, who frowns while reading and has given herself a deep— Oh!' Mallory looked at a spot between my eyebrows and stopped speaking.

'Not yet fifty?' I said. 'I'm not even forty-five! But she is right. Look at your mother, after all. She was the most sunny-natured person and she looked like a girl until the day she died.'

Mallory nodded and her expression grew a little more grave. 'I keep forgetting she *is* dead,' she said.

'And there are still so many questions,' I went on. 'Where did the tramp go after the foul deed? Will he strike again? *Has* he struck again?'

Mallory said nothing.

'Not to mention why she was out there in the middle of the night for him to strike in the first place,' Alec added.

Mallory looked up at that. 'Why do you say "the middle of the night"?'

Alec frowned at her as if puzzled. 'The house was full, wasn't it?' he said. 'You and your sister. Her husband. Your father. The Tibballs. The servants. I suppose I just assumed that getting three items of luggage out without being seen must have been done after everyone went to bed.'

'Besides,' I added, 'we know she was dead by the next morning, under the untrammelled snow. And we know she was alive the previous evening, giving messages about dining in her room, cancelling church and ordering breakfast.'

'She always just left a note in the kitchen if she was having a bad night,' Mallory said, 'and that way Mrs McReadie knew to take up a tray.'

'So that's breakfast,' I said. 'What about the rest of it? When did you last actually speak to her?'

'She and Cherry and I all went upstairs together. We had just found out Cherry's happy news, if you remember, and we went up together to sit and enjoy it for a while, work out dates and that sort of thing. Talk about names. Mummy wanted to look at old photographs of us when we were babies, but that was going a bit far. We were both as fat as butterballs and the fashions of the day didn't help. Of course, now I wish we had stayed with her and studied every last snap and lock of hair. But we didn't know it was our last chance, did we?'

'In the midst of life,' I said, cringing a little to be such a ghoul. 'So you're saying it was then – while you and Cherry were in your mother's room talking about the happy news – that she decided not to go to church after all and not to come down to dinner? It *was* you who announced that we should go in to dinner without her, I suppose.'

'It wasn't me who decided not to go to church,' Mallory said.

'Who was it?' I asked her.

But she did not answer. She stopped and walked over to the edge of the road, to the sea wall, and stood looking out over the bay with her hair streaming back in the stiff breeze and her thin dress blowing out behind in a bell shape. She was a very pretty girl, when one saw her out from her mother's shadow.

'Mallory?' I said, going over to stand beside her. 'Who cancelled the expedition to the church? Do you know?'

'Why must you ask all these questions?' she cried. 'Nothing will bring her back. What's the point of making it worse?'

'We are trying to make it better,' I said. 'I am rather older than you, my dear, and have seen more of life. It helps, when something unjust is done, to bring the culprit to book and have justice restored. It really does help. Simply covering up the mess isn't the same.'

'Or wheeling it away,' said Alec. 'That's not much good either.'

'What do you mean by that?' said Mallory sharply. 'Wheeling it away? What do you mean?'

Alec shrugged. 'Just an expression.'

But Mallory Dunnoch was made of sterner stuff than I thought. 'No, it's not,' she said. '"Brushing it under the carpet" is an expression.'

'The thing is,' I said, jumping in to try to cover Alec's blunder, 'that if your mother told you – about cancelling church and missing dinner – while you were in her room with the photograph albums, Cherry would have known too. And she didn't. Did she?'

'Didn't she?' There was a note of strain in Mallory's voice. She turned away from the sea and leaned against the wall, hugging herself as though cold. 'Well, I don't remember every detail after all this time.'

'I would have thought you'd go over all the details until they were burned into your brain for ever like cattle brands,' said Alec.

'What does it matter?' Mallory said. 'What difference does it make?'

'All the difference in the world,' I said. 'If we can find out when Lady Love died we have a much better chance of finding out who killed her.'

'Then down it would all come, crashing on our heads,' said Mallory. 'And Mummy would still be dead. A passing tramp killed her. That's what the police said. And the newspapers said it and Daddy believes it, so I believe it too.'

'But your father doesn't believe it at all, my dear,' I said.

'Daddy?' Mallory said. 'Don't tell me he thinks it was the kelpie? That's what the village thinks, you know.'

'What's a kelpie?' Alec said.

I was a little surprised that he had never heard of them, steeped in Scottish lore as he was these days. 'A sea monster,' I said. 'But your mother was not on the shore that night. Was she?'

'Ah but there's a kelpie out of the sea at Applecross,' Mallory said. 'There's a deep pool at the base of a dry waterfall, up behind the house. And the legend is that a kelpie lives there, washed inland on Maelrubha's flood and then stranded when the waters went down again.'

'I see,' I said. 'Well, your father doesn't suspect a stranded kelpie. No, you see, the thing is he was in the library with the lights out when your mother's body was discovered. He saw you heading round the house with the wheelbarrow.'

All of Mallory's breath left her body in a huge rush that left her staggering. 'He thinks I did it?' she said, when she could speak again.

'And wants to protect you,' I said.

'But why would I kill Mummy?'

It would not have swayed a jury but I was convinced she was telling the truth.

'Why would anyone?' said Alec. 'Miss Dunnoch, please help us find out what really happened.'

'I *know* what happened,' said Mallory. 'And I am not going to help you drag it all out into the harsh light of day.'

'What were you doing with the wheelbarrow?' I said.

'I was taking it to fetch my mother's body,' said Mallory. 'And then I was going to go down to the shore and put it in the sea to be carried away. Then Daddy would think she had left and no one would be hanged for killing her.'

'Why would you do that?' I said. 'Why would you protect your mother's killer?'

'Because I love my sister,' Mallory said. 'And I don't want to break her heart.'

'Your sister!' said Alec. 'Do you know that for sure?'

But I had seen the true meaning Alec missed. 'Break her heart,' I said. 'Not her neck. You think it was Mitten, don't you?'

Mallory nodded miserably. 'Cherry is easily led,' she said. 'It was Mitten who saw the figure out on the moor and

161

persuaded Cherry it looked like Daddy. It was Mitten who was ahead of the others when everyone chased the dog. He said it had disappeared but he could have let it out of the garden gate before anyone else got there. And he's very good with birds. He could have trained a crow to go into the dovecote.'

'Those are nasty tricks,' I said, 'but they are not evidence.'

'And it was *Mitten* who said we shouldn't go to the church that night,' said Mallory. 'It was his idea to scotch that plan. He said he was worried about Cherry being out in the snow and ice, in case she slipped or a caught a cold, but Cherry is as strong as an ox. She still is, two months later. She'll probably be stacking hay the day before the baby is born and again the day after.'

'But why do you suppose,' I said, 'even if you're right, that it had to be that night? Or the next day? Did things suddenly come to a head in some fashion?'

Mallory shook her head in wonder and stared at me. 'Don't you know?' she said. 'Has no one told you? Has Donald not told you? I thought Daddy told Hugh, at least.'

I resisted the urge to shout, 'Told me what?' and instead simply shrugged.

'Mummy was going to be free when she was fifty,' Mallory said. 'Free of all the trusts and entails and all the nonsense my grandfather put in place to protect Applecross when he realised that he was never going to have a male heir and it was Mummy or nothing.'

'Yes, we know,' I said. 'At least, we didn't know there were legal trusts involved, but we knew she was planning to make a few changes. Moving to the Clachan manse with your father, leaving the way clear for Cherry. Why would Mitten mind that?'

'You seem to have got the story rather garbled,' Mallory said.

162

'No, dear,' I insisted. 'Your father told Hugh that Cherry was staying on here and your dowry was going to be in the form of cash. Sorry to be blunt.'

'And where do you think the cash was coming from?' Mallory said. 'Mummy was breaking up the estate.'

'No!' I said, proof, were it needed, that some of Hugh has rubbed off on me.

'But oh yes,' said Mallory. 'She and Daddy were going to stay at the manse, the crofts were to be handed over to the crofters, save one for Cherry and one for me—'

'No wonder old Michael and the rest are grateful!' I said.

'—and the house, park and moor were to be sold.'

'Sold to whom?' said Alec.

'There were two interested buyers,' Mallory said. 'One lot was monks, which would have been quite fitting in a way. And the other plan was to sell it to His Majesty's government to open a school. A boarding school. Well, a sort of children's home, I suppose. For the sort of children who are best kept out of harm's way.'

'But that's an outrage,' I said. 'A borstal? Here? And your father and sister camped on the doorstep. Not to mention the villagers, suddenly having to lock their doors and chain up their bicycles.'

'She hadn't decided,' Mallory said. 'It might have been the monks after all.'

'But why?' Alec said. 'She loved this place. Didn't she? Even if she was leaving why did she have to rip it up as she went?'

'She wasn't leaving,' Mallory said.

'That's right,' said Alec. '*You* packed her bags, didn't you?'

'No,' said Mallory. 'No, as it happens, I didn't. No, Mummy was planning to stay at the manse with Daddy. In the only bit of Applecross that was still a sanctuary. *A' Chomraich*.'

'After the rivers moved out of their paths,' I said. 'Yes, we know. Someone thought she was leaving though. Someone

163

put dolls in the flower-room drawers to bind your parents to the place.'

Mallory gasped. 'That's dreadful. Someone tried to stop Mummy from getting to her sanctuary?'

'And your father,' I reminded her.

'Daddy's in no danger,' said Mallory.

'But getting back to the bags,' said Alec. 'Someone packed them and took them away. A trunk, a jewel case, a dressing case and her garden journal.'

'Her garden journal?' Mallory boggled at that.

'Yes, we wondered about that too,' Alec said. 'Did she keep strictly to gardening in the pages of those volumes?'

'No,' said Mallory. 'No, she tended to note events of particular significance, whether horticultural or not. Her war journals are remarkable.'

'So, presumably,' I said, 'her killer packed them and hid them somewhere. Mitten, if you're to be believed. Do you have any evidence or just a hunch about motive?'

'Motive?' said Mallory. 'There's certainly that. All those thousands of acres, the house, the manse, the cottages, hundreds of crofts. I don't think he married Cherry for it. I think he loves her. But he did expect it.' She smiled at me. 'Not everyone is as lucky as I am. I know Donald was happy to plight his troth before he'd heard a thing about any dowry.'

I forbore to mention various things at that point. I forbore to mention the fact that her father wanted the union dissolved. He might change his mind if he could be persuaded that the guilty party was a son-in-law and not his own daughter, but equally he might decide he did not want to contract alliances with the cloud hanging over any part of his family at all.

'I have to say, I'm surprised by your take on all of this, Mallory,' I told her. 'Cherry is young and could have a long happy life with a much nicer chap if you were to ring up the police and tell them what you know. Your father would have peace of mind and justice would be done.'

'Hear hear, Dandy,' Alec said. 'Frankly, I'm astonished that you are standing by while some gold-digging brother-in-law plans and carries out such a scheme. Why shouldn't he hang for it? What if he kills again? What if Cherry displeases him, or if this baby that's on its way turns out to be disappointing?'

Mallory had stopped leaning against the wall. She had, in fact, shot upright and was standing practically bouncing on the balls of her feet, waving her hands to make Alec stop talking.

'No!' she said. 'You've got it completely wrong. It wasn't planned. It wasn't a scheme. Mitten didn't know what Mummy had in mind until she told him on the eve of her birthday. That's what I think. I think she told him and he flew into a rage and lashed out.'

'With a shovel,' said Alec.

'Peat-cutter but yes,' said Mallory. 'It's horrible. But if you were told that your life was to be pulled down around your ears and you happened to be carrying a peat-cutter at the time . . .'

'I would not lunge at a defenceless woman with it,' Alec said.

'Do you have any actual proof that this attack happened?' I said.

'Of course!' said Mallory. 'Good grief, of course I do. I saw him about five minutes *after* it happened. I saw him washing the blood from his hands.'

Alec and I stood in stunned silence at her words. 'Wh- When was this?' Alec said.

'Much earlier than you thought,' said Mallory. 'When Cherry and I left Mummy in her room, she said she was going to pop down and check that no harm had come to the apple crosses during the great chase. And about half an hour later, I went down to the flower room.'

'Why?'

'Because that's where we keep the gumboots and oilskins.

165

It's the nearest door to the church path. I wanted to secure a good mackintosh for the trudge. Cherry has a habit of bagging all the best clobber.'

And what did you find?' I said.

'Mitten was in there. I half-opened the door and saw him washing his hands in the sink. The water was bright red. And he was crying and muttering.'

'Muttering what?' I said.

'"She's dead, she's dead, she's dead." He was scrubbing at his hands so hard I thought he would take the skin off them. And so I asked, "Who is dead?" I knew it wasn't Cherry because I had heard her singing in the bathroom as I passed. I wondered if it was an animal. Or rather I hoped it was an animal.

'Anyway, when I disturbed him he came out into the passageway and put his arms round me. I asked him gently who was dead and he told me. He spoke in a great rush of words. "Your mother. My darling Cherry's beloved mother. Did you know she was going to sell up from under us? Did she tell you? She was going to shut down the whole show after all the those years. Is that why you're leaving for somewhere you can be sure of?" Then he said: "I'm sorry, Mallory. I'm so very sorry. I'm so, so sorry." And so I decided to pack her bags and make everyone think she had left us.'

'But you just said you didn't pa—' Alec began.

'That's right. When I went to her room to start, I saw that someone had got there before me. Her writing case and jewel case were already gone. And quite a lot of her clothes too.'

I was speechless. The three of us were rooted to the path just staring at one another, when a voice hallooed from the distance. Mrs McReadie had come down the drive to the Applecross House gateway and had her hands on her hips in that unmistakable posture of feminine outrage.

'Miss Mallory!' she bellowed. 'Your dinner is on the table and getting cold! You!' – she jabbed a finger that I guessed was aimed at either Alec or me – 'were supposed to be fetching her! What are you doing? Grease horse!' I took that to be Gaelic. 'Get a move on.'

14

'What *are* we doing, Dan?' Alec said when Mallory had scuttled off, leaving us staring at her back. 'We have no client here. This is not a case. The body is buried and the family is recovering. If you want my opinion, we should take Donald by the scruff of his neck and get out before we turn over another stone and find another seething nest of white maggots.'

'What a delightful phrase,' I said. 'And just in time for luncheon.'

Neither Cherry not Mitten were present in the dining room when we arrived a few minutes later. Lord Ross sat withdrawn and austere at the head, Mallory pale and quiet at the foot. Hugh was still glowering. Donald and Teddy were marooned together on one side looking very much as though they wished the earth would open and swallow them. David Spencer on the other side was watching the company with short flicking glances, as though wondering what on earth had caused such an unspeakable atmosphere: crackles like an approaching thunderstorm and waves of misery emanating from all around and meeting to hover above the table in a sickening cloud.

Dickie and Biddy Tibball alone seemed unperturbed. They were engaged in a long story about their engagement party, but Biddy broke off to welcome us, actually standing up and flapping a napkin to shoo me into the seat where she wanted me. I glanced at Mallory to see what she made of the woman assuming a hostess's bearing, but that young woman was concentrating fiercely on shaking pepper into her soup.

'Don't worry that you're a tiny moment late,' said Biddy. 'Mrs McReadie sends out the soup so hot we've all got time for a stroll round the garden before it's safe to sip.'

Perhaps it was the conversation we had just been a part of, but that 'stroll round the garden' struck me as terribly thoughtless. Any mention of the garden was tainted now. Biddy was right about the soup, though. The dining room was not chilly but billows of steam rose in rolls from the ten plates. Dickie Tibball's spectacles clouded as he bent over his serving.

It was, I saw with horror, so thick as to be not quite flat on top, still showing signs of the ladle's last drops sitting proud on the surface. I diagnosed barley and mutton from its dark grey colour and the viscous skin over the lumps beneath. It was, in short, Scotch broth, the very concoction that made me weep with homesickness when I was first served it, just after my honeymoon all those years ago. Mrs Tilling, my cook, had been running through the entire Scottish repertoire in my honour, from haunches of venison to plates of humble porridge. Scotch broth, I was to understand, was the jewel in the crown, studded with chunks of Swedish turnip and threaded with scraps of bitter kale.

I jabbed my spoon into the current bowlful and lifted. There was a sucking sound as the soup below reluctantly loosened its grip. Just as reluctantly I put the spoon to my lips. It was powerfully flavoured, of course; as though a whole sheep, after a long life, had been boiled in the pan with the barley.

'Do excuse my treat,' said Lord Ross. 'I thought I'd never get through the party tonight – a lot of silly little nibbles of nothing – without a decent luncheon. Supper is cold cuts and shift for ourselves, I'm afraid.'

'Nothing to apologise for,' said Hugh. 'Scotch broth made me the man I am.'

169

Alec glanced at me and raised one eyebrow about an eighth of an inch.

'I can eat it as long as I don't see it being made,' said Biddy Tibball. 'Mrs McReadie is terribly old-fashioned. She has a sheep's head delivered right from the killing and she burns off the wool with a hot poker. She swears by it, but the smell would make you faint, Dandy.'

'Jolly sensible,' Hugh said. 'Put the whole thing in the pot, brains and all.'

'No,' said Mallory. 'Brains on toast was always a supper-time treat for Mummy. Mrs McReadie splits the skull with a cleaver and removes them.'

At last, this grisly conversation had strayed too close to recent memories and it petered out. After a few moments of silence, broken only by the swamp-like sucking noises as spoonfuls of soup were separated and then by the gurgling whistles of them being drunk, I felt the spirit of Nanny Palmer move within me and attempted to get things afloat once more.

'Is there anything I can do to help with the party prepar-ations, Mallory? I am quite at leisure this afternoon if you need me.'

Mallory took a minute to think. 'The flowers are done,' she said. 'The food is in hand. I'd appreciate it if you'd take a quick look at the ballroom. See if I've got everything laid out in sensible places. The drinks and so on. Are you any good at calligraphy?'

'I can write without making blots.'

'Only there are some people coming who've never been in the house before,' she said. 'I wanted to make a couple of signs pointing the ladies towards the withdrawing rooms.'

'Mallory!' said Biddy Tibball. 'Really, dear, not at the luncheon table, please. But of course I'm very happy to write the signs if you would show me where you've put the card. I was well-trained by a very peculiar headmistress in the village school,' she said, in explanation to Alec, Hugh and me as if we cared. 'Miss Alva. We all went off to big school already with perfect penmanship, if rather haphazard ideas about arithmetic.'

The conversation became general, then, and stayed general until we had drained our coffee cups of the nasty bitter coffee the Dunnochs served and gone about our afternoon's business. Hugh elected to take Bunty for a good tramp over the high ground. I thanked him fulsomely, but I was not taken in. He needed the walk more than she did and once he was away from prying eyes he would shower her with kisses and come home in a better temper.

Alec and I went to the ballroom, ostensibly to approve Mallory's arrangements, but actually to discuss her bombshell and plan our attack on Mitten.

It was a newish wing, as they tend to be, with a billiards room downstairs and this great barn above, and was as unappealing as any ballroom empty at two o'clock in the afternoon with daylight pouring in and showing up all its little imperfections. The folds in the curtains were darker than the planes, the floor was shinier at the edge than in the middle, the wallpaper was sooty behind the sconces and faded from washing at the chair rail. Later that evening, in gentle candlelight, the floor covered in dancing couples and the air filled with music and laughter, it would take on a satisfactorily fairy-tale quality, but for now it was drear.

The one feature I had not expected, although perhaps I should have, was Grant, on a high stepladder in the middle of the floor, stringing what looked like ropes of beading between the two chandeliers.

'It looks like a cobweb,' I said. 'Are you sure?'

'They're glass,' said Grant. 'They'll twinkle when the lamps are lit. It's going to be magical. And I see you glaring at the curtains, madam, but I have glass roses to poke into the folds there too to catch the light.'

'Glass roses,' I said. 'Where did you get them? I assume you didn't blow the glass yourself this morning?'

'They were decorations for Lady Love's fortieth birthday,' said Grant. 'Held outside in what they call the "apple crosses", which is inviting confusion if you ask me. But since it was such an unhelpful time of year for real flowers they brought in false ones. It must have been a picture, madam, don't you think? Glass roses on sticks and electric lamps to light them up. I wish I'd seen it. Anyway, there they were in the attics doing nothing but gathering dust so I brought them down, had those footmen of theirs' – she meant Lairdie and Mackie – 'wash them and now I'm nearly finished.'

'What do you mean, "there they were in the attics"?' I said. 'What were *you* doing in the attics?'

Grant opened her eyes very wide and spoke in tones of injured innocence. 'I was searching for the missing bags,' she said. 'The trunk, the two cases and the all-important diary.'

'Pull the other one,' I said.

'Oh very well,' Grant said crossly. 'I was looking for "something old" for Miss Mallory's going-away outfit. I've convinced her she doesn't have to have it as part of her wedding costume itself. It's far from practical with the clean lines of this year's silhouette. Not like your wedding dress, madam, where any bit of old ribbon tied on just merged into the overall . . . fun.'

'Clean lines?' I said. 'Don't tell me Mallory's going to be one of those sylphs in a nightie? They're barely decent at all and certainly not for church.'

'She has a lovely *ligne*,' said Grant. 'No point hiding it under a milkmaid costume.'

'Or in other words, Mallory had a perfectly respectable pretty dress all picked out and you've nagged her into ditching it for a scrap of chiffon that will make the vicar blush.'

'Personally, I don't mind young girls making the most of

their bloom even if mine is faded,' said Grant. 'It's a shame to resent them.'

I opened my mouth but found myself to be speechless. When I turned to Alec to see if there was support in that quarter I saw him over at the wall of windows, staring out of the central one.

'What time did it start and stop snowing?' he said. 'Could Mitten really have killed Lady Love out there in the early evening and counted on the snow to cover her?'

'He must have,' I said. 'She was there. She was there by nine the next morning anyway, when Hugh and I feasted our eyes.' Alec grunted but kept staring. 'So either she was left there before the heavy snow started or she was moved there long before it stopped.'

'What's this?' said Grant, coming down her stepladder and walking over to join Alec.

'There is a way it could have been done,' he said.

I hurried over and stared down at the view. It had changed entirely since I stood at the landing window with Hugh. Then it had been stark and white with the naked apple boughs a kind of cross-hatching above. Now it was like looking down on clouds of blossom with a few dots of green grass peeping through. Alec shifted to another window and then yet again to a window in the corner, before returning. He looked at the garden through first one eye and then the other.

'What are you doing?' I said.

'I'm pretty sure,' he answered, 'that there's a route from the far side – from the potting shed where a peat-cutter might be kept – to the middle where her body was found, where the top bit of the arbour or whatever you call it hides every inch of the ground.'

'And?' I said.

'Imagine Lady Love met her killer – Mitten, for the sake of argument – in the potting shed. And she was killed there.

173

I think he could have dragged her body to the middle without his footprints being visible from the house.'

'Which would only make sense if he happened to know that there was a route where his footprints could not be seen,' I insisted. 'And anyway, why would he drag her there at all?'

'To make sure she wasn't discovered,' said Alec. 'As Mallory said. If the snow had started and no one was allowed to step on it then she was safe under the dovecote until it melted.'

'It would have been very risky,' Grant said. 'Why not leave her in the potting shed and lock the door?'

'Depends how many keys there are,' I pointed out.

'But leaving her out in the open would have been madness,' Grant insisted.

'Look,' said Alec. 'Can you see the dovecote? Yes, all right, I know you can see the weathervane, but can you see the base of it? Can you see the ground?'

'Alec, dear,' I said, 'Hugh and I not only saw the base of the dovecote; we saw the handle of the peat-cutter sticking up. Honestly, you can see everything through the branches in winter.'

'Well, either she was killed there or she was moved there,' Alec said. 'Because she was there! So someone must have left her there or put her there. I'm just trying to work out who and when. And why.'

'And how, darling,' I said. 'Because snow is the most unhelpful surface to drag a bloody corpse through, wouldn't you say?'

'Perhaps if you lean hard on the suspect he'll tell you,' said Grant. 'Mitten, you say?' I rather thought she wanted rid of us so she could get back to her strings of glass beads and roses. But she made a good point and so we obeyed her.

On our way down the stairs, we passed Mallory on her way up them, with Donald in tow. 'I'm going to dust the chairs

174

and Donald said he'd carry them one by one to the ballroom,' Mallory said.

'Jolly good,' I said. 'It's nice to see you pitching in, Donald. Where's Teddy?'

'Out with Father,' Donald said gloomily. Carrying dusted chairs, even with his beloved, was dull stuff compared with racketing about the countryside, I surmised. And Hugh, on the topic of other landowners' shortcomings, can be inadvertently entertaining.

'The room looks lovely, by the way, Mallory,' I said. 'We've just come from there. All shipshape.' She beamed and then I ruined it, by adding: 'Do you happen to know where Mitten is?'

Donald shot me a poisonous look and put his arm round Mallory, drawing her away.

'We really do need to find him,' I said, as we descended to the ground floor. 'We can't follow him up and down the rows in the potato field asking the kind of questions we need to ask.'

'They were getting on too well this morning to still be at it now,' said Alec.

In fact, we stumbled upon him without effort. As we crossed the hall in search of anyone who might give us directions to his cottage, a loud groan came from the offshoot leading to the flower room. Alec shared a frown with me and then walked softly towards the door. I followed on my tiptoes, lest the metalled rims of my country shoes ring out. When we were halfway, another groan, even deeper and more pained than the first, met our ears.

'I say, are you all right?' Alec said.

'Nothing an hour in Epsom salts won't cure.' It was Mitten himself. Alec pushed open the door and entered the room with me at his heels. Mitten sat on a low stool in his stockinged feet, a pair of muddy boots unlaced before him. He wiggled his toes and groaned again.

'The tatties are planted!' he said, like an emperor making a proclamation. 'It's back-breaking work but one can hardly complain when one's wife and old women in their eighties are hard at it alongside. Oh!' he said, as some bit of him cracked with an explosive report. I could not help wincing.

'I applaud your dedication to the crofting life,' I said. 'It's quite remarkable the way you and Cherry join in.'

Mitten smiled. He was a pleasant-looking young man, even when begrimed and perspiring. His hair was reddish and sat in crisp curls on his head and his jaw was strong and square. I glanced at his hands, workworn and reddened. And something that should perhaps have occurred to me before occurred to me then. If Mitten Tibball had killed Lady Love by bashing her in the head with a peat-cutter, why would he have blood on his hands? Even if he had dragged her to the middle of the garden after the blow was delivered, he would have pulled her by the feet or by the arms, surely. Certainly not by the head anyway. Once again, where would blood have come from?

'We have been given permission by Lord Ross to ask a few questions,' I said. Alec did his best not to appear startled by my bold opening. I did my best not to blush with shame about the egregious lie of omission I had just told. We had been given permission to ask questions, certainly, but of Mallory, and we had asked them.

'Oh?' said Mitten. 'Questions about what?' Then he winced and dipped his head. 'Forgive me. Of course. About what happened on Valentine's Day.'

Alec and I shared a glance. I shrugged, for it seemed to me that the only way to do this was head on. 'Mallory just told us she thinks you killed her mother,' I said. 'But she loves Cherry so very much she's willing to go along with this tramp nonsense.'

Mitten let his head fall back so sharply it knocked against the wall. He rubbed it absent-mindedly as he stared up at us.

'I didn't kill Lady Love,' he said. 'I *found* her. I tried to help her but I thought it was too late.'

'You found her body?' Alec said. 'By the dovecote?'

'No.'

'In the potting shed?' I said.

'No,' said Mitten with a puzzled look. 'Why the potting shed? No, I found her in here.'

A shudder ran through me from head to toe and left every hair on my head standing up.

'When?' I said.

'What do you mean "when"?' said Mitten. 'The day she died, of course. The eve of her birthday. I came in here to fetch my thick boots to go to church and found her, sprawled on the floor with that . . . dreadful thing sticking out of her.'

'The peat-cutter,' I said.

'Lawn-edger,' said Mitten. 'Not peat-cutter. It was a little demilune Lady Love and McReadie use for edging the grass paths. But yes. I tried to remove it. It looked so horrific, dug into her. I thought she was dead. She was so cold and felt so wooden when I touched her arm. I was sure she was dead.'

'She *was* dead,' I said. 'What do you mean?'

'She moved,' said Mitten. 'So she can't have been. She must have come round and gone outside. It's where she would go if she was in extreme distress, I'm sure of that much. To the centre of the garden; that was the centre of her life. I don't know how to forgive myself for not raising the alarm when I should have. Maybe she would be alive today if I had.'

I did not want to make the young man feel foolish, but I could not allow him to persist in his delusion. 'Of course she was dead,' I said.

'But she moved,' said Mitten. 'She wasn't found where I found her.'

'She *was* moved,' said Alec. 'No doubt about that. Someone moved her.' He did not say that someone was just about to move her again when that disembodied scream had come out of the darkness.

'Why didn't you tell anyone?' I asked.

'I . . .' He bowed his head as though a wave of shame washed over him. When he raised it, he said, 'I put it in Mallory's lap. I left it to her and I didn't try to persuade her. Well . . .' He gave a short laugh. 'I can't actually remember what I said to her exactly. I was distraught. But she understood me. It was her decision to make.'

'She did *not* understand you,' Alec thundered, making the young man flinch. 'Haven't you been listening?'

'Mallory thought you were confessing,' I said. 'She reported to us that you apologised. You begged for forgiveness.'

'Confe . . .' He ran out of breath as though he had suffered a blow in the middle of his chest. It took two gasping gulps get him right again. 'Why did *she* not tell someone then?'

'She was protecting her sister,' I said. 'She loves Cherry and Cherry loves you. So Mallory decided you were to be kept out of harm's way.'

'That's mad,' said Mitten. 'I can't believe it of her.'

'Even though you did the same thing?' said Alec. 'Who were you protecting? By washing your hands and keeping quiet?'

'Yes,' I said. 'Answer us that, at least. Who do you think did it?'

'My father,' Mitten said. 'I thought he'd seen red and set upon her. He had good reason. She was going to throw my mother and father to the dogs after years of loyal friendship and service. Marooned up here, miles from anything, my father lugging the old man from bed to bath to chamber pot.'

'Don't scorn an old solider for his injuries,' said Alec. 'That's not cricket.'

'And my mother, a glorified companion, pretending it was good fun, just like when they were girls. I reckoned when my father heard about the scheme— You know what it was, I suppose?'

'To sell the house, give away the crofts and live in the manse,' I said.

Mitten nodded. 'I reckoned when he heard he had a sort of a brainstorm and blacked out. It happened once before, just after he came home from the war.'

'And so you suspect him,' I said. 'I understand that you suspect him. But do you have any proof?'

'Yes,' said Mitten, the word torn from his mouth with him biting at it as if to hold it in. We waited. 'My mother told me that my father had encouraged Cherry to do the flowers for the party. At breakfast time when she was teasing Lachlan about taking part in a snowball fight and Lach was breathing fire about her "delicate condition", my father made a strong case to Cherry that she should go to the flower room and do the birthday flowers instead. There was no explanation for that. He has never taken an interest in feminine matters such as party decorations in his life and I don't think I can remember him ever telling Cherry what to do before or since.'

'It struck me as odd at the time,' I said, remembering.

'My father left Lady Love in the flower room to die and he sent Cherry to "find" her. He didn't know she'd come round and wandered off. Or – if you're right – been moved by someone.'

'But it's hardly conclusive,' said Alec. 'Even if you're right.'

'That's not all,' said Mitten. 'He had her woollen necklace in his pocket. It was bloody and soaked but I knew what it was.'

That was rather damning. I struggled to find an innocent explanation and failed. 'How did you find it?' I asked him.

'He collapsed,' Mitten said. 'After her body was found in the garden that night. He went to pieces, shaking and . . . well, drooling, if you must know. It was a terrible sight. He looked like a lunatic, sitting curled up with his hands round his shoulders and his mouth hanging open. Long trails of spit hanging down to his chest.'

'Steady on,' Alec said. He still, on occasion, acted as though I were a delicate flower to be protected from life's ugliness.

'I found him like that. In his bedroom. Well, the room they sleep in when they stay here overnight. He doesn't have a dressing room. All these empty rooms and they're expected to bunk in together.'

'They have a cottage,' I said. Perhaps unkindly, but it was hard to take this boy complaining that the Dunnochs' generosity was not generous enough.

'And so I put him to bed,' Mitten said. 'And it was when I was undressing him that I found the necklet, folded in his shirt pocket – he was still wearing a soft shirt, you know. We hadn't changed, what with all the worry and upset that day. I didn't know what was in the pocket at first. It had soaked through and made a stain, but when I drew it out, it was Lady Love's woollen necklet that Mrs McReadie had given her the night before.'

'Are you sure about the blood? Might it not have been dye from the wool?'

Mitten shook his head. 'It was blood. I could smell it.'

'And it was definitely Lady Love's necklet?' I said.

'Oh yes,' said Mitten. 'When Mrs McReadie brought Cherry's and mine to us the night before, Cherry made a point of looking at what knots Mrs Mac had tied into her mother's necklet. Since it was her birthday, you see. It was Lach we were supposed to be favouring, but . . . It's going to sound quite mad if I tell you.'

'On her fiftieth birthday, Lady Love would be particularly interesting to all manner of demons and spirits and if she was going to bring herself to their notice by wearing a spell asking for help, then she had to be protected while she did so.'

180

Mitten stared at me round-eyed and I have to say I was caught between pride and horror at how it had all tripped off my tongue.

'We spent one wedding season with Aberdeenshire fisherfolk,' Alec said. 'They make you Highlanders look like scientists in white coats.'

'Well, at least you see what I mean,' said Mitten. 'I would have recognised Lady Love's necklet anywhere. It was quite different from the others.'

'And why do you suppose your father had it in his pocket?' I said.

'Because killing someone with it round her neck would bring all the black luck back to the killer,' said Mitten.

'So he removed it beforehand.'

Alec whistled.

'I know it makes him sound like some sort of credulous fool,' Mitten said. 'But he had a very hard war and he hasn't been the same since.'

'If a man is a murderer, I don't really worry about how foolish or credulous he is when deciding what I think of him,' I said. 'But if your father removed the necklet before the attack, why would it be bloody?'

Mitten sat back again, just as slackly as before, although this time he managed not to knock his head on the wall behind him.

'That,' he said, 'is a very good question, Mrs Gilver. Why *would* it? That doesn't make any sense.'

'So do we have your permission to talk to your father, please?' I said.

'Yes!' Mitten seized on it, as I thought he well might. It did not last, however. 'Well, no,' he added. 'As I told you, he's not as robust as he looks. It might be better if I took care of it, actually.'

'Or I,' Alec said. 'I think I'm probably the one out of the three of us best qualified for the job, don't you? Where was

Dickie when he picked up his shell shock? Do you know? Does he talk about it?'

Mitten shrugged. 'France,' he said.

'What year?' said Alec.

'Fifteen.'

'Wipers probably,' Alec said. 'Don't worry, Mitten. I won't add a single iota of upset to what he's got on his back already. I would never forgive myself for it. And I've got about half a platoon of chums who'd come back and haunt me the rest of my days.'

15

In the time we had spent interrogating Mitten in the flower room, Applecross House had shifted into a higher gear on the journey towards the party that evening. I suspected Grant's hand in much of it; I thought I recognised the dazed look on the faces of the two footmen as they rushed about and my hunch was confirmed by the news that Dickie Tibball – whom we asked after, casually – had gone along to the Clachan manse.

'To escape the dervish,' said Lord Ross. 'Although the official explanation is that I might need me chair before the end of the night and the one along there is less battered and muddy. LL bought me a spanking new one for the new house, don't you know.'

Cherry and Mallory too were exhibiting the signs of having been whipped up into silliness. Cherry was out of her overalls and wrapped in a white satin robe with her hair wound around rollers and pinned to her head so that she looked a little like a cauliflower. She and Mallory were both sporting blood-red fingernails and when I raised an eyebrow Mallory shook off her slipper and revealed toenails to match.

'Don't worry,' she said. 'They won't show under my dancing slippers. But it does feel rather delicious. Are all Perthshire ladies' maids as splendid as Grant? I wasn't going to bother but look at my eyebrows! I'd put Greta Garbo to shame.'

'Can I come with you?' I said to Alec once I had detached myself from the giggling. 'Or do you think you need to speak to Dickie soldier to solider?'

Alec snorted. He has a marvellous menu of snorts and I had grown to recognise most of them, but this latest was something new.

'Do you despise me for even asking?' I said. 'I apologise in that case. But can I at least ask you to do something for me? Please take notes. Take my notebook, if you like. Take my propelling pencil. But don't leave it to chance.'

'You'd trust me with your propelling pencil?' said Alec, putting a hand to his chest.

'Oh, shut up,' I said. 'Just indulge me.'

'No need,' said Alec. 'I want you to come along. I'm not worried about Dickie Tibball. He's faking.'

'What? How do you know? You've barely met the man.'

'He witnessed a great big dog crashing through a closed window and was fine?' Alec said. 'He heard a bloodcurdling scream in the night and went rushing straight towards the source of the noise? He committed a murder, then sat calmly at breakfast encouraging his daughter-in-law to go and find the body? I think not, Dandy.'

'But isn't it a sort of mounting scale?' I said. We were on our way northwards round the bay, and I was glad to be out of that house, away from the rooms where dogs crashed through windows and screams were heard; rooms where dolls were hidden in drawers and corpses moved.

'How do you mean?' Alec said.

'Lashing out and then backing away, telling oneself it can't have been real. He could have managed that. And then at the end, out in the dark and the rain, seeing it again, knowing it *was* true. That might have just been the straw that broke him. Couldn't it have happened that way?'

'We'll see,' Alec said and we walked in silence the rest of the way.

The Clachan manse, I saw upon entering it, could not have been more different from Applecross. Instead of ancient stones here was new plaster, freshly distempered. In place of the cavernous fireplaces, here were radiators hanging on the walls and joined together by pipes that snaked round the skirting boards. There were no mouldering Turkey carpets here, nor tapestries, nor crumbling faded curtains needing glass roses in their folds to hide their dusty age. Here the floorboards were pale and polished and the walls were smooth and unmarked by sooty candles. White shutters flanked the windows and the empty rooms smelled of newness and cleanness. Most remarkable of all was that there were no flowers: no chintz, no sprigged muslin, no horticultural wallpaper, no rosebud carpet.

'I wouldn't turn this place down if someone offered,' Alec said.

'It's a bit poky,' I said. 'A drawing room and dining room and that's your whack. One would have to be very chummy with one's family. No separate fiefdoms.' I saw him grinning. 'Yes, that *is* what I mean. Hugh and I wouldn't last ten minutes. Between his pipe-smoke and my devotion to Bunty we'd be at daggers drawn.'

'Who is it that sits in a white room without a fire?' Alec said. He had wandered over to the back of the long dining room and was looking out, presumably at the gardens.

'Fanny Price,' I said. '*Mansfield Park*. Insufferable prig, sitting by an empty grate with nothing but her rectitude to keep her warm.'

'There was one thing Lady Love didn't want to change,' Alec said, turning and beckoning me over. I joined him and looked out. There were no apple trees and no labyrinth, but the little patch outside the Clachan manse was an exact replica of the knot garden at the centre of the labyrinth along the way, with a dovecote, a weathervane and numerous little teardrop-shaped flower beds formed by the loops and twists of hazel hurdles ten inches high, there to act their part until the spindly little box hedge got its roots down and spread its arms out. At the moment it was no more than a few well-spaced twigs. In the dark earth of the teardrop beds themselves, the few green nubs of early growth were beginning to burgeon. Nothing could have been more piteous and I heaved a sigh.

'Is this a tryst?' came a voice from behind us. Alec and I jumped and turned to see Dickie Tibball sitting in a gleaming basketwork wheeled chair, silhouetted in the doorway. The rubber tyres on its wheels had given him his silent approach.

'Just checking that it's in good working order,' he said, leaping out of it and kicking its brake. 'Lach thinks he might tire tonight and that chair he uses every day is a disgrace. He has never seen a path or a patch of grass or gravel he doesn't firmly believe it can traverse. He once persuaded me to wheel him into the river so he could cast for salmon. It was a warm day but Lady Love just about throttled me when she found out.'

'I'll bet she did,' I said. 'Did he catch anything?'

'There's a good reason fisherman usually stand up to cast, even if they settle down to ruminate for quiet hours afterwards,' said Tibball. 'It wasn't successful, no. But the main thing is that we tried. He tried. He kept trying all these years and look at him now. Up on his feet again. He'll take Mallory down the aisle in June. Just you see if he doesn't.' He took a ragged breath at the end of all this.

'Well, we'll see,' I said. 'I'm sure you must understand, Mr Tibball, that I feel somewhat ambivalent about the wedding at the moment.'

He cocked his head and gave me a sharp look. 'You think it's too soon?' he said. 'I wondered about that too. But Biddy said I was being Victorian.'

'I'd listen to Biddy, if I were you, old man,' Alec said. 'If one's lucky enough to have a wife and all that.'

Tibball nodded uncomfortably, but said nothing.

I tried again, turning the tap just a little to let a slightly louder hiss of gas seep out and see if it reached his nose. 'I wish I could be sure the police had got to the bottom of it, with this tramp story. I think that's the sticking point for me.'

Perhaps the sanguine reactions of Cherry, Lachlan, Mallory and Mitten had lulled Alec and me into an unwarranted expectation of how my statement would be met. Certainly, what happened next came as a shock to both of us. Dickie Tibball's face drained until it was an ugly grey and he folded in on himself, crumpling to the floor like a puppet with its strings cut. His eyes fluttered and his head lolled to the side.

'Would you say that's a confession?' I asked Alec in a whisper. Tibball was already coming round. He blinked, then shuffled until he was sitting up, shaking his head and clearing his throat.

Alec put his hand out to the man and pulled him back to his feet, shushing away the mumbled apologies. 'Not at all,' he said. 'Don't even dream of mentioning it. Is there anything we can do to help? Let me give you an arm over to the . . . Yes, just sit and rest on the windowsill for a moment. There's no need to explain. Your son told us, but I'm afraid I didn't realise the extent . . .'

'It's been twenty years,' Tibball said. 'Twenty years and every time I think it's gone for good, back it comes.'

'Would you like me to go away?' I said. 'I know women are no help at a time like this.'

'No, no, quite the reverse,' said Dickie Tibball. 'You're quite wrong there, Mrs Gilver. Gosh, there was a time when a man's voice – the doctors and the orderlies – had me cowering in a corner and only a friendly girl of a nurse could coax me out again. And Biddy—' His lip trembled. 'I'd have been carted off to the loony bin long ago if it weren't for my darling Biddy.'

'It's a rum old do, isn't it?' Alec said. 'I keep thinking I've seen every kind of shell shock there is. What is it that sets *you* off, so we know not to do it? Or say it. Or whatever it is. If you know, that is. And just tell me to keep my nose out if you don't.'

'Oh, I know,' said Dickie Tibball. 'It's got a fancy name and everything. Agoraphobia. Fear of open spaces.'

'From the trenches?' I said. It did not seem to add up.

'No-man's-land,' said Tibball.

'And – forgive me,' I went on, 'but how can you bear to live in this place? It's all sky and sea and moortop.'

'I don't quite know how to explain it,' Tibball said. 'It was the name of the place at first. *A' Chomraich.* The Sanctuary. And then Biddy told me that there was no road. No way in and no way out except by sea in a little boat. And when the sea is rough even that's a non-starter. It sounded – when Biddy told me about the place she'd grown up – as if life here would be pretty much as snug as a bug in a rug. And so it was. More so than I imagined. Life at Lachlan's pace suited me down to the ground, Biddy had Lady Love for fun. *I* wasn't much fun in those early years, let me tell you. And when Mitten and Cherry's eyes met across a turnip field and they married, it was a fairy tale.'

'Then Lady Love built the *bealach na bà*,' I said.

'But I was so much better by then,' said Tibball. Alec had produced a flask from his inside pocket and he wrested the stopper off. Dickie accepted it with a grateful nod and took a restoring swig. At last his colour grew a little less ghastly. 'Besides, it's a terrible road! Well, you were on it yesterday; I don't have to tell you. And it's useless half the year.'

'What about the pier?' Alec said.

Tibball took another swig and nodded as he handed the flask back. 'Yes, the pier did give me some mild collywobbles,' he said. 'But again, I'm rather better than I was. Perhaps it'll be just what the doctor ordered when the time finally comes.'

'And – do stop me if I'm prying too much,' I said, 'but what was it I said that caused you such anguish today?'

'Well,' said Tibball. He swallowed hard. 'It's this. If we

have to leave. If I have to leave. If I lose Biddy and don't live here any more I think I'll be back as bad as I ever was again. Shaking in corners like an ill-used dog.' He rubbed his hands over his face and then made a noise as though he had just splashed himself with cold water. 'Of course, the tramp is nonsense. Everyone knows it and no one says it. But when you spoke of it, right out like that, the whole house of cards came tumbling down. Ha! And I with it.'

'You mean . . .'said Alec.

'I mean,' said Tibball, 'if the local bobbies actually solved the murder instead of playing along with this mythic tramp idea, I'd be out of here quicker than you could say knife.'

A thought formed in my head and was out of my mouth before I could stop it. 'But wouldn't a jail cell suit you down to the ground? One can't get much more enclosed than that. And a crime of passion with a few doctors to give you a filthy bill of health wouldn't be a matter of the noose. Would it?'

'Me in a jail cell?' said Tibball. 'As an accessory, you mean? But I wasn't thinking of myself, Mrs Gilver. I was thinking only of my darling Biddy. And a prison cell wouldn't do for her at all.'

'You . . .' I said.

'You think Biddy killed Lady Love?' said Alec.

'What have we been talking about for the last five minutes?' Dickie said. It was, apparently a genuine question. Alec and I stared at one another, each wondering how to escape having to answer. Alec folded first.

'I've been talking about the fact that your son thinks it was you,' he said. 'Mitten believes you killed Lavinia.'

'Why on earth would I have done that?'

'Why on earth would Biddy?' I countered.

Tibball gave a yearning sort of look at Alec's breast pocket but, when the flask reappeared, he shook his head. 'I'll be tipsy before the first champagne cork pops,' he said. 'Why would Biddy kill Lady Love? Where do I start? How far back do I need to go?'

'They're best friends!' Alec said. 'Lifelong chums. Aren't they?'

It was one of those moments when I loved him most. Such innocence and optimism about his fellow man. Or rather, and this was very much to the point, woman.

'Lifelong chums who started more or less as equals,' said Tibball. 'Of course, Applecross was always more ancient and romantic than Biddy's family place at the Shieldaig. But it was two gentlemen with two estates and two daughters who went to dancing classes together, fell off their first ponies together and were bridesmaids at one another's weddings. Biddy left home after we married, of course, and LL stayed, but otherwise they were on – what do you call it – parallel paths. There was a time, even, when Biddy looked to be doing a little better, if one was in the mood to call it a competition. We had a son to carry on the family name and Lady Love and Lachlan produced only daughters. Then our fortunes began to diverge, is the best way to put it. And here we are. Still chums, and related of course, by the marriage of our boy to their girl. Perfectly happy. At least, I'm perfectly happy. And Biddy is a good, loyal friend and a good, loyal wife.'

He nodded as if satisfied with his account of the lives of the Dunnochs and Tibballs. If we had not been trying to account for one murdering another, that would have been marvellous. As it was, someone needed to nudge him on to the next chapter. It was my turn, Alec told me with a glare.

'But something went wrong?' I said. 'To upset the . . .' Apple cart was too close to a pun for this solemn matter.

'Something went wrong,' Tibball agreed. 'Something in LL's head went badly wrong.'

'But if she did any of the reckless things she talked about,' said Alec. 'Selling the house and giving away the land. Even if she and Lord Ross moved to the manse and did not need

190

a nurse and a helper any more, your son wouldn't turn you out. I don't quite see the problem.'

'It was nothing to do with keeping a roof over our heads,' Tibball said. 'We are fine on that score. Although, I must say it's nice to be in the big house rather than in that bloody hut that passes for a cottage. Lachlan likes the company, you see. And Cherry is useless anywhere except a sheep dip, so Biddy is essential to keep the house ticking over.'

We waited.

'I don't suppose there's any chance you could just forget all about this, is there?' he said. 'Or even just forget about it until after the party? Poor Mallory. She deserves one night before the horror comes crashing down on her, doesn't she?'

We waited again.

'Yes, of course,' said Tibball. 'Silly of me. Oh Lord, it's just all so very exhausting to think of what's ahead of us. Not to mention painful. But very well. Biddy found something out, you see. Lachlan told her something. Something he should either have told her long ago or taken to his grave.'

'Yes,' I said. 'Those are often the two best options and yet people so very regularly plump for a third one.'

'Which is what happened here. A secret kept and kept until life relies on its keeping, like some ancient wisteria holding a house up. Then for some silly reason the gardener decides to prune the thing and crash. Roof falls in, walls crumble to nothing, family of six trapped inside as dead as doornails.'

'What was the secret?' Alec said.

'Simply this. Biddy found out that Lachlan loved her all those years ago when she was a girl. He loved her and Lady Love knew it, but she wanted a title and some money and had an estate to offer in return and she stole him away.'

'Phew,' said Alec. 'That most definitely should have been kept for ever. Why on earth would Lachlan suddenly tell Biddy after all these years?'

191

Tibball shook his head. 'I don't know, but Biddy saw red. She said to me she went out for a walk and thought about the night that Lady Love and Lachlan met. It was at Biddy's dance in London, the season they both came out. She'd met Lachlan a few times before, of course, but he was playing his cards very close to his chest and she had no idea that he cared for her. She saw him dancing with Lady Love and thought they made a handsome pair. The next day – the very next day! – at a luncheon, LL introduced Biddy to me. She said to me Biddy had pestered her. And she said to Biddy that I had clamoured to be presented.'

'But did you never compare notes after you were married?' I said.

'Of course! On our honeymoon. How we laughed. We thought she was matchmaking and we were glad she had. But really what she was doing was taking Biddy off the market so Lachlan was fair game, you see?'

'But haven't you been happy?' I said. 'You seem happy.'

'We've been happy enough,' said Tibball. 'I mean, yes of course we've been happy. But the thing is, well, Shieldaig – Biddy's father's place, you know - is long gone. Sold up and turned over to sheep. They took the roof off the house to avoid the death tax when Biddy's father went. And Lachlan's money – if Lachlan had married the girl of his choice – would have kept the place afloat. Shieldaig would be thriving and Applecross just a memory. And then Lachlan wouldn't have gone out to save the Applecross gardener's son, because Biddy and he would have lived at his place. Lachlan might have been in a different regiment altogether. I wouldn't have had anything to do with the Highlanders and I wouldn't be living out my days with this wretched shell shock always waiting under the next bridge to leap out and drag me down.'

It was a horrible image and if accurate, my sympathy for Dickie Tibball would be increased markedly.

192

'But that's a fool's game,' Alec said, with somewhat less pity than I was feeling. 'I mean, who knows what would have happened to any of you if Lachlan had married Biddy. She might have died in childbirth, you might have been crippled on the battlefield. Lachlan . . . well, all right, it is hard to imagine many things worse than twenty years in a bath chair and burnt hands but he might have been blown to bits in a different battle altogether. Anything might have happened.'

'I know, I know,' Tibball said. 'But that's where all the silliness about the monks and crofters comes in. That LL was willing to steal a man to keep the estate and then a few short years later – speaking in terms of how long *A' Chomraich* has been in existence, I mean – she's changed her mind and wants the place broken up? It's the caprice, you see. It's worth scheming for and then the wind changes and she's ready to let it all go.'

'So Biddy and she argued,' I said. 'When?'

Tibball gave me a sudden sharp look and seemed almost pleased.

'Exactly,' he said. 'The night before her birthday. It was the night before. You see? It wasn't the day she was found. It was the night before. No one else could have killed her so early and hidden it so long.'

'What makes the task easier for Biddy than for anyone else?' Alec said. 'I don't understand.'

'I asked Mrs McReadie how she found out that LL wanted dinner on a tray the night before,' Dickie said. 'And she gave me a long, silent, staring look and said, "A note on her door, sir, like always".'

I nodded. Inspector Hutcheson had surmised as much.

'Notes!' Dickie repeated, with a fervour that was lost on me until he continued: 'I was terrified Mrs McReadie would know why I was asking. That she'd realise only Biddy could get away with it.'

'The handwriting!' I said. 'The dame school! Miss Whats-ername?'

'Miss Alva,' said Tibball. 'We used to laugh about it. Lachlan and me. I can't imagine ever laughing again now.'

'So, you're saying only Biddy could have faked up notes about dinner and breakfast and managed to cloud the time of death?' Tibball nodded. 'But there was another social fixture beyond meals,' I went on. 'Mallory told us earlier today that *Mitten* cancelled the plans to go to the church. You don't think *he* knew what his mother had done, do you?'

'Not a chance,' said Tibball. 'No.'

'So do you think the reason he gave is true: that Cherry – in her condition – shouldn't be out in the snow on a cold dark night?'

'Cherry?' said Tibball, and despite his claim that his laughing days were over he gave a hearty chuckle. 'She's out in the potato field today with Mitten egging her on,' he said. 'In her condition! Nonsense.'

I stared at him. Something was bothering me. Those words were acting on my memory like a tuning fork, setting me thrumming. But what was it? 'So why then?' I said.

'Didn't you ask him?' said Tibball. 'When you were getting Mitten to reveal that he thinks his father is a murderer, didn't you ask him why he cancelled the church plan? And why on earth *was* that, anyway? What made the boy think I was the one?'

'He found her necklet in your pocket when he was helping you undress.'

Tibball gasped. 'Good God!' he said. 'Oh Lord! I completely forgot! I picked it up. I picked it up and put it in my pocket and I absolutely utterly and completely forgot from that moment to this!'

If he was acting then it was the best act I had ever seen, including West End plays and the talkies.

'Picked it up where?' I asked.

'On the path,' said Tibball. 'When I was following Biddy. After that ungodly scream, we went out of the library doors – poor Lach was stuck there – and Biddy was running hell for leather. She tripped and put a hand out. I thought she was going to go head over heels but she righted herself and kept moving. I glanced down to see what had tripped her and it was one of those bally woollen necklets we all had to wear. I picked it up and shoved it in my pocket to save anyone else getting tangled in it and then I went to see what was amiss wherever Biddy was. She was yelling by then. Well, not so much yelling as sobbing. Good heavens, and so Mitten found it in my pocket, did he?' He thought for a moment. 'How did it come to be on the path though?'

'I wonder if Biddy dropped it as she ran,' Alec said.

'Maybe LL dropped it there on her way to the dovecote,' Tibball said. 'Before she died.'

'I don't think so,' I said. 'Mitten told us it had blood on it.' I was thinking furiously. If someone had dragged Lady Love's body feet first, her woollen necklet might well have come off and it might well have got bloody, but if she was dragged at all it was from the potting shed side, where the arbours would hide the marks from anyone who looked out of a window. Then a thought struck me.

'This has been troubling me even though it was buried so deep I couldn't have told you it was there,' I said. It was a sensation familiar to Alec and me from cases of old but I wondered if it would sound like nonsense to Dickie Tibball.

'Like the pea under twenty feather beds,' he said.

'Exactly! Ross told us about the unearthly scream. You were in the library and the windows were shut, isn't that right?'

'But they are French windows,' Tibball said.

I shushed him. 'The scream came from the dovecote, did it not? And you were in the house and heard it. And you say that Biddy was in the lead, running, and you followed her?'

Alec gave a low whistle.

'What? What?' said Tibball. 'I don't understand.'

'How did she know where to go?' Alec said. 'A scream from outside, from round the corner of the house, heard through the closed windows. There is no way Biddy would know to run to the knot in the middle of the dovecote unless she already knew what she'd find there.'

16

I will never quite understand how he persuaded us to let the engagement party go ahead as planned. To be sure, if Biddy Tibball was the murderer then my worries about Mallory joining my family were somewhat allayed. Her sister's mother-in-law hanged for murder was much better than her father, her sister or herself. I thought the Gilvers could probably weather a scandal at that remove. And I did so want to let her have her happy moment. The poor child had earned it, after all those months keeping Mitten's secret and aching for her family, not to mention mourning her mother. My mother was an irritating woman: she landed me with the name Dandelion for one thing and she ruined a perfectly nice house with a lot of pale paint and pre-Raphaelite pictures. Still, when she died, it took me a few months to stop suddenly bursting out into fits of weeping and a few years to stop suddenly feeling sad whenever I remembered her. A woman like Lady Love plucked away from her daughter by violent means when the girl still lived at home must have left even more furious storms of weeping and bouts of sadness behind her.

So we set off back to Applecross House ready to drink cocktails, dance reels and toast the happy couple and it was just as well, for the house had gathered the momentum of the party and was skidding downhill towards it unstoppably. The maids who Mrs McReadie was so keen to stress did not live in the house had arrived from the village by the handful. They were not dressed in black, but in whatever dresses they happened to be wearing, although they had crisp white pinnies on top and someone had persuaded them to put little hats on too. A trio of them was busy carrying bud vases of flowers across the hall when we entered, presumably for supper tables.

'Lamb ma,' one of them called out to us.

'Good afternoon,' I hazarded.

'Are you here for the celebration?' said another. 'And come in time for a wee ceilidh to yourselves. See and get in the library there. See, listen?'

Indeed, when I cocked an ear I could hear strains of fiddle music through the library door. Once again, it seemed, the guests had landed hours early and were making themselves at home.

'No, Mornie,' said another, digging her compatriot in the ribs with an elbow. 'This here's not guests. This here's Donald's mother and her man.'

I could not be bothered to correct her, so I simply nodded and smiled.

'A fine boy you've had there,' said Mornie, giving it rather an agricultural ring, to my ears. 'And thanks be to you taking our Mallory away to safety. Thanks be.'

'Safety,' Alec repeated.

'Thanks be,' the other woman chimed in and then they all bustled off with the little vases clinking in their hands. It was a cheerful sound but it did not drive away the chill I felt.

'Ignore them, Dan,' Alec said softly. He had seen my shudder. 'How many times have we been embroiled in cases with ghosts and goblins coming down every chimney? And every time the answer to our question is a plain ordinary fact of human failing.'

I thought he was overstating it just a little, for there have been many odd little queries I have been forced to walk away from, leaving them unresolved. Instead of answering, I drew him towards the flower room.

'I want to check what we've been told about these garden diaries,' I said.

'Why?'

'Because,' I answered, lifting one of the gilt-stamped volumes from a shelf, 'it was the middle of February.' I flicked through the pages of the book I was holding and nodded. 'She started a new diary each year on the first day of January and wrote through until the thirty-first of December.'

'I see,' Alec said. It is one of my very favourite things about him that he always does see. 'So she packed a heavy book full of blank pages.'

'Don't you find that odd?'

'Very. I wish we knew where her belongings had got to.'

'Do you suppose anyone searched?' Alec said. 'Who shall we ask?'

'Grant,' I said.

'Grant,' I said, entering my bedroom. 'Those bags you were pretending to look for. Lady Ross's luggage. Has anyone actually been looking?'

Grant had the grace to blush. 'Yes,' she said. 'Lord Ross had the beaters out all over the estate as soon as the weather cleared after Valentine's Day and Mrs McReadie ransacked the house and turned up nothing. I apologise for my little white lie earlier, madam.'

I barely heard her, because I had just seen what was laid out on my bed.

'No,' I said, pointing and then folding my arms.

'Oh come now, madam,' Grant said. 'Simply because you are about to be a mother-in-law and – if we are lucky – a grandmother very soon, is no reason to give up.'

'Nice try,' I said. 'I see through you as easily as I see through that.' I snatched up the dress she had draped over my counterpane and held it up to the window. The light

199

shone through the diaphanous silk so clearly that we could see the transoms. 'It's obscene!' I said.

'It's got an underskirt,' said Grant.

'And it's not just the fact that one could . . . what's that marvellous phrase?'

'I have no idea what you mean,' Grant lied.

'You "could spit peas through it",' I said, in triumph. It was one of my laundrymaid's sayings, most usually employed in relation to linens worn thin from use but just as apposite to this ludicrous garment that started life thin by design. 'And what's this?' I said, flicking one of the enormous shoulder ruffles so that it danced up and down like a can-can petticoat.

'It's this year's silhouette,' said Grant. 'Shoulders are back.'

'But how is one supposed to walk?' I demanded, for the skirt portion dwindled from hip to knee before bursting into another explosion of ruffles.

'Elegantly,' said Grant. '"One" is supposed to float. "One" is not supposed to march about like a soldier on parade. It's called a "mermaid hem".'

'Hmph,' I said. 'Mermaids are, after all, noted for their walking. I refuse to have anything to do with it. What else have you brought?'

Grant stuck her chin in the air and said nothing.

'This better be a joke,' I told her.

'I have no idea what you mean,' she said, but the spots of colour on her cheeks said otherwise. Grant used to buy startling garments and try to persuade me to take them to parties. Then she bought them and started packing them when we went away to parties. She would hang them on the back of the wardrobe door and nag me while I dressed in my respectable frock. Recently, she had taken to laying out the backless wonders, the Turkish pants, the Chinese cheong-sams, and only very begrudgingly letting me see the alternative once I had made a fuss. If she had finally taken the last step, if she had not brought anything else for me to wear, tonight of all nights, then she was going to be in a great deal of very hot water.

'Have you brought another frock?' I said.

'No.'

'Have you brought anything that can be ripped up and made into side gussets so I can walk in this frock?' I said.

'No.'

'Very well then,' I said. 'This is an extremely difficult evening for me, Grant. It would have been a difficult evening in a bathrobe and slippers. I am juggling a good many different calls on my ingenuity: to act the proud mother, the innocent bystander and the willing recent recipient of more confidences than I can even remember. Not to mention the detective who is still trying to get hard evidence about a murder and has more or less promised not to rock the boat until tomorrow despite the fact that a cold-blooded murderess is going to be at this *bloody* party with me. Doing it trussed up like a string of onions is not going to help.'

'Murder*ess*?' said Grant.

'Biddy,' I told her.

'A lifetime of jealous envy bubbling up and boiling over?'

I sank down onto the dressing stool and sighed. 'Exactly,' I said. 'What a sorry mess. For the proverbial two pins, I'd stay up here with Bunty and a chocolate pot.' Bunty thumped her tail at the sound of her name but the fight had gone out of me. I would wear the ridiculous garment. I would let Grant do whatever she wanted to my hair. I would even let her paint my face as she deemed necessary. I just wanted to be done with it.

Hugh, edging round the connecting door after a perfunctory knock, addressed me in a bewildered voice

'Was that you cursing, Dandy?' he said. 'Have you decided I'm right to be angry after all? Because I've spent the whole afternoon trying to see it from your point of view. And, I have to say, failing.'

'What?' I said, trying to work my way back through the maze to whatever state of affairs Hugh and I had last discussed. 'Oh. Well, yes. I mean, no. There's no need to get Donald to jilt Mallory after all. Look, I'll explain everything tomorrow. We need to get through tonight first.' I could not bear the idea of telling Hugh about Biddy Tibball and having him lurk at her elbow glowering the whole evening through.

'And is that what you're planning to wear?' he said, picking up the frock. 'Won't you be chilly?' Grant gave a snort that she turned into a sneeze. 'Especially if there are colds going about,' Hugh added and withdrew to his dressing room again.

I *was* chilly. I was, frankly, frozen to the marrow by the time I was dressed. For one thing, the hot-water boiler at Applecross House was not equal to the number of baths suddenly required to get all the Dunnochs, Tibballs and Gilvers ready for the ball. Mine, rather late in the running, was tepid and then Grant took an age to set my hair. When at last I wriggled into the mermaid frock my arms were mottled gooseflesh and the tip of my nose was pink. Even given that, though, it was spectacular. The shoulder ruffles made me look like a Hollywood star and the way the skirt clung to my hips and the tops of my legs made me blush, which at least warmed me up a little.

'You're going to make such an entrance,' Grant said, working a bracelet over my hand and then, for some reason, shoving it up my forearm until it stuck.

'So I imagine,' I said, 'given that the only way I can hope to get to the ground floor is to lie on the landing and roll down the stairs. And anyway, it's Mallory's night. I shouldn't be taking any attention away from her.'

Grant gave an entirely unconvincing start of surprise. 'Didn't you know I've been in correspondence with Miss Dunnoch about her dress for tonight?' she said.

'What have you done to the poor girl?' I asked. 'Is that

202

where you've been until now? Is that why I hung about until the hot water was finished, waiting? Because you were dressing Mallory?'

'As you said, madam, it's her night,' replied Grant. 'Go down and see for yourself. And it's perfectly simple to descend the stairs, by the way. You just turn about forty-five degrees to the left, to make use of the bias, and go down right foot first onto each step, with a good firm grip on the banister in case you forget.'

'Oh, is that all?' I said. 'Silly me.' But I did want to see Mallory; that much was true. So I set off across my bedroom and along the corridor, flinging each leg forward from the knee and feeling the unaccustomed but unmistakable sensation of my rear end twitching from side to side as I did so. Another, deeper, blush saw off my goose bumps before I was halfway to the stairs.

I descended them with a lack of speed and an excess of wariness I had never seen outside an egg and spoon race and was thankful no one was around in the hall to watch me. Back on solid ground again I wiggled off in the direction of the dining room, where the cold cuts were to have been laid out. I tried not to think about how to get back up the stairs to the ballroom. Grant had not touched on that and I could not imagine.

'Good Lord above,' was Hugh's pronouncement as I shimmered towards him. He was sitting in the middle of a group of men who had gathered at the north-east corner of the long table, putting much distance between themselves and the group of women gathered in the south-west near the fire. Cherry was in an empire line frock of an attractive deep coral that brought out the chestnut glints in her hair and took the top off her sunburn. Biddy was in the sort of matronly frock, solid and comfortable-looking, that I wished I was wearing. Mallory, though, was a wonderment. She was standing eating from a small plate on the mantelpiece, either because she could not sit without creasing her frock or, more likely, because she simply could not sit. Grant had triumphed. Her dress was paler than mine, more see-through than mine and clung even harder to her for even longer. She was encased like a sausage from rib to calf and there were no ruffles. The dress simply had a low cowl of fabric – exceedingly low! – across her décolletage and a slit up the front to let her fling her legs in front of her and approximate something that might be called walking. Her hair was pulled over from just above one ear and had been worked into something like a lotus blossom just above the other. Her eyes were twice their natural size and her lips were claret coloured and sharper than daggers.

Donald stared at her, apparently astonished by the dis-appearance of the chummy, friendly girl he cared for in his way and the advent of this silver-screen vision sprung to implausible life before his eyes. Despite the fact that he was steadily forking folded slices of mustard-slathered roast beef into his mouth and could not possibly be feeling hungry, *hungrily* was the only word for the way he was looking at Mallory.

'Can you sit, Dandy?' Mallory said. 'Or will you join me at the other end of the mantelpiece?'

Biddy Tibball got fussily to her feet and started loading a plate for me from the sideboard. 'Charred end or rare middle?' she said, with a serving fork hovering over the beef plate.

'Oh, whatever's there,' I said. 'And not too much. I'm short of space.'

'You do look lovely,' Biddy said, so cravenly I wondered if Dickie had tipped her the wink and she thought sucking up would endear her despite everything. 'And look at Mallory! She looks like an angel, doesn't she? Oh, my heart breaks that her mother's not here to see her.'

I craned over one shoulder – much easier than trying to

turn my body unless I was prepared to hop – and caught Alec's eye. He nodded imperceptibly. Too far, his expression said. We could barely stomach it anyway, but if she was really going to wring her hands about the woman she had killed she really had gone a step too far.

Accordingly, as we filed out of the dining room again – after the cold beef and a dish of stewed gooseberries that made me hope Mrs McReadie was saving her efforts for the party and that this was not an indication of the supper tables to come – I put a hand on Biddy's arm.

'Might I have a quiet word?'

She turned on me a look so open, so frank, so friendly, that I wavered in my suspicions. Alec approaching from her other side, however, looked steely enough for both of us.

'How can I help you?' she said. 'Oh. It's not . . .? I mean, do you need to pay a visit? Do you need assistance?'

I had not even considered that aspect of my incarceration in this silken straitjacket and my face fell. 'No,' I said. 'It's not as bad as it looks, actually. They're very clever, these fashion designers, you know.' It was a bare-faced lie. Whoever had designed this dress and Mallory's was a practical joker whose victims were women and whose final triumph was that we paid him. 'No, it's just that we feel, Alec and I, increasingly uncomfortable about the way matters have been left.'

Biddy had heard Alec coming up behind her and she turned to include him in her question.

'Matters?' she said. 'What "matters"?'

'We don't believe, you see,' said Alec, 'that Lady Love was killed by a passing tramp. We believe that you know rather more about it than you have said.'

Biddy's face fell, the innocent curling smile replaced by welling tears and whitening cheeks. 'Yes, you're right. I do,' she said. 'Please let Mallory have tonight. If you let her have tonight, he will be gone in the morning.'

'Who will?' I said. 'Death? One of its harbingers? Another crow? A bigger, blacker dog? A prefigurative vision of the next corpse?'

Biddy blinked at me. 'No,' she said. 'Are you feeling quite well, Dandy? You're talking wildly.'

I shook my head. 'Forgive me,' I said. 'That vision out on the moor was Lachlan himself, wasn't it?' Was it? It still troubled me that Cherry had called her father 'fit as a fiddle' on Valentine's Day. 'Who will be gone?'

'The killer of course,' Biddy said. 'David Spencer.'

I could not speak but Alec was made of sterner stuff.

'Keep your voice down,' he hissed. 'The man's still crossing the hall. He'll hear you. But for God's sake tell us what you know.'

'Why would David Spencer kill Lady Love?' I asked. 'What would he care if she sold the estate?'

'Sold the . . .?' said Biddy. 'Have you been talking to Dickie? He's convinced I'm in a rage about Lady Love's latest scheme. He never can believe that I adore him and wouldn't change a thing if I had my life over again.' She smiled, then grew solemn. 'He wanted her to go away with him,' she said. 'That's why he came. I – it's terrible to admit it, I know – but I overheard them talking in the knot garden the day before her birthday. He was trying to persuade her. Oh he didn't call it that. He said she had to see sense, face facts, admit that she had made a mistake, not let pride ruin the whole of her life but have the courage to call it quits. He told her he loved her. And she said she knew he did, had always known, and loved him too.'

'He *was* rather cagey about why he had come all the way up in such treacherous weather,' said Alec. 'But we'd put him down as a friend of the family, hadn't we Dandy? Or at least no more devoted to Lady Love than anyone else.'

'He asked her to meet him at the dovecote after dark on the eve of her birthday, once everyone else was in bed.' Tears gathered in Biddy's eyes as she remembered. 'I thought, when she was missing and yet he was still here – on the morning of her birthday itself, you know – that she had gone away to think it over. Packed her bags in case she decided to go through with the scheme and then curled up somewhere quiet to ponder it. When I heard the scream coming out of the dark that night, my first thought was that she'd met him at the dovecote like he asked, albeit a day late, but that she'd said no and he'd flown into a rage and set upon her.'

'That's why you knew where to run to!' I said. 'Straight out of the library to the dovecote like a homing pigeon. We thought that was suspicious, you see. We thought the only reason you'd know where to go was that you knew where the body was.'

'I?' said Biddy. 'You thought I knew that my dearest LL was lying there in the cold and wet and I just left her? Why on earth would I? How could anyone who loved her do such a cruel heartless thing?' She looked between Alec and me beseechingly, the tears in her eyes now so many that they sparkled. 'Oh!' she said, far too loud. She clapped her hands to her face. 'You thought I killed her? You thought I killed my best friend? My oldest friend? The warmest, kindest, most beloved woman I have ever known in my life?'

'Sorry,' I said, and it sounded so ludicrously inadequate that I almost laughed. 'We didn't believe that she was still alive when you seemed to suggest that she was still alive, you see. We thought you wrote the notes saying she wanted dinner in her room and then breakfast in bed.'

'No,' said Biddy. 'No, I didn't write them. I mean, I could have, of course. Our handwriting is very similar, and I've seen enough of it over the years to be able to mimic her style, but I didn't. I can't prove it. You'll just have to believe me. Or not. But it would be wonderful if you would believe me. Because then there would be three of us keeping an eye on him tonight. Instead of me alone.'

That was inarguable. I nodded and glared at Alec, who nodded too.

'Do you have any evidence that it was David Spencer?' I said. 'It's a compelling motive, but unless there's hard evidence about the deed itself to back it up, we can't really let a motive sway us. There are, after all, motives everywhere we turn.'

'Are there?' said Biddy. I opened my mouth but she put her hand up. 'Don't tell me. I don't want to hear it. I loved LL like a sister and I don't want to hear ill of her.'

'Your husband said you were angry when you found out she stole Lachlan from you,' I said.

'Yes,' she said, squirming a bit. 'That's what I said to Dickie and he believed me.'

'When in fact?' said Alec.

'I did find something out, but it wasn't that.'

We waited but she shook her head. 'It doesn't matter now. Spencer is the thing.' She shook her head even more vigorously, as though driving all extraneous nonsense from it. 'And I don't have any "hard evidence", as you put it. All I've got is more motive. His wife died recently, you see. He took a young wife in a bid to get LL out of his heart once and for all. And she died. That was why he came north when he did, to try again.'

'And when you say she died,' Alec said. 'You don't mean that he killed her to get her out of the way, do you?'

'No!' said Biddy. 'She was expecting a baby and she caught a severe chill and it went to her blood and she died. He told Mitten about it. He was dead set on getting Mitten to cancel the plan for us all to go along to the church that night before LL's birthday. And that was the reason. The thought of Cherry out in the cold in her condition brought back all his dreadful memories, you see.'

'I don't see,' I said. 'I think Lady Love was already dead by then. I think he went to her room and killed her. I think he had to quash the church expedition because Lady Love would have been part of it and her absence could not be explained. If it was just dinner and then breakfast she missed, no one would be worried. She often dined off a tray and breakfasted in bed, didn't she? But the church service was something else again.'

'But,' said Biddy, 'even if he had some sort of mania for LL and even if he struck out when she refused him, that's not to say he's a cold-hearted monster. He probably did mourn when his wife died and the baby with her. He probably did feel a twinge of worry at the thought of Cherry going out that night.'

Alec gave her a kindly look. This woman was a goose. She was telling us more clearly than we could have desired that she did not have the wit to plan and stage and then hide a murder. 'Biddy,' he said. 'I rather think the tale of the wife who died of a cold was made up out of whole cloth to get Mitten to cancel the church service. Do you see?'

'Oh!' said Biddy again. 'Yes. But that's a terrible thing to say if it's not true. And it's rather awful to be able to think up something like that. I mean, if I had gone into a blind rage and whacked someone with a peat-cutter, I'd be a jelly. I wouldn't be able to make up stories to help cover my tracks.'

'No, I don't believe you would,' I said. 'But I believe David Spencer did some very quick thinking. I think he almost managed to persuade Lady Love to go. I think she packed her bags and wrote a couple of notes to go on her door, saying she wanted dinner and breakfast alone. But then, for some reason we may never know, she changed her mind. And when she changed her mind, Spencer saw his chance. He could take her bags away, put one note then the other on her door. Perhaps he even cleared the dinner tray that must have been delivered, making it look as though she'd eaten. All this to convince the servants and her daughters that she was still alive.'

'Still alive when though?' Alec said. 'All of that only makes sense if he also manufactured an alibi for the supposed time of the killing.'

'He was away all day on Lady Love's birthday,' I said. 'Until the late boat.'

'Does anyone know why?' said Alec. 'Where he was supposed to be?'

'We can ask him,' I said. 'It would be odd if we didn't interview him, when we're interviewing everyone else.'

'We'll have to be quick,' Alec said. 'If Biddy's right about him leaving tomorrow. But, Biddy, what makes you think so? What makes you think he will leave tomorrow when he has stayed on since Valentine's Day? Why wouldn't he just stay indefinitely, making sure no one starts to pick at his story and unravel it?'

'He told me,' she said. 'Well, he told all of us. He's going to take LL's place on this plant-hunting expedition she was so excited about. He leaves tomorrow. He's going to New Zealand to search for this fabled true black lily to add to their score of discoveries.'

We both took a while to digest this startling piece of new information coming at us out of nowhere.

'He is, is he?' Alec said at last.

'Lachlan is underwriting it,' Biddy said. 'In Lady Love's memory. And McReadie is going, of course. He's the plantsman. He's needed to make sure the cuttings or bulbs or seeds or whatever Spencer finds are properly handled so they survive the journey back here.'

'We'd heard as much,' I said. 'But this is the first news that David Spencer is part of the plan. New Zealand is a very exotic destination to keep quiet about.'

'That's just the starting point,' Biddy said. 'If they don't find one there they're going to move on to China and then the Americas. Lachlan wants a memorial to her. David Spencer probably wants it too. And the way I see it is that if he's in New Zealand he's nice and far away from all of us. And the reason he hasn't mentioned it is that he doesn't want to steal Mallory's thunder. He's going to slip away tomorrow.'

'Unless the police stop him,' Alec said. 'Do you have any shred of proof? Anything at all? The fact of his being out of the way on the day of the birthday is suspicious but not conclusive. Likewise the things you overheard. Is there anything else?'

'Well,' Biddy said. 'What you were saying about an alibi. Making it seem that she was alive and making sure he was out of the way – that's only half the story, isn't it? There's also the matter of needing to be on the spot to do the deed when it really was done.' We nodded. 'And I think I saw him.'

That set Alec and me back upon our heels. 'After tea on the day before LL's birthday, he said he was walking along to the street, to the grocer's shop. He made a great fuss about it, asking everyone if they wanted anything while he was there: tobacco or anything. And off he went. But I was in the turret room with its windows all round, and I saw him sneaking back. He wasn't on the road. He was crouched down behind the wall on the landward side and he was scuttling along the edge of the field there. Keeping his head down so no one on the road could see him, you know. The only windows on that side below the turret are the French windows out of the library and the hedge screens them, even if the curtains are open, so it was the merest chance that I saw him. I watched him all the way until he was too close and then I heard the little side door bang as he came into the house. Now, that door is kept locked, you see. It used to lead to the outside privies before Lachlan updated the plumbing and it doesn't lead anywhere now. It's never used. So David Spencer must have unlocked it specially. He wouldn't have tried it on the off-chance.'

'And this was before supper on the thirteenth?' Alec said.

'The eve of her birthday,' Biddy agreed.

'Do you know where he went after he came into the house?' I said. Biddy shook her head. 'And why were you in the turret room?'

'Fetching the pictures to set out for her birthday the next day,' Biddy said. 'I don't know where he went when he came back. And I don't know when he scuttled back along to the street. But I know he came banging in the front door with a lot of noise and bluster about half an hour later, with some leeks done up in newspaper that he said he'd seen in the shop and couldn't resist because they were such fine specimens. He went straight to the kitchen to give them to Mrs McReadie. As if McReadie didn't grow good enough leeks for us!'

'He was definitely establishing an alibi,' I said. 'He must have been disappointed that no one in the family asked for peppermints or a picture paper. He had to buy something to make it clear he had been out.'

Biddy nodded. 'And then he killed her and left her lying at the dovecote, put those notes on her door night and morning, then went off on the early boat hoping we'd find her while he was away.'

I gave a glance at Alec, wondering if we should tell this woman about Lady Love's peregrinations. She clearly did not know that the body had spent time in the flower room. Alec shook his head slightly and I agreed. It was a pointlessly unpleasant image to put into Biddy's head for all eternity.

'What I don't understand,' said Alec, 'is why, having got away with it, he didn't hoof it. Why was he still here when the snow melted? Why is he here today? Why couldn't he wait somewhere else for this expedition to begin?'

'I think he's watching us to make sure no one suspects him,' said Biddy. 'He couldn't bear to be somewhere else and all of us talking behind his back, putting it together and tightening the noose. So he stays and watches. It's been driving me demented. I daren't even tell poor Dickie in case it floors him.'

'I don't imagine he's been troubled by you all talking,' I said. 'Since no one is saying a word to anyone. Yours is the sixth version we've winkled out. All different. Spencer must be cock-a-hoop.'

'And on that note,' Alec said. 'Let's the three of us get up to the ballroom, shall we? If he's as watchful as all that he'll be wondering why we're in a pow-wow.'

'I'm just glad I've got you two to help tonight,' Biddy said. 'We should make sure that one of us can see him at all times. It would have been awfully suspicious if it was just me on his tail – and I couldn't follow him to the cloakroom – but this way we should be able to manage it.'

'I'll mention it to Teddy,' I said. 'And Grant. No doubt she'll find some excuse to attend.'

With that, we left the dining room. Alec strode ahead and Biddy kept pace, then, realising that I was nowhere near them, they turned back and waited for me to wriggle my way across the floor. They did not notice, for that reason, David Spencer descending the staircase. He had one hand tucked into his dinner jacket and the other resting lightly on the banister rail and looked the picture of ease and suavity.

'There you all are!' he said. 'I've been sent to round you up. Carriages approach and you are needed, Dandy.'

'I?' I said.

'Mother of the bridegroom,' said Spencer. 'Mallory wants you to greet the guests as well as her, Donald and Lach. She's feeling the lack of her mother terribly tonight. And Cherry thinks she would excite a little too much comment from the neighbours, given her . . . ' He waved a hand in front of him.

'Very well,' I said, wriggling to the bottom of the stairs. I could, indeed, hear the sound of revellers mounting the steps

213

towards the front door. Lairdie, the footman, was making his way towards it to open up for them. He was dressed this evening in Highland dress, his kilt swinging and various bits of him glinting as the chain of his sporran, his silver buttons and the dagger in his sock caught the lamplight. I gripped the handrail and tried to lift one of my legs to make a start on the bottom step. Nothing happened. I tried the other one.

'Oh, Lord!' said Alec. 'Would an arm help at all?'

'I don't see how,' I said. Lairdie was opening the door and a rush of cool night air and happy voices poured in. I looked back at the stairs and then, before I knew what had happened, David Spencer bent down, grabbed me round the silk-encased thighs and straightened again with me over his shoulder. He set off up the stairs at a trot, me squeaking my disapproval and trying not to get dizzy looking at the steps falling away behind his heels.

In less than half a minute we were on the first floor, I was back on my feet and Spencer was smoothing his hair.

'Forgive me,' he said. 'It's not usually my style to cart women off without permission but there was nothing else for it.' And he left me.

Alec, arriving at my side, was fuming with impotent rage. 'Cheek!' he said. 'Upstart! I could have lifted you, Dandy. I'm just as strong as him.'

'Hardly flattering,' I said, 'to reassure me that you're hefty enough not to buckle under my weight.' Biddy Tibball was up beside us on the landing now. Her face was pale and drawn.

'The sight of it,' she said. 'The sight of him carrying you like a . . . well, like a dead weight. As if he's done it before. And we know he has. I feel quite sick.'

'Steel yourself, Mrs Tibball,' said Alec.

But I, another frail woman, and currently hobbled by my outfit to boot, felt just as shaken. 'You're right, Biddy,' I murmured. 'We keep him in sight this evening. We keep one set of eyes on him at all times.'

17

It made for a rather less dull party than I thought was in store. Brought up as I was to train my full attention on whomever I was currently speaking to, never to glance over a shoulder to find more interesting goings-on, I usually find myself stuck with curates and aunts. Tonight though, I stood at the edge of the ballroom while Alec was dancing and kept my beady eye bouncing around the throng.

The youngsters, of whom there was a lively crowd, managed to dance terrible modern dances to all but the very slowest dirges provided by a five-piece band and, when the dirges outwitted them, they went to stand by the open windows, smoke black cigarettes that someone had produced from somewhere – not the Applecross grocer's shop – and drink brimming glasses of champagne until they cooled off. While their jabbing elbows and knees were off the dancefloor, the elders ventured out, doing some terrifically complicated reels at a snail's pace, while the fiddles moaned on and the drums boomed out their death knell.

I had never seen the point of those reels. They are unnerving to be in, as one is thrown from man to man like a skittle, always in danger of going wrong and wrecking the set or of missing the arm held out towards one and simply spinning off into the tables and chairs and breaking limbs. Watching it, however, was rather moving. The couples were absolutely stony-faced and in perfect time with the plaintive music. I was even quite proud of Hugh, swishing round so knowledgably, no matter how involved the patterns became.

Perhaps I was turning Scottish after all these long years. I blinked as David Spencer passed close by me, catching then flinging away a woman in a blue cotton dress, a white apron and a little hat. The serving maids were dancing.

Perhaps he had made a bet with someone that he would partner every woman in the room before the night was done. Biddy had been grim-faced as she did her stint, but I applauded her nevertheless. If he had killed my best friend, I might not have been able to stomach his hands upon me. I had also marked him, before this maidservant, with Mallory, with Cherry and with several of the jolly neighbours. It was inevitable, I suppose, that eventually he would come up and proposition me.

'It's a very slow waltz,' he said, 'and I promise to stick to the time-honoured shuffle and not put in any fancy steps. Would you care to?'

'Delighted,' I said. As we took to the floor, Alec grabbed Biddy Tibball and muscled his way towards us, setting up just behind Spencer's head with a glower. I was aware of Hugh watching with rather a lot of interest and foresaw that I should have to explain the glower.

'It's all going off very well,' I said, as the music started up and we spun away, in something far from the promised shuffle. At first, I clutched his shoulder and tried to sort my feet out, but he was what they call in professional ballroom circles a 'strong lead' and so instead I let myself be rattled round like dice in a cup without worrying. 'I thought it would be sad. I thought no matter how many people were here, all we would be able to think about was who was missing.'

'I can't say she's been far from my mind,' he said. 'But one must try, for Mallory.'

'Indeed.'

'He's a splendid boy, your Don,' Spencer said next.

'Boy rather than man?' I said. 'If you are asking me what I think about the difference in their ages—'

216

'I'm not.' He pulled his head back and gave me a startled look. 'He's a boy and Mallory is a girl, viewed from my great number of years.'

'Mine too,' I said, with a laugh. It was hard to remember that this man was a cold-blooded killer. 'If I had ordered up a bride from a menu I would have ordered one younger and I wouldn't have ordered her so soon. But she's lovely and he cares for her. I mean, look at them!'

Donald and Mallory were dancing a rather more ambitious waltz, thanks to the split in the front of her skirt, but despite that they did not seem to be concentrating on getting the steps right, but were gazing deep into one another's eyes, with small smiles on their faces. I turned the problem over in my mind: did a mother killed by a spurned lover taint Mallory? No, I concluded. When this was over, she would be his bride. Then, I cast an eye around to see if Hugh was witnessing the display of affection and caught sight of Grant watching with as much triumph on her face as though she was not just the wardrobe mistress and hairdresser, but at least the matchmaker if not the proud mother. I chuckled.

'So stately his form and so lovely her face that never a hall such a galliard did grace,' said Spencer, smiling at them too.

'What's a galliard?' I said.

'A kind of dance, although I'm taking licence since they're actually doing a waltz.'

'You certainly are steeped in Highland . . . what-have-you,' I said. 'For a Londoner.'

'I'm not a Londoner,' he said. 'Not even the home counties. Chaucer would think me a Midland man. And anyway, Walter Scott isn't from the Highlands.'

'Scott, is it?' I said. 'I just about know "Oh what a tangled web we weave", and that's my lot.'

I bit my lip after that, but Spencer did not seem to read anything into it. 'I'm very glad Mallory is going to be settled,' he said presently. 'Changes are coming to Applecross, I fear.'

'Inevitably,' I said. 'But changes were coming anyway.'

'What do you mean?' I thought I felt his hand grow warm in mine; an unpleasant sensation, and I briefly regretted the demise of long evening gloves, like the dowager I was.

'Lady Love was going to leave Applecross,' I said. My throat felt dry as I considered, too late, the wisdom of speaking. But I was safe enough, with Alec and Biddy watching and surrounded by people.

'Do you think so?' David Spencer said. 'What have you heard?'

'What do you mean?' I said, hoping I sounded innocent. 'She fitted out the manse for her and Lachlan, didn't she?'

'Oh!' he said. 'Leave this house, you mean? I thought you meant leave the estate. Leave Wester Ross. Leave this place and make a new life.'

'With you,' I added, my heart in my mouth and my throat now dry enough to click when I swallowed.

'So you did hear something,' he said. 'Of course, in this house of women it was ridiculous to believe that the secret would be kept. Yes, I hoped to persuade Lavinia to come and live with me. I came up for her birthday to state my case and sweep her away.'

'And on her birthday, when you disappeared for hours, were you making preparations?'

'No, no, it was all wrecked by then. By that time I was trying to avert an even worse disaster.'

'You failed,' I said.

'I did,' said Spencer. 'I loved her. And it killed her.'

'It?' I said. His hand was now so slick with sweat that mine was slipping out of it. '*It* killed her?'

'Don't tell me you believe in this "tramp"!' he said, with a sneering laugh. 'You're a detective, for one thing, and not a stupid woman even without that. I've been on tenterhooks every minute since you got back, waiting for you to gather us all up and lay the truth out on the table.'

'I take it you wouldn't care for that?' I said.

'Not at all,' said Spencer. 'Although I'd be interested to know how you uncovered that truth, since you know less than I do of the matter. I don't suppose you'd do me the great favour of just looking the other way until tomorrow. Once I'm gone, you can tell who you like and say whatever you choose. But if it's all right with Lach and the girls, why can't you just, for tonight, look the other way?'

He had pulled back again to see into my eyes and suddenly he lunged forward as if he was going to kiss me or, I feared, bite me. It was, however, just that he had been bumped from behind. The male half of another couple was holding his head too and the village woman staring over her partner's shoulder at us had a look of alarm on her face.

'Gammon his cart!' she said.

'Not at all,' I said. I was getting very good at guessing. 'Don't mention it. No harm done.'

I was wrong about that, though. David Spencer let go of my hand, put his to the back of his head and brought it away with red fingers.

'Good heavens,' I said. 'You're bleeding.'

'Yes, it was quite a smack.'

'Shall we get you a bandage?' I said. 'Some ice at least?'

'Best not fuss,' he said. 'It's terribly bad luck as far as these Highlanders are concerned, to shed blood at a wedding or a christening. I don't want to chance an engagement party. If you'll forgive me.'

He took me to the edge of the dancefloor and then shot off towards the doors. I signalled frantically to Alec, who – I am afraid to say – simply left Biddy standing alone in the middle of the room and hightailed it off after him. Biddy came to stand next to me, naturally enough given the fact that we were two orphans abandoned in the middle of a dance.

219

'What happened?' she said. 'I was looking the other way.'

'Tell me,' I said, 'is it bad luck to shed blood at a Highland wedding?'

'It's rather bad luck to shed blood at all,' she said, reasonably enough, 'but there are no particular taboos about it. Why?'

'In that case,' I said, 'I've definitely tipped our hand. I am sorry. I couldn't resist it, while I had the chance. You did much better than me.'

'Not really,' Biddy said. 'I'm afraid I dropped a hint or two of my own. We were talking about architecture.'

'That sounds harmless.'

'And I asked if he knew why there were no windows on the east side of the house. I said it seemed odd not to have any way to see if there were strangers approaching unless one stood in the turret.' She rubbed her nose. 'And he stiffened. I felt his shoulders go quite wooden.'

The waltz ended with one last long whine of violin and the couples on the floor sprang apart and clapped desultorily. When the band picked up again, in a lively air almost too fast to imagine dancing to at all, the clapping from the youngsters quickened and a couple of cheers went up. The elders smiled and began to leave the floor, including the village woman who had bumped us. I smiled again but she was frowning and looking about herself, paying no attention to me. Of her partner there was no sign. I scanned the crowd and as I did so, Alec came in at the door, his eyes wide. He shook his head and mouthed something.

'What's the matter with Osborne?' said Hugh, suddenly at my side.

'He's been looking for David Spencer,' I said. 'And I don't think he can find him.'

Alec pushed across the floor and spoke in an angry hiss when he reached us. 'Vanished. I know he didn't get down the stairs because they're thronged with people coming up.

I checked the bathroom on the landing that's being used as a gentlemen's cloakroom. Then I'm afraid I checked the ladies' cloakroom, which caused rather a stir. I have to say you do yourselves very well in there. He must be somewhere in the bedrooms or up in the attics. How can we organise a search?'

'Hugh,' I said, 'you're tall enough to see over all these heads. Can you cast your eyes around and just check that Mallory and Cherry are here? Donald? Teddy? Dickie and Lachlan?'

'All present and correct,' Hugh said, after a long searching look. There were quite fifty people in the room by now.

'Biddy,' I went on, 'would you be willing to station yourself at this door and make sure none of them leave? Spencer hiding is one thing; Spencer cornered is another. As long as none of the family gets in his way we can search for him and track him down, by hook or by crook.'

'Not you, Dandy!' Hugh said. 'Osborne and I. That is, I take it we're tracking him down because he's the murderer? In which case, I must put my foot down and say no.'

I chewed this over briefly, but the memory of how strong Spencer had felt when he hoisted me over his shoulder was hard to dismiss and so, with ill-grace, I nodded. 'I shall station myself at the head of the staircase,' I said. 'If he passes me, I'll raise the alarm.'

'Righto,' Hugh said. 'No one has noticed anything. Let's disperse and carry out a clean operation. Osborne, take the attic floor and I'll sweep round on this one, then we'll both do the ground together.'

'And what can I do, madam?' said Grant. I had not seen her standing by me, attracted like a bear to honey by the unmistakable signs of trouble.

'You could go and stand unobtrusively by the front gate to see if he takes a motorcar and gets clean away,' I said.

Grant boggled. 'It's coming on heavy rain,' she said.

'Oh?' I answered. 'Do you feel inappropriately dressed? Do you feel that your wardrobe is unequal to the prospect before you?'

'Grant would be more use at the foot of the servants' stairs, checking that he doesn't slip down that way,' Hugh said.

I withered him with a look and propelled myself forward, kneecaps first, towards the ballroom door. Hugh got ahead of me in two strides and marched out.

'We'll find him, Dan,' said Alec as he passed me in turn.

I reached my station at the head of the stairs without mishap, after which my biggest problem was resisting efforts to be taken back into the ballroom on someone's arm or another. The late crowd was just arriving; twenty or more of them, well-refreshed after their late dinners and inclined to be chummy. I pled a need for air, a dancing partner who had stepped away and was soon returning, a promise to my husband to meet him there if we had got separated and, finally, a plan for an engagement surprise that was just about to come off and needed my presence on the landing. These Highlanders, I thought crossly, were far more forward than the Scots I was used to.

When not fending them off, I looked all around me, a bland smile upon my face even though my heart banged so high in my chest it felt as if it was sitting just behind my jaw. There was no sign of David Spencer. I saw Hugh once or twice, flitting across from room to room in the bedroom passageway. I saw Donald and Mallory twirl past the open ballroom doorway on their passage round the dancefloor, still gazing deep into one another's eyes. I even saw Teddy sweep by, gazing deep into the eyes of what looked horribly like a village girl. At least she had on black leather shoes and wore a hairband with lace flowers stitched to it.

I turned away. Outside the landing window the night was as black as a coalhole but Grant was wrong about the rain.

222

Unless, I thought, catching sight of something, that was rain making the weathervane shine. Certainly, something had glittered down there in the garden suddenly. And there it was again. I turned and put my face close to the glass, cupping my hands to cut out the glow of the lamps. It was a torch. I saw it very clearly this time. A beam of electric torchlight lit up the dovecote and sent the shadow of the weathervane leaping like a witch across the pale bank of apple blossom beyond. He had got himself out to the knot garden. He was getting away. Without thinking, I grabbed the window latch and wrenched it open. 'Stop!' I shouted. 'Stop!'

The torchlight snuffed out and I was staring blankly into perfect darkness again. I swung back. Biddy was out of sight inside the ballroom. The bedroom corridor stretched ahead of me, quite empty. There was no sign of Alec on the stairs leading up again to the second floor. There was nothing for it. I bent, gripped the hem of my frock and ripped a slit in it up to my stocking tops. Then I kicked my dancing slippers off and plunged down the staircase, headed for the nearest door to the outside.

No one saw me except a red-faced old gentleman heading towards the card room who said only, 'Hijinks starting early,' and chuckled. I checked my headlong dash, wondering if I could ask him to join me. But it would take too long to explain, so I sped up again, making for the flower room and the garden beyond.

The gravel that looked as smooth as sand was torture under my stockinged feet but I gritted my teeth and raced along. I was certain to be too late, but if there was even a chance of him getting lost in the labyrinth, without his torch-light, it was worth trying. All I had to do was stay on the path all round the outside until I reached the door in the wall at the far side and could lock it. *Then* all I needed to do was find a rock and hide. Before I could terrify myself

223

with any more details of what I was pelting towards, it was too late. I was there.

And he was there before me. Or so I thought, because I could see movement, faint but unmistakable, at waist height, and could hear stertorous breathing. It was the oddest sound, almost like a snore. I peered desperately into the darkness and saw a faint gleam. It was joined after a second by another gleam and then the two tiny lights remained trained upon my face as the strange rumbling snore grew louder. I was frozen in mystified horror, transfixed by a sight and sound I could not decipher. Then, just as I thought I must shriek aloud from the creeping terror of it, the two pinpricks blinked.

'Ursus!' I hissed and lunged forward. The cat sprang down and streaked away as I made sharp contact with the garden roller where he had been perching. It was indeed a raker, as Hugh had said, barbed as well as solid, and one of its teeth pierced my toe. I winced and hopped until the throbbing might recede, but at least that slowed me down enough so that I noticed the shadow of the garden gate gleaming faintly ahead of me, its white paint no more than a ghost of light in the blackness. I slowed and stopped and put my hand out. It was locked. I scrabbled around a bit and my fingers felt the key.

So. He was still in here with me. Silently, not even breathing, I eased the key free and crept away from the gate. I listened so hard, straining against the silence, that my ears crackled and hummed, but there was no sound of footfall, no sound of movement, nothing but the shushing of the night breeze in the apple trees.

I felt the flood of perspiration that had washed over me begin to cool and dry on my skin. It was such an airless night, at least in here where the walls stilled the air and turned it foetid with the smell of damp grass and rotting blossom.

I blew upwards into my hair for relief and then froze. How could I be gasping in the airlessness while listening to the sound of the breeze?

As if in answer, the rushing changed to a gurgle. Numb with the knowledge I could not deny, even while I refused to give it a name, I blundered forward onto one of the paths leading to the centre of the maze.

I made what felt like fifty wrong turns but must only have been a handful, following that dreadful gasping, gurgling sound to its source. It grew fainter as I got closer and, by the time the clouds had thinned enough for me to see my way, it had stopped. When at last I arrived in the opening, stumbling over one of the little flower beds and then seeing the dim mast of the dovecote and weathervane just ahead, the silence was deafening. I crouched down and groped and there, as I knew it would be, was a shoe with a foot in it, a trousered leg, a stiff shirt front and a wetness spreading down from the collar.

He had killed again.

Reaching for a hand to take his pulse, even though I knew it was too late, I felt cold metal and shrank back, before realising that it was the torch. I scrabbled for it again, turned it on and, steeling myself, trained the beam forward.

David Spencer lay twisted on the ground, awash in blood from a wound across his throat.

A scream escaped me just as a door opened up on the terrace and Hugh's voice came, barrack-trained, as loud as thunder across the garden.

'Dandy? Are you out here?'

'She can't be,' came Alec's voice. 'She can't walk in that bloody dress, never mind without her shoes.'

'Hugh? Alec?' I said. 'I'm here. I'm all right. I'm at the middle of the knot. But there's been a— He's dead. You need to ring up the police and stop anyone from leaving.'

I heard one set of footsteps ringing out on the wooden boards of the library floor and another set of footsteps crunch and spatter as someone ran across the gravel to the start of the grass paths.

I did not know who had gone to the telephone and who had come straight to me until he rounded the last corner of the apple-tree arbour and into the torchlight at my side.

18

It was not suicide. The local bobby would have loved for it be suicide, clearly. The sergeant from Lochcarron, likewise. The inspector from Inverness would have greeted the possibility of suicide – while the balance of mind was properly disturbed by the remorse that goodness demanded be felt – with profound relief.

Unfortunately for them, it is well-nigh impossible to whack oneself in the front of the throat with a long-handled pruning saw and it is utterly impossible to leave that saw leaning against the wall of the house forty feet from one's corpse, having done so.

That left no other possibility but that the local bobby, who puffed along from the street on his bicycle while the party guests were still stampeding like frightened horses, the sergeant from Lochcarron, who arrived in a motorcar with the klaxon going while the guests were sitting exhausted but restive all over the ballroom floor with nothing but strong tea and the sad remnants of the party supper to comfort them, and the inspector from Inverness, who tried to sweep in with dignity as the sun came up the next morning but failed, had all let a murderer slip through their hands for the second time.

It was the inspector for whom I felt the hottest anger and the coldest disdain. The bobby, one Constable Petrie, usually concerned himself with Sabbath licensing, stray dogs, children chalking naughty words on the paths when playing hopscotch and the odd case of disputed grazing. He was horrified. His face ran with tears as well as with the perspiration engendered by suddenly pedalling around the bay at top speed after a long day. He stood in the knot garden, wrung his hands and wept openly.

'I knew it was wrong,' he said. 'That's the worst of it. I knew. What tramp would there be all the way out here in the winter, getting in and getting out again and not a soul to see him? I'll take this to the gates, I will. St Peter will read this out at my reckoning.'

'Yes, well that's as may be,' I said crisply. 'But there are pressing matters to attend to before that. The house is full of party guests. Half the county and most of the village is in there. I'm surprised you weren't here already, Constable.'

'We've a new baby in the house and the other three and my wife are down with laryngitis,' he said miserably.

'So you need to get started on witness statements,' I said, but less crisply perhaps. 'We can help, can't we?' I nodded at Grant, Hugh and Alec, who had all gathered by this time. 'We were watching the ballroom and we can tell you, categorically, that all the Dunnochs and Tibballs were accounted for when Mr Spencer was attacked.'

'You were watching?' said Constable Petrie. 'Why?'

I frowned at him. It struck me as a stupid question, but if he had a wife and three children ill in bed and an infant besides, his brain was probably fuddled beyond all usefulness from sleepless nights. 'Because we knew Lavinia's murderer was still at large and suspected – rightly – that he was probably in the house tonight.'

Petrie did not need to know that we had circled around the entire household and had eventually trained our attention on David Spencer himself.

'I'll be glad of your help,' he said. 'But won't you get away in and change your clothes first?'

I looked down and flinched. The ruined dress gaped, showing more of my legs than I had ever displayed outside

228

of my bathroom in my life and, more to the point, both dress and legs were smeared with David Spencer's blood, from me kneeling at his side, feeling for his pulse and then stretching over him to close his eyes. I looked at my hands and shuddered, seeing blood dried dark in the creases of my palms, caught in among my rings.

'I didn't kill him,' I said, looking up at Petrie.

'Of course not,' Petrie said. 'Why would a lady like you do such a thing? I didn't mean to suggest it.'

'No, no, no, this will never do,' said Alec. 'That's what went wrong last time, Constable. You were all far too quick to believe that people "like us" would never commit murder. No convenient tramps this time around. Mrs Gilver is a suspect like any other.'

'Steady on, old man,' said Hugh, rather mildly in my view.

Alec smiled. '*I* know Dandy didn't kill David Spencer,' he said. 'But this investigation needs to establish that fact on the grounds of timing, witnesses and other evidence. That's all I mean.'

'Thank you for that,' I said.

'So maybe you shouldn't change your clothes just yet,' said Petrie. 'Until the sarge gets here and sees the . . . evidence.'

'Constable,' I said, 'the gravel is extraordinarily smooth and nicely kept and you will notice that I'm not wearing any shoes. You will see, if you look, my footprints on the gravel leading clockwise round the outside of the garden from the flower-room door to the gate at the far side. You will also find the prints of stockinged feet all over the damp grass between the garden gate and this spot of the maze, showing where I ran hither and yon trying to get here, while Mr Spencer lay dying. You will not find any such footprints on the gravel path anywhere between the garden gate and the east wall of the house where the murder weapon has been discarded, nor on the grass path between the dovecote and the house. And you will find neither my fingerprints on the murder weapon, nor any discarded gloves with which I might have disguised them. Do you see?'

'I see,' said Petrie.

'I saw someone out here,' I said. 'I saw torchlight. I opened the window and shouted. The torch went out. I left my shoes on the landing, ran downstairs, took the gravel path around to the garden gate, ascertained that it was locked, removed the key, heard the sounds of someone in distress, followed those sounds and found Mr Spencer.'

'I really do see,' Petrie said. 'The murderer did his foul deed, turned on a torch for some reason—'

'To check that he had made a proper job of it,' Alec said. 'Or to pick up the weapon if he dropped it.'

'You opened the window and he ran off,' Petrie said. 'He took the weapon with him and went back inside the house to the party.'

'Leaving the pruning saw on the terrace where I fell over it on my way out,' said Hugh. 'Why didn't he leave it with the body? Or take it away completely?'

'My guess would be that he took it to wipe fingerprints off it on the way,' I said. 'But I imagine it would be somewhat tricky to hold a saw and wipe it, while running in the dark, without leaving at least a smudge behind. So, Constable, it will be worth dusting it very carefully.'

'It will at that,' said Petrie.

Alec raised his hand, covered with a white silk handkerchief, the pruning saw dangling from one finger. It was such an innocent object, but with blood darkening its blade and scraps of skin caught in its teeth the sight of it made me suddenly light-headed.

Grant, Hugh and Alec all stepped forward, by which fact I deduced that my face must really be as white as I felt it to be. Grant was quickest. She put an arm across my back and led me away, back the way I had come.

'The long way round, I'm afraid,' she said. 'For the

footprints, you know. There might be something useful for the police.'

'Ow,' I said. The gravel was like shards of glass under my tender soles, all the worse since I could barely see it in the darkness.

'I'm sorry about the dress,' said Grant.

'I'm sorry I ripped it to shreds,' I said. 'And splashed it with blood.'

'I can salvage the bodice and turn it into a little—' Grant said, then subsided, seeing my face and finding a shred of pity.

The sergeant had arrived by the time I was back downstairs in skirt and jersey and with hands scrubbed and face wiped clean of make-up if not of shock. Lachlan was back in his wheeled chair with Ursus on his lap. Dickie Tibball had been put to bed with a sleeping powder after Constable Petrie took pity on him, shivering and white with shock.

'This is Mrs Gilver, that found the body,' Petrie said, when I entered the library.

Sgt Morrison nodded gravely. 'You were very brave, madam,' he said. 'Very enterprising to go haring off on your own like that into the garden, rather than get help or raise the alarm.'

It might have sounded like praise but I knew it was admonishment. I refused to hang my head. 'I was trying to keep things quiet because of the party, Sergeant,' I said. 'If I'd known the man was being murdered I'd have taken a different tack, obviously. Have you any ideas? He didn't get away through the garden gate. We know that much. He might have got away round the house and out the front way, though.' It occurred to me then that if Grant had been stationed on the drive, instead of guarding the servants's stairway, she would have seen him. I sighed.

'I've sent men along the street, knocking at the doors

231

telling folk to check their outhouses and lock up tight,' the sergeant said, but as he spoke I was aware of a figure hovering in the doorway, shifting heavily from foot to foot. McReadie came forward diffidently, tugging at his tight collar.

'Begging your pardon,' he said. 'I need to tell you something.'

'Who are you?' said Sgt Morrison. 'The guests were supposed to stay upstairs until I spoke to them.'

'Don't let this mislead you,' McReadie said, waving a hand that was meant to take in his Brilliantined hair, his shiny suit and his dancing shoes, a pair of cracked patent-leather antiques I supposed had been Lachlan's many moons ago. 'I'm the gardener. I'm Lady Love's gardener. I'm—' He sniffed and put a work-roughened hand up to his face to wipe his nose as his eyes brimmed. 'I can tell you nobody got away down the drive.'

'Oh?' said Morrison.

'I saw the kerfuffle upstairs,' McReadie said. 'I saw Mr Spencer go rushing out and you after him, Mr Osborne. I saw the ladies go off in different directions and Mr Gilver go into Miss Cherry's bedroom. So it wasn't hard to guess that you were looking for him. But no one went to keep an eye on the drive. And all those cars were parked there. So, I just slipped out and stood in the shadows. Kept my eyes peeled.'

'Very fortuitous,' Morrison said.

'And so it's true, is it, your lordship?' McReadie said. 'Mr Spencer is murdered, is he?' He drew a sharp breath in over his bottom teeth and wrung his hands. 'I can't go on my own. I'm sorry to be thinking of myself at a time like this but I can't go all that way on my own. I wouldn't know where to start with the money and the tickets and what have you.'

'No, no, of course not,' Lachlan said. 'Don't fret, McReadie. I wouldn't expect you to set out across the seas.'

'Although Mr Spencer did write it all down,' McReadie said. 'And the passage is paid. Coal boat in the morning, train to Edinburgh, ship from Leith. Can I sleep on it, your lordship?'

'Sleep on it, by all means,' Lachlan said, 'but don't worry. Ask Dolly what she thinks and be guided by her. She's a woman of sound sense.'

'Who's Dolly?' I whispered to Alec.

He nodded at McReadie. 'His wife, I think,' he whispered back.

McReadie looked black affronted to be urged towards her counsel. He glowered at Lachlan as he withdrew. I watched him leave, troubled I knew not why. Then I shrugged it off. No doubt he had only offered to sacrifice his trip for form's sake and was annoyed to have it taken at face value instead of batted politely away.

'Now then,' said Morrison. 'The inspector will be here by morning. I would like to have a tidy pile of witness statements and an empty house by the time he gets here. I can clear a fair few of the village folk, but there's more than that to contend with.' He turned sharply in his seat and gave me a look I could not quite decipher. 'I believe you were drafted in as a special constable in Edinburgh a while back, Mrs Gilver.'

'1926,' I said. 'Yes. How did you know?'

'Oh, Inspector Hutcheson gave me the benefit of a lot of his insights and opinions after what happened here in February. Didn't you know? Yes, well. So then I can't see why you shouldn't take a few of the witnesses yourself. You're a detective, aren't you? Detect.'

'I'm not the only one,' I said. 'Mr Osborne here is my partner and co-detective. We could make even shorter work of it with three.'

'And I'm not related to any of them,' said Alec. 'I can do the family.'

'And I can take care of the household servants and casual staff,' said Grant, stepping forward from wherever she had been lurking. I thought briefly that a bell round her neck was not by any means an unwarranted option. 'I'm an assistant detective with Gilver and Osborne,' she added. 'With special responsibility for household liaison.'

I rolled my eyes at Alec. But Sgt Morrison wanted the case in order before the inspector descended and he agreed readily enough.

It was a long night even at that. Hugh appointed himself steward and conscripted Donald and Teddy as his staff, and between them they shepherded guests one by one out of the ballroom and into the card room for Alec, the library for me, the drawing room for the sergeant or the breakfast room for Grant. I took names, addresses and endless breathless reassurances of perfect ignorance until my head rang and my pen hand cramped from all the writing.

By dawn, when the fleet of police motorcars made their stately way up the drive and an austere military figure climbed out of the first one, knuckling his back and smoothing his moustaches, we were all back together in the library, amalgamating our night's findings and agreeing that they added up to nothing.

'Did you speak to the woman whose dancing partner bumped David Spencer on the head?' I said to Grant.

'Yes. She's a Miss Roderick,' said Grant. 'From the street. She pops along and helps out whenever there's a party.'

'And who was the man?' I said. 'I asked everyone and no one admitted to it.'

'What's this?' said Sgt Morrison.

'Probably nothing,' I said. 'Someone banged into Spencer, but very hard, while we were dancing. I wondered if it was deliberate. If someone was angry enough to bump into him, perhaps that same someone was angry enough to attack him more seriously.'

'Yes, but it *wasn't* deliberate,' Grant said. 'It was Miss Roderick's brother and he was drunk. He threw his head back laughing at something she'd said and made the unfortunate contact. Miss Roderick said it sounded like a mallet hitting a croquet ball.'

'She must have been dancing cheek to cheek to have heard it over the din,' I said.

'Holding him up, I think,' Grant said. 'He really was quite pickled, they tell me.'

'And did he confirm this version, Mr Roderick?'

'He's gone,' Grant said. 'His sisters had been at him to take himself off before he embarrassed them and that bump was the last straw. He left straight away.'

'We can get him at his house and ask him about it,' said the sergeant. 'Strange that Mr McReadie never mentioned him leaving. That's all.'

'Oh, but he did,' Grant said. She leafed through her notebook, which – I was amused to see – was a replica of mine. 'In his statement, Samuel McReadie said he saw a Mr Roderick make his way, unsteady but without falling, down the drive and no one else left until Constable Petrie arrived on his bicycle.'

'And with that our one wee wisp of a solution blows away,' said Morrison, as steps rang out on the marble floor of the hall and the fabled inspector arrived.

I was banished rather smartly. The inspector, whose name was Snell, took my notebook with a pained look, as though picking slugs out of his salad, and dismissed me. He looked no more approving of Alec's untidy sheaf of loose pages, scribbled over with a pencil and, when it came to Grant, his top lip almost turned itself inside out from the strength of his sneer. I was too exhausted to protest. I simply trailed off up to bed, past the burned-out candles, past the discarded dance cards and abandoned champagne glasses, averting my eyes from the dusty sadness to be glimpsed through the half-open ballroom door.

Grant was too tired to be waspish. She stared dully at my pot of hairpins as I shrugged out of my skirt and jersey, then she took a silk scarf and wound it tightly round my head.

'Try not to toss about,' she said. 'I'll mend everything in the morning.' Then she left me, not even taking my stockings to wash or my shoes to polish. I pulled my nightgown on and was just getting into bed, trying not to wake Bunty, when Hugh appeared.

'Boys all right?' I said.

'Sound asleep,' said Hugh. 'Are *you* all right?'

'Nothing a week's sleep won't fix,' I said. 'Did Donald say anything?'

'He didn't have to,' Hugh said. 'His devotion to Mallory, his assumption that a second murder will not make any difference, his loyalty to this benighted place and the horrors it contains apparently go without saying.'

'We have to take him away,' I said. I lay back against my pillows. 'I mean detach him from her and take him away.'

'Of course,' said Hugh. 'I shall speak to Lachlan in the morning.'

'Even if she sues for breach of contract.'

'Of course,' Hugh said again. 'But I'd be very surprised if they had the gall to attempt a suit.'

He swung his legs up onto the bed, nudged Bunty with his knee until she rolled over and made room, then lay back on the pillows beside me.

'Thank you for flying to my side earlier, by the way,' I said.

'Of course,' said Hugh a third time and, as I turned out the light, he reached for my hand.

He was gone in the morning. Bunty was long gone too. I awoke alone in a cold bed with the sun high in the sky and the sound of someone shouting somewhere in the

236

house. My eyes flew open and I bolted upright, but whoever it was was not shouting 'murder' or 'help'. As I strained to hear, I thought I caught the words 'fool' and 'disgrace' and 'full extent of' and something that was probably 'law'.

'What on earth?' I said, as Grant came round the door with a tray of tea and toast. 'Who's that?'

'Inspector Inverness,' said Grant. 'Whatever his name is. Snell? He is most displeased and he's got no one but himself to blame.'

'What's happened?' I said.

'The inspector and sergeant and constable between them have got as far as deciding that someone killed David Spencer and then slipped back into the house.'

'Well, *we'd* got that far,' I pointed out.

'They conjectured that it was someone who knew that David Spencer killed Lady Love.'

'And avenged her,' I said. 'It makes a certain amount of sense. But why the commotion? Why the raised voices?'

'The police think the only way to catch the murderer is to take everyone's fingerprints and try to match them to whatever smudges they can lift from the pruning saw.'

'Very sensible,' I said. 'Is there a problem?'

'Samuel McReadie has gone by boat to catch the train to Edinburgh and has taken his pruning saw with him.'

'*What?*' I said. 'How did he get his hands on it? Wasn't it under lock and key?'

'Yes, of course it was,' Grant said. 'But his wife is the housekeeper and she has a key to every lock. She gave it to him while he was packing.'

I caught sight of myself in the dressing-table mirror across the room and closed my mouth, but I could not do anything about my eyebrows. They refused to climb back down my face to where they belonged.

'Is she some kind of fool?' I said.

'That's what the inspector thinks,' Grant said. 'He called her a disgrace to the Highlands and promised her she'd feel—'

'The full extent of the law,' I joined in as she finished. 'I heard that bit. So she helped him pack, did she? That's remarkable. It's not every wife that would be so loyal when her husband sets off halfway round the world to get a flower for another woman.'

'She's Applecross born and bred,' said Grant. She gave me a sly look. 'She has family here to comfort her until he comes home.'

'What are you getting at, Grant?' I said.

'I'll give you a clue,' she said. 'It wasn't Miss Roderick's *brother* who clonked Mr Spencer on the head last night while dancing. It was her brother-*in-law*.'

I narrowed my eyes, thinking. 'What is the name of Mr and Mrs McReadie's son?' I said at last, my eyes widening again of their own volition. 'The one at Oxford. The one whose life Lachlan saved? I know I've heard it.'

'Roddy,' said Grant, smiling. 'Short for . . .'

'Roderick!' I said. 'He was given his mother's maiden name as a Christian name.'

'As they do in these parts,' said Grant. 'You've got it now.'

'So,' I said. 'Sam McReadie was, dancing with his sister-in-law.'

'Sam McReadie!' said Grant. 'He was that close to you and you never knew it was him.'

'All men look the same in black tie and Brilliantine,' I said. 'And I was concentrating on Spencer anyway. So, he was close enough to Spencer to bang heads, close enough to hear what he thought was a confession. He followed Spencer and killed him and now he's hopped it.'

'Yes,' said Grant. 'He wasn't stationed at the front gate at all. He didn't see any "Mr Roderick" staggering home. He made that up. And the Roderick sisters closed ranks.'

I whistled. 'Will they catch him at Leith before he sails?'

'I don't know if they're going to try,' said Grant. 'I don't think the police have put it all together. They think McReadie is peculiarly devoted to his favourite implements and his wife is peculiarly stupid, or loyal, or both.'

'What are we to do, Grant?' I said. 'What on earth shall we do?'

19

Of course what we did was tell the austere inspector everything. As soon as I was dressed – flat of hair but otherwise quite buoyant, considering – I sought out the troika of Inspector Snell, the Inverness sergeant and the Lochcarron sergeant, Constable Petrie having gone back to stray dogs and scrumped apples. I did not walk unaided into the lion's den. In fact, between the three of them and the fact that Grant was at my left hand and Alec at my right as we advanced, the meeting was more like an ambassadorial summit than a witness coming cap in hand to men of law.

'He confessed?' Inspector Snell thundered. 'And you just kept dancing?'

It sounded rather marvellous, almost a philosophy one could live by, but I attempted to look grave. 'He didn't confess to murder,' I said. 'He confessed to love. He confessed to being here to try to whisk Lavinia away with him. He didn't confess to killing her when she refused him.'

'As good as,' the inspector said. He winced as a gunshot rang out. Hugh and the boys had gone out early, more to get away from the torrid atmosphere in the house than from any desire to kill stags, for Hugh usually undertakes a scrupulous fast from his shotgun as spring progresses, to let excitement build for the birds come summer. I was not sure whether the inspector – a Highlander after all – disapproved on account of the Sabbath or if he simply disliked the noise, but I was glad Hugh was annoying him.

'And even at that,' I said, bringing my attention back to

the inspector's point, 'we tried our best to track him down when he left the ballroom.'

The inspector waved an impatient hand. 'I need to get on to Edinburgh and Leith,' he said. 'McReadie'll not get on a ship, if I can help it. He'll not get off the *train*, if I can help it.' He looked around Lord Ross's desktop with an irritation it was momentarily hard to account for.

Grant correctly identified his concern. 'The only telephone is in the little alcove in the hall,' she said. 'It's not exactly private, but Mrs McReadie is in the kitchen with the door shut and so she'll not hear you and get upset.'

'The question of upsetting Mrs McReadie does not concern me,' the inspector said. 'I could live with Mrs McReadie being beside herself with anguish. That would be fine by me.'

He was reaching the pitch of ire where he might start lashing out indiscriminately at whomever was to hand and so the three of us left the three of them, closing the library door softly and then all breathing out in unison.

'Is that that then?' said Grant. 'Is the case closed, madam? Are we done?'

I might dispute the choice of the word 'case', not to mention the word 'we', but it was a good question otherwise.

'We certainly can't join in with a manhunt in any useful way,' Alec said. 'They'll catch him before he gets on the ship.'

'In that case,' Grant said. 'I think I'll start packing. We always meant to leave today, didn't we?'

'Scandalising the locals with our Sunday driving,' I agreed. 'Easter Sunday, no less.'

'But I'll just stop by Miss Mallory's room,' Grant said, as she was walking away. 'Try and persuade her to come with us. You wouldn't mind that, madam, would you? Different for Miss Cherry. She's got her husband and her in-laws as well as her father. And she's got the daily round of crofting.

But it's going to be awful for Miss Mallory if we go off and leave her now.'

'Grant,' I called after her. 'You are not fooling me. You are probably not even fooling Mr Osborne.'

'On what score?' said Alec.

'She has probably already rung up shops and ordered samples to be delivered to Gilverton,' I said. 'She's going to dress Mallory for this wedding if it kills her.'

'But she's right,' Alec said. 'We can't disappear and leave the poor child here after this.'

'I'll broach it with her at church,' I said. 'I take it we're going to church, are we? It is Easter, after all.'

Alec was staring at me.

'What?' I said.

'It is indeed,' he said. 'It's Sunday. Easter Sunday. The most Sunday-like Sunday of the entire year. And yet McReadie has gone away by boat?'

I whistled. 'I've grown so used to talk of the coal boat that it failed to register,' I said. 'But there can't have been one today. Do you think one of the local fishermen could have been persuaded to take him over to Plockton? Or down to Kyle?'

Alec shook his head. 'I think a Wester Ross man putting out to sea today would be as conspicuous as you or me walking down Piccadilly stark naked, playing bagpipes.'

'But how else could he get down to Leith in time for the sailing?' I said. Even as I spoke, I answered myself and could not help a laugh escaping me. 'He's not going to Leith, is he? He's not going to New Zealand to look for black flowers for Lady Love's memory.'

'Of course not,' said Alec. 'Who knows where he's gone. Let's go and ask Mrs McReadie what she'd put her money on.'

From Grant's words 'in the kitchen with the door shut' I expected the cook to be sitting in her Windsor chair weeping

242

into a handkerchief and letting the household go to pieces around her, but far from it. She was trussing a leg of lamb when we entered the room and had Lairdie busily shelling green peas at one end of the table and Mackie peeling potatoes at the other. She wiped her hand across her brow and faced us down with a look like a cow protecting newborn calves, or like my own Mrs Tilling if I try to talk to her about menus when she's busy with her marmalade.

'What boat did Mr McReadie take?' I said. Lairdie stopped with his thumb halfway along a plump pod and Mackie let a half-peeled potato plop into the bucket of water, splashing his trousers.

'What's this you're coming asking?' said Mrs McReadie, looking up, her black eyes as bright as ever.

'There can't have been a coal boat today. On the Sabbath.'

'There's ways round everything,' Mrs McReadie said. 'We are God-fearing folk here at Applecross, but we all loved her ladyship. And sometimes you have to choose.'

'So one of the local boatmen broke the Sabbath to help him escape?' said Alec. 'Because everyone applauds him for avenging Lady Love's murder?'

'But wasn't someone going to break the Sabbath anyway?' I said. 'To help them get off on their expedition? That's rather odd, isn't it?'

'They were going by motorcar,' Mrs McReadie said. Mackie had fished his potato out of the bucket of water but now stalled again. Lairdie had finally managed to strip the little peas out of the pod, throw it down and start on another one.

'The police are going to try to stop him at the port,' I said. 'What do you think of that?' Mrs McReadie shrugged with a commendable show of unconcern. 'But we don't think your husband has any intention of going near the port,' I added. Mrs McReadie faced me calmly, both her hands resting on the haunch of lamb as if it was a comfort to her.

'We think it would be a better idea to search the islands across the sound. Do you have any more relations or connections there? Someone who'd be just as happy to meet the boat as someone evidently was to set sail in it?'

'Unless the whole story of a boat is nonsense from start to finish,' Alec said. 'If we were to search the estate would we find him holed up in an abandoned croft cottage with a flask and a loaf?'

'There are no abandoned cottages on the Applecross estate,' said Mrs McReadie. 'Lady Love wouldn't hear of it.'

'We shall suggest it to the inspector anyway,' I said, watching her carefully. There was no flash of fear upon her face nor any shuffling of her feet. 'And now,' I said, with a glance at my watch, 'we'd better get ready for church.' I turned away, then whipped my head back quickly. I could not mistake what I saw when I did so. Mrs McReadie, for some reason I could not fathom, was deeply relieved.

Mallory met us in the hall. She was white around the eyes and I suggested walking to the service. 'I know people will be staring, my dear,' I said. 'But you must hold your head up and ignore them.'

'Yes, I know,' Mallory said. 'One day of sticking my chin in the air and then I can escape. Thank you so very much for inviting me down, Dandy. Let's see what Cherry says about walking.'

I nodded. 'Will your father be all right without you?' I said. 'If you do come away.'

Mallory's face grew rather fixed at the mention of Lord Ross. 'I expect so,' she said. 'David was very much Mummy's friend, not his. As we've all come to see only too well. He won't grieve for the man who was trying to ruin his life with a divorce and actually ruined it with a murder. Why would he?'

I did not agree with her rather cut and dried view of grief. Lord Ross, still reeling from the death of his wife, might well be profoundly shocked by this latest round of horrors. He might even be miserable that it took a servant to avenge her, while he looked helplessly on.

The household was beginning to assemble en masse. Mrs McReadie had washed the lamb blood from her hands, rolled down her sleeves and put on a dark coat and a black straw hat. She came out of the kitchen passageway with the two footmen at her heels. They, in tweed caps and coats, looked as unlike servants as ever. Cherry, descending the stairs, was in full mourning. Her coat was black and dead plain and she wore a black felt hat pulled down hard over her ears, although she clutched her prayer book in gloveless hands.

'You're very sombre,' said Lord Ross, spying her. 'I don't think you wore such a lot of black to church the first Sunday after Mummy died.'

'Shall I change?' said Cherry.

'No, dearest,' Mallory said. 'We don't have time if we're going to walk. And I want to walk.'

'Does anyone know where he is?' Cherry said. 'David. Is he still here or have they taken him away? I hate to think of his body lying alone in the police house. What if one of the little Petries sees it? They are always playing housey in the jail cell. But then there's no way Roderick would have picked him up on the Sabbath.'

'Don't think of it,' said Lord Ross. He had opened the front door and held it for his daughters and me to pass through. 'I do wish you'd try not to dwell on such morbid thoughts. I've been trying to get you to take better care of yourself since the very day you shared your happy news. I wish you would indulge me. Truly, I do.'

'Roderick?' I said. The name had caught my attention, but even as it did I knew it had distracted me from something more important. I tried to see past it to the back of my own mind. Unfortunately, Mallory came up beside me and took my arm, talking in my ear and driving the idea away completely.

'The undertaker,' she said. 'Well, undertaker, carpenter and smith combined. There isn't enough work for three men in such a tiny place.'

I murmured politely but all hope of concentrating was gone now. For at the end of the drive a slow procession of black-clad men, women and children was snaking along the shore road.

'Aren't they going the wrong way?' I said.

'No,' said Mallory. 'Easter, harvest and Christmas Eve, we use the Clachan church.'

'And everyone will be there?' said Alec. 'I don't suppose your minister would make a plea from the pulpit, would he?'

'A plea for what?' Lord Ross said.

'Information, cooperation, civic duty,' said Alec. 'Someone must have seen McReadie go. If he left after daybreak someone must have seen something. I cannot believe that a whole village full of people whose houses face the sea missed a boat setting sail. Or, if he went up and over that road – whatever it's called – someone must have been out feeding beasts, even on a Sunday. They'd recognise him, wouldn't they? A local man. Or even if they just saw a figure, they would be able to confirm now that it was McReadie. Why have you stopped walking, Dandy?'

'I don't know,' I said. In truth, I did not even know if it was the same something troubling me again or if Alec, with his little speech about witnesses to McReadie's departure, had started another one.

'I don't think our minister would be willing to do that,' Cherry was saying. 'What do you think, Mall darling? Police business strikes me as that which is Caesar's, although no doubt he'll have plenty to say about last night. The champagne, the dancing, the bare shoulders.'

'But that's rampant hypocrisy!' I said. 'He was there

dancing! With his wife, admittedly, but he definitely danced. And I'm sure I saw a glass of something in his hand that didn't look like lemonade.'

'Oh but the poor man,' Cherry said. 'He'll be so angry with himself. He prides himself on having a kind of *nose* for evil. He came after Mummy died and cast out the spirits from the knot garden, for instance. But he missed David right here in our midst. He'll be inconsolable on that score.'

'So, you see, Dandy,' Mallory added, 'he'll be very down on the old ways and very up on the church this morning. Even though it's Easter.'

'Even though?' I said. 'Especially because, surely.'

'Oh well, you know,' said Cherry. 'Springtime and all that. It gets rather tangled. And he does usually manage to tread a very nice line.'

They were making no attempt to speak in low voices and I glanced about myself at the knots of villagers who were keeping pace with us. There was no susurration of whispered Gaelic this morning. All were listening intently as we turned off the path up across the velvety, sheep-nibbled grass towards the church, just as the bell began dolefully to call us.

'Daddy,' Mallory said, as we approached the door. 'The Gilvers have asked me to go down and stay in Perthshire for a bit. What do you think? It's only if you can spare me.'

'Well now, how can I answer that?' said Lord Ross, with a fond smile. 'I cannot "spare" you. But I cannot bear you to be here with all of this sadness either. On you go, my dear. I've got all the Tibballs to keep me spirits up. On you go.'

The inside of the Clachan church was as cold as the grave and as dark as a chimney. There was nothing so flamboyant as a single chip of stained glass but somehow the plain windows did not let in as much light as they ought. We shuffled onto the front pew and I pawed the ground like a horse, groping for a hot pipe upon which to rest my feet. There was nothing there. The board panels of the hymn-book stand met the stone slabs of the floor without so much as a hassock for comfort. I sat back, working my hands up into my coat sleeves, and gazed at the altar. A plain table with a dark cloth, an oak lectern with a plain black ribbon marking the place in the Bible and a pulpit, entirely unornamented and looking exactly like the air-raid watchtowers I had seen in the news reels during the war, all promised a very dull hour on this happiest day of the Christian year.

Needless to say there were no flowers and I spent a few sad moments wondering what Lady Love had made of that all her life. If she had married an Englishman and embarked on her years of horticulture in the south she would have been granted the chance to mount astonishing displays every week. Easter Sunday in the church of a lady who loves flowers is exuberant beyond all reckoning. Even my mother, who tended towards reverence for weeds and grasses, could hardly help producing beauty at Easter.

As the pews filled behind us, I was watching Mallory out of the corner of my eye. When Donald had first told us that there was a girl he wanted to marry, all I had felt was profound relief. That she was thirty was news, I admit, but she was of good family and fortune, nicely brought up and apparently steady. The divorce of her parents would have given me pause. The murder of her mother did give me pause. And so one might have thought that this second murder would have finished her off for me altogether as a candidate to join my family and as the star by which my son would now chart his life's journey. Strangely, though, I found myself feeling rather fierce and determined on Mallory's behalf. Still I was glad the thing was done.

We would take her away to Gilverton. We would have the wedding there. I would fill Gilverton chapel with flowers. I would lean hard on Hugh until he coughed up a honeymoon for them both as a wedding present, and none of the usual three weeks with an aunt in Devon and the sleeper home.

248

Donald and Mallory would go to Paris, Rome and Vienna, staying in hotels and going to nightclubs.

Except that nightclubs made me think of Berlin and I wondered if a trip to Vienna was a sensible idea. I wondered if any part of Europe was a sensible idea. 'Luftwaffe' still struck me as a comical word, but in the last month alone Germany had rejected the very idea of disarmament and then there had been the business in Sudetenland. 'They've won an election, Dandy,' Hugh had said, reading the headlines. 'Those Nazis have actually won at the ballot box now.'

I must have sighed, because Mallory turned and gave me an inquisitive look.

'Are you all right?' she said.

'Very much so.' I managed to get a smile onto my face. 'I'm thinking about the wedding. I was wondering where you wanted to go on your honeymoon.'

Mallory was smiling too now. 'It's going to be so beautiful,' she said. 'June is lovely here. It's light until midnight and the meadows are so sweet. The apple blossom will be finished but Mummy's roses will be absolutely at their peak.'

'Here?' I said.

'Where else?' said Mallory. 'Delia says June will be fine. She's ordering my veil from Brussels and it takes a month.' It took me a minute or two to place the name and when I did I thought, quietly to myself, that I was going to have to take Miss Cordelia Grant firmly in hand. 'It won't interfere too badly with the farming,' Mallory said. 'It's after the shearing but before the first cut of hay. And before Cherry is too enormous to be my matron of honour and so Donald can get back from honeymoon – he wants to go to Norway – before the grouse.'

'Norway?' I said. '*Nor*way? What for? And what about you? You are the most accommodating bride I've ever seen, I must say. If you want to get married in late November with no veil and spend Christmas in New York, you should just say so. You've got the rest of your life to fit yourself around others, dear. Your wedding is the one time you can suit yourself.'

'I don't mind,' Mallory said. 'I'm sure it'll all be tremendous fun whatever we do.'

'Even Norway?' I said.

'He's interested in the softwood plantations,' said Mallory. 'The inland climate isn't so different from Perthshire and we both think it would be a good idea.'

I simply stared. I was going to put my foot down about this. I saw Hugh's hand in it and I was going to put my foot down hard on top of that hand. This child was not beginning her married life looking at pine trees in Norway.

Before I could say any of that, however, a door opened at the side of the altar and the minister, swathed in black and with a face like a poker, came in to begin the service.

There were no words of comfort from him for the family who had been visited once again by tragedy, nor even for the many villagers who had spent the night sitting on a ballroom floor waiting to be grilled by policemen and hangers-on like me. There was not even any fire and brimstone, which would have been some sort of relief. There was just a steady drone from some oft-neglected book of the Bible, dead dull and unrelenting. I found my head starting to droop after ten minutes. A hymn revived me but then he started in on the sermon itself and now there was only his voice and his own deathly words, not even the music of scripture to catch at one's ear. And it was not getting any warmer in here, despite the breath of all the people and their packed bodies. I shrank down in my pew and stared at my feet. If my eyelids closed perhaps he would not notice. Even if he did, he might take it to heart and liven things up a bit before next time.

Cherry fell asleep before me, as well she might, being both with child and at rest after a hard week's work crofting. I was aware of her sagging against my shoulder on my right side and could hear little popping noises as her gentle snores pushed her lips apart each time she breathed out. I listened to them for a moment or two and then I realised that the popping sounds were actually caused by pieces of gravel shooting out from under my feet as I walked with heavy shuddering tread along one of the paths in the apple crosses. I was trying to get to the knot garden in the middle, to get something out of the dovecote, but my feet were heavier and heavier. The popping had stopped now and slow dragging groans began instead. When I looked down I was heaving myself through snow up to my knees, the heaviest snow I had ever known. I pulled at one foot and shifted it forward, then I leaned over at an impossible angle and brought the other one under me again. Before I could take a third step the ground changed a second time. It was not snow after all; it was ice, brilliant and crackling, and I was skimming along as though on skates, swinging round the corners, hanging onto the branches of the criss-crossed apple trees. I was following someone. There was a trail in the ice ahead of me where something sharp had been dragged, leaving a deep score-mark. I peered closer and closer as it grew fainter and fainter, until I was bent double and it was gone. The ice was unmarked, polished and clear, the trellis patterns of the apple boughs reflected perfectly in it, because it was glass I was standing on. The paths between the apple trees were made of smooth, clean, plate glass. I could feel it tremble under my weight and I could see through it to the earth below, from where the face of Lady Love and the face of David Spencer were looking back at me. She opened her mouth to speak and I saw the earth shift and seethe as David Spencer lifted his hand, shovelling through the heaped dirt and apple-tree roots to cover her mouth and silence her. He was too slow but McReadie was there too. I saw him in the glass below my feet, working at her with a little trowel, scraping

251

the earth up and patting it smooth, like a pillow behind her head. She closed her mouth and then closed her eyes and was just beginning to darken and fade into the soil itself when the glass gave way and I crashed through.

I must have gasped, possibly even snorted, as I awoke. The minister sent me one cold flick of a look but did not pause in his droning. Mallory smothered a giggle and Cherry cleared her throat and sat up.

I bent my head, partly to hide the flush of shame in my cheeks but mostly to try to catch at what my dream had been telling me before cold wakefulness drove it away.

20

We made our arrangements to leave the next morning. Inspector Snell had given his consent, barely pausing. He knew where to find us, his casual wave seemed to say, but we were beneath his notice. All of his quivering attention was on the telephone that would bring him news of McReadie apprehended at the port of Leith.

It was breakfast time when at last the telephone rang. After Snell snatched it up, there came a silence, then an angry cry and the sound of the earpiece crashing into the cradle hard enough to shatter it. Mallory let her knife and fork fall to her plate with a clatter and Lord Ross half rose from his seat.

'They've let him get away,' she said.

'No, I don't think so,' I told her. 'I rather think the inspector has just been told the ship sailed without him and has only now realised his mistake.' I took a sip of coffee. 'I ought to have shared my suspicions on that score, I suppose.'

The truth was worse than any of us expected. The inspector was too angry to speak of it, and the sergeant entered into his feelings so far that he too drew a veil. It was left to Constable Petrie to regale us, when sergeant and inspector had pulled their remaining shreds of dignity about them and left.

Alec and I sat in the kitchen, watching Mrs McReadie ice a loaf of gingerbread and drinking it in. Petrie had his helmet off, his tunic unbuttoned and a saucerful of strong sweet tea before him.

'You would hardly credit it,' he said, 'but it's true. They warned the port polis that a Mr Samuel McReadie might try to board and should be stopped. They never said anything about a David Spencer. Well, why would they? The man's dead.'

'And yet he presented himself with a passport, boarded the ship and took to his cabin,' Alec said.

It had not occurred to me either that McReadie would simply pretend he was Spencer and begin his journey. 'He took a terrific risk,' I said. 'How could he have dreamed he'd get away with it?'

Alec gave Mrs McReadie a stern look. 'Perhaps he was told the police were only looking for McReadie,' he said. 'Perhaps someone overheard the inspector telephoning to Leith and got word to him.'

'Me?' said the cook. She was scraping round her mixing bowl with a palette knife, making an ungodly screeching sound that set my teeth on edge. 'I wouldn't help him run away, even though he is my own husband. I wouldn't give him the steam off my porridge after what he did. And anyway, it would never have crossed my mind. If it never struck an inspector and two famous detectives, why would it strike a servant?' She spread the last of the icing over the dark loaf. It was the perfect consistency, just runny enough to drip down the sides but stiff enough to stay thick and white on top. For a moment it reminded me of the snow turning to glass in my dream and I shivered.

'And they're not turning back,' I said. 'The line office was very clear about that, although they might try to put him off at the first port, if they can get the consulate organised in time.'

'And if someone owes someone a favour and the stars align,' Alec said. 'But if it's Gibraltar I think we can forget it. Lachlan was just telling me that Lady Love's father was in India for a while with the current ambassador's grandpa, all very chummy. There will be little appetite in *that* quarter for bringing her avenging angel to justice.' He was watching the gingerbread with close interest, and he smiled as Mrs McReadie took a breadknife and began cutting thick slices from it. 'No,' he said, comfortably, 'I think "David Spencer" – Samuel McReadie as was – has got clean away.'

I was watching the woman's face, and had half an eye on her cutting hand. The one was calm and the other steady. 'I'm very sorry for your troubles, Mrs McReadie,' I said.

She nodded, but every bit as calmly. 'We'll do all right, his lordship and me,' she said. 'We'll do fine.'

Something was not right. I knew it, Alec knew it, even the constable knew it somewhere deep in his placid soul. But all we did was take a slice of gingerbread each and turn our faces away.

Lord Ross and all four Tibballs were on the front step the next morning to see us off. It was a gusty day, with puffs of white cloud scudding across below the banks of grey cloud and the tide in the bay dancing. I was glad the *bealach na bà* was open and that we would not be upon the water. By night we would be back in the bosom of our Perthshire valley and I would be glad of that too.

'I am most grateful to you for taking Mallory,' Lachlan said. 'I can't be worrying about both of them all day long.'

'Are you especially worried about Cherry?' I said. 'She's in fine fettle as far as I can see.'

'I worry about her lugging those Highland cattle uphill and down dale by their horns,' he said. 'And lifting yearling lambs over walls to save driving them round by the gates. I've seen her at it. And of course, I've been worrying even more about her since I found out about the baby coming. That was the darkest day of my life and yet had such a bright spot in it. Losing my wife and getting tidings of my first grandchild. The gods do like to laugh, don't they?'

'Indeed they do,' I said. 'But put your mind at rest. We shall take very good care of Mallory. Except that Grant might wear her out with shopping trips and fittings. And you can always come down for a while and stay yourself. Have a look at where she'll be living.'

'I think I'll stick here,' Lord Ross said. 'With LL and McReadie both gone, someone will have to keep at the under-gardeners if we're to have the place fit for a wedding come midsummer. But I'm grateful for so many things.'

As well he might be, I thought to myself, although I said nothing. Mallory's mother had spurned a lover and been killed by him in a jealous passion. The killer had been unmasked by a devoted servant and meted out rough justice. None of it was to Lady Love's detriment, much less poor Mallory's. Still, she was under a cloud and would remain under that cloud for many years. Even when I was white-haired and wrapped in shawls and Donald's children were grown and going to parties, people would look at them – these imagined grandchildren of mine – from behind lowered eyelids and drawl to one another that was there not some story or other there, from ages back, of course, but what was it exactly?

'It was very odd, was it not, that McReadie took the imple-ment with him?' I said. That was still troubling me for reasons unknown and I thought that Lachlan's debt of gratitude to me should at least buy me the right to talk things over as I saw fit.

Lachlan stiffened as though he had been turned to stone.

'Not now, Dan,' said Alec, perhaps feeling more kindly.

'Took it with him?' Lachlan said.

'The long-handled pruning saw,' I said.

'Was it?' he said. He shook out his handkerchief and used it to do something I could not quite identify. He was neither wiping his mouth, blowing his nose nor even mopping his brow. He was, I realised, simply hiding his face. The entire operation lasted only a moment before he refolded his hand-kerchief carefully and put it back in his pocket.

'Here we go,' said Hugh as Lairdie came round the corner of the house in Alec's motorcar. It was piled high with Mallory's suitcases and hatboxes. 'Goodbye, Ross. We shall ring up to let you know we're home safe and sound. And we shall see you soon.' He waited. 'Dandy? Have you changed your mind? The boys can go with Osborne if you'd rather sit with me.'

I was watching Mallory and Cherry saying goodbye and one of the many things that had been troubling me was closer than ever.

'Write every day, darling,' Cherry said. 'Or you know – ring up, if it's easier.'

'I shall ring up *and* write,' Mallory said. 'I promise, dearest. You will be sick of the sound of my voice.'

'Impossible,' said Cherry. 'Darling Mallory.'

'Dearest Cherry.'

'Not now, Dan,' I repeated. Then in a louder voice, I said, 'Cherry. What did your mother call you?'

'Call me? She called me Cherry like everyone else does. Why?'

'No, I mean you call Mallory "darling" and she calls you "dearest". What did Lady Love call you?'

'She called both of us *mo ghoal*,' said Mallory and her eyes were awash with instant tears at the thought of it. 'We should start trying it out, Cherry. Keep it alive.'

'And when you went to your mother's room on the morning of her birthday,' I said, 'you asked to be let in and you thought she said "not now, my sweet", is that right? About twenty minutes past eleven.'

'Dandy, what *is* this?' said Hugh. Even Alec looked uncomfortable and Donald was bright red in the face with his brows drawn down together. Teddy alone watched with simple interest to see what I was up to.

'It can't have been your mother in her bedroom, calling to you through the door,' I said. 'Because by that time . . . well. Who was it then? A woman's voice? So either Biddy or Mallory.'

'Or Mrs McReadie,' said Cherry. 'It was muffled. I thought she was dressing, perhaps towelling her face even. It might have been Mrs McReadie. I was translating, you see, Dandy. I knocked and said, "Foot me heen a sty, mammy?" meaning "Are you all right, Mother?" and a voice said "Hunn ooten drasda, *mo ghoal*." Which means "not now, my sweet".'

'So it wasn't me,' said Biddy. 'I never took to the Gaelic like Lady Love.'

'Nor me,' said Mallory.

'I wonder what Mrs McReadie was doing in her mistress's bedroom,' I said. All eyes were upon me. 'She it must have been, since there are no maids at Applecross.' Lairdie had climbed down from the motorcar and was holding the door open. 'I wonder there was no sign in the room that Lady Love's bags were packed and gone. Her jewel case. Her writing case.' Cherry shifted from foot to foot. Perhaps she was beginning to feel uncomfortable standing for long periods. I hoped Biddy Tibball would soothe her and comfort her through the months ahead, which would be so much worse when the summer heat came. Finally, human kindness reasserted itself within me. I might even have blushed a little. 'Forgive me,' I said. 'Mulling is an occupational hazard, but that's the last of it.' I pecked Cherry's cheek, shook Lord Ross's hand and then from the very depths of me a thought bubbled up fully formed.

'How did you know Cherry was pregnant?' I said.

Hugh, pushed beyond his capacity to tolerate me, stamped off down the steps and round the side of the house to seek out his own motorcar and begin a few glorious hours of masculinity without me dropping bricks and letting off bombs.

This time, though, I was not alone. Alec had not been

here in February but he had learned our book of hours and he was nodding.

'Yes, indeed,' he said. 'That day. The day of the *cù sìth* and the *feannag*. Cherry told the womenfolk her news round the hall fire at teatime. Lady Love went upstairs to her room, supped up there, slept up there, breakfasted up there and died. Lord Ross, your room was downstairs. You were keeping the news of your walking as a birthday surprise. So you, presumably, did not go up the night before. And yet you claimed your wife told you Cherry's news, isn't that right?'

'That's right,' I said. 'Cherry came into the breakfast room talking about snowball fights and you advised against it. She asked how you knew and you said "Mummy told me". Does no one else remember?'

Everyone else, on the contrary, was looking aghast at Alec and me.

'Does it matter?' said Mallory.

'We like to have all the loose ends tied up,' I said.

'She came down to say goodnight,' said Lord Ross. 'She always came down to say goodnight to me and that night was no different.'

'She did?' I said. 'What time? And did you tell the police? Do they know that you saw her last, and long after the time we've been navigating by?'

'Good God,' said Ross. 'No, I don't expect so. What possible difference does it make?'

'It makes all the difference in the world!' I said. 'The question of where Lady Love was and when and who spoke to her is absolutely of the very essence. Perhaps she never went back upstairs. Perhaps she went outside then, after saying goodnight. If we had known this before, perhaps—' I finally caught my lip and managed to stop talking.

'I'm glad you brought it up, Dandy,' said Cherry. 'Daddy, I never knew Mummy used to come down to say goodnight to you. I love knowing it. Thank you!'

They were still smiling at one another when Mrs McReadie came round the side of the building where Hugh had disappeared. She was wiping her hands on her apron.

'Mister said you've got a wee question,' she said. 'About how the news got up and down the stairs when her ladyship didn't and his lordship couldn't. There's a simple explanation, Mrs Gilver. I told his lordship. I told him when I went in with his hot water. Just on ten o'clock it was, sir, don't you remember?'

'This will never do,' said Lord Ross. 'We're both telling stories now. The truth is, Mrs Gilver, that I can't remember and neither can our good Mrs McReadie. It was a very strange night and the next day was even stranger. Me mind is quite a blank about a great many things that took place around then. I want nothing more than to put the whole boiling behind me. Life goes on, my dear lady. Life goes on and we must live it.'

Mrs McReadie was nodding, in satisfied agreement. The Tibballs began nodding too and Cherry caught it until the whole lot of them looked like a chorus of puppets, unnerving in the strangest way.

I gave Cherry one last peck on the cheek and then fairly bolted for Alec's motorcar.

We were silent all the way up the twisting road past the graveyard and the walled fields, all the way up to the high tops where the sheep and cattle ran free. We were just as silent all the way down the other side to Lochcarron too. When we got to flat ground and were trundling along the side of the loch, Grant took a deep gathering breath, but Alec got in first.

'This case is not over,' he said. 'When we get home we need to have a pow-wow. I have no idea what is going on, but something certainly is.'

'Thank you,' I said. 'If I'd had to try to persuade you I think

I would have run mad, because it's nothing I could put my finger on. But it's no less real for being somewhat ineffable.'

'Like a gas leak,' said Grant. 'And you haven't even heard what I picked up in the kitchens yet. Some of it was in Gaelic and will need checking but if I've got them aright, there's more here than the police know.'

'Is Mallory part of it?' I said.

'Not in the way you mean,' said Grant. 'Master Donald has nothing to fear from her. She and Miss Cherry – that is, young Mrs Tibball – are the innocents here.'

Never have I been happier to turn off the Dunkeld road and onto the lanes of Gilverton. Usually, upon returning from a trip, the deep valley, the gloomy shade of the elm trees and the dripping damp of the mossy hedgerows depresses my spirits, whether it is city lights, sea breezes or southern meadows with which I am comparing them. But, set against the bleak, scoured landscape of Applecross, our valley was like a familiar armchair, soft to drop into and moulding itself to my shape with the ease of long years. The sight of Gilverton's lighted windows, the disdainful lift of Pallister's eyebrows as he descended the steps to meet us and even the joyous yips of Hugh's dogs as they dashed out onto the drive and plunged about the motorcars, scraping paint and preventing the opening of doors – all of it made me want to weep with the relief and contentment of coming home.

I was keenly aware, though, that Mallory alone of our party was not enjoying a homecoming but an awkward introduction to her future, too late to change her mind if it failed to appeal to her. Rather than flopping onto a sofa in my sitting room, I would need to show her round, settle her in and entertain her.

She stepped down rather stiffly after the long journey, but made a tremendous first impression by greeting all of Hugh's dogs with neither a gush of affection nor a cringe of anxiety.

She simply patted each one firmly on its head and glared at the pair of terriers for jumping up and putting paws on her tweed skirt. Hugh nodded approvingly.

'Come in, Mallory dear,' I said.

Pallister did not turn his head but he fairly sprained an eyeball following Mallory's passage up the steps and into the house.

'Donald doesn't have a butler, you might be relieved to hear,' I said. 'He shares a factor and steward with Hugh and inside he has a darling of a cook and a very pert head housemaid who needs taken in hand. I can help, of course.'

'And I can help if you're going to look for a maid of your own,' said Grant, on our heels. 'Drafting the notice for *The Lady*, interviewing candidates. I could take care of the whole enterprise if you'd rather.'

'Gosh, it will be lovely to have a maid!' said Mallory. 'If we can affor— I mean, I'm not accustomed to it and I've managed beautifully without one. But . . .'

'What is the nature of the Applecross ban on maids?' I said, but Mallory had that fixed look on her face that we call 'needing to wash one's hands after a long journey' and so I waved off her attempts at an answer and showed her to the cloakroom by the stairs.

'That's what I was trying to tell you, madam,' Grant said. 'That's what I heard in the kitchens. They haven't had maids at Applecross since they changed the course of the rivers to build that road. They cut off the sanctuary from the house, you see. So's not to have to build two bridges. They diverted the burn into the river upstream. And now they're seaward of where the streams converge.' She was waving her arms around like a windmill as she spoke, clearly trying to draw a map of Applecross in the air for my edification.

'What on earth are you raving about, Grant?'

'Sea monsters,' she said, unhelpfully.

Before I could interrogate her any further, Mallory was back. I tucked her arm in mine and drew her upstairs to the best guest bedroom to let her rest. 'It's not nearly as pretty as the bedrooms at Applecross,' I said.

'Oh, all those flowers!' said Mallory. 'Poor Daddy nearly had a fit when he climbed the stairs again and saw what Mummy had wrought. This is lovely.'

Privately, I agreed. This room had blue walls and white linen and no more flowers than a very few peonies worked into an Aubusson carpet.

'But then,' Mallory went on. 'Daddy is not as superstitious as Mummy always was. She never chose flowers for the look of them, you know. They were always working hard to cast their magic and protect us.'

'What do you mean?' I said. 'Lavender for sweet slumber and the like?'

Mallory, unpinning her hat, caught my eye in the dressing table looking-glass. 'I'll tell you if you promise not to think she was peculiar and I might have inherited it,' she said. 'It was just her Highland way, really. She wasn't feeble-minded and nor am I.'

I nodded with what I hoped was an encouraging look upon my face but, to own the truth, an assurance of sound mind tends to raise the question even while it seeks to quash it.

'Mummy knew we needed a road,' Mallory said. 'It never occurred to her that the road-makers would move the burn. I can still remember the day she found out. We were out on a lark together, she and I and Cherry. On one of our favourite fairy walks. Up round the caves and down by the kelpie pool. We were laughing and talking and we didn't notice how quiet it was until we were almost at the waterfall. The pool at its bottom had the coldest water I've ever known and we always used to dip our toes in and then snatch them out when we felt the kelpie nibble.'

'What fun,' I said, mindful of my promise not to question her mental state.

'But when we got there that day,' Mallory went on, 'the waterfall was gone. The face of the rock was dark green slime going pale as it dried and the water in the pool was quite still and lower than it should have been. It was still emptying out down the hillside, you see, but was no longer being replenished.'

'Because of the culvert,' I said. 'To make the road with just one bridge.'

'Exactly. It's the most terrible bad luck to strand a kelpie in sour water. It angers her and that's when she climbs out of where she belongs and walks the land.'

I opened my mouth to respond but came up short.

'Don't look at me like that, Dandy!' Mallory said. 'I'm only telling you the story.'

'It's not a story I've heard before.'

'There are remedies,' Mallory said. 'Kelpies don't belong on land and so they are helpless against myrtle and rowan and lots of other dry-land plants. And it's only maidens that interest them. And if they ever get back to the sea they're perfectly happy again. It was Applecross House being slap bang in the path between the stagnant pool and the open bay that worried Mummy so terribly. And she was very angry! I've never seen her more furious. I'd never heard her shout at anyone, but that day she screeched at the Roderick boys like a banshee.'

'The Roderick boys?' I said.

'Men in their fifties, really,' Mallory said. 'Mrs McReadie's brothers. They had made the road. Well, they were in charge of it, with a team of navvies over from Ireland to do the heaviest of the work. And it's the heaviest work I've ever seen anyone do. Nothing in the crofting year comes close. So Mummy filled our rooms with a witch's brew of flowers and put in that knot garden and, of course, the pier was going to be no end of help too.'

'Was it?' I said. 'In what sense exactly? For the kelpie to slither down?'

Mallory blinked and bit her cheeks to keep from laughing at me. 'No,' she said. 'So that we could get away without having to wait for high tide and willing arms. A nice long jetty with boats tied up would mean that we could be out at sea as soon as we heard it coming.'

I felt a slight warmth rising from my collar and decided not to answer. 'What about all the little girls along the street and in the cottages?' I said. 'All the crofting maidens?'

'Their mothers all know very well how to look after them,' Mallory said. 'And none of them has Maelrubha's blood in their veins. The kelpie set on vengeance would want Maelrubha's daughters ideally.'

'And why would that be?' I asked.

'Well, it was Maelrubha who made the sanctuary of Applecross Bay,' she began. 'It was the flood of his tears that tricked the kelpie. She swam in salt water and didn't know she was stranded until the flood went down.'

'Ah,' I said. 'And do you suspect the Roderick brothers of ignorance or malice? Do they *believe* this tale? Did they decide to put you and Cherry in harm's way? Moving the river's run like that.'

'To be perfectly frank, I don't know what the Roderick brothers were thinking. McReadie refused to talk about it and Mrs McReadie was pretty tight-lipped too.' She heaved a sigh as though tired out by all this talking, as I could imagine she might be.

'Rest, dear,' I told her. 'I'll send up a tray of supper and see you in the morning. Breakfast's at nine.' I kissed her cheek and left the room, with my head reeling. Kelpies and curses and mediaeval monks danced through my thoughts and threatened to drown out the very real question of the Roderick family's doings and Mrs McReadie's part in it all.

Grant was in my room, unpacking so fast I could tell she

wanted to be done with me and get onto Mallory's bags as soon as she could.

'I've heard from Mallory's own mouth what you picked up in the kitchens,' I said. 'And in English too. So I can probably confirm it.'

'She knew?' Grant said.

I frowned. 'Knew what? About the kelpie? Of course she knew.'

'What kelpie?' said Grant. 'What are you talking about, madam?'

'What are *you* talking about?'

'The plan that David Spencer scuppered,' Grant said. 'There was a secret plan. Not the scheme we uncovered. Not the break-up of the estate and the move back to sanctuary in the manse. Something else. It was hatched a while back but it had to wait until Miss Cherry and Miss Mallory were both settled in homes of their own and then it was all set to go ahead. Only, David Spencer wrecked it.'

'What was it?'

'I don't know in any detail. Everyone who spoke of it knew what it was so they didn't need to elaborate. The most they ever said was that "she loved him". She "truly loved him".'

'Whom? Spencer?'

Grant shrugged. 'Lairdie said it one night after a few drams. "The sin of it is that she loved him". But I think he said "sin" meaning "pity", not "sin" meaning "sin".'

'So perhaps the thought was that she loved Spencer and if he'd been patient and willing to wait until Mallory was married, she might have agreed to go away with him. But he rushed things and spoiled— No, it makes no sense to say he spoiled his own plan. He'd only have to go back to waiting again. And Spencer's plan can't have been Lady Love's plan. Hers was long-established, you say. And he came up on her birthday to *present* his.'

I sat down on my bed. Bunty was already installed there, curled up in as small a ball as a Dalmatian can ever make, tired out by the journey.

'You have a very peculiar look upon your face,' Grant said. 'But at least you're not frowning for once.'

'I'm shocked by my own thoughts,' I said. 'I suddenly realised I was inwardly cheering that we're going to get a third crack at solving this, when we go back for the wedding.'

'What's shocking about that?'

'I shouldn't even be thinking about agreeing to the wedding going ahead while there's still a mystery to be solved. In case its solution concerns Mallory. Mr Gilver and I should be bringing all our influence to bear on Donald to get him detached from the Dunnochs and then using all our persuasive powers to make him forget he ever saw Mallory.'

I did not notice Grant signalling until it was far too late. Donald had entered my bedroom without knocking and stood, pale and still, in the doorway.

'Is that what you're planning?' he said. 'To separate Mallory and me? I shall just elope, Mother. I shall just take her to Gretna Green and present you with a fait accompli.'

'You don't have to go down to Gretna Green if you're already in Scotland,' I said.

'And it would be wicked to make that poor girl marry without a wedding dress and trousseau,' Grant put in.

But there was no consoling Donald. He marched into the room and strode up and down on my bedroom carpet in his outdoor shoes, slapping his hand against his leg in a display of irritation. 'Good grief. Her poor mother is killed because she's so loyal and proper that she won't give the time of day to an old flame. Then her devoted servant, who can't bear seeing the man get away with it, avenges her. And a whole village who loves her decides that he's a hero rather than a villain and you think all of that makes Mallory – Mallory! – unsuitable? I think it makes her even more splendid. And her father! Her father risked his life to save the son of a servant and is putting him through Oxford. Her father learned to walk again and kept it up his sleeve for a birthday surprise. And her sister! Her sister is as sweet and unspoiled and charming a girl as I've ever met. She knows more about farming – well, crofting – than even Father does. I'd like to hear what anyone in this family has ever done that stacks up against any of that? I'm lucky Mallory is willing to settle for *me*!'

'Very well put, dear,' I said. 'I agree. Tell me, do you know anything about a secret scheme or plan that was being hatched, that was scuppered by Lady Love's death?'

'No,' said Donald.

'Would you ask Mallory if *she* knows?' I said. 'She made references to complicated matters that could be simplified by frank discussions. Would you open one of those discussions with her, for a change. Instead of ranting at me.'

'No,' Donald said. 'I won't do your dirty work, Mother. If you want Mallory grilled, you grill her.' He gave me one last glare and then slammed out.

'Well,' I said. 'That's me told then.'

Grant's eyes were misty. Passionate declarations of love were much to her taste.

'I'm going to keep digging,' I said. 'And if I find scandal in the Dunnoch family before they say "I do" I shall take great pleasure in putting a stop to it. In fact, I've always rather wanted to stand up in the middle of a wedding service and say, "Yes, vicar. *I* have a reason". Meanwhile, on we go.'

Grant tried to look sober, but I knew she was thinking of tulle and lace and seed-pearl embroidery. Of underclothes and bathing suits and evening gowns.

'Did you know,' I said for sheer spite, 'that they're honeymooning in Norway?'

PART 3
Summer

21

Mallory was long gone home again, of course, by the time the Gilver party made its third pilgrimage to Applecross one balmy midsummer afternoon. She had been thoroughly kitted out by Grant, on three trips to Edinburgh followed by many quiet evenings of pinning and trimming, and had departed with exactly twice as many articles of luggage as when she arrived. The wedding dress itself was under strict embargo and if Mallory had not been such a very sensible girl, not to mention having thirty summers to her name, I should have been worried. As it was, I had extracted assurances from Grant that it was white, that it reached the floor all round and that it was a dress, and had to make do with that.

The change of season from spring to summer had wrought another miracle in the glens. Those wobbling knock-kneed lambs from Easter were now lusty and muscular, no longer racing around and bouncing with *joie de vivre*. They had settled into their lives as sheep, eating steadily and ambling unconcerned across the road no matter how one leaned on one's horn. As we reached the summit of the *bealach na bà*, Alec turned off onto the cropped grass, finding a flat spot between the outcroppings of rock, turned off the engine and stepped out.

'Glorious day,' he said.

'I hope it lasts until after tomorrow,' I replied.

Alec tutted. 'Do you know, Dandy, that you have managed

271

to get Donald's wedding into seven out of ten conversations since this morning? I've been counting.'

'I'm glad I gave you such innocent diversion on the long drive,' I said. I swung my arms and lifted my face into the breeze, breathing deep the sweet-scented air.

Alec sneezed. 'Haymaking going on somewhere,' he said. 'We did not need innocent diversion. We had pressing matters to discuss.'

I groaned. 'We have discussed our pressing matters to death. I can recite them like a creed. "When exactly did Lady Love die? Did Spencer move her from the flower room to the knot garden? Why? Was it someone else? Why? Or was Mitten Tibball lying about where he saw her? Why? Or was he perhaps right that she wasn't dead and she came round and wandered outside herself? And if she was killed in the flower room, was there a peat-cutter—"'

'Lawn-edger.'

'"—was there an implement used for cutting peat and edging lawns that just happened to be in there? Why? It's not a tool store. And if it wasn't in there already, did David Spencer bring it to his rendezvous with Lady Love? And why?" There are no revelations to be got from saying it all again and again.'

I was wrong, of course.

'And on the subject of David Spencer,' said Alec. He had filled his pipe and lit it and now he leaned back against a sun-warmed rock and waved it around. 'Since Lady Love refused to go away with him and he killed her in a fit of frustrated rage, why on earth did he not immediately hop it and put as much distance between him and the Dunnochs as he possibly could? Once the story of the tramp was established – and I can't say I think much of the Inverness constabulary for that one, I must say – why did he not scarper? Why on earth stay put until Mallory's engagement party and risk discovery?'

'It was a bold strategy,' I said, nudging him until he moved over and then leaning against the rock beside him. 'Staying put and hiding in plain sight. Not to mention leaving on a trip with someone who adored Lady Love. But at least he was leaving, at long last. It wasn't going to work, of course. If McReadie had somehow got wind of what had really happened to her, Spencer would have been lucky not to get himself tipped overboard.'

Alec stopped, mid-puff, and spat his pipe out. 'What did you just say, Dan? He was leaving "at long last". We think he should have gone at once, but he was leaving at last.'

'So?'

I watched awareness dawn on Alec's face. His eyes widened and his mouth dropped open as a new idea filled his mind.

'What? What?' I said.

'We've made a mistake, Dandy,' said Alec. His voice was solemn but I could hear excitement bubbling away somewhere underneath. 'Not the first time, of course,' he went on. 'but this one's a whopper.' He drew in a deep breath and prepared to lay it out for me. My own thoughts were a jar of bees, ricocheting uselessly around my head as I tried to see what, in the tangle, I had overlooked. 'He was free to go,' Alec said. 'David Spencer didn't have to wait for anyone's permission to set sail to New Zealand as his only means of getting away! In fact, he didn't have to go on *that* trip to get away at all. Unless, for some reason, he wanted to. Do you see?'

'No.' It pained me to admit it.

'*He* was free to go. *He* didn't need permission.'

'As opposed,' I said slowly, 'to Samuel McReadie.' I still could not see where this was leading.

'Who *couldn't* just up sticks and leave without it raising suspicion. Who had to persuade Lachlan Dunnoch to let him go on the trip. To fund the trip, in fact.'

'What are you saying? That McReadie wanted to go on the trip to get Spencer alone and avenge Lady Love's death?'

I mulled it over briefly. 'But how could McReadie expect Spencer to join the expedition? And anyway, when he made his plans to go, he didn't know Spencer had killed Lady Love, did he? He found out at Mallory's party, when he and his sister-in-law danced so close to Spencer and me and he overheard us talking. The trip was much in his mind even before that. And when he did find out, he *didn't* take his time, or go on any trip and tip Spencer overboard. He bashed his head as soon as he heard the bombshell and killed him with a pruning saw minutes later.'

'Yes,' Alec said, infuriatingly. 'It doesn't seem to make any sense, does it? But think, Dandy. One of the two men could have left at any time but didn't. The other – a servant – had to set up a trip to get away.' He waited. 'One of them might have wanted to tip the other overboard on some quiet stretch of an ocean. The other lashed out at great personal risk.' He waited again and then took pity on me. 'One of them killed Lady Love and the other one knew.'

'Good Lord in heaven,' I said, turning to face Alec and staring at him, knowing I was now his mirror image, *my* eyes wide, *my* mouth open. 'We've got them the wrong way round. Samuel McReadie killed Lady Love.'

'Yes. And when he discovered that Spencer knew, he killed Spencer as well.'

'But why, Alec?' I said. 'Why would McReadie do such a thing? He adored her. And they had a grand old time of it together in that garden. Why? At least with Spencer we had a motive. He was a spurned lover.'

'True,' Alec said. 'He was. And I don't know the answer to your question, Dandy. But now we've got a better motive for McReadie killing Spencer, haven't we? Not to avenge his mistress – and why wouldn't he simply have told the police, if that were the case? – but to save his own neck!'

We were quiet for a moment then, testing the theory to see if it held. It almost held, with a few loose knots.

274

'Why though,' I began, 'between Valentine's Day and Easter did David Spencer not simply tell the police that McReadie had killed Lady Love? Why not put it in the hands of the law instead of what he was planning to do? Taking off on a jaunt with the man.'

'I don't know,' Alec said. 'Perhaps to protect her reputation? The family's reputation?'

'I suppose so,' I said. 'I do wish I understood more about this "scheme" that Spencer spoiled. It occurs to me that perhaps *that's* what he was keeping under wraps by planning to exact revenge instead of letting justice rain down. This plan, or secret, whatever it was.'

'We could ask Mrs McReadie,' said Alec. 'At the moment her position is secure: her husband avenged Lady Love's death and the Rosses owe her gratitude. If the real story is that her husband killed Lady Love and killed again to get away . . . she might help us, if we promise not to point the finger at her husband.'

'I don't think we can promise that,' I said. 'But she has a lot to lose, as you say, and she might just blurt something useful if we sniff around.'

'Not her,' said Alec. 'Not after the way she kept her nerve on the night of the ball and the morning after.'

'Or perhaps we don't actually need to know the scheme. Perhaps it's irrelevant.'

'Perhaps,' Alec said, somewhat reluctantly. 'Although, I do hope not. We've got Spencer scuppering a secret scheme and the mystery of McReadie's motive. It would be nice if the two were connected.' He puffed at his pipe again, but I knew from the whistling sound it made and the look of chagrin he gave it that the thing had gone out again. 'I don't suppose you're edging towards a brainwave?'

I had all but given up on brainwaves and told him as much with a sigh. It is one of the perennial frustrations of a complicated case. Somewhere, in the midst of the cascade of tales we had been told at Easter-time – each of them suspecting another, no one suspecting the true culprit – someone had said something that shone a thin beam of light into a corner so dark I had not even fully apprehended that there was a corner there at all. I could not remember who said it and I could not remember to whom it was said. It might even have been the dream about the glass paths in the labyrinth, still hanging about me as the most unsettling dreams sometimes do.

Who knows how long we would have carried on picking it over and worrying at it like ratters with a catch. As it was, we turned, when a horn tooted, to see Hugh's Daimler coming over the brow of the hill with Donald and Teddy each hanging out of a side window.

'Engine trouble?' Hugh called hopefully, or so it seemed to me.

'Just having a breather,' Alec said. 'All's well.'

'You looked rather blank,' Donald said, with a wary look. 'Nothing wrong, is there?'

'Just puzzling, as usual,' I said.

'Now Mother,' said Donald. 'You promised you'd put all of that out of your head and simply enjoy the wedding.'

'Did I?' I had no such memory.

'You could promise now anyway,' Donald said. 'I'd be most awfully grateful.'

I beamed at him. It was a non-committal beam and, besides, the most fervent beam ever hoisted onto a face is not a binding contract. Donald, however, is not the most intellectually supple child, and he beamed back, satisfied, as Hugh drove away.

As we descended the hill, past the graveyard, past the first of the crofters' cottages and into the woods, I became aware of a great clamouring filling the air. It sounded, from a distance, like a revolutionary horde, but as we drew closer to sea level, the shouts and shrieks were revealed in fact to be baas and bleats. And as we came to the walled paddocks nearest the parkland, the unmistakable scent of a great many warm sheep began to fill the air.

'They're shearing,' Alec said, as we rounded a bend and came upon a little huddle of sheep crossing the road in front of us. They were newly shorn down to their milky-white skin and had looks of enormous affront upon their naked faces. Alec stamped on the brakes and managed to avoid ploughing into them. The shepherd was herding them from behind by clacking his crook against the ground and shouting – unintelligibly to our ears, although the sheep were paying close attention.

Alec leaned over the steering wheel and peered in at the field gate. Then he opened his eyes very wide. 'Good grief, Dandy,' he said. 'Can you see that?'

I could see nothing except the high stone wall and so I stepped down from the motorcar and wandered over. The scene in the shearing field was straight out of Bruegel the Elder: men, women and children swathed in long aprons with cloths upon their heads, sheep of every age and size, from proud rams with curling horns, to anxious ewes, to struggling hoggets new to the experience, to lambs who were not to be shorn for a year yet and who stood forlorn, crying their mothers' names. The men grabbed the beasts and wrestled them to the shearers' stations, the women picked over the fleeces and rolled them tight, the children chased about after stray wisps, filling little sacks. In the middle of it all was a strange sort of gibbet, taller than a man, and hanging from it a long sturdy sack, half full of fleeces already and filling all the time as new ones were flung up to a woman straddling one of the top beams and deftly flicking them in.

'Cherry!'

She looked down, squinting against the sun, and then waved madly.

'Dandy!' she said. 'I thought I heard a motor but I was concentrating. Welcome back! Welcome back, Mr Osborne! Oh, happy day.'

'Cherry, what are you *doing* up there?' I said. The beam was hefty and she had her ankles wound round it but I could tell from the ground that she was as plump as a dumpling, her round stomach resting on her lap.

'I'm the best at flicking the fleeces in,' she said. 'Years of tennis. I'm quite safe. There's a ladder to get me down again.'

'Well, I can't watch you,' I said, turning my back and hurrying away.

I was more glad than ever for Mallory when we drew up the drive of Applecross House minutes later. She came out onto the step, holding Donald's hand, dressed in a pretty frock of pink crêpe and with her hair in shining curls. Grant had been here for half a week and already it was showing.

'Do you know what your sister is doing?' I said, as I kissed her on both cheeks.

'Shearing,' said Mallory.

'She actually *shears*?' I said, astonished. 'She bends double with a sheep held between her knees and . . .?'

'Not this year, thankfully,' Mallory said.

Inside Applecross House, a subtle change had taken place. I could not put my finger on it at first. The hall was furnished as before and, despite this being Midsummer Day, there was a fire burning in the grate. There were perhaps a few more newspapers on chair-backs and there were certainly fewer flowers around. Only one bowl of roses sat in the middle of the big table and some petals had fallen. Mallory picked them up absent-mindedly and threw them onto the fire.

'You must excuse the state of the bedrooms when you go up,' she said. 'We haven't done very well with our forced blooms, having no McReadie and no Mummy. They were the experts. And so we're saving most of the best stuff for tomorrow. In fact, it should all be in the flower room now,

278

plunged in cold buckets, to let the earwigs scramble out. I hope you'll forgive us bedside bud vases instead of the extravaganza Mummy used to do.'

'The bedrooms are so very pretty anyway,' I said. 'Even without extra flowers added, I can't imagine they'll be drab.'

Mallory laughed and tucked my arm in hers just as I had when she arrived at Gilverton. 'Yes, if it was me taking over this place, I might try to do something about the floral nature of the upstairs decor, but Cherry and Mitten really don't care. As long as the stable yard is swept every morning and the hay is made and dried before the rains come, I think the inside of the house could be given over to mice and cobwebs.'

'Cherry and Mitten are definitely taking over then?' I said. 'What about your father?'

'He's along in the manse.'

'Alone?'

'Oh no, not at all,' said Mallory. 'He doesn't need Dickie any more, of course, but Biddy's such a good housekeeper and so at home in the kitchen that we don't need Mrs McReadie *here*. So she's looking after him. And they seem to do very well.'

'Biddy and Dickie are living here in the house, are they?'

'Yes, it's all worked out neatly enough,' Mallory said. 'The cottage they used to have has been given to a family who needed it and Cherry's so hopeless at anything domestic, she's delighted to have Biddy take the reins.'

Her voice grew rather strained towards the end of this speech and I glanced at her from the corner of my eye. Something about this latest upheaval was troubling Mallory. I assumed it was not the same thing that was troubling me: namely, that Lachlan was now living alone with the wife of a fellow who had killed and killed again. Mallory might think he did not need Dickie Tibball's nursing but I would have been happier if some protection for the old man was guaranteed.

279

I would also have been happier if Mrs McReadie was still in the kitchens of the main house. It was a great deal harder to think up a reason to enter the servants' quarters along at the manse and strike up conversation with her there. I decided, therefore, to start with Lairdie and Mackie, the footmen.

I swept into the servants' hall the next morning at an unconscionably early hour, hoping to catch them unawares. I was alone since Alec had told me he was not going to risk a meal to go fishing for an unknown catch. 'Weddings do terrible things to a household economy, Dandy,' he said. 'Lunch is bound to be a crust of bread and a rind of cheese. I am not willing to miss my porridge and kippers too.'

'Mrs Gilver,' Lairdie said, leaping to his feet. He was in shirtsleeves and his braces hung at his hips. 'Did you ring?'

'I want a chinwag,' I said. 'How's your tooth?'

'Gone back to Kyle for the dentist's collection,' he said. 'But my gum's fine. Thanks for asking.'

'A chinwag?' Mackie said. He was polishing medals. I took it that Lord Ross was going to walk Mallory down the aisle in full regalia.

'It's about the trouble in the spring,' I said. 'Winter and spring. Mr Osborne and I have a few questions outstanding, you see.'

I did not acknowledge the look that passed between them but neither did I miss it.

'Fire away,' Lairdie said and, seized by a deep desire to sort this out before my son joined the benighted Dunnoch family in seven hours, I fired.

'What plan did David Spencer spoil by coming up here in the winter to talk to Lady Love?' I began.

I had no reason to think the two boys were related, except by the sort of inevitable cousinhood that tends to arise in places like Applecross, but they looked very similar at that moment, with their eyes growing round and their faces turning pale.

'I- I- I don't know,' said Lairdie. 'We never heard anything about it.'

'About what?' I said.

'What?'

'You never heard anything about what?'

Lairdie flushed, realising his mistake, and began to speak very fast, almost babbling. 'Ocht, her ladyship always had some scheme or another,' he said. 'The pier was the latest, after the road, and then the move to the manse. That was her idea. And a new school. She was all for another schoolhouse so the bairns could stay home with their mammies instead of taking off on the boat to Plockton all week. I don't know what she was planning, the poor lady. Before she was taken.'

'How could David Spencer do anything to interfere with plans such as those?' I said. 'He wasn't a speculator, was he? He hadn't persuaded Lady Love to invest in something?'

'No, indeed,' said Mackie. 'He was a soldier turned poet, was Mr Spencer.'

'A poet?' I said, startled. 'Right enough, he did always seem well-read.'

'Yes, writing poetry and teaching a wee bitty and editing for the . . . what was it called. The University Press.'

'Gosh,' I said. That sounded like much more than writing "moon" and "June" on the back of an envelope. 'Which university?'

'Cambridge?' Lairdie said uncertainly. 'I was valeting for him and I saw some of his papers. But I'm blessed if I can remember.'

'No,' I said, clicking my fingers as the truth rose in me, 'it's Oxford. Chaucer wouldn't call Cambridge the Midlands, would he?' I only became aware that I was staring at them when Mackie cleared his throat and looked down at his polishing cloth. 'Oxford University Press,' I repeated.

'Handy for his work,' Lairdie said.

'I had only heard "down near London",' I added.

'And so it is near London,' said Lairdie. 'What with the trains and roads. No waiting for spring or the coal boat down that way.'

I nodded absently. Oxford. Where Roddy McReadie was studying. The boy whose life Lachlan saved, thereby ruining his own. David Spencer lived there. David Spencer rushed up to Applecross unexpectedly and scuppered a plan. And the McReadies were neck-deep in his death.

Alec was wiping his mouth with a napkin when I found him in the breakfast room. 'We need to get to the manse and lean very hard on Mrs McReadie,' I said. 'Something in this infuriating tangle is at last beginning to loosen.'

I regaled him with my news as he, I and Bunty walked – fairly marched – along the shore road to the manse. I prayed that he would not pooh-pooh my discovery and squash my excitement back down.

Far from it, he whistled and sped up even more so that I was obliged to trot to keep up with him. We skirted the garden wall of the manse and came up on it from behind, entering the kitchen after a sharp rap on the door but not waiting for an invitation.

Mrs McReadie was there and, even better, was alone. She had, I thought, made a great deal of effort for Mallory's wedding day. Her hair was no longer in its scraped-up bun, but had been cut short and was shining. And although she was wearing an apron to protect her clothes while she dusted trays of little cakes with icing sugar, the clothes she was protecting were a smart lilac skirt and a crisp cream-coloured shirt.

'Busy day, Mrs McReadie,' I said. 'But still we wanted to stop in and ask how you've been.'

Mrs McReadie cocked her head to one side and regarded me.

'It's a hard road, Mrs Gilver,' she said. 'I hope you never have to walk it. But then if you go first there's Mr Gilver

282

will have to walk it instead. And you're not married yourself, sir?'

Alec was startled, and shrugged while his cheeks coloured a little.

'But you speak as if McReadie is dead,' I said. 'Have you heard that he's dead?'

Now it was her turn to colour. She turned to face the range in an attempt to hide it, but there was nothing there that had to do with sugaring cakes and she soon turned back again.

'Gone is gone,' she said. 'I suppose I'm trying to make myself face that I'll never see the *bodach* again. If that's strikes you as cold, then I'm cold.'

'The *bodach*?' I said and shivered. 'Is it like the *cailleach*? It's unnerving how the same word is used for one's nearest and dearest and for . . . well, witches and ghouls too.'

Mrs McReadie merely stared at me. 'We have our own ways,' she said at last.

'You do indeed,' I said. 'Like those little models of Lachlan and Lady Love that used to be in drawers in the flower room?'

She stared even longer this time before she selected a suitable remark. 'Why would you think I made them?'

'Because they were wool and it was you who made the necklets,' I replied.

'That was just for luck.'

'Good or bad?' I asked and her eyes flared.

'Depends which was on the left and which the right, doesn't it?' said Alec. Months late he had provided just the expertise on Scots folklore for which I rang him up that fateful day.

'But let's not dwell on it, this happy morn,' I said, seeing that the swift change of topic had unsettled her as I meant it to. I gave her a bright smile. 'Has your son come up for the wedding?'

Mrs McReadie shook a thick blot of sugar over the edge of the tray as her hand jerked. Even Bunty could sense the woman's discomfiture. She pricked her ears up and wrinkled her brow. 'My son? Why would he be here?'

'Hasn't he known Mallory all his life?' I asked. 'And given his history with Lord Ross too.'

'He's got his exams,' said Mrs McReadie.

'As late as this?' said Alec. 'I'd have thought finals would be long past by now.'

'He's had to resit one,' she said. Finally she raised her eyes to ours again. 'I'm that ashamed of him. I don't want his lordship to know. I'd be grateful if you wouldn't mention it.'

'I can sympathise,' I said. 'My younger son did nothing but drink cocktails and study form for about a year. I wanted to go down there and box his ears more than once.'

Mrs McReadie swallowed. 'What year is he in?' she said. 'I wonder if they know each other?'

'Oh, he's finished,' I said. 'He scraped a lower second in the end.'

Mrs McReadie's shoulders dropped a good inch and a half.

'Your lad must be a good bit older than most of the undergraduates,' Alec said. 'One would hate to think he was lonely. But then there are other soldiers who've gone back to studying. Of course, he won't have Mr Spencer any more. He did know Mr Spencer, didn't he?'

'What makes you think that?' said Mrs McReadie. 'I never heard that they met.'

'Really?' Alec said. 'I just assumed that what with Spencer being such a friend of the family and being right there, they'd have been sure to run into each other.'

She shook her head and when she stopped I noticed that her jaw did not quite stop trembling. Bunty was keening in Mrs McReadie's direction; she is always ready with comfort for the troubled.

'Well then, we'll leave you to it,' I said. 'I'm sure you've got a lot on your mind. On your docket, I should say.'

Mrs McReadie nodded bleakly and we departed by the back door.

The garden along here at the manse was not quite as glorious as the labyrinth at Applecross but it knocked anything the Gilverton gardeners had ever achieved into a cocked hat. The roses were leggy adolescents still but they had put on a good show for midsummer, each of their trained stems hanging heavy with blooms. The paths between them were not as smooth as the paths at Applecross, having the marks of barrow wheels running through. I got a twinge that might have been the memory of the deep scores through the gravel on the night of the engagement party or might have been the last lingering shivers from my nightmare. The new knot garden itself was looking rather better than the original had been last time we saw it, with profusions of flowers blooming. Just as a troubled thought rose through the layers of confusion to the top of my brain, Alec voiced it for me.

'That was odd, wasn't it: McReadie grubbing out plants when he did?'

'He was in the throes of great grief,' I said. I held up a hand as he threatened to interrupt me. 'Even though he killed her. But perhaps the feud with his mistress over her plantings was too well-known by all the house-hold. Still, one would think he'd nurse those ill-judged little seedlings like his own sickly child with a fever.'

Alec nodded. 'And yet he couldn't rip them out fast enough.'

'What were they?' I said. 'Did he say?'

'Can it possibly matter?' said Alec.

I shrugged. 'I just wonder if there was some element of sorcery about them,' I said. 'Perhaps they were planted not for scent or colour but for protection. I wouldn't put it past Lady Love. And so he feared they might invite harm to him that killed her.'

'I don't think so,' Alec said. 'I mean, *this* was where she meant to live through the current summer, wasn't it? And these are just cottage-garden flowers. Speedwell and suchlike. What's that thing?'

'*Dicentra*,' I said. And at Alec's look: 'I can't help it. Hugh has dinned it all into me over the years. And this is *lunaria*. I have no idea if they have protective qualities.'

'I never understood the lure of the Latin name,' Alec said. 'The folk names are so much prettier. What could be sweeter than speedwell?'

'It's also known as forget-me-not,' I said. 'Forget-me-not, honesty and the bleeding heart certainly do sound more poetic than *myosotis*, *lunaria* and *dicentra*.'

'Rather *too* sweet for my taste,' Alec said. 'Do you think they were perhaps chosen for the messages they send? I'd love to know what was in the other knot, in that case. Wouldn't you?'

'No doubt the planting plan is in the journal,' I said. 'Wherever *that* is. Look, let's get back to the house, shall we?'

And yet what we found ourselves doing – partly because Bunty was tugging us but partly because we could not resist the lure – was climbing the hill behind the house, up to the graveyard, up to where the walls stopped and the land opened and up again, until we were standing on the summit, surrounded by shorn sheep and uninterested cows, panting slightly and looking down on the buildings and the little patchwork of fields as if we were giants or they a model.

'We should be able to see it, don't you think?' Alec said.

I put my hands on my knees and bent over, breathing hard. 'Is that what we're doing up here?' I said. 'Yes, I've been thinking the same. When the boys were tiny, they had a charming little book of painted pictures with objects hidden in them. A seaside scene with ten shells disguised as shadows. Or a circus with top hats everywhere. Of course, they became

286

familiar in the end and then the book was only wheeled out for visitors, but this case makes me feel as though I'm reading another one for the first time. This is a farming scene.'

For there was indeed a hay-cutting going on in the lower fields, as Alec had guessed earlier from his fit of sneezing. The crofters looked like toy figures as they scythed the virgin sward, then tossed the cut hay, raked it and gathered it, straightened it into bundles and spread it along the walls to dry in the sunshine.

'Or a garden,' Alec said. 'With lawn-edgers everywhere.'

'Peat-cutters.'

'Well, there's one thing we *can* do,' said Alec. 'We can check to see if they're the same thing and, if not, why the confusion.'

'Let's ask the haymakers,' I said. 'They're bound to know and they'll be glad of a rest, don't you think? It must be hot work.'

'Surely Cherry isn't amongst them,' Alec said. 'She can't be going straight from a hayfield to her bridesmaid's dress.'

She was not. We saw, when we had descended the hill and hallooed the workers, that neither Mitten nor Cherry was part of the fun this morning. Everyone else from the sheep-shearing was there, though, and we were hailed as old friends.

One of the women brought two tin cups of water over to us and raised her own horn water bottle in salutation.

'You'll think we're daft,' she said. 'But it's to rain on Monday and tomorrow's the Sabbath so it's this or nocht. We'll be washed and in our best for the wedding and we'll enjoy it all the more with the hay cut and drying there.'

'Not at all,' Alec said. 'I'm a farmer myself. I quite understand. And we won't keep you any longer than we have to. Only, we have a question. About farm implements.'

'Scythes?' the woman said. 'Hoy! Wullie. Gentleman's wanting a lookie at your scythe.'

287

Alec waved his arms back and forth to tell 'Wullie' not to interrupt his rhythm. 'Not scythes,' he said. 'Peat-cutters. I don't think I've ever seen one and we were just wondering . . . how big is the blade?'

The woman wiped her lips and recorked her bottle, frowning at us. 'You were "just wondering" what like the spit depth is on a peat-cutter?' she said. It did sound foolish when she repeated it that way.

'Look,' Alec said. 'It's about the night Lady Love was killed. Unbelievable as it sounds, no one is entirely sure what weapon was used. It's been called a peat-cutter and a lawn-edger and we'd like to make sure – doubly, trebly sure – that we've got it quite straight.'

'A lawn-edger?' said the woman. 'Likes of for the garden? That's a wee half-moon thing, isn't it not? Aye, and a peat-cutter's a great big thing, bigger than a shovel. They're nothing like.'

'Well, but is there perhaps a small peat-cutter, for cutting small peats, for a small fireplace?' I said. 'One that would do service as a lawn-edger?'

Now the woman was staring at us as though we were children, and not particularly bright ones. 'Naw,' she said. 'If you're after small peats you split big ones.'

'So it's impossible to mistake one for the other?'

'Aye, only a softie would think they're the same.'

Alec made a strangled noise and nudged me.

The woman frowned at him. 'But why are you intere—?

'Nothing you need to worry about,' Alec said, with an unmistakable note of triumph in his voice. He had solved the puzzle; I knew it. 'Don't let us keep you.' He lifted his hat politely.

When, with a troubled backwards glance, she had returned to her work, he lit his pipe and waggled his eyebrows at me.

'Oh go on then,' I said. 'Don't milk it. Just tell me.'

'I know why no one can say whether Lady Love was killed

288

with a lawn-edger or a peat-cutter,' he said. 'You'll kick yourself.'

'Probably.'

'Remember that McReadie took his pruning saw with him even though he'd used it to kill David Spencer.'

I thought for a moment and then felt my gorge rise. 'Oh God,' I said. 'He killed her with his favourite lawn-edger. Mitten saw it. But by the time McReadie had moved the corpse to the knot garden he'd put a peat-cutter in its place.'

'Exactly,' said Alec.

'But why did he put anything in its place?'

'Exactly again,' Alec said. 'It's too gruesome for words.'

'It is,' I agreed, 'but if a peat-cutter's right there, still lodged in the wound, it does stop one wondering what the murder weapon was, doesn't it? It does stop one deciding it was a gardening tool and casting one's eye at the gardener.'

'Ssshh,' Alec said. He had seen another woman, older, broader and somewhat threatening in her foursquare stance, coming up. 'What's this you're asking Kate?' Her face was stony under its sheen of sweat and sprinkling of hayseeds.

'Just chatting,' Alec said. 'She was kind enough to give us some water.' He handed back the empty cups.

'You're the detectives, are you not?'

'Not today,' I said, smiling. 'Mother of the groom and family friend. Why would you be thinking along the lines of detection?'

The woman shook her head wordlessly then turned away, wiping her brow with her forearm. I saw the glint of a wedding ring there and took a guess. I had an even chance of being right.

'Oh, Mrs Roderick?' I said.

She turned at the sound of her name, as one will, helpless not to.

'Good work, Dandy,' Alec whispered. 'Oh jolly good work indeed.'

22

'We should be getting back,' I said, as we walked into the blessed shade of the woods down near the house. 'Grant is much taken up with Mallory and Cherry, of course, but I'm sure she's got plenty in store for me too.'

'I've never understood why it takes so much time for women to get dressed,' Alec said. 'You wear far fewer clothes and no cufflinks.'

I decided it was not worth the effort to explain. Besides, we were not alone. There was a rhythmic knocking noise coming from somewhere off to our left. I peered through the trees and realised that we were just outside the high garden wall that formed the back of the hothouses.

'We could take a shortcut if that gate's open,' I said.

Alec led the way, chivalrously whacking away a nettle or two with a stick. The gate was indeed open and we passed through. The source of the knocking noise was then revealed to be a carpenter who was constructing some kind of bower out of smooth pine poles. The two legs were complete and he had got as far as nailing the top piece into place.

'Fur photies,' he said, and nodded in through the open hothouse door where, upon the staging, lay the kind of extravagant floral garland – quite ten feet long and as thick as a chimney brush – that I had not seen since my Victorian girlhood.

'Good heavens,' I said. 'What an enterprise.' Hoping I was not disparaging his efforts, I nevertheless went on, 'But why not take the photographs under the arbours already *in situ*?

You could poke a fair few flowers in amongst the apple boughs, surely? Or you could do it at the manse against roses.'

'Wrong flowers,' said the carpenter. 'Lady Love left a list.'

I did not understand how roses could be the 'wrong flowers' for a wedding day, but the news that a list had survived Lady Love's death made me hopeful of a planting plan too and I was round the first corner of the labyrinth, on my way to the flower room, before I noticed that Alec was not beside me. I retraced my steps and saw him standing staring down at where the carpenter was kneeling. He nodded his head to draw my attention to the man too.

I looked. He was a middle-aged chap dressed in rough corduroy trousers, a woollen waistcoat and a collarless shirt, and was bare-headed on this warm morning – made even warmer, no doubt, by his industry. He was hammering the bower together with such long nails so closely spaced that the resulting structure would be sturdy enough for its job even if the Dunnochs decided to add a marble pediment to the garland of flowers. As he selected yet another six-inch nail from his collection, finally I too saw what had struck Alec. The box where the man's nails and screw nails were arranged in natty compartments, where hammers of various sizes and chisels too were arrayed, was not a toolbox in the usual style. It was rather more sumptuously lined than any toolbox I had ever seen, rather more intricately constructed and more stylishly shaped. And I had never, in my long life, seen a toolbox with gold hinges.

'Do you mind, my good man,' Alec said, 'if I close this case, just for a minute?'

The carpenter, pausing the rapid percussion of his hammer briefly, sat back on his heels and stared up. 'My box?' he said. 'Help yourself. It's a good one, is it not?'

'It's a beauty,' said Alec. He lowered the lid. It fell to with a soft click and we found ourselves looking at some rather fine marquetry – swollen and sprung here and there but well mended – with a mother-of-pearl inlay at its centre where gold initials curled and twisted a great deal but still just about managed to convey the short message 'LAPM'.

'Lavinia Something Mallory,' Alec said softly; then, in a louder voice, he added, 'Where did you get this?'

'My box?' said the carpenter again. 'From the *ciste-ulaidh*.' At our looks, he translated. 'The treasure chest. From the sea.'

I do not know what emotions passed over Alec but I was flooded with shame. We had asked ourselves incessantly what had happened to Lady Love's bags and had never once considered the obvious place for someone to ditch them. Even when Mallory admitted she meant to tip her mother's body into the sea we did not make the short leap.

'It washed up on the beach,' the carpenter was saying when my flood of shame receded. 'Finest thing I've found on that beach for many's a long day.'

'When was this?' I said.

'Winter time coming spring,' said the man. 'That's the best time for jetsam. The currents, you see. Terrible for the fishing but grand on the tideline.'

'Was it sprung open when it washed up?' I asked. I thought not, for the wood inside the box, not to mention the satin lining, showed no water damage. Only the exterior was warped and stained.

''Deed it was not,' the man said. 'It was locked tight but I gat at it with my pins and hooks and gat it opened.'

'And was there anything inside it?' I said.

''Deed there was. Chock-full of papers.'

'Papers?' said Alec, the leap in his voice matching that in me.

'Letters, mostly. And a good big bookie quarter-full of scribbles. A diary, maybe it was. Or suchlike.'

Alec and I shared a glance that did not dare to be hopeful.

'Did you read any of the letters?' Alec said. 'Or the scribbles in the . . . bookie?'

'I don't read that English,' the man said, with a bite of scorn in his words. 'I speak it but I read the good Gaelic just. And so I just put them in the basket for lighting the fire, for I hate to waste a good newspaper on the fire and the sticks were wet as haddock that February there.'

I saw Alec's shoulders slump and felt sure mine did the same. Then a thought struck me. 'You used the letters – envelopes too, I imagine – to light your fire? Very practical. But what about the book? With the scribbles? Did you rip the pag—'

''Deed I did not!' said the man. 'Twould have been a waste of it. I gave it to my little granddaughter there to draw in. She's not five but she can draw any animal in the land.'

Alec's shoulders had straightened again. 'Your granddaughter,' he said. 'And where might she live? Here in Applecross?'

'Where else?' The man looked astonished. 'Down the street with her mammy and daddy and the *cailleach* and me. Behind the workshop there. The smithy.'

'Ah,' I said. 'Mr Roderick, I believe? I think I heard you were the carpenter and smith here. And undertaker too.'

The man inclined his head in acknowledgement of his standing and then sent a longing look at his closed toolbox. Alec raised the lid, handed the man a coin for his trouble and then, gripping me firmly under my elbow, steered me away.

'Dare we hope the child still has it?' he said. 'If it was a diary, it only had a month and a half's entries in it and surely that left too many blank pages for young Miss Roderick to have filled already.'

'Even if she has,' I said, 'she's more than likely kept the book. If it's as fine as the writing case, it will be a treasure for her.'

'A treasure from the sea,' Alec said. 'Can he possibly be as innocent as he was making out, Dan? Did he really think that box happened to wash up the sound from an ocean liner exactly when Lady Love went missing?'

'I think so,' I said. 'If he had anything to hide he would have hidden it and, on the contrary, he was quite open, wasn't he? Besides, the villagers can't have known that she packed bags.'

'The villagers who're Rodericks? Don't you think Mrs McReadie would have told all her relations and connections every bit of the business?'

I shrugged. We were almost at the terrace now. When we reached, it I grabbed Bunty's collar, sprinted up the steps, shoved her in at the nearest French window, telling her to go and find Grant, then scampered back down to rejoin Alec. He was standing staring down at the edge of the gravel path.

'What is it?' I said.

'Look,' he said and pointed. The writing case had been well worth pointing out and looking at and so I peered closely. I could see nothing,

'What?' I said again.

'Look at the gravel,' Alec said. 'It's as smooth as a skating rink almost across the width but there's a churned-up rim of untidiness along each edge.'

'I don't know why that's bothering you,' I said, 'but – did I ever tell you? – I had a dream about these paths. A dream in which they turned from snow to ice to glass.'

'Smoother and smoother,' said Alec. 'If you were rolling these paths wouldn't it bother you to leave the edge in this state? There's a perfect ditch!'

I could not quite imagine pushing the heavy roller and I only shrugged. 'I'm not trying to sway you from your concern about an untidy path-edge,' I said, 'but imagine if this very minute, young Miss Roderick is playing at the shore, about to drop her sketching book into a rock pool.'

Alec nodded and started walking again. We skirted the house and set off down the drive at a trot.

'Grant will string me up,' I said.

'If you'd rather leave it to m—'

'Fat chance,' I said. 'I want to read these scribbles just as much as you do and this is one of the many times when a woman's touch is essential, wouldn't you say?'

'Oh?' said Alec. 'What reason are you planning to give for storming the undertakers this nuptial morning then?'

It was a very good question and I had not come up with a sensible answer by the time we arrived at the smithy. Thankfully, such is the nature of Highland hospitality that we were not asked our business when we knocked on the blue-painted door up the narrow close to the side of the workshop. We were simply invited in, ushered to chairs and informed that we would take a cup of tea and a bannock.

'Mr and Mrs Gilver, is it not?' said the round, smiling woman as she plied her kettle and drew her griddle pan onto the flames. 'Parents to the nice young man who's stolen Miss Mallory's heart away.'

'Mrs Gilver,' I said. 'And Mr Osborne, a friend of the family.'

'And today the wedding day!' the woman said. 'You must be very proud. And you're getting a lovely girl to call your own.' It was a welcome thought, and one that had not struck me before this, so many years since I had given up all thoughts of daughters.

'Do you have any children?' I said. 'Have you seen them marry yet?'

'Four boys to my name,' she said. 'And four fine lasses wedded onto them.'

'How lovely! Do you have grandchildren?'

'I have seven!' She was beating me into a cocked hat at this game. 'Two away at the big school, three in the wee school here, one a babe in arms still and then there's Grizzle.'

I was not sure enough of what this extraordinary name could possibly be to attempt to repeat the sound, but I felt sure that 'Grizzle' must be the artistic toddler and accordingly I enquired into her age and current whereabouts and, before too long had passed, Mrs Roderick was at her back door, calling the child in from play.

'She's needing to be got washed and brushed for the wedding anyway,' the woman said. Indeed, the stout little person who arrived in from the garden was lavishly filthy and tousled. Her grandmother tutted and set about her with a flannel, dipped in the kettle and wrung out hard, scrubbing energetically and scolding the child in Gaelic.

'You will have to stay indoors and stay clean once your granny has got you dressed up for the wedding,' I said.

Grizzle, so buffeted and jostled by her grandmother's repeated scrubbing that she could barely keep on her feet without staggering and certainly could not speak in a steady voice, nevertheless replied, 'I can stay clean outside. It's not muddy.'

'It's dusty,' I said. 'What do you like to do best inside? Can you read?'

'Nearly,' Grizzle said. It was an admirable attitude.

'I used to like to draw pictures,' said Alec. 'If I was ill with a cold or if it was raining. Do you like drawing?'

'I can draw!' Grizzle said.

'Houses?' I said. 'I used to draw houses. And people.'

'I can draw cows and sheep and deer and horses and rabbits and mice and birds and cats and dogs!' Grizzle said all in one breath.

'That you can,' her grandmother said.

'And I can draw the kelpie and the *feannag* and the *bodach* and—'

'Hush now,' her grandmother hissed softly. 'Don't show off.'

'Oh but I'd love to see your pictures,' I said. 'Golly, horses are the very dickens to draw.'

Grizzle had to wait until her face was shining like a polished

apple and her hair was scraped into pigtails so tight I was
sure her scalp must be stinging, but at last she escaped her
grandmother and went off into an adjoining room, returning
a moment later with a familiar-looking calfskin book, whose
pages were gilt-edged and whose cover was stamped with
an ornate '1935'.

'A diary?' I said. 'What a pretty one. Was it a Christmas
present?'

'The *bodach* found it thrown away,' said Mrs Roderick.
'And we let the bairnie have it. I've no use for paper and
the school gives jotters.'

'Might I see it?' I asked Grizzle. She was only too happy
to display her work. I caught one tantalising glimpse of a
page filled with writing as she leafed through and then spent
the next ten minutes admiring a zoological garden of animals
all of which looked remarkably similar. We had a little help
from the fact that the beasts of the air were drawn amongst
fluffy clouds, those that crept upon the earth were depicted
against a garish green quite unlike the grass of these hills
and the creatures of the deep were superimposed upon a
strident background of azure blue.

'Is this a . . . sealion?' I said, of a particularly shapeless
blob.

'A beastie,' said Grizzle. 'It's a—'

Mrs Roderick had fidgeted more and more as the private viewing wore on and eventually, at this moment, she
broke in.

'Come away,' she said. 'You've got your frock to get on
and it's pressed and laid out. You just stay and enjoy your
tea, Mrs Gilver, and you too, Mister.'

She and the child disappeared into the other room again.
I hesitated, wondering if we would have time to read the
entries before they returned, but Alec was bolder. He took
the book from my hands, ripped out the written-upon pages
with one wrench and got to his feet.

'Must dash,' he called. 'See you at the wedding.'

'Lovely bannocks!' I added and dove out after him.

Grant was standing in my bedroom like a pillar of fire when the two of us hurried in minutes later. 'Do you know what time it is?' she said. 'Madam.'

'Time to read Lady Love's diary, that washed ashore in her writing case,' I said, as Alec tipped Bunty off my bed and began spreading the pages in order.

Grant spent exactly half a minute in further resentment, then slipped over to stand beside us, hungrily reading.

The first pages were filled with new year's resolutions and garden notes concerning how graft buds were faring in the frosts and how saved seeds were faring in the damp. It was all very dull and reminded me of listening to Hugh on evenings when we dined alone. Then in the third week of January came something quite different.

> *Sam asked again. And again I had no answer. I have been happy here my whole life through and yet to follow in the footsteps of the great plant-hunters of the past, to go to lands that even Tradescant never knew, and find there strange and beauteous blooms to give my name to? For Maelrubha's name to live on, despite me? What a thing that would be.*

'*She* was going on this plant hunt to the new world then?' Alec said. 'It should have occurred to us that it was all arranged too quickly for Spencer and McReadie. "Sam" *is* McReadie, isn't he?'

'I think so,' I said. 'Rather unusual to go off round the world with one's gardener. I can't imagine it myself.'

Grant had been reading ahead and now she gasped and

298

pointed a shaking finger at a page dated 28 January. Alec and I bent close.

'I hardly know how to write what has happened today,' Lady Love had scribbled in untidy script with much blotting.

Sam has declared his love for me. Of course, I knew he was fond of me. I am fond of him. But this afternoon in the peach house, he declared a true serious attachment to me, an intention to divorce his wife, a desire for me to divorce my husband, and he actually proposed. He got down on his knees on the damp tiles and proposed that he and I marry!

'Good Lord above,' I said. 'This is incendiary! This has been sitting in a village house in a little girl's drawing book for four months and no one *read* it?'

'We must be getting close to a motive now,' Alec said.

'I thought I would laugh,' the entry went on.

But somehow, standing there, looking down at his dear face so sincere and so affectionate, the last thing I wanted to do was laugh at him. I felt what I can only describe as a surge of excitement. He is so vital, for all he is my age and more and we were children together. Lachlan has been an invalid for twenty years and lately has withdrawn even from pleasant evenings together, almost from conversations with me. He would rather be with Dickie than with his own wife.

'Oh God,' said Alec. 'He was going off with Dickie practising his walking for her birthday surprise.'

I nodded but was too engrossed in the next entry to answer.

*Sam kissed me! We were pruning, chatting as
we always have when we work in the garden
together, and suddenly he seized my hand
and pulled me towards him and kissed my
lips. I wrenched away, of course, but then I
stood very close to him and looked deeply into
his eyes and for a moment I swayed towards
kissing him back. In my mind, I swayed and
perhaps I leaned forward physically too! Then
a door opened on the terrace and I sprang
away. I do not know who it was and I do not
know if we were seen. But afterwards, when we
were in the potting shed, oiling our secateurs
and sharpening the long loppers, Sam pressed
me harder than ever. He said he knew my
feelings were the same as his and he knew
that we could be happy, two adventurers
together. But I could never do such a thing to
Lachlan. I made vows for better or for worse,
in sickness and in health. I could never.*

'Plants, plants, plants,' Grant said, under her breath, running
a finger down the next few pages, then, 'Aha!'

*A most extraordinary thing has occurred.
Somehow Lachlan has learned of Sam's feelings and desires. But that is not the extraordinary thing! He is not opposed to the plan. I
do not know what to think. My husband of so
many years is not opposed to the plan to
divorce and for me to marry my gardener
and go off to New Zealand with him. It is
hardly flattering.*

'He *what*?' said Alec, catching up.

300

Of course, it's chivalry. Lachlan thinks I should not be tied to a cripple.

'But it can't have been chivalry!' I said. 'Lachlan was learning to walk again.'

And Cherry is happily settled. If Mallory means to accept that Gilver boy, then my girls will no longer need me here. I will speak to Mallory this evening when she returns from her house party. Perhaps the attraction will have worn off. I cannot say he was enormously appealing the one time I met him. His father's family is unobjectionable, I suppose.

'His father's family?' I said hotly. 'His *father's* family? What about his mother's family? What a ruddy cheek.'

'Ssshh,' said Alec. 'Read on. And don't skip the bits about plants, Grant. If we had paid more attention to the plants in this case it would have done well for us. Patience, honesty, bleeding heart and forget-me-nots were planted in the manse knot garden for Lachlan to pine by after Lady Love had hopped it.'

'Oh!' I said. 'And whatever McReadie was grubbing out of the knot garden here in the depth of winter was probably just as blatant. If he planted it as a message of love, anyway. Why did we ignore the oddness of him doing that, Alec? We knew it was important.'

'Never mind rehashing it now,' said Grant. 'Look at what comes next.'

Mallory is truly in love. We must invite his family on a visit for it seems that there is no stopping it. He is younger than I thought. Very

301

stodgy young men sometimes do seem middle-aged before their time. But Mallory set my mind to rest on one score. She admires the mother greatly.

'The mother!' I said, but I was mollified.

Apparently, she's a very original, enterprising and modern type. My Mallory thinks she's a marvel and plans to learn at her elbow, by all accounts. It seems that for all my affection and attention, I have been lacking as a role model. Detectives are much to be preferred to gardeners.

I was embarrassed now and perhaps Grant and Alec were too, for we all read on in silence. The next entry was absorbing and unsettling. It was very strange to read the woman's thoughts as she recounted events we knew were leading so very soon to an unknown and unbearable end.

10 February. Help is at hand. My dear David is coming up for my birthday. The sweet old thing rang up in a flap and said he had to speak to me urgently and could not tell me what it was over the telephone. I said I was delighted because I needed to speak to him too. He is on the train this minute and will be with me tomorrow. I am going to lay it all at his feet and ask his advice. If he says Lachlan must be allowed his chivalry, if he says there is nothing shocking these shocking days about such a misalliance as Sam and me, if he says my girls would be fine without me . . . such a lot of ifs! But if he does, then I

might - I really might - do this mad thing.
I might go. To New Zealand! As Mrs McReadie!

And then the thunderbolt. But it would
throw everything off, wouldn't it?

12 February. My dear old David arrived
yesterday but we did not have our tête-à-tête
until this morning. It began like a farce, with
yet another man declaring his devotion to me.
Hardly news, but it surprised me that he would
suddenly make it overt after all this time. I've
known for years and thought we were past the
crisis when it might make waves. But then came
the bombshell. David knows why Lachlan wants
me gone. It's not chivalry at all or anything
like it. He is as chivalrous as he is heroic. He's
not giving me my freedom. He is getting rid of
me. Well, he is not getting rid of me. I refuse to
be made a fool of. I shall not go. I shan't tell
Sam until after my birthday if I can avoid it.
And then I cannot imagine what will happen.
Perhaps he would like to go to New Zealand
anyway. Will he still send me back plants and
seeds after I've disappointed him so?

'No he will not,' I said. 'He will kill you for disappointing him so.'

'And then what does she write?' said Grant.

'That's the last entry,' Alec said. 'Look: the back of this page has Grizzle Roderick's best attempt at a seagull on it.'

'Because by the next night she was dead,' I said. 'Killed by Samuel McReadie. He truly believed he had persuaded her and when he discovered that she meant to refuse him he struck out in rage and disappointment.'

'As we said all along,' said Alec. 'It was a spurned lover. McReadie killed what he could not possess.'

'And Spencer definitely knew that,' said Alec. 'He meant to kill McReadie out in the wilds of Borneo or somewhere where murders go unpunished.'

'They go quite unpunished in Applecross,' said Grant; an inarguable point. 'But what on earth did Mr Spencer tell her, madam? That caused her to change all her plans.'

'I don't know,' I said. 'It's hard to imagine what he could have found out, in Oxford, that would reveal that Lachlan wanted rid of his wife.'

'Whatever it was, presumably he heard it from McReadie's son. That's the connection.'

'Did they know one another?' said Grant.

'Dolly McReadie says not,' I told her. 'But they must.'

'Perhaps they merely bumped into one another or passed in the street,' said Alec.

'But would they even recognise one another?' said Grant. 'Had they met?'

'Too late to ask Spencer, but we could still ask Roddy McReadie,' said Alec. 'If he hadn't made some excuse to miss the wedding we could have asked him today.'

I stared at him. 'Do you think it's the same thing?' I said. 'The thing Spencer found out and the reason Roddy McReadie is staying away?'

'What sort of thing could that be?' said Alec.

I shrugged, but there was a germ of an idea in there somewhere. 'What did you just say, Grant?' I asked, turning to her. 'About them knowing each other? Bumping into one another?'

But before Grant could answer, my bedroom door opened and there stood Mallory.

She took my breath away. The dress was not peculiar at all. It was not vampish, nor overly modish. It was simply a very pretty white satin and lace dress that fitted her like a glove and made the most of her figure. The veil and head-dress were elegance itself on her smooth curls, and her flowers, naturally, were exquisite. She was the perfect picture of a bride.

Except for her expression, which showed extreme distress. 'Mallory, my dear, what's wrong?' I said.

'What's *wrong*?' she repeated, aghast. 'Dandy, it's twenty-five minutes past two. Everyone's waiting for you!'

23

Alec had a point. I managed to get myself dressed, hatted, painted and powdered in ten minutes flat, although for the rest of the day I was never quite comfortable; finding my stockings twisted and my undergarments not quite sitting true against my form. Perhaps I can credit my physical discomfort, however, with keeping me alert through the interminable wedding service. And I shall always be grateful for that, because it was during the ceremony that so many shadowy notions burst into glaring light inside me. A perfect fireworks show went on behind my eyes as I sat there in the front pew of the Clachan church watching my son be married.

He melted my heart, standing waiting at the altar in his new suit, his brother as stiff as a board at his side, and when I turned to glance in Hugh's direction I was amazed to see what looked like a tear or two in his glaring eyes. I told myself there was a great variety of seeds and specks of chaff floating around after the morning's haymaking and turned back from this most startling sight.

When the pianist, an energetic woman with her sleeves rolled up and wearing very sturdy shoes to help her pedal foot, broke into 'Here Comes the Bride', a ripple of excitement and wonder passed through the congregation. Of course, no one turned. It is thought scandalous in a Scottish church to turn one's head and greet a bride with smiles. The poor thing must pace her way to the altar on her father's arm looking at everyone's hats.

I did shoot a look from the corner of my eye – that much

is allowed. She had recovered enough from finding me so very recently so very unprepared as to be smiling again, a ready open smile, perhaps not quite bride-like; but then the shyness and simpering of brides is tiresome. Donald met her with just such another ready open smile and suddenly I felt sure that they would do quite nicely, these two. They were friends, for which a lot can be said when one lives in close quarters.

As Lachlan handed his girl over to my boy, I watched him closely. He had lived at close quarters with his Lady Love, and also with the Tibballs, and now was alone except for a housekeeper. I turned as far as was appropriate – the rules slacken a little once there is nothing to look at – wondering where Mrs McReadie was sitting. She was alone too now and—

The first of the fireworks went off in my head. Mrs McReadie was *not* alone. She lived with Lachlan. Lachlan had wanted rid of his wife and was perfectly happy for her to go off with the gardener. The reason he did not find it shocking that a woman of Lady Love's class might get entangled with a servant was suddenly obvious to me. And, as if to drive the last nail home, I remembered Lachlan telling McReadie to ask 'Dolly's' advice about his long sea journey and McReadie's quick frown of annoyance. Perhaps the man could stomach the notion of a cabinet reshuffle but did not want to be faced with the bald fact of his master using the familiar name.

Or was I building castles? I knew that the formality of mistress to servant rankled with Mrs McReadie. She scorned Lady Love for calling her by her honorific and her surname, as though they had not been children together. The bond between the two families was stout and many-threaded, after all. Besides the fact of childhood friendship, there was the saving of a son's life.

I looked at my own two sons, standing solemnly before me, and saw with a flare of astonishment that they really were no longer boys. They were men. Donald was looking more and more like his father every day. I felt my mind begin to turn to the drumbeat from Europe and turned it, as ever, resolutely away.

This time the burst of the firework was more like a bomb going off and it made me gasp. Most unfortunately, the proceedings had just reached the point where objections were being sought and everyone upon the altar stiffened at the sudden conviction that I was going to speak.

'Oh! No!' I said. 'Do carry on.'

Donald simply smirked and rolled his eyes but Hugh, at my side, froze in rectitude and mortification. Alec leaned forward on Hugh's far side and raised his brows. He knows what it means when I suddenly gasp. He might not know exactly what had just struck me but he knew something had, and hard.

The son who no longer visited his home, but stayed away at Oxford. The stranger, glimpsed by Cherry on her mother's birthday, who seemed to her like a younger and heartier version of her father. The piece of shocking news that David Spencer brought north, having run into someone in Oxford who should have been a stranger, but whom he recognised. Lady Love's disgust about Lachlan's machinations and her sudden realisation that the act of heroism, dragging the boy to safety, was not the selfless act of heroism she had always thought it but was rather that most natural, most inevitable act of all: a parent saving his child.

And a third firework exploded. Dolly McReadie's relief when she heard that a man had travelled on David Spencer's ticket and was sailing away. She was not an angel, happy for her wicked husband to be leaving. She was a mother, happy to know her child was safe from harm.

The rest of the wedding was a blur to me. I stood, sat, prayed and sang but when Donald and Mallory had made their triumphant journey back down the aisle, Cherry waddling behind on Teddy's arm, and the feathers on the hat of the pianist wagging in time as she banged out Mendelssohn, Hugh had to push me to get me walking out behind them.

The happy couple stopped in the churchyard to be showered with rice and congratulations and Alec sought me out.

'Well?' he said.

I told him.

'Good God almighty,' he said, then ducked as though to avoid a smiting and shot a guilty look at the minister a few feet away. 'Lachlan and Dolly McReadie had a child? Roddy McReadie is Lachlan's son?'

'I think so.'

'And he's the spitting image of his father. How unfortunate.'

'Which is why he stayed away from home.'

'Until Spencer ran into him in Oxford, whereupon he came north, knowing Spencer had twigged and was going to blow his cover?'

'Yes, I think – on Lady Love's birthday – Spencer was escorting him away again. He hinted as much as we danced. Lady Love's anger at Lachlan had made her perversely determined not to leave after all. So David Spencer's own fond hopes of a future with her were dashed – as were Sam McReadie's, by the way – but the two men had vastly different responses to the same bit of news, didn't they? Spencer hustled the boy away again, to stop the scandal spreading, and McReadie saw red and killed her.'

'Hm,' said Alec, a habit he had picked up from me. 'But if only David Spencer had kept his mouth shut about the child, instead of belting up here full of gossip, his fond hopes wouldn't have *been* dashed. What a sorry mess he made of it. If he hadn't been so ready to make trouble for Lachlan he might have got his wish, wouldn't you say?'

I shrugged. 'Not if we believe her diary,' I said. 'It was McReadie that tempted her, not poor David Spencer. Very odd.'

'As odd as Lachlan and "Dolly",' said Alec. 'I agree.'

'Do you suppose *that* pair mean to marry? Would that make Roddy a legitimate heir?'

'I don't know the law,' Alec said. 'Does it count if his parents marry years too late?'

'We could ask someone, but you know lawyers. They'd be agog to discover who we were talking about and it wouldn't take much digging to unearth it all. Best leave well alone.'

'I must say, Dandy, all of that certainly knocks my little brainwave for six.'

'Tell me anyway,' I said, all magnanimity since he had given my tale such a warm reception.

'The roller,' Alec said. 'Remember I noticed that the edge of the path had a deep ditch?'

'Yes,' I said. 'I didn't see the point then and I don't see it now.'

'It's not a roller.' Indeed I did find it difficult to be amazed by this nugget of insight. I had missed the point of it, though.

'I know. It's a raker. It rakes the gravel.'

'The weight is borne on the rims so that the material – usually gravel – isn't pushed to the edges. And the teeth rake the surface of the material – usually gravel – smooth.'

'Why do you keep saying usua— Oh!' I caught up at last. 'Usually gravel, but sometimes . . .'

'Snow. Yes,' Alec said.

'Good grief! I dreamed it and I didn't pay attention to the dream.' Alec and I stared at one another. 'So,' I said after a while. 'She could have been put there any time then? And then the roller could smooth away the tracks afterwards?'

'Yes, I think so.'

'Well then it falls into place. When Lady Love found out – from Spencer – that her husband had betrayed her, that all his so-called sacrifice and the years of her living with an invalid, had all been to save his bastard son . . . she changed her mind about leaving.'

'Sour grapes,' said Alec. 'She didn't want Lachlan but she didn't want it to be mutual. Her famous sweet nature begins to curdle rather.'

'So McReadie killed her. He stashed her in the flower room – where poor Mitten saw her – then moved her to the dovecote and smoothed the path. Spencer knew it.'

'How?' Alec said.

'Or worked it out, rather. Perhaps Lady Love told him of McReadie's devotion and told him she was planning to disappoint the man. If *we'd* known that, then Lady Love killed in her garden with a garden tool and the gardener grubbing out all her last plantings would have struck us as evidence of guilt too.'

'True,' Alec said.

'And so Spencer planned to kill McReadie when they were on their trip together. But when McReadie found out that his crime was uncovered – the night of the engagement ball – the two men had a confrontation and Spencer died.'

'And Roddy McReadie – aided by his mother and perhaps his father too; who knows? – has left the country, using the passport Sam McReadie had ready for the plant-finding trip.'

'Only one question remains,' I said.

'Where,' said Alec, 'is Samuel McReadie?'

We pondered it as we walked back round the bay to Applecross House as part of the joyous wedding procession. The sun shone down on the green hills and the silver shore and the sea sparkled blue as cornflowers in the bay. Ahead of us, a gaggle of children skipped and larked along. They spoke in high little chirrups, half-English and half-Gaelic, telling jokes, teasing one another.

'Kelpie pool,' was the first snippet I really noticed. A small boy was pointing up the hill and dancing around.

'I'm not allowed to,' another tiny boy said. 'In case the *bodach* gets me.'

'Whit *bodach*?' said a larger girl. 'Scaredy-cat, scaredy-cat! Wetted your pants and lost your hat!'

'There's a *bodach* in with the kelpie now,' another girl confirmed. 'My Granny Roderick told me. He'll come and get you if you don't mind your mammy.'

Alec and I stopped walking and waited until the children were out of earshot.

'What's a *bodach*?' said Alec.

'An old man,' I said. 'What better place to tip a body than a pond everyone already avoids for the curse of bad luck it's had for years?'

'But how can McReadie be in a loch? Suicide? Unbearable remorse leading to suicide?'

'Or a ruthless woman tidying up loose ends when the neat plan to swap partners fell through.'

'And what shall we do about it?'

'Nothing until after the wedding dance at least,' I said. 'When they are safely off on their honeymoon, we shall have to see.'

I stopped talking as Hugh turned back, fought his way through the waist-high mob of children and came to chivvy us.

'What's the matter now?' he asked.

'Nothing,' I assured him. 'I like Mallory. She loves Donald and he loves her too. That's what matters. Changes are coming, Hugh, as you never tire of telling me. The old concerns of family and society are falling away. None too soon, if you ask me.'

'What are you talking about?' Hugh said. 'What do you mean "family and society"? Is there more scandal yet?'

'I'll tell you later,' I said. 'Let's dance. The sun is shining and this is a happy day.' I took Hugh's arm and Alec's arm and began to skip. 'Come and dance a Dashing White Sergeant with me, you two.'

Epilogue

There was little warmth in the September sunshine, but its low, golden dazzle was a joy to behold. The bracken had reddened until every hill was ablaze with it and the leaves of the birch trees were spangles of bronze. The last cut of hay was silvering on the fences too and the water in the sound glittered. I caught my breath as we crested the *bealach na bà* and saw the whole treasure box open before us.

'It's such a beautiful place,' I said, 'to contain such ugliness.'

'The purge will surely be almost done after today,' said Alec.

I sighed mightily and let my mind range back over the months as we descended to the shore side. A hopeless tangle of loyalties had rendered me unable to act at midsummer. My fear for Cherry's safe confinement, for Dickie's fragile state of mind and for Lachlan's inevitable heartbreak was bad enough. But there was also poor Roddy McReadie, who had not chosen to be born, nor to be saved on the battlefield, and whose hapless role in the mess would be a perfect opium pipe to the lower sort of Sunday newspaper. I foresaw a manhunt throughout the empire for him. And then there was Mallory, whom I loved more with every passing day, finding in her an alliance I had not even known I was lacking before her arrival. She was another woman in my house of men and a sensible ally to stand shoulder to shoulder with me against Grant's excesses, after the wedding day was past and life went back to its humdrum tweedy round again.

If all that meant that Dolly McReadie reigned at the Clachan manse, paying nothing for her scheming and nothing for her sins, I did not see what could be done about it.

Had not Inspector Hutcheson taken to visiting me I might have let the whole sordid business slip into the past, with my face turned doucely away. But visit he did. He parked himself in my sitting room, a cup of tea in his hand and his most bloodhound-like look upon his face. And there he waited. He kept coming back, before his shifts of duty, and after them, and on his free days. Alec started staying away to avoid him and heaven only knew what Mrs Hutcheson made of his absence from home. After a few weeks, Bunty barely raised her head to greet him, such a fixture had he become. And Becky brought a second cup in on my coffee tray without being asked. Even Hugh took to strolling in for help with the crossword and looked surprised if only Bunty and I greeted him.

It was the end of July when I cracked and told Hutcheson everything.

'I thought as much,' he said when I was done. 'In broad strokes. I couldn't have guessed at all the incidentals, dearie me no. So. There were two men in love with Lavinia, but her husband wasn't one of them. She could have scandalised the county and gone off with the gardener or she could have scandalised only the minister by flitting down to Oxford with the man Spencer. But she took a huff to think her husband had a by-blow, not to mention a plan of his own, and she dug her heels in. Well, that's women – that's a certain sort of idle woman for you.'

'It's David Spencer I could shake,' I said. 'If he were alive to be shaken. Rushing up on the sleeper to tell a tale that was guaranteed to cause pain and turmoil. If he hadn't been so quick to point fingers at Lachlan, none of this would have happened. But that's *men* for you.'

Inspector Hutcheon inclined his head in acknowledgement.

314

'You do see that I can't just leave this be, Mrs Gilver?' he said. 'Like Mr Spencer before me, I'll be rushing up to Applecross to tell a tale, spreading pain and turmoil. You do see?'

I nodded glumly. 'Yes, I suppose so,' I said. 'There was never going to be a happy ending after Spencer stuck his oar in. But how very nearly! They kept Roddy's parentage quiet all those years, right through his schooling and the war and the tragedy of Lachlan's sacrifice. Once Lady Love had gone off with her beloved – either of her beloveds! – then Lachlan and Dolly McReadie could have let their son back into their lives. Cherry wouldn't have cared, as long as it didn't interfere with the lambing, and even Mallory would have weathered it in the end.'

'It looks like that, viewed from here,' Hutcheson said. 'But if no murder had ever come along to upend their lives, I think their father with his cook and their mother with her gardener would have struck those two girls as a very grievous step. Add a bastard brother – excuse my frankness, Mrs Gilver – and they'd both have had the vapours. We wouldn't have thought to say, "Thank your stars your mother wasn't hacked to death in her garden and your old family friend not long at her back".'

I shuddered. 'True,' I said. 'Very true. Well then, Inspector, you must do your duty. Truth will out. Blood will out.'

'Love will out, I've heard,' Hutcheson said. 'But that's not so much to do with me, in my profession. I shall let you know when Mrs McReadie is about to be arrested and whether we reckon to scoop up Lord Ross too and you can help your daughter-in-law take it in, eh? Break it gently.'

I smiled at the phrase 'daughter-in-law', for it still delighted me. I *would* help Mallory take it in. That was my job here. I would leave the villains to be dealt with by the long, encircling and muscular arm of the law.

In the end, the arm of the law barely had to stretch to

grab its prey. The prey walked, all unknowing, into its reach. Mrs McReadie, lulled to complacency by her triumphs, made a fatal error. One evening at the Clachan manse while Lachlan sat with his pipe by the fireside and she sat opposite, sometimes bent over her mending and sometimes looking up to smile at him, she gravely miscalculated the depth of his love.

She told him. Dolly McReadie revealed that her husband had not avenged Lachlan's wife and fled to the colonies, but instead had killed Lachlan's wife, then killed his wife's good friend and had, in turn, been murdered by the very woman who was right now sitting with a half-darned sock in her lap, telling this tale in such a calm, confiding way.

'He's tipped in the lochan,' she said. 'Dead as a doornail.'

'Why . . .' Lachlan began in a voice stretched dry. 'Why are you telling me?'

'Well,' said Mrs McReadie, with a smile and a little movement of her shoulders that was close to a simper, 'I'm a widow, you see. I shall have to divorce him for desertion to keep the courts happy, but we'll know I'm a widow and we'll know that any second marriage I enter into will be a marriage true in the eyes of God.'

Lachlan stared. 'The eyes of God?' he echoed. 'The God who saw you kill the man? The God who knows you stitched dolls and whispered spells into them?'

Mrs McReadie put her needle carefully into her darning ball out of harm's way and clasped her hands in her lap. 'Now, Lach,' she said. 'Don't distress yourself.'

Lachlan Ross stood and, on his sturdy legs that were getting stronger every day, he strode to the telephone and asked the exchange to put him through to the police at Inverness.

So, this September morning, as Alec and I coasted down to Applecross, Dolly McReadie, murderess, was in her prison cell, an object of fear and fascination to the other women and to the warders, who saw her twisting her little bits of wool and muttering. Samuel McReadie, murderer, was lying in the cold earth of a corporation cemetery in Glasgow, no churchyard in the Highlands willing to find a plot for his sorry bones.

And now Lachlan was to be laid to his rest. He had started to fail as soon as the trial began and his final illness had been such a brutal one that the end came as a relief.

'I'm looking forward to seeing Mallory,' I said as we trundled along the shore road. Mallory had been at Applecross since summoned to her father's deathbed and I was missing her and getting rather sick of Donald mooning around missing her too. 'I'm going to try to get her to come back straight after the funeral. Cherry has plenty of help up here, between Biddy, Dickie and Mitten, and Mallory needs to take care of herself. For once.'

'Is she in an interesting condition?' said Alec, who picks up some dreadful slang from his maidservants.

'I refuse to answer such a vulgar enquiry,' I said. 'But that reminds me: we'll be seeing Cherry and Mitten's little boy. Mallory tells me he's a lusty chap. Came to no harm from all the excitement.'

'Not to mention the shearing,' Alec added. 'What's his name?'

'Lorrimer,' I said.

'Fine name.'

'They call him Lollipop.'

Alec made a disgusted noise in his throat and I did not blame him. We were nearing the gates to Applecross House now and I was looking into my compact mirror to tidy my hair when I heard Alec gasp and felt the car swerve.

'What on earth?' I said.

'Nearly hit a dog,' Alec said. He had come to a halt and was looking back over his shoulder. I twisted round to look too. A large black dog, very familiar to me, was trotting away along the middle of the road. As we watched, a crow came

317

circling down and landed on the dog's back. The dog continued to trot along, untroubled by its passenger.

'Well, I've seen everything now,' said Alec. 'Is the circus in town? Or has someone in the village trained a pet crow to do that? Have they escaped from somewhere? Should we round them up and send them home?'

The two creatures were turning up the hill to take the cattle pass away from Applecross. The dog disappeared behind the hedgerow and all I could see was the tip of the crow's black beak as it threw its head back in a farewell caw.

'No,' I said. 'I think they're leaving. And we should let them go.'

Facts and Fictions

Applecross is a real place. These days, the Applecross Trust runs the estate and several of the houses, including the Clachan manse, are available for holiday lets. The walled garden is open to visitors and you can have a delicious meal in the Potting Shed.

The topography is pretty much as I've made it here, although I have taken various small liberties. For instance, 'Michael's Cottage' is further round the north arm of the bay, beyond the Clachan. I've taken larger liberties with such aspects of local history as: the ownership of the estate, the effect of the clearances, the source of funds for infrastructure improvements. And I'm not at all sure the apple variety exists that's hardy enough to grow in Wester Ross.

As for the folklore, that is almost entirely the product of my imagination. Maelrubha was real but the tales I've spun about him here are not. All the harbingers I mention have a basis in Celtic mythology but the real Applecross peninsula is not so beset with them as I've suggested.

None of the human characters are based on real people, but Ursus the cat and his table habits are borrowed from the late and great Bear Hoenisch.

Acknowledgements

As ever I would like to thank Francine Toon, Jasmine Marsh, Sophia Brown and all at Hodder & Stoughton; Lisa Moylett, Zoe Apostolides, Jamie Maclean and Elena Langtry at Coombs, Moylett, Maclean; and all my family and friends in the UK and US.

This time I would also like to include thanks to: Ruaridh and Kate Cameron at the Applecross Heritage Centre for information and guidance; and Donald and Ishbel Ferguson for tea, pancakes and lots of patience as they guided me through the spelling, grammar, pronunciation and honorific system of Applecross Gaelic. Any mistakes that have squeaked through are mine.